Stolen HEART

HEARTS OF SAWYERS BEND
BOOK 1

IVY LAYNE

GINGER QUILL PRESS, LLC

Also By Ivy Layne

THE HEARTS OF SAWYERS BEND

Stolen Heart
Sweet Heart
Scheming Heart

THE UNTANGLED SERIES

Unraveled
Undone
Uncovered

THE WINTERS SAGA

The Billionaire's Secret Heart (Novella)
The Billionaire's Secret Love (Novella)
The Billionaire's Pet
The Billionaire's Promise
The Rebel Billionaire
The Billionaire's Secret Kiss (Novella)
The Billionaire's Angel
Engaging the Billionaire
Compromising the Billionaire
The Counterfeit Billionaire
Series Extras: ivylayne.com/extras

THE BILLIONAIRE CLUB

The Wedding Rescue
The Courtship Maneuver
The Temptation Trap

Contents

Chapter One

GRIFFEN

I HATED MY DESK. THIS OFFICE HAD BEEN MINE FOR the better part of a decade. It should have felt like home, but I'd never been a desk kind of guy. Any excuse to get in the field. I did my job, didn't slack on the paperwork, but I never felt truly alive sitting behind a desk.

Now, it looked like I'd be stuck here for the rest of my life.

Fucking Andrei Tsepov and his fucking idiot goons. I should be glad it was just a bullet to the shoulder. More than a few men had died that night. I could have been mowed down by one of the AR-15s they were using. If a bullet from an AR-15 had hit my shoulder I would have lost my arm.

One shot from a handgun and I'd been down. Shoulder wounds are a lot more complicated than people think. The bullet had nicked an artery and torn through ligaments and tendons, breaking bones along the way.

Hours of surgery, weeks in a sling, followed by months of physical therapy. I was almost as good as new.

Almost.

For a guy with a regular job, almost would have been good enough. For me, *almost* meant the end of my career. It had to be my right fucking arm, didn't it? My brain might have the reaction time I needed, but my right arm would always be a fraction too slow.

No matter how much I wanted to be in the field, wanted the adrenaline and the rush, I wouldn't risk a client's life to soothe my ego.

I was grounded. I'd have to find a way to live with that.

I'm not a brooder. I grew up in a family of volatile personalities, surrounded by rage and betrayal, malice and grudges. I'd walked away when I was twenty-two, resentful and angry, but once I'd tasted the freedom of life away from my family, I'd made a decision.

I wasn't going to let the bullshit get me down.

There's always a bright side, always a reason to laugh. I'd never give in to hate. I'd seen what happened to people who did that, seen the way it sucked the life from them, leaving them dried-up, bitter husks.

That wouldn't be me. That would never be me.

For fifteen years, I'd managed to hold on to that, always ready with a smile, always looking for the silver lining. And now this. Holed up in my office during the day, hiding in my condo at night. Grumbling, growling, and snapping at my friends, the friends who'd become my family.

I knew I was being an asshole. I tried to smile, to laugh, tried to pretend everything was great, but we all knew it was a lie.

Everything wasn't fucking great. Everything was all fucked up.

A buzz sounded on my phone. Alice at the front desk. I picked up the handset and winced as I heard myself bark, "What?"

I was being a bastard. Alice was like a sister, now married to my best friend. She was family. She deserved better than me being a dick.

Before I could apologize, she let out her sparkling pixie's laugh and said, "Hello to you, too, sunshine. You have a visitor. Says her name is Hope Daniels. Should I bring her back?"

Hope Daniels?

Not possible.

What were the chances the name could be a coincidence?

None. No chance.

I cursed the universe. Kick a man while he's down, why don't you? Whatever dark force had brought Hope Fucking Daniels to Atlanta, it could just take her back.

Twenty-year-old Griffen would have welcomed her with open arms. The Griffen of six months ago would have at least been curious. Now? With this fucking bum shoulder aching like a rotten tooth, I wanted to tell Hope to fuck off and get out.

No good could come of Hope Daniels walking back into my life.

"Griffen? You want me to just leave her standing here until she gathers dust?"

I couldn't help the tiny smile that spread across my face. I shut it down. Might as well get this over with. I'd find out what Hope wanted and get rid of her. No big deal.

"Bring her back."

"Righty-ho!" Alice hung up.

Hope fucking Daniels.

Alice was going to want to know who she was. Cooper, Evers, Knox, everyone would want to know who she was. When was the last time a woman had walked into the office and asked for me? Never. I kept my personal life separate from work. Always.

Hope wasn't personal. Not like that.

She wasn't a woman, she was a sign of the fucking apocalypse.

3

All too soon, Alice swung open the door of my office. My first thought was that she must have made a mistake. The woman standing beside her was not Hope Daniels.

She was tall and slender like Hope, with the same sandy brown hair and cognac colored eyes, but this was not my Hope.

With her hair scraped back into a tight knot at the base of her skull, her face pale and eyes flat, she looked more like a scarecrow than a woman. Hope had always been slender, slight of build despite her height, but this woman was scrawny. Brittle. Her face was devoid of makeup. She lacked all ornamentation outside of a simple set of gold studs in her ears.

The woman who called herself Hope Daniels stood in front of me wearing a beige suit that fit her as if it had been purchased for someone else, the jacket and skirt boxy, overwhelming her frame and hiding any hint of the body beneath.

Her matching pumps were dull and serviceable. She was neat and clean but utterly and completely bland. Forgettable. I studied her, searching for any hint of the Hope I'd known so well.

My Hope had reminded me of Alice. She'd been far quieter than our outspoken office manager, but Hope had the same core of steel and, like Alice, a funky, quirky style all her own.

I'd loved keeping an eye out for the secrets she'd hide in her school uniform. A headband embroidered with skeletons. Socks with mermaids woven into the pattern. She'd spent her allowance looking for ways to be different despite her guardian's demand that she fit in. My Hope wouldn't have been caught dead in beige.

Alice waited at the door, expectant, her eyes ping-ponging between me and Hope. When neither of us said a word, she raised an eyebrow and offered, "Coffee? Tea?"

"No, thanks, Alice. Hope won't be here long enough for that."

4

Narrowing her eyes at my rudeness, Alice shrugged a shoulder and excused herself. I had no doubt her next stop was Cooper's office. Whatever. They were my friends, and this absolutely qualified as gossip. If the tables had been turned, I would have done the same.

Not only was a female visitor unusual, I was never rude. Well, lately, yeah, but it was only to the friends I knew would put up with my bullshit. Not in the office with a stranger. But then, Hope Daniels was no stranger.

In a low voice that held no inflection, Hope said, "May I take a seat?"

I leaned back in my chair. "Suit yourself."

No reaction from Hope. There'd been a day when an unkind comment from me would have filled her eyes with tears—not that she'd ever been subject to an unkind comment from me. Not until the end. In the end, there'd been tears all around.

She sat, smoothing her ugly skirt over her legs and crossing her feet at the ankle. It was like the Hope I'd known had been wiped clean, an automaton substituted in her place. This new Hope grated against every nerve.

Hope had been a girl when I'd walked away from Sawyers Bend. Only a girl, but she'd been the spark that set the fire, the one who'd turned the gears that ended in heartbreak and loss, in a grudge that would last the rest of my life.

"What do you want?"

Showing her first sign of weakness, Hope drew in a long breath and looked down at the purse she'd stowed neatly on her lap. When she looked back at me, her eyes held the faintest glimmer of emotion.

The last words she'd spoken to me had shattered my life. This time was no different.

"Your father's dead. Ford is in jail for his murder. All the assets, corporate and personal, are frozen until the will is read."

5

I swallowed, fighting the burn of her words. Those people meant nothing to me. Not anymore. Hardening my heart, I forced myself to say, "Then read the will and leave me out of it."

"We can't. Your father stipulated the will couldn't be read without you."

Her words lanced through me, cauterizing the wound as they went, leaving me numb and hollow.

My father was dead.

I hadn't seen him in fifteen years. I'd hated him far longer than that.

I wasn't alone in hating my father. Prentice Sawyer was one of the most hated men in our patch of North Carolina. Hell, he was probably one of the most hated men in the country. Stalling, I said, "How? What happened?"

"Sterling found him in his office at Heartstone Manor. He was shot. He'd been dead a while."

Sterling. My little sister. Half-sister. Most of my siblings were halves. Prentice collected wives, but he was shit at keeping them. I resisted the urge to ask if Sterling was okay. Sterling wasn't my problem. None of them were.

"Where?"

"His office," Hope repeated more slowly, as if I were hard of hearing.

"No, where on his body was he shot?"

"His forehead."

Execution style. A crime of passion, I could have seen. An angry husband or a betrayed lover, sure. Not an assassination. And Ford was in jail for killing him? No way.

I had a lot of reasons to hate my brother, but there was no way he could have killed our father with a single shot to the forehead. Ford didn't have it in him. He knew his way around a gun, all the Sawyer kids did, but that kind of cold-blooded murder? No.

How much had changed since I'd left?

I pushed Ford from my mind. *Not your problem,* I reminded myself. "The bastard changed his will after I left. Again."

My father was famous for changing his will. He used that thing like a weapon, setting my siblings and me against one another in a constant play for dominance.

It wasn't enough that the Sawyers practically owned the town of Sawyers Bend, owned hundreds of millions of dollars of real estate and industry in North Carolina and the surrounding states.

Prentice Sawyer wasn't happy unless the rest of us were dancing to his tune like puppets on strings. That will had been changed so many times the fees he paid to the family estate attorney had bought the man a second home.

I'd walked away from Sawyers Bend, turned my back on my family after they'd betrayed me in the worst way. My father's will was not my problem.

"He kicked me out fifteen years ago," I reminded her. "I have my own life now. Solve your own problems."

A ghost of emotion flitted across Hope's face. Fear? Worry? Desperation? It was gone so fast I couldn't tell.

She leaned forward a scant inch. "Griffen, you need to understand—everything is frozen. Everything. Personal funds. Business funds. Everything. People won't get paid. Businesses will go under. The town will go under. You don't have to stay. Please, just come home so Harvey can read the will. As soon as it's done you can leave, and you never have to see any of us again."

Fucking hell. My goddamned father. He always knew how to twist the knife.

He wanted me back in Sawyers Bend for some godforsaken reason, and he was an expert at getting his way, even from beyond the grave.

He knew I wouldn't come back if he asked. I didn't need the Sawyer fortune. I'd been raised to take the helm, groomed to follow in my father's footsteps, but I'd walked away. I'd made my own money, and I didn't owe those people a fucking thing.

My family was poison, but the town of Sawyers Bend was a different story.

Sawyers Bend was filled with people just trying to live their lives. Good people. People dependent on Sawyer Enterprises for their livelihood. Without the free flow of Sawyer cash, Sawyers Bend would grind to a halt, and it was the people of the town who would suffer first.

I wanted nothing to do with my family, but I wouldn't destroy the town.

"When is the reading of the will?"

"Tomorrow at two o'clock. Harvey's office."

"I'll be there. And then I'm leaving."

I watched Hope walk out of my office, her back straight, posture perfect, the girl I'd known nowhere in sight.

Two o'clock. I'd be back on the road to Atlanta by five, finally done with Sawyers Bend.

Nothing on this earth could convince me to stay a second longer.

Chapter Two

GRIFFEN

HE DRIVE FROM ATLANTA TO SAWYERS BEND ONLY took three hours, but it felt like an eternity and was over far too soon. As I left the highway for the two-lane road winding through the mountains, I was catapulted back in time. I hated every second of it.

I don't look back, I look forward. Forget all that 'past is pro-logue' bullshit. We can't change what's come before. Hell, we can barely control our futures. If we could I wouldn't be speed-ing toward the home I'd left behind with a bum shoulder that carried a chip the size of North Carolina.

Driving into the town of Sawyers Bend was surreal, to say the least. Lost in a hazy fog of memory, colored by childhood, I'd remembered it as a perfect slice of small-town Americana.

It still was, minus the patina of memory. This version of

Sawyers Bend was thriving in the now. I drove slowly down Main Street, taking in the couples strolling hand in hand, the crowd waiting at the corner for the light to change.

I hadn't expected so many tourists on a Thursday in early March. The first few months of the year aren't the most hospitable around here. The mountains are always pretty, but it's cold by the standards of the South, and the icy wind can be a bitch. Not to mention the way the temperature swings from freezing to pleasant and back to freezing. And the sudden snowstorms. They didn't happen often, but they were all the worse for their unpredictability.

None of my memories of winter in the mountains matched up with the scarf-wearing, rosy-cheeked tourists strolling the streets of Sawyers Bend. The town itself was cheerful and welcoming despite the weather. Neatly painted shop windows lined Main Street, framed by striped awnings that were vaguely familiar.

I didn't recognize most of the businesses. Restaurants, galleries, tourist shops. Two craft breweries. More restaurants. Sawyers Bend was taking advantage of the foodies and beer lovers who flocked to the area along with the nature lovers. Not a surprise. The Sawyers had always been good at profiting off trends in the market.

At the end of Main Street, just after the last of the shops and restaurants, a massive stone and timber building loomed over the street. *The Inn at Sawyers Bend.* I'd grown up running in those halls, had eaten more than one meal in the family booth in the elegant dining room.

I drove past, averting my eyes. I wasn't here for a trip down memory lane. I was here so Harvey could read my father's will. That was it.

I passed the Inn and turned away onto a road that curved behind Main Street. I parked in front of a perfectly maintained

Victorian that hadn't changed in twenty years, the sign out front swinging gently in the breeze. *Harvey Benson, Attorney at Law.*

Only two cars were parked in the gravel lot. One was a late model Mercedes sedan. Harvey's, I guessed, probably paid for by the umpteen-million changes in my father's will.

The other was a beige four-door sedan. Not old, not new, it was bland, with absolutely nothing to distinguish it from any other car on the highway. Hope's car. I don't know how I knew. I hadn't seen her car in Atlanta. I just knew.

It was a burr under my skin, digging deep when I shouldn't even care. What the hell was Hope doing driving a car like that? Hope belonged in a bright red Volkswagen bug or a Mini Cooper. Maybe a jeep. Hope did not belong in a beige sedan. What had happened to her?

Why do you care?

Hope was the past. Hope was a liar who'd screwed me over. Hope was the reason I'd been kicked out of my childhood home in the first place.

So what if she was a ghost of herself? So what if she'd changed? Hadn't we all?

Just get this over with, I reminded myself. *Listen to Harvey read the will and then get back to your life. You don't belong here. Not anymore.*

I shoved my car key in my pocket and strode up the front steps, not bothering to knock. The door was unlocked.

"Harvey?" I called out.

A round face with apple-red cheeks poked through a doorway, a jovial smile that didn't fit the occasion lighting his eyes. Harvey Benson didn't look a day older than he had the last time I'd seen him. Maybe a little more gray at the temples, maybe his belly was a little bigger, but otherwise, this was the Harvey I'd always known.

He strode forward and stuck out his hand. "Griffen, my boy. It's good to see you. Sorry about the circumstances. Your father left us a big pile of shit, but now that you're here we can get it sorted out. Come on in, come on in."

I'd always liked Harvey's upfront manner. My father spun webs of nuance and manipulation, but Harvey just laid it all out. I had a feeling that was going to come in handy.

He led me into his office and rounded his desk, sitting in his big leather chair and gesturing to one of the seats opposite. I almost didn't notice Hope in the other chair by the desk. How did she disappear like that?

Today she wore a black suit, identical to the suit she'd worn the day before except in color. Ill-fitting but expensive. It should have been well-tailored considering the quality of the fabric. So why—

Focus, Griffen, I lectured myself. *You're here for the will. Not Hope. Hope can deal with her own problems. You've got enough of those yourself.*

I rolled my stiff shoulder. Yeah, I had my own problems. Whatever was wrong with Hope had nothing to do with me.

"We need to head on out to the cemetery in a minute, but before the zoo starts, I wanted to have a word."

"I thought I was only here for the will," I said. "He hasn't been buried yet?"

"Prentice was specific about how he wanted this handled," Harvey explained. "Nothing at the church. Family only at the cemetery, then back here to read the will. We've been waiting for you."

At least the whole town wouldn't be there. Harvey cleared his throat and gave me an apologetic look. That couldn't be good.

"I want you to know before this ball gets rolling, I was your father's estate attorney, but he rarely took my advice. None of

12

this was my idea. I'm going to remind you again after the service, but I'll tell you now while we're private—you don't stand a chance in hell of fighting it."

Harvey looked remorseful. I flicked a glance at Hope, surprised to see a hint of confusion in her eyes, hidden beneath her mask of composure. So, Hope didn't know what he was talking about either.

"Are you that good, or was my father that crazy?"

With a rueful laugh, Harvey shook his head. "Both, son. Both."

"Why is Hope here?" I asked. "Did my father leave her something?"

Harvey shuffled a few papers on his desk, avoiding my eyes before clearing his throat again. Hope answered for him. "Uncle Edgar wasn't feeling well this morning. He asked me to attend in his place."

That made sense. But then, why did Harvey look even more ill at ease? I wasn't sure I wanted to know.

He checked his watch. "About time to head to the cemetery. The rest of your family will meet us there. I'll drive."

Bracing inwardly at the thought of seeing my siblings, I didn't argue with Harvey. I didn't care who drove, I just wanted to get this shit show over with.

I got into the passenger seat of Harvey's Mercedes, barely noticing the tight turns as we made our way down the winding roads to the cemetery. The Sawyer family plot was packed with my ancestors, going back to Alexander Braxton Sawyer, the first Sawyer to make his home in North Carolina.

I hadn't been to the family cemetery in years. Not since my grandfather died when I was a teenager, only months after my father had executed a takeover of the family company and put his own father out to pasture. I'd always thought that my father's betrayal had killed my grandfather. Not that Prentice had cared. He had what he wanted. Control of Sawyer Enterprises.

I tromped across the perfectly-maintained grass behind Harvey, Hope silent beside me. She'd buttoned a heavy black overcoat up to her chin, her shoulders hunched against the biting wind. The breeze that had seemed almost springlike in town turned into an icy blade in the open of the cemetery. I hadn't dressed for the weather. I was too used to Atlanta and hadn't expected to be outside. I'd deal. Hopefully, the burial wouldn't take long.

Harvey led us to the graveside, nodding in his friendly way at the pastor waiting for us, at my siblings standing in a loose jumble on the other side of the deep hole in the earth. The gray metal casket gleamed from the depths of the grave. Only Hope stood beside me, silent but there. I shouldn't have been grateful for her support. It shouldn't have mattered. I nodded at the group opposite but said nothing.

I hadn't seen or heard from any of them in fifteen years. Only Ford was missing. The only sibling who shared my mother, we'd been close as kids. He'd been my best friend right up until he'd stabbed me in the back. Now he was locked up for the murder of our father. Ford was an asshole, but he was no murderer.

The rest of them... Fuck, I barely recognized my youngest sisters. Sterling had been a child when I left, Quinn and Parker not much older. Avery, the oldest, had been learning to drive. I still remembered guiding her down the long driveway to Heartstone Manor, half afraid she was going to crash my beloved truck. Now she looked at me with hard, unforgiving eyes.

Royal, Tenn, and Finn stood in a semi-circle, all ignoring me. They'd been teenagers when I was exiled. Old enough to speak up, but not one of them had taken my side. They'd circled the wagons and let my father banish me from our home. They'd stood by and let Ford take everything from me.

Hope had set it all in motion, but these people, my brothers and sisters, had let it happen.

Braxton, the same age as Sterling and her bitter enemy, stood on the opposite end of the group, studiously ignoring me. I'd always found it ironic that despite their mutual hatred, Brax and Sterling could have been twins. Their gilded beauty was almost unreal. Golden hair, perpetually tanned skin, and our father's electric-blue eyes.

Brax's jaw was hard, his eyes averted from mine, but Sterling glared across our father's empty grave, looking like a movie star in a perfectly-fitted black sheath, her chin set in the same angry thrust as Brax's. Her eyes were red. Tears or something else? Seeing the way she wobbled, her arm wound through Quinn's, I'd have bet alcohol, not tears.

Quinn, her dark hair and electric-blue eyes a mirror of our father's, watched Sterling in concern. Beside her stood Parker, on the arm of a stranger in an expertly-tailored gray suit. She'd been only thirteen when I left and already showing a hint of the beauty she'd become.

Parker looked the most like her mother, Darcy, the only one of my father's wives who was even the slightest bit maternal. Darcy had made up for the rest of them. If we had any memory of a mother's love, it came from Darcy. I'll never know how a woman that kind tolerated being married to my father.

Darcy bound us together. One of the only things the Sawyer children shared was a soul-deep ache at her loss. She'd been gone for seventeen years and I still missed her.

Looking at Parker was a stab to the heart. That pale, straight, blonde hair. Those gold and green hazel eyes. Her slight, fragile build. She was a perfect reflection of her mother and I grieved all over again.

We'd never stood here for Darcy. My father had buried her without ceremony, too distraught to think about what Darcy would have wanted. What the rest of us might have needed.

She lay beneath the dirt only a few feet away, as missed today as she had been the day she died. If Darcy had lived, none of this would have happened. She never would have let Prentice drive me from my home. Never would have let him set us against each other. Never—

Chapter Three

GRIFFEN

I WENT STILL AS NARROW FINGERS CLOSED AROUND mine. Hope kept her eyes on the open wound in the earth holding my father's coffin, but she held my hand in a firm grip.

She held my hand. That should have thrown me as much as the sight of my siblings.

Instead, it anchored me. I hadn't realized I'd been holding my breath until my lungs eased and my racing heart slowed. Neither of us looked at each other, but I squeezed her fingers back, standing beside her in silence, waiting for the torture to end.

Finally, the pastor cleared his throat to get our attention. When we turned to face him, he opened the Bible in his hands and began to speak. I didn't hear a single word. I stood there by my father's grave, Hope's hand in mine, just waiting for it to be over.

The pastor droned on, a pained expression on his face. Probably from the effort of finding nice things to say about the deceased. Every eye around the grave was dry as a bone. Across the way, a flash caught my eye as Sterling lifted a flask in her namesake metal and tipped it to her mouth.

She saw me watching and narrowed her eyes, her glare bleary. Classy. I wasn't going to give her a hard time. Sterling had barely even had Darcy as a mother. She'd grown up under the loving care of our father. If she needed a drink to get herself through this circus, I wasn't going to criticize.

The pastor closed the Bible and made to leave. Before we could flee, Harvey raised his voice. "I need to see all of you in my office. No exceptions."

The drive back to town passed in a blur of leafless trees and bright blue winter sky. Cars filled the small lot in front of Harvey's Victorian as we filed into his small conference room.

A long, shining table dominated the room, surrounded by leather chairs, the heavy drapes and wood paneling giving the space a cozy, intimate feel.

A cart holding a flatscreen TV and a laptop was arranged at the end of the table, Harvey waiting patiently beside it. I started to sit when Harvey pulled out the chair next to the screen. "Griffen, you sit here. Hope, take the seat beside him, please."

Harvey's jovial smile was nowhere in sight. Whatever was about to happen, he wasn't looking forward to it. I glanced at the door, but it was too late to run.

Harvey rolled the screen closer to the end of the table and raised a slim remote. My father's face filled the screen. He'd aged. Why did that surprise me? It had been fifteen years. Of course, he'd aged.

There were streaks of white at his temples. Was his hair a little thinner on top? Maybe it was a trick of the light. Those electric-blue eyes were just as vibrant. Just as cagey. Just as smug.

My stomach knotted. This was going to be bad. How bad, I couldn't guess. I didn't need anything from Prentice or the rest of the Sawyer family. I'd left home with nothing and created my own life. I had money in the bank. A job I loved. Friends who were like family.

Prentice Sawyer couldn't take any of that from me.

I'd quickly learn how wrong I was.

Harvey interrupted my thoughts. "Your father preferred to deliver his final words to you himself. Prentice recorded this six weeks before his death. Changes were made to his will at that time. When he's finished, I'll go over the particulars."

Harvey hit another button on the remote and my father's laugh filled the room.

"If Harvey is playing this I must be dead. Are you all patting yourselves on the back at getting rid of me? I'm betting Ford did it, the cagey bastard."

Another cackle of a laugh. *What the fuck?* What had been going on before he died?

"You've all been plotting against me for years. Don't think I don't know. And Ford was at the root of it. I knew what he was up to. Never expected the way he'd screw me over, though. He got me good. Now he's out. As far as my estate is concerned, Ford is no longer my son."

On the screen, his eyes shifted, landing precisely on me.

No, not on me. He was dead, and I hadn't been sitting here when this video was filmed. Still, the effect was uncanny.

"Griffen. My oldest son. My heir. Your siblings are ungrateful little shits. Every one of them tried to walk out on me, but you're the only one who did it. The only one who went out there

19

and made something of himself without trading on the Sawyer name. The only one who hasn't been a pain in my ass for the last fifteen years. Now, you have to pay for your freedom."

Prentice shook his head, an almost rueful smile curving his lips. "Always thought I got one over on all the other Sawyers. Every ancestor going back to Alexander, and none of them could manage more than one or two offspring. It's a miracle the Sawyer line lasted this long. I learned the hard way—you have to work at it. I went through a lot of wives, but I bred my own little army of Sawyers. Did what none of the rest could do."

He laughed again, triumphant and smug. Prentice had always prided himself on his fecundity compared to all those only children that came before. His laugh morphed from triumphant back to rueful.

"The ancestors had it right. Children are more trouble than they're worth. Should have stopped after the first. The rest of you are liars. Deceivers. You thought you'd get the best of me. You're wrong."

I took a second to process my father implying that I wasn't a liar. Ironic, since he'd booted me out of town for planning to betray him. He must have forgotten that under the avalanche of my siblings' more recent offenses.

I hadn't. I hadn't forgotten anything.

Another maniacal cackle of laughter dragged my attention back to the screen. "You weren't fast enough. Should have killed me yesterday. You forgot all of it is mine. You're nothing but employees, and I decide what happens to my legacy. If you thought you could get rid of me, you're about to discover how wrong you were."

On that threat, Prentice straightened, arranging the papers in front of him. When he looked back at the camera, he was all business, the taunts and triumph wiped away.

"Here's how it's going to work. The bulk of my assets are in a trust. That trust is reserved for the care and maintenance of Heartstone Manor. It will pay for upkeep and management well into the next century. Heartstone Manor is the foundation of the Sawyers. None of you ungrateful cretins appreciated it. That's going to change. Harvey's got a list of do's and don'ts, but basically, they amount to this—don't fuck it up, don't turn it into a tourist attraction, and take care of your legacy."

His eyes moved around the table, resting on each of his children. I had to remind myself that this was only a video, recorded weeks before he'd died. My siblings shifted uncomfortably under his gaze. Sterling tipped her flask to her lips, drinking until it was empty. I couldn't blame her.

"Before you have a collective stroke, I did set aside a little something for my beloved children. An amount of money has been put in trust for each of you. Except for Griffen.

"Griffen is the executor of all the trusts. Excepting the money in the Heartstone trust, Griffen has control over all of your trust funds. If he wants to keep every penny for himself, he's more than welcome to. I would. And who knows? He walked out on you just like he walked out on me, so maybe he will."

Beside me, Hope sucked in a breath. I was right there with her. That was some serious revisionist history. I hadn't *walked* anywhere. I'd been tossed out and told never to set foot in town again.

My father went on with his insanity, every word that came out of his mouth stacking the crazy a little higher.

"If each of you agrees to move back into Heartstone Manor and do what you're told for Griffen the way you never did for me, Griffen will release your funds to you after five years. If he hasn't spent it all on himself, that is.

"Ownership of Heartstone Manor as well as Sawyer Enterprises and associated business interests all pass to Griffen. The

Inn, the brewery, the real estate, the investment portfolio... All of it is Griffen's. He can live comfortably off that income, as I did. If that's not enough he can loot your trusts and buy himself a fleet of yachts."

His eyes came back to me. I stiffened, grateful when Hope's hand closed over my arm.

"Griffen. Bet you're feeling pretty smug right now. You walked away and now you have it all. Well, brace yourself and get ready for the stinger."

At that, the screen went black.

Chapter Four

HOPE

So, what's the stinger?" griffen's brother royal cut into the babble of voices, getting right to the point.

Stinger.

I didn't like the sound of that. I'd known Prentice Sawyer my entire life. He hadn't left Griffen everything as a reward, as some kind of recompense for kicking him out years before. No, this was just another punishment, a final stab in the back from beyond the grave.

Sitting in silence beside Griffen, I wanted to disappear. I wanted to get up and walk out, to get in my car and drive until I hit the ocean.

I needed to stay exactly where I was. Griffen's siblings looked at him with suspicion and dislike. They were strangers, and Griffen hadn't asked for any of this. He wasn't my biggest fan—for good reason—but I was the only one here who was on his side.

Harvey rolled his shoulders, and the entire room braced.

"There are conditions," he began. "You have until Tuesday to relocate to Heartstone Manor. You may leave for a total of fourteen days every quarter, but your primary residence must be Heartstone for the next five years."

"And if we don't?" Royal asked.

"If you don't, your trust will be dissolved, the balance added to the Heartstone Manor trust, and you'll be barred from family property. Including your place of employment, if applicable."

Royal sat back and let out a low whistle. "He's got us over a barrel."

"Fuck that," Sterling said, throwing out a hand that almost smacked Quinn in the face. "We'll just do that thing. What's it called? Protest it! We'll protest the will."

"*Contest* it, you mean," Brax corrected with a withering glare at his sister.

"Whatever," Sterling mumbled, looking balefully into the open mouth of her empty flask.

"Can we?" Quinn asked after sending Sterling a worried look.

Harvey slowly shook his head. "I don't recommend it. If you choose to contest the will, the will as written is void, and everything—the trusts, the house, the various entities owned by Sawyer Enterprises—all go to your cousin Bryce."

Bryce. I slumped back into my chair. Prentice was a bastard, but he knew his children. He might have spent most of their lives playing them against each other, but they were united in their hatred of their cousin Bryce.

For good reason. Bryce was spoiled, selfish, and mean. He'd been a nasty little boy and from what I'd seen he hadn't improved with age. The idea of Bryce walking away with the

Sawyer fortune made me a little sick. I wasn't the only one. The faces around the conference table all looked faintly green.

"I guess I'm moving back home," Finn said under his breath, with a sidelong glance at Royal and another at Tenn.

"Make whatever arrangements are necessary and be prepared to move into Heartstone by Tuesday at midnight," Harvey finished, checking his watch.

"Does it really matter?" Sterling shot out. "Griffen's going to loot our trusts anyway." She crossed her arms over her chest and glared at Griffen across the table. Griffen stared back at her, his face hard as stone.

Quinn wrapped her hand around her younger sister's arm and pulled her to her feet. "I guess we're just going to have to take that risk, huh?"

She gave Griffen an appraising look before she turned to leave. Over her shoulder, she met Harvey's eye. "That's it? We're free to go? And we get our money in five years if we behave and Griffen doesn't spend it all on hookers and blow?"

"That's about it," Harvey agreed.

"See y'all on Tuesday then," she said and pulled Sterling from the room.

I watched in silence as the rest of Griffen's siblings trickled out, grumbling to themselves. Royal paused at the door, looking back at Griffen as if he wanted to say something. Tenn came up behind him, shoving at his shoulder to move him through the doorway. Royal shook his head and went.

In a low voice only Griffen and I could hear, Harvey said, "You two stay put. We're not done."

Beside me, Griffen didn't say a word. Was he in shock, or did he still hate us all this much? I didn't have time to think about it. When the room was empty of everyone but the three of us, Harvey walked to the door and leaned out. He said something to the receptionist before closing the door and flipping the lock.

Pushing the cart with the screen away from the table, he sat, flattening his palms on the shiny surface. He appeared to be lost in thought. I wondered what was left—paperwork probably—when Griffen cut into the quiet.

"The thing with Bryce wasn't the stinger, was it?"

Harvey shook his head. Not in denial. In remorse. "You always were a sharp one, Griffen."

"So?" Griffen prompted.

Harvey sucked in a breath and let it out slowly before he dropped the ax. "To fulfill the requirements of the will you and Hope have to get married. It has to be a real marriage, and it has to last at least five years. If either of you refuses, the will as I explained it to you earlier is void and everything goes to Bryce."

Griffen let out a breath as if he'd been punched in the gut and sank back in his chair. I felt like he looked. My lungs were too tight. I couldn't get any air.

Marry Griffen? What the hell?

Marry Griffen?

Why? What purpose could it serve? I struggled to find the logic. Prentice was cruel, but he never did anything without a reason. Neither did my Uncle Edgar.

Edgar had called that morning and ordered me to attend the service and reading in his place, claiming a headache. Uncle Edgar didn't get headaches, even after late nights with too much whiskey, but I did as I was told. Now it all made sense.

There had been no headache, and Uncle Edgar was as much the architect of this disaster as Prentice.

Why?

He wanted me to marry Griffen. It was a brutal irony. Ten-year-old Hope had dreamed of growing up to marry Griffen Sawyer. Instead, he'd been driven from Sawyers Bend, hating all of us.

Me most of all.

With good reason. If his attitude in the last two days was any indication, he still hated me. I didn't blame him. I deserved it.

I was the reason he'd lost the fiancée he'd loved. Now, he'd be forced to marry me in her place.

I couldn't do it.

I didn't have a choice.

How could Prentice ask this of him?

Stupid question. Prentice wouldn't have cared how Griffen felt. Prentice Sawyer cared about nothing but himself.

Beside me, Griffen croaked out a single word, the one I couldn't stop thinking.

"Why?"

Harvey shook his head, looking between the two of us. "I don't know the *why*. The only thing I know is the how. I'm sorry. I tried to talk him out of it."

"What if I'd been married? Seeing someone?" Griffen asked.

"He knew you weren't."

"What happens if one of us dies before the five years is up?" Griffen pressed.

Harvey raised an eyebrow. "One Sawyer in jail for murder is enough for now, don't you think?"

Griffen scowled at Harvey, then at me. "That's not what I meant."

"It would solve a few problems," I commented dryly.

"This isn't funny," Griffen said, still scowling at me.

"No, it's not," I agreed.

"To answer your question," Harvey said, "It depends. If either of you dies, everything goes to Bryce, unless there's a child. If there's a child, he or she inherits with the surviving parent as guardian. Unless you're both dead, then Royal would be the guardian."

"And if something happens to the child?" I asked, my

stomach pitching at the idea of my future offspring at the mercy of Bryce's greed.

"If something were to happen to the child, Royal would inherit."

"And we can't contest it?" I had to ask, even though I knew the answer.

"You can," Harvey said, "but I don't recommend it. The will is legal. If anyone contests the will, Griffen's trusteeship is revoked, the trusts are dissolved, and all funds go to Bryce. And that's not your biggest problem."

All at once the picture came into focus, and I knew what Harvey meant. "If we contest the will, Griffen can't take over Sawyer Enterprises. He can't access the bank accounts, can't sign payroll checks."

Griffen finished, "It's the same as just walking away. By the time everything is sorted out in court, the town would be dead."

"In all likelihood, Bryce would win anyway," Harvey added.

"And you have no idea why?" I pressed.

Harvey gave me a remorseful look. "Prentice didn't share his motives with me, Hope. You know who you can ask, but I doubt you'll get an answer."

Harvey Benson was Uncle Edgar's lawyer, too. He knew who he was dealing with. Harvey was a tool to Prentice and Edgar, just like the rest of us.

I looked down at my hands in my lap, my nails short and unpolished. Invisible bars pressed on me, squeezing the air from my lungs. I was in a cage. I'd been in a cage for so long I'd gotten used to it, trapped by loyalty and history and obligation.

My uncle had saved me. I owed him everything. He never let me forget it.

This was my life. Stuck in the cage of this town, working for my uncle, doing what I was told. I'd given up on any dreams to the contrary not long after Griffen had been exiled. I'd grown so used to it I went months at a time without remembering that once I'd been a different woman. A different girl.

But this—trapping Griffen in the cage with me—this was wrong. He'd gotten out. He had a life, friends, a career he loved. I'd followed him over the years, unable to keep from picking at the wound. Unable to forgive myself for what I'd done.

"This isn't fair," I whispered.

Harvey gave me a sad smile. "You do this job long enough, sweetheart, you realize nothing is fair. Do you want to hear the terms?"

Chapter Five

HOPE

*L*AY IT ON US," GRIFFEN SAID, HIS VOICE GRIM.

I couldn't bring myself to look at him, couldn't stand to see the accusation I knew was in his eyes. He'd think I was in on it. Of course, he would. How many women had dangled after that position? Lady of the Manor. Wife to the Sawyer heir.

Not me. Never me. I'd had girlish dreams, but I'd never imagined I could fill that role. Even back then, when I'd ruined his engagement, I never thought to take her place.

How could I? It was only that she'd been wrong for him. She'd been a nightmare, not that it excused what I'd done.

Harvey's voice interrupted my thoughts. "You have to be married for five years, as I said. To the outside world, it's a love match. No one can know about the will, excluding the three of us, I'm assuming Edgar, and your witness."

"Witness?" I asked, not understanding. Did he mean the witness to the ceremony? Why would they need to know?

"Apparently, Prentice didn't trust either of you to adhere to the spirit of the arrangement. It has to be real. No separate bedrooms. No separate lives. No adultery. You can't be apart for more than twelve hours at a time in the first year. No more than thirty-six hours at a time for the remaining four years or until you've produced two children. The witness is there to provide testimony, if needed, that you're conducting yourselves according to the terms. And Hope has to sign a prenup. If you divorce in five years, she gets nothing from the Sawyer estate."

"That's bullshit," Griffen said. "She gives up five years of her life and she gets nothing?"

"I don't want anything." Dizzy, unable to draw breath, my heart pounded against my ribs, beating against its own cage, desperate to take flight. Sitting beside Griffen, I appeared composed, but on the inside, I was screaming.

I couldn't do this. I could read between the lines. They didn't just want me to marry him, they wanted me to have his children. I had no illusions about how a custody battle would work out once Griffen divorced me.

I had to be realistic. I didn't know him. Didn't know what he was capable of. Not anymore. Pushing back my chair, I rose, not sure where I was going. I paced to the window and stared through the blinds, seeing nothing.

Behind me, I heard Griffen say something to Harvey. Harvey excused himself, the door shutting with a click as he left. I couldn't bring myself to turn around.

"You didn't know," I heard Griffen say.

I forced myself to turn. He stood there, hands shoved in his pockets as he watched me appraisingly, his sandy blond hair falling into his eyes. I thought I'd exaggerated him in my memories, the strong line of his jaw, the sea green of his eyes. All these years later and he still stopped my heart.

I was too shocked to bother with anything but the truth. "I had no idea. I didn't know why I was here. Uncle Edgar said he had a headache, asked me to come in his place. They sent me to Atlanta to get you because they didn't think you'd—"

"They didn't think I'd come back if one of my siblings showed up, right?"

I shrugged a shoulder. It had made sense at the time. Now I could see it had been nothing more than an elaborate ruse.

"This is absurd," I said. "You don't want to marry me."

"You don't want to marry me either," Griffen said.

"No, I don't," I agreed. I'd stolen one fiancée from Griffen Sawyer. The last thing I wanted was to saddle him with one he didn't want.

He came closer, close enough for me to feel the heat of his body, smell the faint woodsy scent of him. Spice and green trees. It was winter, but he reminded me of fall, of brightly-colored leaves and bonfires, pumpkins and apple festivals. I wanted to curl up in that scent and—

Get your head straight, Hope. None of this is about you. You're a tool and you don't even know what you're being used for.

"Edgar and Prentice did this. Did it occur to either of them that you might say no?" Griffen asked gently.

My laugh startled me. "I'm sure it didn't," I admitted.

In all their machinations, I doubted Uncle Edgar or Prentice Sawyer had considered that I wouldn't do exactly what I was told.

"And are you?"

"Am I what?" I asked, stalling

"Going to say no?"

"Are you?" I asked, curious.

33

Either of us could walk away and damn the consequences. We didn't *have* to do this.

He tilted his head to the side as he studied me. "Why wouldn't I? I have everything to gain. Prentice didn't leave me a trust, but if I marry you, I get everything. The house, the company, you—so why wouldn't I?"

I couldn't tell if he was asking or taunting. It didn't matter. I replied honestly, "You don't want any of that. You know you don't."

The mask dropped from Griffen's face as he let out a long breath, his eyes angry. Trapped. I knew what that looked like. I saw it in the mirror often enough.

"No, I don't. No offense."

"None taken," I said, automatically, lying only a little. I knew what I was. My uncle's boring lackey. I wasn't hideous, wasn't stupid, but there was nothing particularly appealing about me either. Nothing that would attract a man like Griffen.

"What do you get out of it?" he asked. "The prestige of being the lady of Heartstone Manor?" There was laughter in his voice.

I let a small smile curve my lips. I hadn't changed that much. "Sure," I said, "I'll start throwing tea parties and join the Junior League."

"Then why, Hope? Why haven't you walked out of here yet? What does Edgar have on you?"

So many years away, but Griffen still remembered how things worked around here. Layers of loyalty and history, secrets and lies. My motives were simple. I didn't have any secrets, no lies to protect, but I did have loyalty. Loyalty and a lifetime of debt.

I owed Griffen. I owed Uncle Edgar. I owed this town. "When Uncle Edgar brought me home, this town was good to me. You and I are the only thing standing between Sawyers Bend and Bryce."

Griffen barked out a laugh. "Jesus, when you put it like that—"

"You know what he would do. If anyone could burn through the Sawyer fortune, it's Bryce."

He was exactly the kind of idiot who'd buy himself a dozen Lamborghinis, throw a million at the roulette wheel just because he could, who'd sell off everything for one more dollar to spend.

Alexander Braxton Sawyer had founded this town after fighting in the Revolutionary War. Some of these families had been here just as long. Griffen's great-great-grandfather had built Heartstone Manor as a gift for his beloved wife. A gift that was now a piece of American history. If we said no, all of it would fall to dust.

"It's only five years," I said.

Griffen took a step closer, crowding me with his body. I'm tall, but he was taller—much taller. "You realize Harvey said it has to be a real marriage. You didn't miss that part?"

He caught the shiver that ran through me at those words. His eyes flared, and I stepped back before I could stop myself. I jerked my head in a nod and looked down to see my hands fisted at my sides.

I'd cross that bridge when we came to it. If I tried to think what a *real marriage* with Griffen Sawyer implied, my head would explode.

"We don't have all day," Griffen commented, crossing his arms over his chest. "Do you need time to think?"

I shook my head. There wasn't anything to think about. We could pretend we had a choice, but both of us knew the truth.

"I guess the only question is will you marry me, Hope Daniels?"

I looked up into Griffen's sea green eyes, so familiar and so distant, and said the words I never thought would cross my lips. "Yes. I'll marry you, Griffen Sawyer."

Griffen gave a brisk nod and left to call Harvey back in. We took our seats at the table again and carried on as if nothing momentous had happened. Calmly, I read and signed the prenup Harvey put in front of me as a part of me was completely freaking out.

Stop! What are you doing? Don't sign that! Run, run far, far away!

I couldn't listen to my fears. I had to do this. I didn't have a choice.

"So," Harvey said, reviewing my signature, "did you discuss your witness?"

"What about Miss Martha? Was she still working for dad?" Griffen asked, mentioning the Sawyer family house-keeper. Harvey was shaking his head in a negative as I bit back a laugh.

"Miss Martha quit four years ago," I told him.

"If you could get her to come back, I'd agree to Miss Martha." Harvey made a note in the file in front of him.

"Would you approve of Savannah?" I countered. From what I knew of how things had gone down with Prentice and Miss Martha, she wasn't coming back. Her daughter Savannah had worked in the house when she was younger, and she might be willing to take the job.

Harvey thought it over. "I'll agree to Savannah. If you can talk either of them into taking the job, send her to me and I'll get it set up. Things are a mess over there."

"What does that mean?" Griffen asked, but Harvey only shook his head and went on.

"I took the liberty of having Clary from the Register of Deeds office bring over the license. Judge Wilcox will be here in five minutes. We'll do the paperwork and get this taken care of. The ring is on you," he said to Griffen, who nodded.

I hadn't even thought about a ring. Before I knew it, Clary came bustling in with her seal and the paperwork and two pens, and then the judge was there.

Griffen and I stood facing each other at the end of the conference table and repeated the words that would change our lives.

They went in one ear and out the other. Nothing registered until Griffen looked down at me, his eyes cool and remote as he said *I do*. I had a last impulse to turn on my heel and fly out the door.

My mouth opened and I felt the vow form.

The words fell between us like stones.

"I do," I swore.

And then it was done.

I waited for someone to say Griffen could kiss the bride, but the words never came. We both stepped back, the judge and Clary and Harvey conferring over the license. I stood there, my ears ringing, wobbling a little.

Had that just happened?

Griffen raised his chin at Harvey. "Are we done here? For now?"

"For now. You have my number. I'd suggest taking care of the business we discussed first off, then stop by here tomorrow."

Griffen nodded in agreement and turned to me. "Let's get a piece of pie."

Chapter Six

HOPE

*G*RIFFEN STRODE OUT THE DOOR OF HARVEY'S VICTORIAN, HIS feet crunching in the gravel parking lot. As he reached the street, he raised his head and looked around as if surprised at where he was. "Maisie's place still around?"

"Same as it always was." Maisie's Café served breakfast and lunch. She had the best pie in town. Always had.

Griffen's body was drawn tight, his eyes scanning our surroundings. Nothing about this man said he wanted to climb in a car and sit. Maisie's wasn't more than a few blocks away. Glad I'd worn sensible shoes, I started to move. "Come on. We can just about get there before she starts closing up for the day."

We walked in silence, side-by-side. I looked around, seeing the town through Griffen's eyes. So much had changed in the last fifteen years. Everything and nothing.

Tourists were the lifeblood of Sawyers Bend, demanding a delicate balance between the allure of yesteryear and the need for modernity. Almost every business on Main Street offered free wifi—heck, even Maisie's had it—and the gas station had plugins for electric vehicles, but the iron benches on the sidewalks were the same design as those installed a century before. Ditto for the streetlamps, the window awnings, and most everything else.

All of it shiny and new even as it hearkened back to an earlier day. The booths at Maisie's had been replaced three years before, the surface of the wooden tables shiny and unmarred, but the menu wasn't much different. After a few weeks, Griffen would absorb the changes in town and everything would be familiar again.

Except his entire life had changed.

We were married.

Married.

I snuck a glance at the screen of my phone. Uncle Edgar hadn't called me since that morning when he'd secured my promise to attend the burial and the will reading.

Of course, he hadn't called.

He already knew I was exactly where he wanted me.

Why?

Foolish question.

I knew exactly why Uncle Edgar wanted me married to Griffen. Edgar and Prentice had their business all tangled up together. My official job was as Edgar's assistant, but I knew almost as much about Prentice's business. With Prentice dead, Uncle Edgar would want his interests protected.

If some idiot took the helm of Sawyer Enterprises it could mean big losses for Uncle Edgar. Uncle Edgar didn't like to lose. From his point of view, it made absolute sense that he would position me right next to the Sawyer heir.

What I didn't understand was why Prentice had agreed. None of this made sense. I should be angry that my future had been hijacked for someone else's purposes.

What future?

I worked for Uncle Edgar. That was it.

I got up, did what Uncle Edgar needed, and went home. Sometimes I stopped by the library on my way back to my little apartment. I liked to go for walks when I had time or get a coffee at my friend Daisy's bakery. That was the extent of my social life. I couldn't remember the last time I'd gone on a date.

How could they hijack my life when I didn't have a life in the first place?

Sometimes I thought I'd used up all of my rebellious spirit moving out of Edgar's house and into that apartment. Now, I'd have to leave it behind for Heartstone Manor. I should have been excited. Heartstone was practically a castle, and I would be its mistress. Temporarily.

I followed Griffen through the front door of Maisie's, acutely aware of the way conversation stopped when we entered. Probably drawn by the silence, Maisie came bustling out of the back, stopping abruptly at the sight of Griffen. A wide smile spread across her face as her arms flew wide and she hurtled her small, rounded body into Griffen's arms. He closed his own around her in a tight squeeze.

Maisie liked to gossip, and she baked a mean pie, but most of all she had a warm, loving heart. She leaned back and reached up to cup his face in her palms.

"Griffen Sawyer! Didn't you grow up to be a handsome man? Where have you been?"

She gave him a light smack on the cheek as only a woman who'd known him since birth could do. Griffen reached up to take her hands in his, giving her the charming smile I

41

remembered so well. "Maisie Evans. You don't look a day older than when I left."

She blushed at the compliment, her eyes twinkling. "You always were a charmer." Her eyes skipped to me, narrowing in concern as she took in my dark suit and the mud on my low heels. "Let me get you a table."

She looped her arm through Griffen's and led him to an empty booth in the back corner of the café. "I forgot today was the funeral." Her sharp eyes studied me and Griffen. She nodded decisively. "You two need pie. Peach, cherry, apple, or blueberry?"

"Peach," Griffen answered immediately.

"Just coffee for me, Maisie."

Maisie shook her head at my order but didn't comment, gesturing for us to sit. We did and she bustled off. Griffen smiled down at the tabletop. "She really does look exactly the same."

"Maisie doesn't seem to age."

We sat in the booth, the silence a chasm between us. I didn't know what to say.

I'm sorry you had to marry me.

I *was* sorry. Still wasn't anything I could do about it.

I'm sorry your father died?

We'd already covered that. I wouldn't lie to Griffen. I doubted anyone was sorry Prentice had died.

A cup of coffee slid in front of me accompanied by a slice of blueberry pie topped with a scoop of vanilla ice cream. My favorite dessert since I was a little girl.

I'd never forget the first time Uncle Edgar brought me here, my hair in two uneven braids, my dress the wrong size but clean and new. He'd sat opposite me in a booth almost identical to this one, his face heavy with a dour expression that should have frightened an eight-year-old. Edgar didn't frighten me. He'd saved me.

He was abrupt. He wasn't affectionate. He made it clear I was an annoyance and a burden. But he'd saved me. He'd fed me. Given me clean clothes. He'd braided my hair, albeit badly.

He brought me to Maisie, who wrapped me in hugs and fed me blueberry pie.

I'd cried into that first slice of pie. Cried at the sheer delight of blueberries bursting over my tongue, the sweetness of the house-made ice cream. Mostly I cried because between Maisie's sugar-scented hug and Uncle Edgar's obdurate expression, I knew that I was safe. For the first time in my short life, I didn't have to be afraid.

Edgar didn't love me, but he understood loyalty and family in a way my own parents never had.

Maisie met my eye as she slid a plate in front of Griffen loaded with a healthy slice of peach pie and its own scoop of vanilla ice cream. She inclined her head towards my own blueberry pie.

"Eat that. No arguments. You're too skinny."

It was a frequent complaint from Maisie. Uncle Edgar believed women should look like sticks. I'm an adult and don't live in his house anymore, but the lessons of childhood are hard to forget.

I spent most of the day working in Edgar's office, subjected to his comments on everything from my note-taking skills to the way I wore my hair. It was easier just to go along. I couldn't remember the last time I'd dug into a slice of blueberry pie.

I picked up my fork and sank the tines into the flaky crust. If there was ever a day to forget about calories, it was today. I took a bite of the pie and couldn't help remembering the eight-year-old girl I'd been.

Twenty-three years later I was still just as well-behaved— and I was still just as safe.

For the first time, I had the uncomfortable thought that maybe safety wasn't enough. Maybe safety wasn't all it was cracked up to be.

"We need to make a list." Griffen cut into my thoughts, his voice too low for the neighboring tables to eavesdrop.

A list. I could do lists. I was a champion for lists. Setting my fork down, I dug into my bag and pulled out a notebook and a pen. Flipping to a blank page, I wrote *To Do* at the top in my neat handwriting.

Below, I wrote *#1* and looked up at Griffen in expectation.

"We have a shit-ton of things to take care of, but first on the list is arranging for our witness." He rolled his eyes at the word. I had to agree.

We were adults. We didn't need a babysitter. Prentice Sawyer was an ass, but he wasn't a fool. This forced marriage deal would be easy to fake, and for some bizarre reason, Prentice wanted it to be real. Or as real as he could make it, considering I was the last woman Griffen wanted to marry. I was trying not to think about the ramifications of that.

Griffen went on, "We can start with Miss Martha and Savannah. Hopefully, we can talk one of them into it."

I wrote *Miss Martha/Savannah* after *#1* on my list.

"Next?"

Griffen muffled his sigh with a fork full of peaches and ice cream. He chewed thoughtfully before answering. "We need to see Harvey tomorrow. There have to be papers to sign. I want to make sure payroll gets cut."

I wrote that down next. *#2. Harvey*

"I have to find out what's going on with Ford."

#3. Ford

"You don't think he did it," I said as I finished writing Ford's name.

"No way," came Griffen's immediate response. "Do you?"

I shook my head. I was with Griffen. No way.

Ford was tough as nails when he wanted to be, but he wasn't a killer. He was also extremely intelligent. If Ford had decided to kill Prentice, he was way too smart to get caught.

The idea that he would march into Prentice's office and shoot him in the head then stash the gun in his bedroom closet? No flipping way.

The topic of Ford settled to Griffen's satisfaction for the moment, he went on with his list. "We have to go to Atlanta, at least overnight. I didn't bring anything with me, wasn't planning on staying."

I nodded, adding #5. *Atlanta* to the list.

Griffen took another bite of pie as he read the list upside down. Swallowing, he said, "What happened to number four?"

"Number four is Heartstone Manor," I said, surprised I needed to state something so obvious.

Griffen visibly flinched.

He hadn't seen his home since the day he'd been cast out. Guilt stabbed at me again. I wasn't the one who'd thrown him out. That honor went to Prentice. But it was my fault he'd had to leave.

My foolish teenage yearnings had led me to tell a secret, a secret that had ended up stealing everything from Griffen. His love, his family, his legacy. I'd never regretted anything in my life so much as those few ill-spoken words.

When Griffen's pie was done, I pushed my half-empty plate away and got moving. Our to-do list was only five items, but they were big ones and the clock was ticking. We only had a few days before we needed to be living in Heartstone, our witness in place. That week would fly by before we realized the time was gone.

"You should finish that," Griffen said, looking at my mostly uneaten blueberry pie.

"I'm good," I lied. "Let's go see Miss Martha."

We walked back to Harvey's office and our cars. I got in beside Griffen, navigating as he drove the few short miles to the small cottage Miss Martha had purchased after she'd quit working for Prentice.

Despite her history with Prentice, Miss Martha's eyes lit when they landed on Griffen at her front door. A tall, sturdy woman, bigger than me but not quite as big as Griffen, she pulled him into her arms, patting a callused hand on his back and rocking him from side to side as if he were a child.

With a sniff, she straightened and stepped back. "Come on in before you let in the flies." He obeyed, a grin quirking his lips. Martha's strong hand landed on my shoulder as I passed. "What kind of trouble you in, girl?"

"You won't believe it when I tell you," I said.

We followed Miss Martha back to her kitchen, sitting at the table while she started to make coffee. Griffen tried to stop her. "We just came from Maisie's, Miss Martha. Don't go to any trouble. I need to ask you if you'll come back to work at Heartstone."

Martha let out a *harrumph* and continued setting up the coffee. "Boy, you can't jump right into business. I haven't seen you in fifteen years. Sit your tail down at the table and have a cup of coffee with me."

Griffen sat. Unlike Maisie, Miss Martha had changed over the years. Her red hair had streaks of gray at the temples. Lines grooved her fine skin around her mouth and on her forehead.

"You coming home," she asked after pressing the button to start the coffee maker, "or are you just here for the service?"

"Looks like I'm coming home. We have a situation," Griffen said carefully. "I need someone I trust in the house. Why did you leave?"

Miss Martha ignored his question, arranging a tray with coffee mugs, a plate of cookies, and anything else she thought we'd need. You could take the housekeeper out of the house, but she was still Miss Martha. Finally ready, she added the carafe of coffee to the tray and set it in the center of the table.

Griffen controlled his impatience. Barely. When she was settled in her chair, she said, "I'll say you have a situation, Griffen Sawyer. One brother in jail for murder, the rest of your family falling apart. What are you going to do to fix it?"

Griffen froze, completely unprepared for her demand. Fix it? After what they'd done to him, his family should be falling to their knees in gratitude. He'd turned his entire life upside down to save the town. Save their fortune. Instead, they'd stormed out of Harvey's office like Griffen was the villain. He wasn't the one who needed to fix things.

I tried to cover my grumble with a bite of cookie. I wasn't fooling anyone. Griffen gave me a curious look, but Martha knew what I was thinking.

"Maybe it isn't his fault, but it's his responsibility, girl. He's the only one left."

I knew what she meant. Ford had tried. He really had. In some ways, he'd succeeded. But Ford wasn't Griffen.

Griffen decided to ignore both of us. He repeated his earlier question. "Why did you leave Heartstone Manor?"

Miss Martha threw her head back, her whole body shaking with mirth. When she was done, she met Griffen's eyes dead-on. "I left because your daddy was a bastard and no paycheck was worth putting up with him for one day longer."

Griffen shook his head, trying not to smile. "I can't argue with you about that. Who's been looking after the house since you quit?"

"He's had day staff in and out, mostly out, but what I hear from Sterling, the place is a mess."

"You see Sterling?" I asked, curious. Sterling didn't seem to have much on her mind aside from having a good time, but Miss Martha was the closest thing she had left to a mother.

Miss Martha let out a gusty sigh. "That girl. Only thing I regret about walking out of Heartstone."

"Would you consider coming back?" Griffen asked, avoiding the mention of his youngest sister.

Curiosity lighting her gray eyes, Miss Martha leaned forward. "You're really staying?"

Griffen nodded.

"And what are you doing with Hope? What kind of situation do you have, Griffen Sawyer?"

Before Griffen could answer, I said, "The kind of situation we can't discuss if you aren't willing to take the job."

Miss Martha gave another *harrumph*, but she didn't push. With a slow, almost regretful shake of her head, she said, "I'm tempted to say yes just to find out what you're hiding, but I can't do it. I'm enjoying my retirement, spending time with my grandson and in the garden. I love that house, but it's too much for me to take on."

"What about Savannah?" I asked. "She knows the house. And if we can't have you—"

Tires crunched on the gravel drive and Miss Martha smiled. "You can ask her yourself. She just got off her shift at the Inn."

Chapter Seven

HOPE

I HEARD SAVANNAH'S VOICE BEFORE THE DOOR opened, her tone low and soothing. She strode in with a toddler propped on one hip and an oversized tote slung over her shoulder. Her strawberry blonde curls were falling out of their bun, a halo of frizz around her flushed face.

Her white button-down was stained with something pink and a smear of green. Looked like her shift in the Inn restaurant had been a long one. Long and messy. She came to an abrupt stop when she spotted us at her mother's kitchen table.

"Hope," she said in surprise. "What are you—" Her eyes fell to Griffen and widened. "Griffen? Griffen Sawyer?"

Distracted, she set her son on his feet as Griffen pushed back his chair and crossed the kitchen to give Savannah a hug.

They wouldn't have known each other well as Savannah was younger than me, only ten when Griffen had left home. Still, she was Miss Martha's girl and had been underfoot at Heartstone Manor before she could walk.

"Are you back for your father's service? We were sorry to hear—" Miss Martha's snort cut her off, and Savannah slanted her mother a quelling look.

After a lifetime dealing with Prentice Sawyer, Miss Martha wasn't easily quelled. Griffen shook his head and went down on his haunches, holding his hand out to Savannah's son, who studied him with curiosity.

Absently, he said to Savannah, "I appreciate the sentiment, but you'd be the only one if you meant it." To the boy, he said, "I'm Griffen. What's your name?"

The boy stuck out his hand cautiously. "My name's Nicky."

Griffen's hand closed around the smaller one and shook solemnly. "It's nice to meet you, Nicky."

Savannah's gray eyes, so like her mother's, bounced between Martha, Griffen and me.

Griffen stood and looked pointedly at Miss Martha. "Unless you're willing to sign an NDA, we'll need to talk to Savannah in private."

Miss Martha rolled her eyes but stood, holding out her hand to Nicky and mumbling under her breath, "You know I can keep a secret, Griffen Sawyer." Not waiting for a response, she took her grandson's hand and led him out of the kitchen.

"What's this about?" Savannah asked. "Can I get y'all anything? I'm dying for a cup of that coffee."

"Your mother already took care of us," I said, gesturing to the tray on the table. "We've got some time. Get whatever you need." Savannah fixed herself a cup of coffee and joined us at the table, snagging one of her mother's molasses cookies.

"So, what's going on?"

"Do you have any interest in taking over your mother's position at Heartstone?" Griffen asked bluntly.

Surprise washed across Savannah's face before her eyes narrowed on Griffen. "That depends. Who would I be working for?"

"Us," I said.

Savannah's eyes flared even wider. My heart racing with terror and exhilaration, I dove headfirst into the fiction Griffen and I would have to live for the next five years.

Reaching out to close my fingers over Griffen's, I sent him what I hoped was a loving smile. "Griffen and I—uh—we're together." At Savannah's doubtful look, I sucked in a breath and tried again. I'm a terrible liar. I'd have to learn.

"We, uh, we'd been talking," I fumbled, thinking we should have practiced our story before we tried it out on a real, live person. From the corner of my eye, I caught Griffen's wicked grin. My heart kicked up even faster. I hadn't seen that grin in years.

He scooched his chair a few inches closer and wrapped his arm around me. Looking straight at Savannah, he said "My dad's death changed things. Hope and I don't have to keep our relationship a secret anymore. We got married this afternoon."

Griffen leaned in and pressed a soft kiss to my jaw. My heart thumped so hard I thought it might explode right out of my chest. Savannah stared at the two of us in silence before she let out a snort identical to her mother's and shook her head.

"I don't know what's going on, but you two are going to have to practice that routine if you expect to sell it around town."

Griffen's jaw went hard. He flipped his hand over, closing his fingers around mine. "As far as anyone's concerned, that's the God's honest truth."

Savannah rolled her eyes but withheld further comment. Instead, she asked, "Why me? Why an NDA? Would you be living there for real? Because I'd love to take on Heartstone. I

51

know the house, I know what it needs, but I'm not getting stuck there with Sterling and Brax and whoever else decides to show up."

Griffen let go of my hand and braced his elbows on the table. "I can't tell you about the NDA unless you agree to take the job. I can promise you that Hope and I will be in residence full-time, and if anyone gives you a hard time they'll answer to me."

Savannah took a deep breath and let it out slowly, thinking. Finally, she said, "I need health insurance. I have a decent policy through the Inn—"

With a glance at Griffen, I cut in, "If you decide to take the job, the policy that covers Sawyer Enterprises employees will also cover staff at the house."

Griffen shot me a curious look and I explained, "When they changed insurers a few years ago, I helped Uncle Edgar and Prentice research and set up the new policy they offer their employees. Harvey can double-check because I didn't handle the details for Heartstone, but I'm pretty sure that Heartstone Manor qualifies as a small business as far as the insurance is concerned. I can't promise the coverage would be any better than what you have at the Inn. It's probably the same policy."

Savannah nodded. "The Inn policy is pretty good, considering. What kind of salary are you thinking? Where do we live? I've got Nicky. He goes to preschool a few days a week. I try to organize my shifts around that and my mom pitches in when she can, but otherwise, he's with me. Do you have a problem with him running around Heartstone?"

"Of course not," Griffen said immediately. "As far as salary— excuse me for a second—" He got up and disappeared down the hall, following the path Miss Martha had taken earlier.

He returned a few seconds later and threw out a number, adding, "That's what your mother was making when she quit, plus twenty percent. We need you to be in charge of staffing for the house and grounds, organize a cook, maintenance, daily cleaning—everything your mom used to do."

"Everyone will be in residence," I added.

"Everyone?" Savannah asked, incredulous. "That'll be... interesting."

Griffen ignored her comment and went on, "Heartstone expenses come out of a trust Harvey Benson oversees, so he'll need to sign off on everything. He's already given preliminary approval for you as housekeeper."

I leaned in and caught Savannah's eye. "In fact, you're the only one we've agreed on, aside from your mother."

Savannah sat back and crossed her arms over her chest, still thinking. "Any crap from Sterling or anyone else and I'm out."

"Any crap from anyone," Griffen said, "and you come to me. I'll kick any of them out before you."

Savannah's eyebrows shot up. "You mean it?"

"What are you worried about?" I asked before Griffen could answer. I knew he meant what he'd said. We couldn't afford to lose our witness. If one of his siblings wanted to get themselves kicked out of Heartstone Manor for being an ass, that was their problem.

Savannah gave Griffen a hesitant look. Shifting her gaze to me she said, "You know. Sterling puking all over the bathroom after one too many. Bringing home one-night stands who walk off with the family silver. Being expected to fetch and carry all day when I should be running the house."

With a jerk of one shoulder, she added to Griffen, "I grew up in Heartstone. I love that house. I'd love to put it to rights again, to take care of it, but—your brothers have reputations. I'm not interested in offering additional services."

Griffen's back went straight at the implication. "Has anyone given you a hard time at the Inn? Expected anything from you that you didn't want to give?"

"No. Not really. But living in the house is different. And your father—"

She didn't need to finish that sentence. Prentice had never laid a finger on Miss Martha—if he'd tried he would have lost the finger—but assorted other household staff had warmed his bed over the years. Brax had followed in his father's footsteps until Prentice fired the staff.

Griffen picked up one of the cookies and broke off a piece. "Why don't I lay this out in more detail? You'd work for me and Hope. The only other person with authority over you would be Harvey Benson. Your job is to run the house. Until you get a full staff hired, you'll need to pitch in wherever necessary, but your job isn't to jump anytime a Sawyer rings a bell.

"Your job is to make sure we have meals, a clean and presentable home, that the grounds and the house are in good condition. You'll manage the household budget and staff. You will not act as anyone's personal servant. And if at any time any member of the household crosses a line you don't like, you come to me or Hope and we'll sort it out. Does that work?"

"That works." Savannah smiled, drawing in a deep breath that froze in her lungs as something else occurred to her. "What about security?"

"What do you mean?" I asked.

"Someone walked into Heartstone Manor and shot Prentice in the head."

"Ford is in jail," Griffen said carefully.

Savannah gave a dismissive shake of her head. "I know what the police think, but Mom swears he didn't do it."

"I've spent the last ten years working for the best security agency in the country. I'll get a team out to rewire the house, set up a system so we can monitor the property."

"Good enough for me," Savannah said, the smile returning to her face. "When do you want me to start?"

"First thing tomorrow," Griffen said, "go by Harvey's office. I'll tell him to expect you. He can fill you in on the specifics including the NDA and the reason for it. Hope and I have some business to take care of, but we expect to move in by Monday. The faster you can get started the better."

And that was that. We had a housekeeper. And a witness.

A weight lifted from my chest just knowing that Savannah would be there. She wasn't a friend, not yet, but she was an ally. I needed one of those. Griffen was being decent, but eventually, the shock would wear off and he'd remember that he was married to the woman who'd ruined his life.

Since the day had started I'd been a leaf flowing down a mountain stream, bubbling along wherever the current took me, pushed and pulled by everyone else's demands. I'd married Griffen to save the town. I'd do it again in a heartbeat, but it hadn't been my choice any more than it had been his.

If I had to have a witness in the house, documenting my every move, at least it could be someone I'd chosen. Just knowing I'd gotten my way in this one thing made the rest easier to take.

We said goodbye to Savannah and got into Griffen's sleek Maserati. I fastened my seatbelt and looked over to see him tip his head back against the headrest, eyes closed. He looked utterly exhausted. My heart hurt for him.

He'd come home expecting to put his father in the ground, sign some papers, and never see any of us again. Instead, his whole life had been turned inside out. He'd have to leave his home, his career, the people he'd made his family. All of it to save a town that had turned its back on him.

I wanted to help. Hard to figure out how when I was part of the problem. "What now?"

Griffen rolled his head in my direction and opened his eyes. Raising a brow, he asked, "Honeymoon?"

My stomach turned over in disappointment. In remorse. In the tiniest bit of hopeless longing. This wasn't that kind of marriage. No ring. No kiss. No honeymoon. Just five years of playing a role for everyone except Griffen.

My hands twisted in my lap, fingers twined together so tightly my knuckles were white. I didn't know how to answer Griffen, so I fell back on my usual—dealing with the practical. "You weren't planning to spend the night in town, were you?"

Griffen reached up to rub the back of his neck as he shook his head. "I thought I'd be back on the road by now. Thought I'd put this place behind me for good."

I had nothing to say to that. We'd all thought a lot of things that weren't going to happen.

"Do you want to go to Heartstone?" Griffen's face closed down, cheeks tight, jaw clenched. So that was a *No* on the house. "The Inn?" A sharp shake of his head.

Of course, he wouldn't want to go to the Inn. That was Royal and Tenn's domain. They hadn't exactly welcomed him home. Not that I could blame them. Griffen and I weren't the only ones screwed by Prentice's will. Royal and Tenn had put everything they had into making the Inn at Sawyers Bend a success and Prentice had snatched it out from under them.

If Heartstone and the Inn were out, Griffen didn't have many options. We didn't have any chain hotels in town. They were all back in Asheville. Griffen needed a meal and sleep, not an hour-long drive through the mountains.

"You can stay at my place, if you want," I offered, instantly regretting the impulsive gesture. Backtracking, I said, "It's only one bedroom, but the couch is comfortable—"

"Banishing me to the couch already? We've only been married for a few hours."

My heart stuttered. He was kidding, right?

Except Harvey said it had to be real. Holy crap, did Griffen think—?

Were we supposed to—

Tonight?

I felt the blood drain from my face. Cold sweat sprang up between my shoulder blades as a faint grin spread across Griffen's mouth.

He reached out to bop the tip of my nose before trailing his index finger down my cheek, spreading heat along my frozen skin everywhere he touched. Across my lips, along the line of my jaw, down my neck until he reached my collarbone, leaving me shivering and aroused—and very, very confused.

Chapter Eight

GRIFFEN

I SHOULD HAVE FELT BAD FOR TEASING HOPE. I DID, kind of. But then I trailed my finger over her soft skin, felt her shiver from my touch, and I didn't feel bad anymore.

I felt all sorts of other things for Hope Daniels. Things I'd never expected.

No, not Hope Daniels. Hope Sawyer. She was Hope Fucking Sawyer now.

And she was mine.

In a million years, I never would have imagined the satisfaction I got from that thought.

Hope was mine.

Until she'd walked into my office, I'd thought I never wanted to see her again. Thought I hated her. A part of me did. I'd never forget standing in my father's office, seeing Hope's anguished, guilty eyes as I lost my fiancée, my home, my family, my legacy. She'd been the only one I told, the only one who knew. Like a fool, I'd thought I could trust her.

She'd betrayed me once. Why was I trusting her now?

Arguments swirled in my head. Reasons why Hope was the only one I could trust. Reasons I should boot her out of my car and take off.

My gut had one resounding answer. *Hope.* Just that. *Hope.* Like I usually did, I was following my gut. My gut and the silk of her skin under my touch.

After the day from hell, I was pathetically grateful she'd offered to put me up at her place. I half-expected to hear that she still lived with Edgar. It didn't seem like he'd let her out from under his thumb since I'd been gone.

Hope interrupted my thoughts. "Turn right after the sandwich shop. The stairs to my place are behind the building, next to my parking spot."

"You live in town?" The only places in town were small apartments tucked over the local businesses. Her uncle was wealthy. She was a professional. Surely, she could do better than a place over the sandwich shop.

I grabbed my emergency bag out of my trunk and followed Hope up a set of sturdy wooden stairs to a small landing that overlooked the back alley where I'd parked.

She pulled out her keys, opened the door, and we stepped into a kaleidoscope of color.

I stopped just inside the doorway, too stunned to move. Given those suits, I'd expected beige. Maybe black and white.

I'd never imagined anything like this. The building was old and even the second floor had high ceilings with ornate crown moldings. Hope had painted the walls a deep, burnished gold.

The tall windows overlooking Main Street were framed by thick, bottle-green velvet curtains. The combination reminded me of late summer in the mountains, the heavy sunlight and vibrant trees. I almost imagined I could hear the forest around me. The effect was lush. Inviting. Sensual.

Entirely unlike the woman who'd walked into my office the day before.

Exactly like the woman I'd thought she'd grow up to be.

Here was Hope. She was in the fairy lights strung along the ceiling, twinkling against the gold walls. In the rattan hanging chair in the corner beside a small table piled with books. In the massive, overstuffed, brown velvet couch that should have been too much and somehow wasn't, even covered in blood-red velvet pillows.

There were things everywhere. I could look all day and not catch all of it. A figurine of a girl holding a wand was propped on the windowsill, almost hidden behind the heavy curtain. Flowers crowded one end table, books and a haphazardly placed coffee mug another. A lamp was shaded with fringed paisley scarves. Paintings and photographs filled the walls.

It was disorderly, a riot of color and texture, and the polar opposite of the woman Hope was pretending to be. How did she hang those bland suits in the closet? I imagined the apartment would eject them straight out the front door, unworthy to exist in this fever dream of a home.

Thinking of her suits led me straight to thoughts of her bedroom. What I could see of her apartment pulsed with energy and passion, with pure hedonistic pleasure. If this was her living room, what had she done to her bedroom?

I turned slowly to see Hope beside me, shifting from one foot to the other, her cheeks pink with embarrassment as I absorbed the impact of her apartment.

"You live here?" I had to ask.

Hope nodded with a jerk and swallowed hard. "I... I know it's a little... Uncle Edgar said it's awful, but I—"

"Edgar is an ass. It's not awful. It's perfect. I could sleep on that couch for days."

Hope looked around as if seeing the room for the first time. "I didn't really have a sense of what I wanted when I moved in. I just saw stuff and bought it. I know none of it really goes, but I like it."

"I like it, too. It reminds me of you."

At that, Hope laughed. "It absolutely doesn't remind you of me. It can't. But that's okay." She crossed the room, leaving me behind. "There's beer in the fridge if you want one. I'm just going to change and then we can figure out dinner."

She disappeared through a door at the opposite side of the room. What was Edgar paying her? The son of a bitch was wealthy, but he'd always been tight with a dollar. I wouldn't put it past him to convince Hope she was lucky to have a job and then pay her a pittance.

Her apartment was cool, especially considering what she'd done with it, but it was small and run down. The appliances I could see in the kitchen were far from new. So were the fixtures in the tiny bathroom that adjoined both the living room and the bedroom. I changed clothes in the cramped space, aware of Hope doing the same in her bedroom, just on the other side of the door.

Like the asshole I am, I found myself wondering what she looked like under that ugly suit. Wondering how long it would be before I found out.

I'd been watching Hope in the car. One stroke of my fingertip over her soft skin and she'd shivered under my touch. Not in fear or revulsion. In arousal. She'd done that in Harvey's office, too. So responsive, even when I hadn't touched her yet.

She'd had a crush on me as a girl, but that was a lifetime ago. She was a woman now.

She was my wife.

Five years. No adultery.

She'd had her chance to run, to negotiate, to beg for mercy. Instead, she'd married me.

I'd never trust her again. Not like I had before.

In a fucked-up situation like this, trust is relative.

Did I trust Hope? Not fully. Not to the core.

Was there anyone in Sawyers Bend I trusted *more* than Hope?

Not even close.

We could make this work. It was only five years. We'd team up—work during the day, in bed at night—and when it was done, I'd set her free.

I exited the bathroom to find Hope in the kitchen, standing over a selection of take-out menus spread across the counter. Her hair was still in a bun, but she'd traded the suit for a slouchy gray sweater and a pair of jeans so old they were white at the seams. The jeans weren't tight, but they fit the curve of her ass like they'd been made for her.

Her eyes brightened when she looked up. "You changed. I'm glad you had something else."

"Me too. I like your jeans," I said, checking out her ass again so blatantly she blushed. I'd always liked teasing Hope, though I'd never teased her like this. She'd been a kid. She wasn't a kid now. And she wasn't wearing a bra. She probably thought her breasts were too small to need one.

When she moved her shoulders and the soft sweater slid over her curves, I had to shove my hand in my pocket before I slid it underneath all that loose fabric to see for myself how much of a handful she was.

Her cheeks still pink, Hope looked down at her jeans and shook her head. "I've had these jeans since college. They're comfortable."

"You look great," I said. I thought about commenting on her hideous taste in suits and told myself to shut the fuck up. Maybe she liked her suits. Maybe she didn't want some guy she hadn't seen in fifteen years commenting on her wardrobe.

Especially when the thing that guy was starting to want most was to see her out of her wardrobe.

Get yourself under control, I told myself. *It's been a long fucking day and your head is spun. You're stuck together for five years. Don't fuck it up on day one.*

Innocent of everything tangling in my head, Hope pushed the menus across the counter toward me. "Pizza? They deliver, so we wouldn't have to go out again. There's Chinese. They do take out, but—"

"Pizza sounds great. What do you usually get?"

"Pepperoni, sausage, mushrooms, and olives."

"Works for me," I said.

Hope pulled out her phone and placed the order. "It might be a little slow, but they're usually not too long."

I picked up my beer and headed for the couch. I never would have guessed Hope would choose the clunky, brown, velvet monstrosity. The lines weren't particularly attractive, but damn, the thing looked soft.

I sat, propping my heels up on the wood-and-metal-strapped trunk that served as Hope's coffee table, and sank into the plush velvet. "Where did you find this thing?" I asked on a groan. "It's ugly as sin, but it's insanely comfortable."

Hope curled into the other end of the couch and took an almost dainty sip of her beer. "I know. I saw it at an estate sale and once I sat in it I didn't want to get up. Sometimes I fall asleep reading, it's so comfy."

I let my head fall back into the cushions and took a long drink of beer with my eyes closed. The day pressed on me. All of it. The coffin in that hole in the ground. Sitting at Harvey's conference table, my siblings staring at me like I'd stolen Christmas. My father gloating from beyond the grave. Fucking asshole. And Hope trapped in the middle of it. So fucking unfair.

Eyes still closed, I said, "Hope, I'm sorry—"

"Don't," she said. "You didn't do this. You could spend the rest of your life trying to make up for your father and you'd never manage it."

I let out a bitter laugh. "That's fucking true. Prentice Sawyer was a piece of work." I lifted my beer in salute. "Let's hope the devil keeps him 'cause God knows we don't want him back."

Hope spit out her sip of beer. "Griffen! I can't believe you just said that."

"Did I lie?"

She wiped her mouth with the back of her hand, shaking her head. "No, but still. What about that whole *don't speak ill of the dead* thing?"

"Fuck that," I said. "He's not *the dead,* he's my father. *Undead* is more like it. He's in the ground and he's still controlling our lives. He's pretty much the definition of *undead.*"

"You have a point," Hope agreed. "I don't want to talk about your father anymore. What have you been doing for the last fifteen years? I know some—the Army, Sinclair Security—but that's all."

I could entertain Hope with the stories I'd collected, but we had time for that later. I didn't want to talk about myself. I wanted to know about her.

What had happened to the girl I'd known? I never thought I'd come back to find her buttoned up tight, living alone and working for Edgar.

"There's not much more than you already know," I lied. "After Prentice threw me out I didn't know what else to do, so I joined the Army. Turned out I was good at it. I met Evers

Sinclair not long after I joined up, made Ranger a few years later. When Evers left to join his family's company, he talked me into coming with him. I've spent most of the last ten years in the field handling whatever the Sinclairs threw my way."

Hope's eyes bright with interest, she leaned forward. "You were a Ranger? What's the most dangerous thing you've done? Ever had to shoot anyone? Have you ever been shot?"

At her last question, I rolled my shoulder, feeling the pinch and pull of muscles barely healed. I didn't want to talk about that. Not yet.

"I'll tell you all about it later. First, I want to know—what are you doing here? Why are you working for Edgar? Why are you still in Sawyers Bend? I always figured you'd be out there somewhere curing cancer or building a new internet."

Hope collapsed in on herself, tucking her knees to her chest and cradling the bottle of beer between them, looking down at the label like it held the answers to the mysteries of the universe. She very deliberately did not meet my eyes.

"Hope?" I pressed, "did something happen?"

Chapter Nine

GRIFFEN

"WHY DID YOU THINK I WOULD LEAVE? DO SOMETHING special? I'm not that interesting."

I stared at her, speechless. Not do anything special? Not interesting? The little girl who'd made up stories of fairies under the toadstools, who'd built a drag racer out of scrap wood and an old skateboard, who'd won the science fair four years in a row and never brought home anything less than an A?

It seemed so obvious to me that she was made for anything other than staying home under Edgar's thumb. She looked shocked that I'd expected anything different. "Where did you go to college?" I asked.

A half shrug of one shoulder, her eyes still on the label of her beer, her thumbnail scraping at the damp label so it peeled off in long, curling strips. "I went to UNCA. Lived at home with Uncle

Edgar. He wanted me to work for him, said he needed someone he could trust. I helped Prentice with some of the admin he and Ford didn't have time for."

"And that's it? UNCA's a good school, but you were a straight-A student. When I left, you were already taking college classes in the summer. I would have thought you'd go to Chapel Hill if you wanted to stay close to home. You could have gone anywhere. Even if Edgar didn't want to pay, you could have gotten a scholarship."

Hope's eyes flicked up to mine, the normally warm cognac-brown guarded. Troubled. "Not everything is about money, Griffen. I didn't want to go away to school. I didn't want to leave Sawyers Bend. Uncle Edgar needed me. I owe him."

It wasn't the first time she'd said those words. *I owe him. I owe you.* They irritated me in a way I didn't understand.

"What about what he owes you? More than a life trapped in this town—"

Hope erupted. "There's nothing wrong with this town, Griffen Sawyer." She slammed her empty beer on the coffee table, cheeks flushed, eyes glittering. "Just because you left doesn't mean everyone else wants to."

"We're not talking about me," I shot back.

"Aren't we? Because you don't know anything about me and Uncle Edgar. I *do* owe him. I owe him everything. And no one owes *me* anything. I'm lucky to be where I am. I have a job. I have a home. I have a nest egg in the bank. I'm safe."

"And that's enough?"

Hope shoved up from the couch, her glare scathing. "Griffen, you have no clue what you're talking about. I get that the heir to the Sawyer fortune thinks he's owed something in life, but life owes you jack shit. The lot of you are a bunch of spoiled brats. Sterling aside, you all work hard. I'll give you that. But you should have so much more than money. You should be a family, and you've thrown it away over petty grudges. All of you let Prentice manipulate you, let him set you against each other, then you whine about it."

"I haven't even been here," I protested weakly. Hope wasn't interested.

"You have no idea what it's like to have nothing. To be hungry. To be afraid. So don't talk to me about who owes me what. I know what I have, and I know what I owe." Hope stalked to the kitchen for another beer. I sat where I was, stunned speechless.

I'd wondered where my Hope had gone. Here she was. Her temper was as much her as the fairy lights on the ceiling. I hadn't realized how much I'd missed it.

Or how much I needed to hear everything she'd said.

She was right about us. Sawyers knew how to work, but that was about the only good thing you could say about us. We knew shit about being a family. Maybe if Darcy had lived to hold us all together... but she hadn't.

I didn't think we'd lost all chance of being a family. I couldn't forget the way Quinn had shepherded Sterling out of Harvey's office, or how Royal and Tenn walked out side-by-side. They ran the Inn together and by all accounts had made a success of it. They couldn't do that if they hated each other.

But still, Hope wasn't wrong. We'd been given everything. We hadn't squandered the money, but the rest? Family, history—that, we'd thrown away. We could blame Prentice—he'd sown the seeds of our discord, after all—but we were adults. We'd made our own choices.

I watched Hope come back, her eyes everywhere but on me, and I realized something else. I knew Edgar had brought Hope to live with him when she was a child, but I didn't know why. I'd always assumed her parents had died. After her outburst, I realized there had to be more to the story.

Edgar Daniels wasn't a warm and fuzzy guy. Not the type to inspire such dogged loyalty. I'd seen enough of life to know that there were a lot of things that could make gruff, emotionally distant Edgar Daniels look like a prize as a guardian. I was sick at the thought of Hope suffering any of the scenarios floating through my mind. She knew what it was like to be hungry. To be scared. Scared of what?

I wasn't sure I wanted to know, but I was going to find out. Later.

Now wasn't the time to pry. For better or worse, thanks to Prentice, time was something we had plenty of. I said the only thing I could.

"You're right. I'm an ass. We're all asses who don't deserve what we have. And I'm sorry. If you're happy with the choices you've made, that's all that matters, and it's none of my fucking business."

Hope nodded her acceptance of my apology, her eyes glued to her new beer bottle, her thumb scraping at the label just like she had on the last one. She took a sip, swallowed, and met my eyes, her emotions locked tightly away. "What are you going to do about Ford?"

I wasn't surprised by the change in subject. "I don't know. You said he'd been arrested. I'm assuming since he missed the funeral and the circus at Harvey's, he's still in jail?"

"The judge denied bail."

I raised an eyebrow. Here I was being an ass again, but come on—Ford is a Sawyer. "Are you telling me Ford couldn't get the judge to grant him bail?"

Hope shook her head. "Cole Haywood is his attorney. He's good, one of the best, but the evidence—" She shook her head. "The judge felt Ford was a flight risk and the evidence was overwhelming."

"What do they have?"

"Harvey might know more, or we can talk to Cole, but I know they found shoes that match footprints found outside your father's office window, which was open. A gun in Ford's bedroom closet that matches the bullet that killed your father. He also doesn't have an alibi, and people saw him speeding out of town not long after the coroner says Prentice died."

"Shit. That's bad," I said. Bad didn't really cover it. With that kind of evidence, I'd bet the D.A. was thinking it was open and shut. The press was going to have a field day if this went to court. The Sawyer name wasn't nationally prominent—Prentice made a point of staying out of the news—but we had too much money not to be a factor.

The heir apparent murdering his father in the family manor house? That's news. "How are they keeping this quiet? Why aren't there news vans everywhere? Are they holding Ford in town?"

"They moved him to the county prison after the judge denied bail. Cole is doing everything he can, but all the evidence points right to Ford."

"But you don't think he did it?" I asked.

"The evidence looks bad, but I know Ford pretty well," Hope said. "Uncle Edgar's business intertwines with Sawyer business and I've worked with Ford and Prentice a lot over the years. Your father was an ass, no argument there, but Ford is a good guy. A little distant. Stiff, maybe, but he's honorable. He's not a liar or a cheat."

"Funny you'd call him honorable, considering." Considering he'd betrayed me to our father while cheating with my fiancée. When he was done, I was homeless, and Ford had both my inheritance and my woman. Not exactly *honorable*.

Hope looked away. "He's changed, Griffen. He's not like your father. And he's smart. If Ford had killed Prentice, he wouldn't have been caught."

71

"You think he was set up."

"It sounds so contrived, but I can't get my head around anything else. As far as I know, Ford didn't carry his gun with him. Ford is controlled. I've never seen him lose his temper. I could see him killing Prentice. I could see a lot of people killing Prentice. But not like that."

"Any ideas who might have done it?" I had to ask even though I knew what she was going to say.

"How long do you have? Half the people who knew your father probably thought about killing him at least once. He had his fingers in a lot of pies. There could be enemies we don't know anything about. We have a good police force in town. Weston Garfield is the police chief—you remember him—and the county sheriff is a good guy. But with this kind of evidence, they're not looking for anyone else. Why would they?"

"Then I guess we pencil in a visit to West and Cole Haywood after we get back."

A knock fell on the door. Hope rose to answer. Out of habit, I followed her, checking the peephole to see the pizza delivery kid before I stepped back to let her open it. Sawyers Bend is a small town and relatively safe. Then again, my father probably thought it was safe, and look what had happened to him.

Hope didn't have a TV. We sat at her small kitchen table and ate in silence. When we were done, Hope said, "I know it's early, but I'm beat. We have a long day tomorrow."

"Yeah, me too." As I said the words I realized how true they were. Exhaustion pulled at me, my bones aching with it. Now that my stomach was full and the rest of the world was outside Hope's door, I craved the solitude of sleep for just a few hours.

I wasn't ready for tomorrow. Paperwork with Harvey. Walking through the front door of Heartstone Manor. And the worst part—going back to Atlanta to say goodbye. I didn't want to think of any of it. Hope disappeared into her bedroom, emerging with bedding and a pillow in her arms. "I'll make up the couch for you—"

"I can do it." I took the bundle from her arms and dumped it on the couch. She turned to go. I shot out my hand to close around Hope's wrist. She jumped in surprise. When she turned back, her cheeks were pink.

I looked down at her face, so familiar and yet completely new. Those eyes that saw so much, the honeyed strands of her hair that had fallen from her bun to frame her face.

"Griffen—" She tugged at her wrist. I didn't let go.

"You heard what Harvey said. It has to be real."

Her eyes flared wide in alarm. I resisted the urge to grin. Did she think I was going to toss her over my shoulder like a conquering warrior and have my way with her?

"We have time," I said, "but we got married today. You're my wife. And I never got to kiss the bride."

Her lips parted in surprise and a bolt of arousal shot straight to my cock. I didn't give either of us a chance to think. I tugged her closer until she all but stumbled into me and raised my palm to cup her cheek, bringing her mouth to mine.

I don't know what I expected from the kiss. A dry press of our lips. For her to pull away. To protest.

What I got was something else. Her mouth half-open, her lips soft. Giving. I went back for more, my tongue slipping out, tasting. Testing. I was ready for her to stiffen up.

Instead, she melted, sinking into me, her tongue reaching to stroke mine, her breasts pressing to my chest. And the sounds she made in her throat—half-moan and half-growl, all of it dragging me under.

I fell into the kiss. Fell into her. Hope was made to be here, held in my arms, her mouth under mine. I could taste her hunger, the passion she kept locked away. She pressed closer, her head tilting deeper, her lips against mine taking more of me.

One hand found its way under her loose sweater and I stroked up her spine, absorbing all that warm, soft skin. I itched to cup her breast, to claim more of her.

Too soon.

Hope kissed like it was a discovery, like every press of her mouth to mine was something new. Unexplored. That was the only thing that kept me from pushing it further. Her passion was more than a match for mine. We could have sated ourselves on that wide velvet couch—

Don't fuck it up on the first day, I reminded myself.

Her hands had closed over my arms as if she were holding on for dear life, her mouth moving on mine with hunger, with need, but unpracticed and uncertain.

Too soon.

I eased back, the cold air that rushed between us a punishment. I wanted more.

I would get what I wanted.

Eventually. Not tonight.

"Sleep tight, Hope." I pressed one last kiss to her forehead before I let her go.

Hope stared up at me with dazed eyes, her lips swollen. With a tiny, indrawn breath, she turned and bolted for her room, closing the door behind her.

I spread the blanket and sheets on the couch, stripped down to my boxers and lay down in the dark. The couch was exactly as comfortable as it looked. The day crowded in on me. The funeral, the will. The utter disaster that was my life.

I'd never wanted to see this town again, and now I was stuck here for at least five years.

I'd never planned to get married after what happened with my first fiancée. In one day, I'd skipped the fiancée part and gotten myself a wife. I'd married Hope. Little Hope Daniels, who wasn't so little anymore.

I should have felt resentful. Resistant. About the rest—the will, the trusts, my siblings—I absolutely did. I couldn't let myself think about my father, still yanking my chain even after death. Just a flash of that scene in Harvey's conference room and I wanted to rage at Prentice. He was dead, and I knew better than to waste my time.

I'd made my choice. I'd see it through.

Why didn't I resent Hope? She should be at the top of the list.

But that kiss. *That kiss.*

I lay on the couch, staring at the ceiling until I dropped off from exhaustion. Of all the things on my mind, the only one I kept circling back to was the feel of Hope's mouth under mine, the heat of her body in my arms.

More of that and I might just make it through the next five years.

Chapter Ten

GRIFFEN

THE CREAK OF A DOOR WOKE ME. DUE TO YEARS OF training, I came alert without moving, my eyes sliding open just enough to see the room. The day before came into focus along with my surroundings.

Sawyers Bend. The funeral. Harvey's office.

Hope.

I lay sprawled on her obscenely comfortable velvet couch wearing only my boxers. Sunlight streamed through the split between the heavy velvet curtains. My hostess—my wife—crept across the living room floor, headed for the kitchen.

Hope was wrapped in a fluffy pink robe. I caught the furtive glance she tossed my way as she picked up her pace and disappeared into the kitchen. Faint rustling sounds. Water running. Was it too much to wish for coffee?

I'd take her out for breakfast later, but I could use some caffeine. I let my mind drift as I waited, looking around Hope's cluttered apartment as the luscious scent of coffee drifted into the room. Catching the clink of a mug, I rolled to my feet.

Hope turned as I stepped into the kitchen, her empty mug clutched to her chest, eyes wide as they ran from the top of my head down my mostly naked body to my feet. Only mostly naked. I was wearing boxers. I wasn't trying to give her a heart attack.

I had a feeling mostly naked men were not a fixture in Hope Daniels' kitchen.

"I thought you were asleep," she said unnecessarily. "I didn't mean to wake you up."

"I'm happy to get up for a cup of that coffee."

"Oh. Of course." She poured me a mug, joining me at her small kitchen table.

We sipped in silence, waiting for our brains to wake up. Hope's eyes flicked over my bare chest, snagging on my shoulder and the still-pink scars there. Her lips parted as if to ask what had happened, then pressed together, her eyes darting away. When they returned, she only studied the scars for a moment before her eyes slipped down, over my pecs to my stomach.

I shouldn't have liked the faint flush on her cheeks so much. I leaned back, giving her more to look at. Her cheeks flared red and she took a hasty sip of coffee.

Finally, Hope said, "Do you want breakfast? I have some bread. I can make toast."

"Not much of a breakfast person?"

"Not usually. I snooze my alarm and then have to rush to get into the office," she said, honestly, a faint flush on her cheeks.

I stopped myself from making a comment about Edgar keeping her on a short leash. I'd deal with him later. Or maybe not, I thought, as Hope's phone rang. Edgar's name showed up on the display. She stared at it for a moment before accepting the call. I expected her to get up, to try to have the conversation in private, but she stayed where she was.

"Hello?"

"Get Griffen and be in my office within the hour. We need to talk." Edgar's voice was faint, but I could hear him just fine.

Hope swallowed hard. She didn't protest, just said smoothly, "We'll see you then."

Edgar hung up on her. All charm. Vintage Edgar. Hope set the phone down on the table slowly, probably thinking about what to say to me. I made it easy on her.

"Command performance for Edgar?"

"Something like that. He wants us both there—"

"I heard," I said. "We can get breakfast after. Before we go back to Harvey's."

"Of course," Hope agreed distantly. I wondered if she was thinking the same thing I was.

I hoped so because if she wasn't, the conversation we were about to have was going to be sticky.

"A lot has happened in the last twenty-four hours, Hope," I began. "I don't know if you've thought about this, but it's a serious conflict of interest for you, as my wife, to continue working for Edgar."

Hope shot me a grateful look. "I know. I know. With Ford in prison and Prentice dead, Edgar and I know more about Sawyer Enterprises than anyone. I don't know everything, obviously, but you're going to need help. I'm the best available option, not just because I'm your wife."

"I know you used to do work for Prentice while also handling most of Edgar's business, but that isn't going to fly with me. I don't trust your uncle. I can guess why he maneuvered Prentice into this marriage thing, but I have no clue why Prentice would have agreed."

"I know," Hope murmured. "The only thing I can think is that Edgar had something on Prentice. But I don't know what it could be."

I let out a breath in relief. It made things easier if Hope and I were on the same page. "Considering who we're dealing with, it could be anything."

Hope nodded in agreement. I didn't want to be harsh with her, but Prentice and Edgar hadn't left us much choice.

"I want to trust you, Hope, but I can't do that if you've got a foot in both camps. You have to choose, me or Edgar."

"I know," she agreed. I waited. I knew what I wanted. I didn't know how hard I'd have to fight to get it. It turned out, not hard at all. "I'm going to tell Edgar I can't work for him anymore. I have some money saved up. I can get by for a while, especially if I'm not paying rent—"

I sliced a hand through the air, cutting her off. "I'm offering you a job Hope, not asking you to work for free. What was Edgar paying you?"

She named a number that had me wincing. No wonder she lived in this tiny apartment. What the hell was Edgar thinking? Never mind, I knew exactly what he was thinking.

Just as I'd thought, he paid her just enough so she could live but not enough for her to have any real freedom. Biting back everything I wanted to say about her uncle, I said, "I'll double it."

"Double it? Griffen, I can't ask you to—"

"You didn't ask. That's what our office manager makes at Sinclair Security and she earns every penny. I have no doubt you will, too. I've been paying attention. You know way more about Sawyer Enterprises than I do. I can't do this without you. I'm not going to take advantage of you to get your help."

"Griffen, after everything that happened before—"

I shook my head, feeling my jaw clench tight. Forcing my mouth open, I spit out, "If you say you owe me one more time,

I swear to God—I don't want to hear that from you again. You don't owe me anything. Maybe you did, but my father hijacking five years of your life more than makes up for anything you did over a decade ago. I'll take advantage of your help because I need it, but I won't do it for free."

Her eyes wide, Hope must have decided it wasn't worth arguing with me. "Okay," she said quietly.

"Who's your landlord?" I demanded in what seemed like a change of subject.

Hope let out a strangled little laugh. "You are, as soon as you sign whatever papers Harvey has for you."

"Good, then we don't have to worry about the lease. If you can get your personal things packed, I'll have Savannah arrange for the rest to be moved to Heartstone."

"Okay," Hope agreed, taking a quick sip of coffee, her eyes still wide. She was looking a little shell-shocked.

"Are you worried Edgar is going to make things difficult?" I asked, trying to figure out what had her so thrown.

"I don't know." She sounded dazed.

"I'll tell Edgar if you want me to," I offered.

Hope shook her head. "No, I'll do it. We better get going."

She stood. I followed as she took her coffee cup to the sink, so close her scent wreathed me, sweet and warm, apples and spice. When she was a girl she'd always smelled like cinnamon and dirt. An odd combination, but it fit a little girl who'd loved to curl up under a tree with a good book or bury herself in the kitchen to bake cookies.

She still smelled of cinnamon, but there was nothing childish about that scent. It was spice and heat and woman. I wanted to stick my nose in the hollow of her throat and follow the traces of cinnamon down between her breasts, to feel the weight of them against my cheeks as I tasted to see if she was as sweet as she looked.

81

Remembering the hesitation in her kiss, I had the feeling I'd give her a stroke if I did. Instead, I said, "I need to take a shower before we go."

Her eyes everywhere but my bare chest, she fled from the kitchen, saying over her shoulder, "Let me just grab some stuff out of the bathroom and it's all yours."

I followed her through the living room, waiting while she gathered her things. She was quick, ducking out through the doorway a minute later carrying a brush and a pile of hairpins in one hand. In the other was a red wool dress flowing from the hanger like a banner in the wind. Red as flame, it had 3/4 sleeves that ended in a bell, tiny buttons up the front, and a narrow skirt that flared at the bottom.

I couldn't stop looking at the dress. That red would bring out the warmth in her cognac eyes, the subtle hints of auburn in her hair, the pink in her creamy skin. This was the kind of thing she should be wearing, not those ugly suits.

"What's that?" I asked before she could disappear into her bedroom.

She looked down at the dress and bit her lip in what I thought was embarrassment. Her words spilled out in a rush, "Oh, uh, just something I ordered online. I thought... I don't know what I was thinking. It's too short. And red. It's so red."

The dress was not short. It probably hit an inch above her knee. Not what anyone would consider short.

"Wear it," I said.

Startled, Hope hugged the dress to her chest. "No, I can't. It's too—"

"I'm your husband," I countered. "You promised to obey me."

A snort burst from her elegant nose, dissolving into a laugh. "I did not promise to obey you."

"You did," I insisted. I wasn't paying that much attention to the vows, to be honest, but the flags of color on Hope's cheeks matched her dress, so I egged her on a little more. "I'm your lord and master in all things now, and I say you have to wear the dress."

She laughed harder, snorting again as she tried to get her giggles under control and tell me to shut my trap. Finally, shaking her head, she conceded, "I'll try it on, but I'm not wearing it out."

"Good enough," I agreed, sliding past her into the bathroom. I was in and out of the shower in a flash before brushing my teeth and running my fingers through my wet hair. A towel hiked around my waist, I raided my emergency bag for a clean pair of boxers and pulled on my jeans and flannel shirt. I wasn't putting that suit back on. If Edgar and Harvey couldn't handle me in jeans that was their problem.

The door to Hope's bedroom remained closed. Impatient, I poured myself another mug of coffee and waited. That dress gave me hope, pun intended. That dress fit this apartment. Fit the girl I'd known. The woman I knew she hid deep inside.

When my coffee was almost empty, the door to Hope's bedroom opened. She'd pulled her hair back into another bun, this one softer around her face. She hadn't bothered with much makeup, not that she needed it. Red glass beads caught the light at her ears, an exact match for the dress. And the dress— The dress was perfectly Hope.

It wasn't too short or too red. Skimming her slender frame, it was neither shapeless nor too tight, hugging her hips before it flared just above her knees. The dress showed almost no skin. It shouldn't have been alluring, but the way it framed the curve of her breasts, her narrow waist, and the flare of her hips left my fingers itching to touch.

She curled her fingers over the bell sleeve, tugging, shifting her weight from one foot to the other. "It needs tights and boots," she said.

"Do you have tights and boots?" I asked.

A jerk of her chin, her eyes refusing to meet mine.

I wanted to punch Edgar. Hope had no idea what she looked like. As the man who'd raised her, it was his job to make sure she knew her own worth. Clearly, he'd royally fucked that up.

"Hope," I said softly. She raised her head, nerves skittering in her eyes when they met mine. "You look beautiful. You have good taste. I don't know what's up with those suits, but—"

"Uncle Edgar bought them. He bought all my work clothes."

I didn't know what to do with that. "Hope, that's weird, and he has terrible taste."

"It's not weird. He likes a certain atmosphere in the office, and he didn't like the way I dressed when I picked my own clothes. I got tired of him complaining, so when he bought me some suits, I just wore them."

I shook my head. "It *is* weird. And you're not working in Edgar's office anymore. You're working for me. You can wear anything you want. Though I'll beg you not to wear those suits he bought you. Otherwise, I don't care. Wear jeans or pajamas. Wear your robe. Or, you could just work naked."

The flush in her cheeks matched her dress. Giving in to impulse, I pressed my lips to hers, tasting Chapstick and toothpaste. The second my mouth hit hers, I wanted more.

Not the time, damn it. It kept taking me by surprise, how much I wanted her. There was so much wrapped up in being near Hope. Affection and resentment. Anger so old it was starting to crumble.

And lust.

Need.

I wanted Hope, wanted her naked and in my bed.

I had not seen that coming when I drove back into Sawyers Bend.

With a jerk, she stepped back, mumbling, "I have to get my tights and boots."

I drifted behind her, standing in the doorway of her bedroom, struck dumb. When she swung the door shut in my face I was still standing there.

I'd been right, her bedroom was a hedonist's dream. Like the rest of her apartment, it was a kaleidoscope of color, but all I could remember was the bed. Fuck, that bed. It was burned into my brain. It had to be a king-size, though I didn't want to consider why Hope would need a bed that big. Definitely an antique. Fashioned of heavy brass with four posters, Hope had piled it with pillows, covering the whole thing with a thick blue velvet duvet.

She'd look like a princess in that bed. And, of course, my perverted brain immediately thought about the convenience of that brass frame, of tying her to the bed and joining her there. Touching. Tasting. Making her beg. That was the kind of bed we could lose a weekend in.

That bed was coming to Heartstone Manor.

I was still a little stunned—and more than a little aroused—by the time Hope emerged, tugging up the zipper on her knee-high boot.

Have mercy. The red dress and those boots were going to kill me.

Swallowing hard, I tried to play off the lust practically choking me. "Let's get a move on. I want to hear whatever Edgar has to say and then get some breakfast. We still have to go by Harvey's and then face the house before we drive to Atlanta."

The thought of the day ahead chased the lust from my brain. I hadn't calle   d anyone in Atlanta to let them know what was going on. I wasn't ready to see them, to set in motion the end of that life and the beginning of this one.

I didn't have a choice. Or, rather, I'd already made my choice. Now, I just had to see it through. It tugged at me as I ushered Hope from the apartment, locking the door behind us.

I wanted to go home. I didn't want to stay here, to take my father's place, to deal with my siblings. I didn't want any of it. But when I imagined chucking it all and going home to Atlanta, I kept seeing Hope by my side.

Wouldn't it be ironic if, in trying to punish me, my father ended up giving me the one thing I never knew I wanted? The one thing I needed most?

He would have hated that.

At that thought, a genuine smile spread across my face for the first time since I'd arrived back in Sawyers Bend.

Chapter Eleven

GRIFFEN

*E*DGAR HAD HIS OFFICE IN A BRICK BUILDING A BLOCK FROM the town hall. Hope was quiet on the ride there, staring out the window and fidgeting with the ends of her sleeves. I followed her into the lobby, bumping into her as she swung open the office door and stopped abruptly. A woman sat behind the desk in the outer office, her hair in a steel gray bob, a pen tucked behind her ear.

"Can I help you?" she asked.

Hope didn't appear to have a response. I nudged her in the back, not sure what was going on. Finally, she swallowed hard and said in a choked voice, "Who are you? What are you doing at my desk?"

The woman rose from her seat and held out a hand, appearing unruffled by Hope's question. "I'm Peggy Carmody. Mr.

Daniels interviewed me for the position a few days ago. You must be Hope. He's expecting you. As requested, I put your things together."

I noticed a cardboard box on the edge of the desk, the leaves of a plant sticking out of the top. What the fuck? I knew Edgar was cold, but this... Hope looked from the box to Peggy Carmody. Drawing in a deep breath, she turned to me. Her eyes were blank, all emotion locked away.

In a cool, perfectly-controlled voice, she said to me, "Would you sit out here for a moment?" Not giving me a chance to answer, she strode to Edgar's office door.

Peggy moved as if to stop her, then appeared to think better of it. Maybe I should have taken a seat and waited, but I followed Hope, lingering on the other side of the door, close enough to eavesdrop.

"Can I get you anything?" Peggy asked, the sound of her voice drowning out whatever Hope was saying to Edgar.

"No. Be quiet or get out," I said. She shut up. I listened. I couldn't catch everything.

I'd planned to let Hope handle Edgar herself, but when I heard him demand, "What the hell are you wearing? You look ridiculous," I changed my mind.

Shoving open the door, I found Edgar rising from behind his desk, scowling at Hope. She stood in front of him, her spine so stiff I thought it might break, her face completely blank. Her expression showed nothing, but her eyes were fractured pain. How could Edgar not see it? His glance flicked to me, and he sank back into his seat with a sigh of satisfaction.

Lacing his fingers over his ample midsection, he leaned back into the leather chair. "Peggy," he called into the front office, "go get yourself a coffee or something. Give us about twenty minutes. Bring me back a danish."

"Yes, sir," came through the open door. Hope's replacement was obedient. A minute later the front door shut behind her and we were alone.

"Lock it," he ordered Hope, who stared at him in silence. I didn't know if she was too angry to speak or too shocked. Either way, I locked the front door myself. I had to agree with Edgar. Whatever was about to be said, we needed privacy.

Hope still said nothing. I wasn't sure she'd welcome the touch, but the look in her eyes and the satisfaction in Edgar's had me winding an arm around her waist, drawing her to my side.

"It's done?" Edgar asked. "You're married?"

"We are," I confirmed. "How did you get Prentice to make your niece the queen of Heartstone Manor? What did you have on him?"

"Nothing you'll ever know," Edgar said.

Hope finally found her voice. "Why is there someone sitting at my desk?"

"You're married, girl. You don't need a job. It'll take her some time to get up to speed, but she'll do well enough for me."

Hope just stared at him in mute horror.

"That makes things easier for us, doesn't it?" I said, squeezing her closer to my side. Her eyes flashed up to mine in confusion. In comfort—and to keep myself from crossing the room to knock Edgar out cold—I dropped a kiss to her lips.

To Edgar, I said, "We were planning to tell you Hope was quitting, that she's working for me now. Convenient that you saw it coming and already replaced her."

Edgar leaned forward, his heavy brow creasing. "Working for you? What's this about? She's going to be at Heartstone Manor, taking care of the house and making babies. Raising the next generation of Sawyers."

Hope made a choked sound in her throat. For a second I thought she might be laughing, but no. One look at her face told me that wasn't amusement, that was rage. I waited for the explosion. It didn't come.

Her voice arctic, Hope said, "Why?"

"Because he owed me," Edgar answered as if that explained everything. Maybe to him, it did. Now I knew where Hope got it.

"And that's it?" Hope pressed. "You're fired, now go have babies?"

"Don't get emotional, Hope," Edgar said with a dismissive shake of his head. "I did my duty by you. Now you're Griffen's problem."

Another choked sound from Hope. If she wanted to scream, to hit him, I wouldn't stop her. Hell, I'd help. Hope disentangled herself from me. Turning for the door, she said, "I'll wait for you in the car." Then she was gone.

Disappointed, I looked at Edgar. Beneath his smug satisfaction was a thread of unease. Good. Maybe he had a conscience buried somewhere in there. "You're a complete asshole," I said.

I moved for the door.

"Griffen."

I stopped, curious to hear whatever he had to say.

"If you want to keep everything that just fell into your lap, I suggest you get her pregnant as fast as possible. Until then, you've got a big, fat target on your back."

I didn't need to hear any more. All I could think about was getting back to Hope. I found her exactly where she'd said she'd be—sitting in the passenger seat of my car, hands folded on her knees, face still blank. I got in and started the engine, pulling out of the parking lot before asking, "Are you okay?"

Hope turned shattered eyes to me as she said, slowly and deliberately, "No, I am not fucking okay."

"What do you—"

"Are you fucking kidding me?" she shrieked. "He fired me? I've done everything he ever asked. Went to the school he picked, got the degree he wanted, sat at that desk and took his orders every single fucking day, and he fired me?"

"He—" I started, but she cut me off again.

"And then he sold me to you—to Prentice, but it's the same thing. Like a piece of god-damn chattel. This isn't the fucking fifteenth century for fuck's sake."

That was an impressive number of 'fucks' in a short amount of time. I couldn't remember if I'd ever heard Hope swear before this. She hadn't as a teenager. Not when I knew her.

"What did he say after I left?" she demanded.

Thrown by her anger, I didn't think when I said, "He told me to get you pregnant as soon as possible." Wrong answer. I was distracted by the flash of her eyes, the flush in her cheeks.

"What?" she screeched. "He told you to what? Impregnate me? Like I'm a farm animal? I'm a fucking virgin! I've never even had a boyfriend! He never let me date and now he wants me knocked up! Why? Did he tell you why?"

I had no answer. I was still stuck on the part where she said she was a virgin.

Hope was thirty-one years old. How was she still a virgin? I thought about those suits. Edgar not letting her date. Choosing her college, her career. How long had he been planning this? What was he saving her for? I had to be his backup plan for Hope.

Unless Edgar Daniels had killed Prentice—or known he was going to die.

"Griffen!" Hope's shout cut into my thoughts.

"Do you think Edgar killed Prentice?" I asked before she could get a word in.

Silence. I glanced at Hope to find her staring out the window, lost in thought. "Maybe," she said eventually. "He couldn't have done it personally. He was out of town on a business trip. The Sheriff has already verified his alibi. But he could have paid for it, I guess."

"But you don't think so?"

"I don't know what to think. He must have interviewed Peggy as soon as he found out Prentice was dead. None of this makes sense."

I waited for her to address the baby issue. I wasn't going to tell her what Edgar had said about me having a target on my back. It didn't matter. A baby wasn't going to happen.

Sex was definitely going to happen. When Hope was ready. But children? No fucking way. We were not having a child to appease my dead father and Edgar Daniels. The will tied us together for five years. A child would bind us for a lifetime.

They'd stolen too much of Hope's future. I wouldn't take more than that by getting her pregnant just to save my own ass.

I waited for Hope to say something. Anything. It seemed her mini-rant after we got in the car would be it. No more profanity, no more anger or frustration. She sat beside me in silence, staring out the window, lost in thoughts she didn't share.

When I didn't think I could take the quiet any longer, I dared to ask, "Hope, are you okay?"

Weirdly, she answered with, "Why are we here? I thought we were going to breakfast."

I looked up to see the granite and iron gates of Heartstone Manor rising in front of us, imposing and forbidding. I'd forgotten about breakfast. After the bizarre meeting with Edgar and Hope's outburst, I'd apparently forgotten everything. I'd driven by rote, passing over roads I'd once known like the back of my own hand, and found myself at the last place I wanted to be.

Heartstone Manor.

Home.

Chapter Twelve

HOPE

GRIFFEN STOPPED THE CAR IN FRONT OF THE GATE AND GOT out, staring at the entrance to Heartstone Manor, face blank. He looked as if he wanted to be anywhere else. I couldn't blame him.

I'd been handling things pretty well up until we'd walked into Uncle Edgar's office and I'd seen that woman sitting behind my desk.

I could deal with marrying Griffen to save the town, with giving up my apartment, changing my job, but at the sight of that woman behind my desk, I fell apart. I'm sure it wasn't her fault. She seemed clueless. Peggy whatever-her-name-was had no idea what she was in for. Uncle Edgar wasn't exactly a treat as a boss.

I couldn't get my head around what had happened. Fired? How could Uncle Edgar fire me? Bad enough that he'd handed me over to the Sawyers like chattel in a feudal marriage contract.

But to tell Griffen to get me pregnant? To dismiss me as if my only use was as a broodmare?

Uncle Edgar wasn't affectionate, but I'd always believed he loved me, if just a little. Now I wasn't so sure. Had I just been an investment? A useful tool? But how was pawning me off on the Sawyers useful?

I'd said it before. None of this made sense.

I didn't want to think about it anymore. This was my reality. A temporary marriage to Griffen. Moving into Heartstone Manor. I could spend the rest of my life trying to work out Edgar and Prentice's motives and still come up blank.

I wouldn't think about the hurt. The abandonment.

I couldn't consider that I was suddenly adrift in the world, cast off by my only family and tethered to a man who didn't want me. The weight of it threatened to crush me.

Griffen didn't look like he felt much better than I did. He stood in front of his sleek Maserati, hands hanging loosely at his sides, staring at the open gate as if he'd never seen it before. I got out to join him.

"Do you mind getting breakfast later?" he asked distantly after the *thunk* of my door closing had faded.

At the idea of food, my stomach turned over in protest. "That's fine. We might as well go in. Since we're here."

Neither of us made a move. It had been fifteen years since Griffen had been driven from this place. I couldn't imagine how it must feel to be back. I remembered the feel of his arm around my waist as I'd faced Uncle Edgar. Solid and strong, his support had been exactly what I'd needed as I felt my world crumbling beneath me.

Stepping closer, I took his hand in mine, squeezing tight. "What if we do this like pulling off a band-aid?"

"Huh?" Griffen blinked, looking down at me as if he'd forgotten I was there.

"I know this is weird. Hard. Whenever things are hard, I try to focus on the practical. Just get through it."

"You're saying we should storm the castle armed with lists?" A faint thread of amusement tinged his words.

"Basically. I haven't been here in more than two years. Prentice started coming to the office for meetings. Edgar said he'd fired the staff, said he was acting paranoid, claimed he couldn't trust anyone in the house. He and Ford fought about it. Ford moved into the Inn almost a year ago. At the very least, we're going to need to hire more help than Savannah. And we need to figure out where everyone is going to stay—"

"I assumed they'd stay in their rooms," Griffen said blandly. I didn't take the bait. I was just relieved he sounded amused instead of distant.

"Smartass," I said under my breath. Griffen squeezed my fingers before releasing my hand.

"Okay, General. Let's get your lists and conquer this bitch."

We got back in the car and drove through the gates. The drive to Heartstone Manor was almost half a mile long, the great house cushioned by thousands of acres of land. The Sawyers hadn't sold any of the original acreage, adding here and there as land came on the market.

Most of the land was zoned for agricultural use, and while the orchards and fields didn't bring in the income they had a century ago, they provided a valuable tax break. More importantly, all that land gave them privacy.

We wound through the woods, beneath ancient oak trees, surrounded by dense forest, the early morning sun unable to penetrate the trees. The asphalt of the drive was pitted in places, crumbling at the edges, weeds pushing through the cracks as if the forest wanted to repossess the road, cutting off access to the house.

The groundskeepers should have taken care of that. I made a note on my pad. Hadn't Miss Martha said Prentice fired them, too? Based on the state of the road, I wasn't feeling good things about the condition of the house.

My stomach tightened in anticipation as we came around the final bend before we reached the house. I always felt like this when I visited here. No matter how many times I drove down this road, I never got used to the sheer grandeur of Heartstone Manor.

The house appeared out of the woods as if by magic, so massive it was hard to imagine mere trees being able to hide its bulk. Three stories of granite, it towered above us, every window dark.

Built by William Sawyer in a Jacobean style meant to soothe his bride's homesickness, Heartstone Manor always made me feel like I'd been whisked off to the English countryside. The windows were tall, the front of the house a long expanse that jutted forward on each end, creating a courtyard. The short side sections were rounded in the front, giving the impression the house was flanked by turrets. The real turrets were out of sight on the east and west wings of the house, jutting out behind the main section, hidden by the trees.

Ivy grew up the solid gray stone, reaching the roof in some places.

Wait. I stopped and looked again. I'd always loved the touch of ivy climbing the house. The granite could have been cold and forbidding, but the wooden front door and the ivy had warmed it, made it just a little approachable.

I'd once asked Miss Martha why they didn't let the ivy grow to cover the whole house, imagining fairies hiding in the glossy green leaves and story-book princes climbing the vines to the balconies.

Miss Martha had told me the ivy could damage the house with its roots if it was allowed to grow unchecked. She'd said they kept just enough to look pretty and cut back the rest. Someone hadn't gotten the memo.

The ivy was taking over the granite, evoking stories of Sleepy Beauty and the wall of thorns around her castle, the prince and his sword freeing her from sleep. Heartstone didn't need a prince, but it did need rescue—it needed an army of groundskeepers.

Griffen pulled to a stop in the courtyard, parking just in front of the steps to the front door. When I was a child, I'd rarely had to ring the bell. At the approach of visitors, the staff would alert Miss Martha, who would already be opening the door as we climbed the steps.

I waited in the passenger seat for the door to open. Nothing happened. Of course. No one was here. Maybe Sterling or Brax, but they'd hardly lower themselves to answering the door. Especially if they knew it was us.

I got out and looked up, taking in the general state of neglect creeping over the house. It wasn't just the ivy. The bushes and flowerbeds were overgrown. The courtyard was a mess. It should have been a neat checkerboard of granite squares intersected by strips of perfectly-trimmed green grass. Instead, the grass was long and infested with weeds, almost completely obscuring the stone.

If the front of the house was this bad, I was a little afraid to see the formal gardens in the back. The woods loomed over the courtyard, cutting off the morning sun, the trees far closer to the house than I remembered.

I edged nearer to Griffen as we stood in front of the manor door, waiting to see if anyone would answer our ring. So far, nothing. The house sat silent. Abandoned. Griffen rang again. I heard nothing.

"I think the bell is broken," I said, reaching forward to close my fingers around the heavy iron handle. I stumbled, unprepared, as the door moved, shifting inwards just enough to tell me the door wasn't locked. I pushed harder, to no avail.

Stepping aside at Griffen's nudge, I watched as he tried the handle like I had, then, finding it unmoving, set his shoulder against the solid wood and shoved.

The heavy wood budged a half-inch. Definitely not locked, just very stuck. Griffen stepped back and scanned the full height of the door, eyes narrowing as if the door was an opponent he intended to vanquish.

Seeing the resolve in his eyes, I took another step back, murmuring, "Don't hurt yourself."

Griffen backed up, then launched himself at the door, turning at the last moment to force his shoulder to take the brunt of the impact.

The door shuddered, giving another half inch. Jaw gritted, Griffen reached up to rub his shoulder. Not the one he'd used as a battering ram, the other shoulder. The one I'd noticed him rolling now and then. Odd. Eyeing the door again, sizing it up, he fisted his hands at his side and kicked hard with one long leg.

I'd have to remember to stay on Griffen's good side. His booted foot slammed into the heavy door right beside the handle, the sheer force of his kick shoving the door clear of the frame. Somehow, Griffen managed to keep his balance, shoving his hands into his pockets as he waited for the house to give up its secrets. With a groaning creak of protest, the tall, iron-strapped door swung open, revealing the entry hall of Heartstone Manor inch by inch.

The stale odor of dust hit me first. Heartstone's entry hall was palatial. Two stories high, big enough to fit my apartment a few times over, it was paneled in dark-stained oak from floor to ceiling, an elaborate crystal chandelier hanging in the center.

Straight ahead, a wide staircase rose one flight before it divided, the second set of stairs leading up to the right and left giving access to both the rooms on the second floor and those in the east and west wings of the house. The carpet on the stairs was gray with dust.

Everything was gray with dust.

Heartstone had always smelled of lemons and beeswax, of the flowers Miss Martha set out daily in crystal vases all over the house. Through the French doors at the far end of the entry hall, I glimpsed the formal gardens beyond. All was gray and dead.

Even in winter, the gardens had been beautiful. Not now. Nothing here was beautiful, the artful design of the house disguised by what had to be years of neglect.

Griffen summed it up. "What the fuck happened here?"

Chapter Thirteen

HOPE

I COULD ONLY SHAKE MY HEAD, FENDING OFF THE DIS-
orienting sense that I'd stumbled into an alternate
universe. Prentice murdered. Ford in jail. Marrying Griffen. Heartstone a ghost. It was all a bad dream and I
couldn't find my way out.

"I thought Sterling and Brax were living here," Griffen said,
taking in every detail of the neglected foyer.

"So did I. Brax has a place in Asheville since he does so much
business over there. Maybe that's where he's been staying," I
offered.

"So, Sterling's been here alone?"

Neither of us liked that idea. Sterling was gorgeous, and
reckless, and so very damaged. The idea of her on her own in
this shell of a home, as abandoned as the manor itself—it didn't

bear thinking about. She could be a brat and she wasn't the nicest person I knew, but she deserved more than this. Even a palace wasn't much of a home when you were utterly alone.

"Maybe she's been staying with Quinn," I said, hoping that was the case.

Griffen only grunted in response, venturing deeper into the shadowed interior of the house. I pressed the light switches cleverly hidden by paneling, relieved when the chandelier came to life. Half the bulbs were dead and the crystal droplets were dull with dust, but it was light. I'd take what I could get.

Wide arched doorways opened on either side of the entry hall, one leading into the gallery, the other into the green drawing room. The drawing room was decorated in white and green, with hand-painted silk wallpaper and light, airy furnishings. The original mistress of Heartstone Manor had loved her gardens and it showed in her formal receiving room.

We'd have to figure out how to clean the walls without damaging the delicate vines and flowers some long-ago artist had painted for Lady Estelle Ophelia Sawyer. Darcy—Finn, Parker, Quinn, and Brax's mother—had loved this room. She'd called it the garden room, retreating to its bright space in the gray of winter and the heat of summer both. Her death had been a vicious wound to the family she'd dreamed of making in Heartstone. I doubted anyone had used this room since.

I was almost afraid to look in the gallery. Once, it had been home to the crème de la crème of the Sawyer art collection. Other pieces were placed throughout the house, but the best, most prized pieces had been here. I was expecting it, shouldn't have been shocked at the sight, but I was. The walls were bare, the pedestals empty.

"Do I even want to ask what happened to the paintings? The sculptures?" Griffen should have been angry. Millions in art was missing. He sounded more resigned than anything.

"They were here the last time I was in the house," I said. The surfaces of the pedestals were covered in a layer of dust. Whatever had happened with the sculptures, it hadn't been recent.

"You can ask Harvey," I murmured. "We'd better check out the rest."

The thought of facing almost forty thousand square feet of similar neglect was daunting enough to have me backing up to the front door. Realizing what I was doing, I stopped.

"We don't need to see the whole house right now," I said, pulling my notebook from where I'd stashed it. "Let's check the kitchens, dining room, and the bedrooms. We'll need food, and somewhere to sleep. We can tackle the rest later."

"Or we could just let it go. Let it fall to dust and forget the Sawyers were ever here."

The bleak misery in his voice dragged me from the list on my notepad. His eyes were cold, resentful as he scanned the entryway of his family home, his shoulders hunched forward as if braced for whatever was coming at him next.

"Don't even think about it," I said before I could stop myself.

"What?" He jerked a shoulder in a shrug. "It's my house, isn't it?"

"No, it isn't. It belongs to your children, and their children. It belongs to history and to this town."

"I don't have any children." Griffen glared at me in challenge. I wasn't touching that one.

"Not the point," I muttered. Drawing in a deep breath, I forged ahead. "I didn't marry you and agree to leave my life behind so I could live in a dusty mess of a house, Griffen Sawyer. And if you think Savannah will agree to work here and leave it like this, you don't know her very well."

"I don't know her at all."

That stopped me in my tracks, just as I was gearing up to tell him what a spoiled ass he was. Last night's rant, part two.

He didn't know Savannah. Not really. He didn't know any of us. He'd been gone fifteen years, had been living a life far away from Sawyers Bend, and now he'd been yanked back and had this whole disaster shoved in his lap. Did he look in the green drawing room and see his long-lost mother? The deeply-mourned Darcy? Did the empty gallery bring back his father with his lies and manipulations?

Years ago, he and Ford had run through these halls, closer than most brothers, the white knights who took care of their siblings. Until Ford had stabbed him in the back, stealing his love and his fortune, leaving him homeless and alone.

Not without a little help from you, my conscience reminded me.

Guilt washed away my righteous indignation. Where did I get off calling Griffen spoiled? Maybe he had been, way back then. Then he'd lost everything, been sent from the only home he'd known. And I had been the cause of it all. Because I couldn't keep my stupid, jealous heart under control. Because I couldn't keep my mouth shut.

Where did I get off telling him what to do, how he should feel? I'd made this mess as much as Ford or Prentice.

This house was shrouded in the past, haunted by the ghosts of those we'd lost. Griffen and I were the only ones who could drive them off. Who could make this place into something better. Into a home. And it was the last job either of us wanted.

Griffen glared at me, hands shoved in his pockets, his gorgeous face in a sulk that should have been unappealing. Except that pouty lower lip, those angry green eyes. Inwardly, I sighed. I was not equipped to handle a man like Griffen. Not when I couldn't stop ogling his mouth.

On the other hand, I had plenty of experience wrangling ornery men. Griffen deserved compassion, but my gut told me that wasn't what he needed. We had a lot to do and we were running out of time. I had a list to finish.

I tossed out compassion and dredged up my own ornery. "Get over yourself. We both got tossed in the deep end, and it's too late to walk away."

"And you're going to make it all better, is that right, Hope? With your lists and your determination?"

His voice was silky and dangerous. I took a step back. Ornery I could handle. Not this, not the intention in his eyes, suddenly hot with something that was not anger. Something I had no idea how to handle.

"I—"

"My consolation prize. Little Hope, all mine, with no one to protect her. So fierce when it comes to saving this town, this house, my fucking family. What about me, Hope? You going to save me, too?"

I couldn't stop backing away as he advanced, his eyes narrowing, mine shot wide with panic. *Griffen won't hurt you,* I told myself. Surely, he wouldn't.

Would he?

"Why, Hope?" he pushed. "Because you owe me? Because none of this would have happened without you?"

"Griffen, I—I'm sorry. I shouldn't have said anything. It was a secret and I—"

"But you couldn't help yourself, could you? I know why. I knew why all those years ago."

My back slammed into the cold wood of the paneled wall. There was no escape. Griffen smiled, those lush, soft lips curving into a predator's snarl. His body almost touched mine, radiating heat, tall and broad, trapping me. Leaving me at his mercy.

A whimper left my lips. Not fear. I was flushed with nerves, and need, and the utter terror of the unknown. His head dropped until those lips I'd ogled brushed my cheek.

"You did it because you wanted me. You had a crush, imagined you loved me—"

"I didn't! I—"

"No?" His lips were so soft, brushing my skin, the shell of my ear. "Are you calling me a liar? Telling me you didn't lay in your bed dreaming about me?"

I couldn't get air in my lungs, had no idea how to answer even if I could have formed a word. He lifted a hand, tilted my head to the side and skimmed his lips down my neck.

"You going to say you didn't lie under the covers and think of me with your fingers between your legs? Didn't dream of me when you made yourself come?"

I was shaking, my head and body going in different directions. I wanted to run, I wanted to touch. I squeezed my eyes shut in humiliated, aroused memory. Of course, I'd dreamed of Griffen the first time I'd slid my fingers between my legs, terrified someone would sense what I was doing and burst in my room to stop me. Of course, it was him. It had always been him. And he knew.

His lips tasted my jaw, pressed to my own, his tongue flicking out to touch mine before skating up the other side of my jaw to my sensitive earlobe.

"Is this a punishment or a victory, Hope? You act like you're sorry, but from where I'm standing, you're the only one who got everything she wanted. Maybe you did know about the will. Maybe *you* killed Prentice."

He didn't mean it. He couldn't. How could he think *this* was what I wanted?

Forced into marriage with a man I'd once loved. Adored. Worshiped.

Forced to spend five years knowing he'd rather be with anyone else, that he'd only grow to hate me more with each day.

Once upon a time, I'd wanted Griffen to fall in love with me, to carry me off on his white horse like a prince in a story book. Never mind that Griffen hadn't had a horse.

It was never going to happen then, and it was impossible now. Those were the daydreams of a lonely girl for a boy she'd never really known.

A single tear squeezed from between my tightly closed lids, the salt of it running down my cheek, staining my skin. Griffen pulled back, licking his lips from the taste, his brows pulling together.

"Hope, no. I—"

Chapter Fourteen

HOPE

THE FRONT DOOR SWUNG OPEN WITH A SHRIEKING creak. Boot heels clattered across the hardwood floor, coming to a stop in the center of the entry. I shoved away from Griffen, swiping under my eyes before glancing up to see Savannah standing in the middle of the room, hands on her hips, surveying the formerly impressive entry hall of Heartstone Manor.

"You are not paying me enough for this," she pronounced, her eyes narrowed on Griffen and me as I sidled away, needing distance from my unwilling husband.

I fumbled for my notebook and pen as Griffen said, "Then ask Harvey for a raise."

Savannah gave a *harrumph* that reminded me of Miss Martha as she absorbed the gravelly rasp of Griffen's voice. Had he been about to kiss me? My pounding heart wasn't sure if that idea was terrifying or exactly what I wanted.

Griffen was at my side, looping his arm through mine. I tried to pull away, unsuccessfully. He shot me a glare as he said, "We just got here, haven't seen much yet. Kitchen and dining rooms first?"

"Sure," Savannah agreed, fishing her own notebook from her purse. Her kind gaze landed on me, taking in the flush in my cheeks and my wet eyes. "You okay, Hope?"

I nodded, my throat too tight to risk words.

"You'll tell me if you're not?"

I nodded again.

Griffen scowled at both of us. "I'm not going to hurt Hope, for fuck's sake."

Savannah only rolled her eyes. "It's my job to keep an eye on you two and that's exactly what I'm going to do." Raising her pen, she pointed it at Griffen. "She married you to save this town, not because you're Prince Charming. Don't think I'm going to let you get away with treating her like crap because you don't like how this all ended up. You got everything, including Hope. If you want to keep it, I better see her smiling."

A laugh choked its way out of my throat. I yanked my arm free of Griffen and put some space between us. I was still too twisted up. Aroused, but hurt. Scared, but longing for more.

I wanted to be Savannah, years younger than me and bold enough to tell Griffen off. Bold enough to tell anyone off. She was Miss Martha's daughter. She came by her ball-breaking honestly.

Humor in his eyes, Griffen said, "Yes, Ma'am." He moved to take my arm again. I side-stepped him. I wasn't playing the smiling bride in front of Savannah, the only person allowed to know I was anything but. Griffen's brows drew together but he didn't protest.

Good, it wouldn't kill him not to get what he wanted for once, and we had work to do.

We started with the dining room. Aside from Prentice's office, it was the only room on the main level we needed if we wanted to move in. Designed for formal entertaining, it was big enough to feed fifty, and every inch needed a thorough cleaning.

The kitchens weren't as bad as I'd feared. Located in the lower level, the main kitchen was bigger than most houses, with two long rectangular islands, several commercial refrigerators, and enough ovens and gas burners to cook for an army. Adjacent were the butler's pantry, the prep kitchen, and a room just for baking and making desserts. Heartstone Manor needed a cook.

Savannah was already making notes. "Needs a good cleaning—I'm already working on a crew—and someone to cook. You'll have to put up with my cooking for now. Mom might chip in. Otherwise, everything seems like it's in good shape."

She opened and closed the first dishwasher, giving a hum of approval when the lights on the control panel came to life. A glance in one of the refrigerators had her wrinkling her nose and swinging it shut. Stacks of takeout containers grown pungent with mold along with half-cut limes, bottles of tonic, and four different bottles of vodka.

Sterling. I wasn't sure if I wanted to hug her or smack her.

"I'll get these cleaned out, make a grocery run for staples," Savannah murmured. She scribbled on her pad for a few more minutes, then lifted her head and said brightly, "Bedrooms?"

"First, let's check this," Griffen said, leading us through a narrow hall off the back of the main kitchen. The hall opened into a sitting room with a narrow window set high in the wall. Despite the window's small size, the room was filled with light. A small built-in desk with a corkboard above was against one wall, a comfortable looking chair and ottoman against the other.

Savannah stopped in the middle of the room and turned a slow circle, wonder in her eyes. "I forgot about this. We stayed here when I was little until Mr. Sawyer moved Mom to the cottage." She trailed a finger over the dusty chair, lost in memory.

"Eventually, I figured you could move into the cottage, but I have a feeling it might need some work. And while you're getting a handle on things here, it would be easier to stay in the house. Does that work?"

"Sure," Savannah murmured as she opened the door off the sitting room into a decent-sized bedroom. Like the sitting room and the rest of the house, it was dusty, the air stale. Savannah turned another circle, her eyes darting here and there, the gears in her mind whirring.

"When I move into the cottage, can I turn this bedroom into a proper office and leave the sitting room as a kind of break room for staff? A place they can put their feet up for a minute without worrying about bothering the family?"

"That's a great idea," I said, thinking of the desk in the sitting room. Knowing the scope of Savannah's job, that desk wouldn't be enough. The housekeeper's bedroom wasn't huge, but it was enough space to add a bigger desk, file cabinets, a printer, and whatever else she'd need.

Giving Griffen a sidelong glance, I said, "We need to put the cottage at the top of the list once we deal with the bedrooms and the kitchen. Savannah has Nicky. They need more space than this."

"Shit, you're right. I forgot Nicky," Griffen said with an apologetic look at Savannah.

"I have an air mattress," Savannah said. "Nicky loves sleeping on it, feels like he's camping, so we can make do for a while."

Griffen nodded in agreement. "All the same, once this place is livable, we'll make the cottage top priority. This room makes a better office than bedroom."

"And speaking of bedrooms..." I said, knowing we had to deal with them eventually. Every single Sawyer would be here on Tuesday, and we had no clue if there was anywhere habitable to put them. At the very least, Savannah had a metric ton of laundry on her hands.

When seen from the front courtyard, Heartstone Manor appeared to be a simple rectangle of a building. The original architect had cleverly hidden the east and west wings, angling them out from the back of the house, camouflaged by trees, so the shape of the house was more of a V with a flat bottom, that bottom being the front. The west wing held the garages on the first floor and guest rooms above. The east wing was for family. On the first floor were Prentice's office, two sunrooms, the card room, billiards room, and the family gathering room. Above were the family apartments.

In the kitchens, we were on the opposite side of the house from the family bedrooms we'd need to inspect. Just walking around the house was going to keep me in shape.

I turned to head back to the closest staircase, following Griffen back up the main level and further still to the second floor. As we walked, he said over his shoulder, "Keep an eye out for any improvements or modernizations we need. Your mother might be able to give you ideas. If there isn't a laundry room on the second floor, you need one."

He had a point. As far as I remembered, the laundry was on the lower level, past the kitchens. That was a lot of stairs considering the amount of sheets and towels Savannah would be hauling around.

"I can live with it for now," Savannah said as she made notes on her list, "there's a few dumbwaiters and laundry chutes off the main hall."

Griffen let out a surprised chuckle. "I forgot about those. We used to drive Miss Martha crazy trying to take rides in the dumbwaiters. And once, I threw all of Avery's dolls down the chute and they got stuck. I got a hell of a spanking for that one."

The staircase let us out just where the west wing joined the main house. Savannah stopped in the hall, studying the faded wallpaper in the dim light. After a moment, she reached out and hooked her fingers through a hidden loop of wire, pulling to reveal a door. We stepped into a utility room, the bare bulb on the ceiling flickering, the shelves stacked with sheets and towels that appeared clean enough, if a little musty.

With a look around, Savannah said absently, "We could put in a washer and dryer here. There's plumbing in the mudroom below us." She scribbled notes on her pad. "And enough linens to get started."

We exited into the hall, the door disappearing behind us as if part of the wall. I turned to study the wallpaper, squinting until I could see the faint lines of the door and the tiny round handle hidden in the design of a flower.

Reaching out, I ran my finger over the seam in the wallpaper. "I never knew this was here."

"Heartstone has all sorts of secrets," Savannah said, half to herself. I'd known she'd be a good choice because she'd grown up in this house, first as a child, then as her mother's helper, and later as paid staff herself. Savannah probably knew more about Heartstone than anyone, excepting Miss Martha.

We crossed the hall that ran along the back of the main house from the west wing to the east, passing the main staircase on our right, windows looking into the formal gardens on our left. I only glanced that way once. Once was enough. I'd been right. If the front courtyard was an overgrown mess, the formal gardens were worse.

In the family wing, a wide hall ran through the center, closed doors all the way down on both sides. The sconces in the wall were half burned out, the wallpaper just as faded as the rest. The first door we came to had a cockeyed, hand-painted sign tacked to the door. *Keep Out, That Means You!*

Savannah sighed.

"Sterling," she said, gingerly turning the handle after a brief double knock. The three of us stood in the doorway, no one willing to venture in any further. Calling it a disaster would have been too generous. Sheets half torn off the bed. Piles of dirty clothes almost knee-high. A not-so-faint odor of spoiled food and stale vomit.

With a low growl, Griffen nudged us back into the hall and slammed the door shut. Anger hot in his eyes, he turned to Savannah. "You do not go into that room. When she comes back, hand her a shovel and a bottle of cleaning spray. She can clean it herself or she can pitch a tent in the woods."

He strode to the next door, his jaw set, swearing to himself. Savannah shook her head, giving me a sympathetic glance. "He's not wrong, but I still feel bad for her."

"Me, too." Sterling was a hot mess, no question. She wasn't my favorite Sawyer. She wasn't even in the top five. She was reckless, spoiled, petulant, and generally a brat. She'd also lost her mother when she was three, Darcy only four years later. Since then, Miss Martha was the closest thing she had to a parent. Prentice had barely noticed she was alive. Braxton, the only sibling close to her in age, had hated her practically since birth.

She'd call me a liar if I said it out loud, but Sterling Sawyer was the loneliest person I knew, and I knew a lot about loneliness.

Uncle Edgar was far from perfect—as my current circumstances proved very well—but he'd taken care of me. He might not have been kind about it, but if I'd started to slide out of control as Sterling had, he would have yanked me into line. Sterling had no one who cared enough to save her from herself. Until now.

Griffen was pissed, but if he held any shred of the boy I'd known, he wouldn't give up on his little sister. I refused to believe he had that in him.

The rest of the rooms were anticlimactic after Sterling's. Only Braxton's room showed any sign of current use. As the youngest siblings, Brax and Sterling had single bedrooms. Enormous bedrooms, at least twice as big as my apartment, but single rooms nonetheless.

The other Sawyers had small apartments, each complete with generous bedroom, bathroom, and sitting room. I'd grown up well off in Uncle Edgar's home, thinking it was a palace compared to the pit he'd rescued me from. Heartstone Manor was something else entirely.

We continued on, making notes of any areas that needed extra attention, linens replaced, curtains repaired. Everything needed a thorough cleaning and a gallon of furniture polish, but otherwise, we didn't find anything unexpected.

I was almost relaxing when we opened the door to what had been Griffen's room. The entire space was completely empty, not a trace of Griffen left behind. No furniture, no carpet. Not even a curtain hung in the room. The wallpaper had dark squares showing where paintings and posters had hung, where furniture had been placed along the walls.

Griffen said nothing, his jaw clamped tight, eyes blank in an expression I was growing to hate. In a thin, tight voice, I asked, "Did you take your things with you when you left?"

Chapter Fifteen

HOPE

I WALKED OUT WITH THE CLOTHES ON MY BACK AND my driver's license. Nothing else."

We turned to Savannah, who looked back at us with an embarrassed flush on her cheeks. "I'm sorry. I forgot about this. I wasn't here when it happened, but I think your father—" She swallowed hard, "I think the furniture was moved to the attic, and he had the rest thrown away. My mother might know more. I can ask," she offered.

Griffen shook his head, shutting the door on the empty room. "Forget it. I don't care, I left that life behind a long time ago."

He could pretend he didn't care, but it still had to sting. I made a note to see if Miss Martha knew where his things were. I doubted he cared about the furniture, but the rest—trophies and pictures and books—he had to want those back.

"Where to now?" Savannah asked. "Are you and Hope going to stay in your room? Do you want me to find furniture for it? I know there's a stash of unused pieces up in the attics."

"No," Griffen said shortly and paced down the hall. We followed, waiting to see what he had in mind. He led us to the main hall at the top of the stairs, the dull floor of the entry hall far below.

Savannah gave the dusty chandelier a glance. "I'll get on that once I deal with the bedrooms and the kitchen. I think there's a crank in the attic to lower it."

"I always wondered about that," I murmured as Griffen turned the corner and threw open the double doors to the master suite.

Prentice Sawyer's personal rooms had always been strictly off-limits, even to his children. While I'd run tame through much of this house as a young child, I'd never, ever been in here. What I saw had my breath catching in my throat.

This was a world unto itself. If the older Sawyer children had luxurious apartments, Prentice had a mini-palace all his own. The suite had a small foyer, with art deco black-and-white tiled floor and dark-red silk wallpaper, a table to the side with an empty crystal vase. Oil paintings hung on every wall, mostly of the mountains and rivers of Western North Carolina. A few of what I imagined were Sawyer ancestors.

Once past the foyer, the sitting room spread before us, filled with more antiques and graceful velvet couches, the floor covered by a thick, deep red carpet. A study was off one side of the room, the walls paneled with the same dark oak as the rest of the house. Beside it was an entertainment room with a massive television on the wall and an enormous leather sofa big enough for two adults to stretch out side by side. I never thought I'd see a couch bigger than my velvet monstrosity, but here it was. I still liked mine better.

On the other side of the sitting room, double doors led to the master bedroom. Griffen shoved them open and I stood in the doorway, jaw dropped. *Not to my taste.* That was the most polite thing I could think. *Yuck* was a lot closer.

The bed was massive, covered in a gold spread, with a gold-framed mirror on the ceiling. Ugh, I did not need to imagine Prentice Sawyer and that huge, tacky mirror over that even bigger, tackier bed. Double yuck. Savannah choked on a laugh as Griffen stood motionless, taking in the room.

Finally, he said, "Can you organize movers to clean this shit out? Take that mirror down and repair the ceiling?"

"I'll get it done over the weekend," Savannah muttered, scribbling furiously on her notepad. "What about the sitting room and the rest of it?"

Griffen turned to me. I thought I saw a hint of a plea in his eyes when he said, "Can we move your furniture in here? Your couch in the sitting room and the rest of it in the bedroom?"

Relief spilled through me. I loved my things. If I had one space in this huge house that was all my own, I could relax. I'd still have a nest. A haven. A place that was mine.

In a rush, I said, "Yes, absolutely," never thinking that I was fundamentally wrong about one thing.

No space in this house could be mine. Not while I was married to Griffen. I could hide from the rest of them, but never from him.

The rest of the master suite had me alternating between glee and head shakes of disbelief. At one point as we cruised through the closet, Savannah said, "Now I know how Prentice caught all those wives. I'd marry the devil himself for this closet."

I had to agree. The dressing rooms were massive, with built-ins for everything from shoes to scarves to jewelry. Griffen's section had a whole wall rack just for ties. And the bathroom... decadent didn't cover it. There were two separate spaces for the sink and vanity, each with its own small room with a toilet. That's right, two master baths, joined by the huge bathing room.

I guess the master and lady of the house didn't floss their teeth together. Though they must have taken baths together considering the size of the claw-footed tub. I couldn't even look at the square, glassed-in shower without blushing. No single person needed a shower that size.

"Isn't this all a little big?" I had to ask, trying to pretend I wasn't suddenly obsessed with thoughts of Griffen's sleek, soapy skin in the huge, tiled shower. "I've toured the Biltmore and a few other gilded age mansions. They were all luxurious for the time, but none of them had bathrooms like this."

Savannah answered as I'd suspected, knowing more about the house than Griffen did. "Prentice completely re-did this whole section of the house five years ago. What's now the dressing rooms and bathrooms used to be a guest suite. Or two. My mom would know. She never said exactly, but I had the feeling Prentice was getting it ready for a new Mrs. Sawyer."

Griffen suddenly came alert. "Any idea who?"

"No. And I don't think Mom knew either because she thought it was weird he'd spend so much money renovating for a woman he'd never even brought back to the house. She thought—" Savannah shut her mouth so fast her teeth clicked.

"What?" Griffen pressed.

"He, um— Well, Mom thought she was married. But I don't know if she had a reason to think that or if she was just guessing."

Griffen only said, "Wouldn't be the first time." That was true enough. Griffen looked at his watch. "I have to get to Harvey's to sign some papers and then we need to get on the road to Atlanta. We'll be back by Tuesday. Maybe sooner. Do you have everything you need?"

Savannah consulted her list. "I'll need a key to Hope's place as well as a list of anything she doesn't want moved." She looked to me for confirmation.

"I'll drop it by Miss Martha's on our way out. I'll pay for movers for anything that needs to be packed up."

Beside me, Griffen shook his head. "She pays for nothing. Bill it all to the house. And if Hope is good with it, bring everything. Anything of Hope's that doesn't fit, store in my old room until she can decide how she wants it all arranged."

"Got it, boss." Savannah shot me a wink.

"Any ideas for a groundskeeper?"

Savannah tilted her head to the side, staring at the ceiling as she thought it over. "Not off the top of my head. I can ask around."

"I have someone in Atlanta who might take the job. We can knock out security and the grounds in one shot if he's interested." Under his breath, he muttered, "And if Cooper doesn't kill me for poaching him."

"Got it. The grounds can wait, anyway," Savannah said, scribbling on her pad. "We need the inside done first. What about uniforms?"

"Uniforms?" I asked, confused.

"My mother and the other house staff always wore a uniform," Savannah explained.

Griffen and I stared at her, non-plussed. Eventually, Griffen said, "Do you *want* to wear a uniform?"

"Honestly, I don't know." She looked around at the over-the-top grandeur of Heartstone's master suite. "It feels weird to show up in jeans, you know? The house deserves more."

"Then how about this," I offered, hoping Griffen would agree. "You decide about the uniforms, and if you want them—for you or the rest of the staff—charge them to the house account."

"Will do," she murmured, making another note.

"Can you get this place in shape before the invasion?" Griffen asked.

"You won't even recognize it."

"Then we'll see you on Tuesday."

Griffen moved to leave. I turned to follow as Savannah's hand closed over my wrist.

"You sure you're okay?" she asked.

I shrugged. I didn't want to lie, but I didn't need rescue. I'd agreed to this, foolish though it might be. A shrug wasn't enough for Savannah.

"I meant what I said before. I'm not just here to enforce Prentice's ridiculous will. I'm here to look out for you. I know we don't know each other that well, but my mother loves you, and that's good enough for me. I don't think I'm going to have many friends in this house, but I'd like you to be one of them."

Tears filled my eyes at Savannah's bold honesty. "I don't think I'm going to have many friends in this house either." Impulsively, I threw my arms around her in a tight hug. "One is more than enough when it's a good friend." I had a feeling Savannah could be a very good friend.

A little embarrassed at my unexpected show of affection, I ran from the room, trying to catch up with Griffen's long stride.

Chapter Sixteen

GRIFFEN

BY THE TIME I GOT BACK FROM SIGNING PAPERS WITH Harvey, Hope had her apartment ready for the movers. Three battered suitcases were neatly arranged by the door holding the contents of her closet. A stack of cardboard boxes sat beside them, labelled *Hope Personal*. She'd left the rest for the movers.

My tires ate up the miles between Sawyers Bend and Atlanta, Hope silent beside me, staring out the window, lost in thought. I wanted to hear her voice, wanted to talk to her, but I had nothing to say.

What had happened in the hall just before Savannah showed up? Had I been about to kiss her again? I was pretty sure that's exactly what I'd been about to do. Right after I made her cry.

I was an asshole.

I wanted to protect her and I wanted to punish her.

I wanted to make her pay for what she'd done and I never wanted to see her cry again.

That was the biggest difference between the younger version of Hope and this one—young Hope had never tied me up in knots like this. Not even close.

"Are you hungry? We missed breakfast and it's getting on to lunch."

Hope shook her head, keeping her eyes on the road. "Not really."

She needed to eat. I could go without meals, was used to it when the job took precedence over my stomach, but Hope was thin enough as it was. We wouldn't be in Atlanta for another two hours. I didn't want to wait that long.

"Do you mind if we stop in the next town? I'm starving."

Just a shake of her head to say she didn't mind. Hope's silence wasn't manipulative. I knew that in my gut. She wouldn't play those games with me, and that made her reluctance to speak that much worse. If I thought she was giving me the silent treatment as payback for being an ass, I could play along.

Her retreat into herself, I hated. Hated it to the core of my being. I wanted to hear her laugh, not feel the sadness coming off her in waves.

Fuck it. There was nothing I could do about Hope. Not right then.

If I couldn't fix things with Hope, I could handle another problem. Better to do this before we got to Atlanta. I picked up my phone and hit the contact without looking at the screen. I didn't need to. I'd called Cooper so many times, my finger found his name on its own.

"Where the hell are you, man?" he answered.

"On my way back."

"How was it?"

"An unholy clusterfuck."

A pause. Cooper weighing what he knew of my family and the tone in my voice. "Shit," he said, finally. "I'm not going to like this, am I?"

"Yeah, you can join the club. No one fucking likes it." I drew in a breath, knowing I had to get it out fast. My gut was tight as I slammed headfirst into reality. "I'm not staying in Atlanta. I have to move home, take over for my father."

"Or what?" Cooper's voice was flat. He knew there was a hook, knew I'd never have stayed a second longer than necessary if I hadn't been forced to.

I gave him a quick summary, saving the best part for last. "Oh, and remember Hope Daniels?"

"The woman who came to tell you about your father? The one who threw you under the bus way back when?"

A careful glance at Hope, who appeared completely absorbed by the thick forest flashing by her window. "Yeah, that Hope. We're married."

A string of expletives that would have made a sailor proud came blasting through the phone. Cooper was loud enough to grab Hope's attention. Her eyebrows shot up and the faintest smile curved her lips before it faded back to the sad, almost wistful expression she'd had since I'd picked her up at her apartment.

Knowing it might be exactly the wrong thing, I pinned the phone between my shoulder and my ear and used my now-free hand to hold hers. Her fingers were like ice. I squeezed, sending her what I hoped was a comforting smile. She squeezed back but kept her eyes on the side of the road.

When Cooper wound down, I cut in. "Chill, Coop. In this whole fucking disaster, Hope is the only thing I'm not pissed about."

As I said the words, I realized I meant them. All the way to the bone, they were the truth.

I tried to imagine doing this alone, facing it all by myself: Harvey, that grave, my siblings, fucking Heartstone Manor. As I tried to picture it, all I felt was empty.

Hope had screwed me over. Big time. She'd ruined my life out of selfishness, and still, she was the only one I could trust. The only person in Sawyers Bend I was sure was on my side. Was she there out of guilt? Out of loyalty to our long-ago friendship? I didn't know.

Maybe I shouldn't trust her. I'd had a point with my bullshit accusation in the hall—Hope had what she'd wanted all those years ago when she'd tanked my engagement. But, no. No fucking way. Hope had not killed Prentice. Not in a million years. Maybe Hope was the last person I should trust, but my gut didn't care. I trusted her anyway.

"Earth to Griffen." Cooper sounded faintly annoyed. I realized he'd been saying my name for a while.

"Yeah, sorry. I feel like shit, dumping this on you with no notice. We have to be moved into Heartstone Manor by next week. I'd give you time to replace me if I had it to give."

It was an empty promise. I'd been out of the field since I'd been shot by Tsepov's goons. In essence, Cooper had already replaced me. My desk job had been little more than a time-filler, a pity job, and we all knew it.

"Fuck you," Cooper said without heat. "We'll figure it out. I don't care about work. Is there any way we can get you out of this?"

"Sure. But not without sinking the town and letting my half-wit cousin walk away with everything the Sawyers have built over two fucking centuries."

"And Hope? What does she get?"

"Not a fucking thing worth having," I said, realizing that those words were more truth.

"Except you," Cooper countered.

"And I come with a family of asshole siblings, a white elephant of a house that's an abandoned mess, a business I have to remember how to run, and let's not forget that someone murdered my father. Since we don't know why we have to assume any one of us could be next."

I couldn't forget what Edgar had said about getting Hope pregnant. A baby meant security. Both Hope and our non-existent child deserved more than being used as pawns.

"Fuck. Well, that answers my next question. Now I know how we can help. What is there for security?"

"You can start salivating now because the bill is going to put Petra through college." I wasn't kidding. Securing Heartstone Manor would be no small project. "I have some ideas we can run through, but essentially, we need what we did for Winters House, times five." I thought about those thousands of acres surrounding Heartstone Manor and the sheer size of the house. "Maybe times ten."

"Are you up for a meeting tonight? Dinner at my place? I'll get everyone in. No wives, just business—" He broke off at the sound of a smack and a feminine protest. "Except you, babe. I meant no wives except you." Cooper gave a patient sigh.

"Can I talk to Alice?" I interrupted. "I need a favor."

Alice's chipper voice came on the phone. "You got married? Without letting me vet the bride? What were you thinking?" She was laughing, but under her humor, I heard the thread of concern.

"We didn't exactly have time for you to put my bride through the wringer. Listen, I need a favor. Is one of the safe rooms clear?"

"Sure. No clients in-house. You want to stay in my old place? Why not yours?"

"Because I need you to find me rush movers who can pack up all my personal shit and have it ready to ship to Sawyers Bend by the middle of the week."

"Ahh, gotcha. I'm on it. What about the furniture?"

"We can leave it. We're moving Hope's things to the house and I don't really care about mine. I thought I could rent my place for a while."

"Got it."

"And one more thing..." I glanced at Hope, who was studiously pretending she wasn't listening. I squeezed her hand to get her attention and mouthed, *Don't argue*. At her look of confusion, I said to Alice, "Are you free tomorrow?"

"Sure, I have a dance class, but I can miss it. Why?"

"Would you take Hope shopping? On me. She needs everything."

Hope's brows drew together, and I waited for her to argue. Instead, she gave a wry smile and shook her head. She tugged her hand from mine and turned back to the window, but the smile still tilted the corners of her mouth. I was taking that as a good sign.

"Shopping? On you? I'm in. She needs everything?"

"Everything. Hope's a workaholic and there's no decent shopping in Sawyers Bend." I wasn't going to tell Alice about Edgar and his miserable taste in suits. That was Hope's to share if she wanted to. "The closet at Heartstone Manor is huge. She needs some clothes to fill it."

"I do not," came from beside me.

"I say you do. Don't argue when someone hands you their credit card and tells you to have fun."

Hope shook her head again, that tiny smile growing just a little wider. "You're nuts."

I ignored her. To Alice, I said, "We're stopping for lunch, be there in a few hours."

"What's my budget on the movers?"

"Whatever you need to get it done."

Lunch passed with more semi-awkward silence. Hope tried

to convince me to drop the idea of a shopping trip. I shut her down. Alice loved to shop, and though she had a unique style of her own, I knew she'd be able to figure out what Hope liked and find her what she'd want.

I couldn't get those suitcases by her door out of my head. An entire life in three suitcases and a few boxes. Hope should have more. I was going to give it to her, one way or another.

Chapter Seventeen

GRIFFEN

I PULLED INTO MY PARKING SPOT IN THE SINCLAIR SECU-
rity garage, feeling like a visitor. This place had
been home for over a decade, but since the day
I'd learned my shoulder wasn't going to be the same, something
inside me had been pulling away. I just hadn't realized it until now.

Cooper, his brothers, and my co-workers were my family, but
I didn't belong here anymore. I couldn't work in the field and
didn't want to be stuck behind a desk watching everyone else
out there doing my job.

The idea of running Sawyer Enterprises was different. It
was both a brand-new challenge and one I'd spent half my life
preparing for. I didn't like the way I'd ended up in charge of
the company, but I won't deny I was excited by the prospect of
finally taking the reins the way I'd always expected to.

I used my handprint to get us access to the elevators and rode up to the third floor. Before she'd hooked up with Cooper, Alice had lived in one of the safe room apartments kept for clients who needed heightened levels of protection. Alice's place wasn't the most luxurious of the three apartments, but unlike the other two, Alice's place was familiar. Comfortable.

I dumped our things in the kitchen and turned to Hope. "I want to head upstairs and check in with Cooper, go over some things. You should come—"

She was already shaking her head. "I'm exhausted. I'd rather lay down, try to take a nap."

Hope did look tired, but I'd bet she didn't want a nap as much as she wanted to avoid meeting my friends. I wanted to promise it wouldn't be that bad when I remembered the string of expletives Cooper had spit out when he'd heard about our marriage.

This mess wasn't Hope's fault any more than it was mine. She'd made mistakes years ago, but this marriage, the will— those were all my father and Edgar. Not Hope. And I didn't like the dark circles under her eyes. She hadn't had a minute alone since she'd shown up at Harvey's office. If she needed solitude, she would get it.

I did a quick check of the fridge. Fruit, a bag of coffee, carton of creamer, and a few more odds and ends. Alice was the best. "Alice left us some snacks and coffee. I'm just upstairs. Call if you need anything."

Hope nodded, so deep in her own head I couldn't tell what she was thinking. Acting on instinct, I wrapped my arms around her, holding her against my body for a long moment. "It's going to be okay. We're going to figure this out, Hope."

She nodded against my chest, relaxing into me just enough for more words to loosen in my chest and come spilling out. "I'm sorry about earlier. In the hall. I was an asshole."

She shook her head in denial. It shouldn't have annoyed me. It did anyway. "You were right," she said in a tiny voice I could barely hear.

"You killed Prentice?" I asked, trying to get her to smile.

"I kind of wish I had," she whispered. "But you were right about the rest."

The bitch of it was I *had* been right. So what? Did it even matter now? I couldn't get my head, my heart, around the split. I was right, she was wrong. This was my vindication. Why didn't I want it? Why couldn't I just let her off the hook?

Her slight body against mine, the curve of her waist under my hand, the heat of her breath through my shirt all made it more complicated. Since when did I want Hope Daniels? My body didn't give a shit about the past, about the bad choices she'd made as a teenager. My body wanted the adult woman in my arms, the woman who'd been my friend, today and all those years ago.

I had the terrifying feeling it was more than my body talking here. I had no fucking clue what to do with that. Since I left Sawyers Bend, my heart shattered, I hadn't given it to any woman. I had my friends, male and female, and I had women I saw socially. I didn't do relationships. I never went looking for forever.

I'd learned firsthand—forever was a lie. Seeing my friends all fall in love over the last few years hadn't shaken my basic belief that I was better off going through life alone. Now I was married, and I'd be faithful to Hope, but it was only temporary. None of this was real.

My head was upside down. My body knew what it wanted. My arms tightened around Hope, plastering her to me, absorbing her heat, her warm apples and cinnamon scent. Lowering my head, I pressed a kiss to the top of her head, wishing I could erase everything that had happened in the hall, the ugly words I'd spoken, the cruel tease of that almost-kiss.

"Rest up. If you need anything, call me, okay?"

"I will," she promised.

Unable to resist, I tilted her face up to mine. Her eyes gazed past my ear, refusing to make contact, a faint flush coloring her cheeks. I hadn't even kissed her and she was already warming to me, her body melting into mine, her tongue sneaking out to lick her lips.

Slow, I reminded myself.

I meant to listen. I did. But the second my mouth touched hers, I forgot all about slow. Her soft lips parted, her tongue shyly brushing mine, that little gasp of pleasure kerosene on the flame of my need. I was hungry for her, greedy, and her mouth met mine, just as greedy, with just as much raw need.

I could be rational, sensible when I didn't have my hands on her. Now? With her breasts pressed to my chest, her hips rolling into me in a movement so instinctive I doubted she knew what she was doing—rational was out the window.

I was a breath away from throwing her over my shoulder and showing her how much pleasure I could give her when I realized she was shaking. A bolt of fear drowned my arousal. Had I scared her? Had she tried to stop me and I missed it?

No. Her eyes were glazed with lust, her body trembling. Not with fear, but with too much sensation.

She's a virgin, you fuckhead, I reminded myself. *What happened to slow?*

She was responsive as hell, and she wanted me, but she had no clue how to handle what her body needed. I rubbed my palm roughly up and down her back with a long sigh. She shook against me, her face buried against my neck, cheeks hot on my skin.

"You okay?"

"A little tired and a lot freaked out," she said with more honesty than I'd expected.

"You want me to stop kissing you?" I asked, my breath freezing in my lungs as soon as the question was out.

What if she said yes?

Her head shook in a negative. Thank fuck. I might have wept tears of frustrated disappointment if she'd said yes.

"You'll tell me if it's too much?"

A nod, and a deep, shuddering breath. "I'm sorry—"

"No," I interrupted. "No apologies. Not about this. Never about this. I'm trying to take it slow. It's just harder than I expected."

A quirk at the side of her mouth as she pushed her body into me, pressing against my rock-hard erection. "Isn't it supposed to be hard?"

My burst of laughter was as surprising as her saucy tease. "My cock? Yes. Taking it slow so I don't scare you off? That should be a lot easier."

"Is it usually?"

"Easier? Hell yes, Buttercup." The almost-forgotten childhood endearment slid out naturally. "Control is not usually an issue for me. Not like this."

"Then why is it hard with me?" she giggled.

"Fucked if I know, but it is. So fucking hard." Another giggle. I rested my chin on the top of her head, absorbing the sound of her laughter. "I forgot I used to call you Buttercup. Do you still pick them and hold them under your chin to see the sunshine?"

"Not in a long time."

"We'll have a picnic when it warms up," I promised, remembering all the times I'd found her in the wild of the woods, curled up against a tree trunk with a book in her lap, a bouquet of buttercups at her side. She'd loved the sunny flowers that grew in abundance in the fields of Heartstone Manor.

"Okay."

With another squeeze of my arms, I let her go, more

135

reluctant to leave her than I'd expected, especially after that kiss. "Rest. Take a nap, a bath, whatever. Text me if you're up for dinner later. Otherwise, there's some cans of soup and frozen pizza in the kitchen."

Another "Okay," and she was gone, grabbing her suitcase and disappearing into the first bedroom she came to. I got in the elevator and hit the button for Cooper's floor, feeling like I'd left some essential part of myself behind with Hope.

Buttercup. How had I forgotten that? And if I'd forgotten calling her Buttercup, what else had I buried? I didn't have time to figure it out before the elevator was spitting me out into Cooper's foyer. Time to face the music. I was not ready for this.

I didn't think I ever would be.

Chapter Eighteen

GRIFFEN

HEY WERE ALL WAITING FOR ME. COOPER. ALICE. Cooper's brothers Evers and Knox. All wearing similar expressions of concern. Alice came forward to give me a hug, her arms strong despite her tiny frame. When she let go, she leaned around me, looking back at the closed elevator.

"Where is she?"

Of course, Alice was looking for Hope. "Taking a nap. She needs it after the last twenty-four hours."

"You got married?"

"Yep."

"You going to tell us why?"

"Because we're in love, why else?"

"She didn't know?" Cooper asked, handing me a cold beer

and leading us to the big couches in his living room. Cooper was sharp. He might not know the details, but he knew I hadn't married Hope of my own free will.

"She had no clue." There was a lot I didn't understand, but I was sure about that. Despite the shitty things I'd said earlier, I knew Hope was innocent in all of this.

"And your brother's in jail? Did he do it?" Evers asked, bracing his foot on the table, curiosity in his ice-blue eyes. He was the youngest of the Sinclair brothers, the most like me in temperament. Easy going, charming, hard to ruffle.

Okay, I had to admit, Evers was more like me *before* I was shot. Post career-ending shoulder injury, I was a cranky bastard.

"No," I answered. "No way Ford did it."

"Huh. Isn't he the asshole who got you kicked out of town and stole your fiancée?" Cooper asked. Alice's head pinged between us, taking it all in. Cooper alone knew the whole story thanks to a bottle of tequila years ago on the anniversary of my would-be wedding.

"He is," I admitted. Might as well get it all out there. "It was a long time ago. A lifetime."

"It was her too, though, wasn't it? Hope had something to do with it?" Alice only knew bits and pieces of the story, but she was good at putting things together. They all were.

I set my beer on the table and went for the bar at the side of the room. "I need something stronger than a beer. Anyone want anything?"

"Bring the bottle," Knox said. Always a man of few words, Knox got right to the point. I grabbed the decanter and five glasses.

Knocking back a generous slug of Cooper's excellent whiskey, I started at the beginning of the end. "We were going to elope. My father didn't like Vanessa. We'd dated off and on all through college. Prentice always hated her. When I started talking about marriage, he said it wasn't going to happen. I ignored him. Right around then there was a business he wanted to buy, thought it would fill a hole in our portfolio. The owner didn't want to sell. Prentice was playing hardball. My brother Ford and I were trying to stop him, to find a way to fill the hole without stealing a man's livelihood."

"Did you two get along back then? You and Ford?" Alice asked, sipping delicately at her whiskey.

"Back then we did, yeah. Or I thought we did." Bitterness crept in, leaving a sour taste in my mouth. I took another slug of whiskey to wash it away. *It was a lifetime ago*, I reminded myself.

"What did Hope have to do with anything?" Evers asked. "Was she an ex? Wasn't she a little young for you?"

"Not an ex," I corrected, remembering Hope back then. Gangly and coltish, she'd grown into her adult height but the rest of her hadn't yet caught up. "She was sixteen. Just a kid."

"That's my point." Evers' eyebrow raised. "She was sixteen. You were twenty-two. Little young for you."

"It wasn't like that. She was always around because of her uncle Edgar, Prentice's business partner. We grew up together. She was a kid, but she was smart as hell and funny. She was kind. Hope had a way of seeing through the bullshit. She was... I don't know, it sounds weird, but she was wise." I shrugged a shoulder. "I liked talking to her."

"It didn't hurt that she had a crush on you," Alice pointed out, reading between the lines.

"It wasn't like that," I protested. It hadn't been. At least not for me. I knew she had a crush on me, and I was careful not to encourage it. I knew she felt like she was all grown up, but in my eyes, she was still very much a kid. "I never touched her. I swear. We were friends. She was the only one I told about the elopement, and she told her uncle, who told my father."

"That's it?" Alice asked. "She was a teenager who told a secret?"

I couldn't keep the bitterness under wraps. It hadn't been that simple. "Hope knew exactly what would happen. She was young, but she was smart. She knew my father almost as well as she knew her uncle. She knew he'd stop us."

"Jealous," Alice murmured to herself.

I raised my glass in a salute. "Exactly. One minute I think I'm getting married, and the next my father's kicking me out—of the house, of the company—Vanessa is married to Ford, and I've got nothing but the clothes on my back. The whole fucking family just stood there. Ford played it off like I'd been trying to undermine that business deal on my own. He handed my father what he needed to force the owner to sell, making me look like I'd betrayed our father and Ford was the savior. Prentice bought it."

"And no one said a thing?" Alice pressed. "They just let him throw you out?"

"No one," I confirmed. Whiskey and memories clouded my mind, the truth slowly rising to the surface. "Except for Hope. Prentice made it into a production, introducing Ford and his bride to the family at the same time as he disinherited me. Fuckers didn't even look guilty. Ford just kept smiling. But Hope started yelling at Prentice. I can't remember what she said. He had her removed from the room, didn't want her spoiling his big scene."

There wasn't enough whiskey in the world to erase the memory of my father and Ford's twin smiles. Smug. Triumphant.

"Your father was a royal asshole," Knox commented. Understated, as usual. I gave another bitter laugh.

"Yeah, and then some."

"Sounds like Hope did you a favor," he said.

I went still inside, instinctively recoiling at the idea any favors had been done in that clusterfuck. My entire life had been stolen from me. My future. My legacy.

"Kind of, yeah," Alice agreed. "She got rid of the fiancée—because why would you want to marry a woman who ditched you for your brother? And Hope got you free of your father. Do you really wish you'd spent the last decade-and-a-half like that? With a woman who—let's face it—didn't love you. A brother who stabbed you in the back. A father who tossed you out just because he didn't get his way. You were better off in the army and then here with us."

"Alice has a point," Cooper said. "You're one of the best men I know, and you wouldn't be that man if you'd stayed there. Would you?"

The change in perspective was bending my brain so far I thought it would break. I'd spent so long seeing myself as the victim, all this time focused on what they'd stolen from me. What Hope had stolen when she'd shared my secret.

Sure, I hated the rest of them, too. I was all about equal opportunity hate when it came to my family.

Hope was the only one who'd protested. She started it when she told my secret, but she'd tried to stop it. She'd stood up for me.

Had she stolen my future, or had she set me free?

What if I *had* married Vanessa? I tossed back the rest of my whiskey. That didn't bear thinking about. I'd been a smart kid when it came to business, not so clever about women.

Vanessa was a viper. I hadn't kept up with my family in the past decade and a half. I did know Ford had divorced her but not without her soaking him for a fortune in alimony.

"What makes you think it was Hope who spilled the beans?" Alice asked.

"She admitted it." I'd never forget the guilt on her face. Guilt and apology. "I asked my father how he knew, and he pointed at Hope."

"But surely, he must have known before she told her uncle," Evers added. "The whole thing with the business deal, Vanessa marrying your brother. That didn't all come from a sixteen-year-old's gossip. It's too orchestrated."

"I looked into your father," Cooper said. "He was not a man who'd miss someone fucking with his business. You were what? Twenty-two? Ford was twenty? You're sharp, but I doubt you were clever enough to hide what you were up to. Especially if your brother was undermining you the whole time."

Fuck. My brain was definitely going to break. They were right. Hope had been so easy to blame. So much guilt on her face as she'd wept, begging Prentice to reconsider.

I'd been so angry. So fucking angry. And terrified. All I'd known was my family.

I'd lived a life of luxury, walked right into my job with Sawyer Enterprises. I had no idea how to survive on my own, how to make my way in the world as myself, separate from the Sawyers.

I'd walked down the endless drive from Heartstone Manor to the main road shaking with fear and rage. Acting on instinct and desperation, I'd bummed a ride to the nearest army recruitment center and signed up.

It had been sheer luck that I'd taken to the army, had found Cooper and then Sinclair Security. By the time I was settled enough to think about what happened, looking back felt like a waste of time.

I poured more whiskey into my glass and drank, knowing I was getting drunk and not caring. Of all the places in the world, this one was safe. These people were the only family I'd known since I'd been cast from home, and they were better than anyone I'd left behind.

Except for Hope.

Fuck. *Hope.* All these years she'd carried so much guilt. And I had let her. I'd let her carry it alone. I'd left, hefting my anger and bitterness like luggage I carried through the years and never thought about what I'd left behind. Never thought about Hope, alone, with only Edgar to look out for her.

I stared into the dregs of my whiskey, trying to figure out what to do next. Apologize? Ask her to forgive me? And what about the rest of them?

I glanced up to see Cooper giving me an assessing look, seeming to understand that I'd had enough for now.

"Just what I love the most," he said. "A drunk client who needs our help. Don't think you're getting a break just because you're family." He rubbed his hands together and snagged a folder I hadn't noticed from the coffee table.

"Don't get too excited about hosing me," I said, tipsy but not yet drunk. "I'm taking Hawk. I need a groundskeeper and on-site security coordinator."

"Fuck. He'll be all over that. Thousands of acres of mountains to get lost in, plus formal gardens. You probably have a fucking greenhouse, too," Evers grumbled.

"Yes, we do," I said with a smug grin. Fucking house should be good for something.

"It'll be good for him," Knox added in a low voice.

It would, which was why the Sinclairs might bitch, but they wouldn't mind if Hawk came back to Sawyers Bend with me. Hawk had been a Ranger with Evers and me, then gone black ops when we'd gotten out. No one knew what had happened, but he'd come to us five years before, a changed man.

Where he'd always been quiet, now he rarely spoke. Quick to anger, he had trouble sleeping, spending hours with his hands in the dirt to soothe whatever ate at him.

He knew more about plants than anyone I'd ever met. What he didn't know, he'd learn. He might not be the most qualified for the groundskeeper position, but when I added in his other skills, he was the only man for the job.

We dug into the security plans, me adding to the layout of the property Cooper and his brothers had pulled together since my phone call, tweaking here and there. If Harvey didn't approve the initial budget I'd add to it out of my own funds. I wasn't installing Hope in Heartstone Manor unless I could assure her safety.

Someone called for pizza. Alice refilled my whiskey glass, winking and cracking a joke about padding the invoice. For the first time in years, I felt ever-so-slightly on the outside.

The Sinclair brothers were almost identical. Cooper and Knox were more heavily muscled than Evers. Evers shared Cooper's ice-blue eyes, while their other brother Axel and Knox's eyes were so dark-brown they were almost black. Those minor differences aside, they almost could have been triplets, and they worked together with the ease of years as partners as well as a lifetime as siblings.

Nothing like my family. Ford and I had once been two peas in a pod, almost identical in looks except for his dark hair to my blond. With so many different mothers, even Prentice's dominant genetics couldn't overcome the variation among the assorted Sawyer children. We didn't look alike. We didn't act alike. And for fifteen years, we'd had absolutely nothing in common. A part of me wanted to grab Hope and run from the whole fucking mess.

Grab Hope? Shouldn't I be leaving her behind?

No. I wasn't leaving Hope behind, and I was done lying to myself. Hope was the only good thing that had come of my father dying and saddling me with his will.

I was more than tipsy, not quite drunk, when I made my way downstairs to find Hope fast asleep in the only bed in Alice's former apartment. A better man might have taken the couch.

Without the whiskey, I might have been that man, but I doubted it.

If it had been any other woman sprawled between those soft white sheets I could have talked myself into the couch. In the dim light from the bathroom, her hair spilled across the pillow, her skin warm cream against the cool white sheets, tiny spots of freckles across the back of her shoulders barely visible.

For a heart-stopping moment, I saw all that skin and thought she was naked. Ever unruly in the presence of a grown-up Hope, my cock came to life, not dissuaded when I spotted the narrow straps holding up her nightgown.

A nightgown was almost as good as naked.

No touching. Even half-drunk, I wasn't that much of an asshole.

I wasn't sober and Hope was sleeping. I hit the bathroom, standing under a cold shower, the icy water doing little to shock me sober and freeze my cock into dormancy.

I thought about crawling between the sheets. I would. Soon.

Instead, I poured myself two fingers of whiskey and took a position by the window, looking out over the sleeping city that had once been my home. The glass was cold against my shoulder, unable to reach deep enough to soothe the ache from tendons and ligaments not yet repaired.

I should sleep. Instead, I stood vigil—watching my city, watching my wife—as they both slept.

Saying goodbye to one and wondering what I was going to do with the other.

Eventually, whiskey gone and my body exhausted, I slid between the sheets beside Hope. I didn't touch. Not on purpose. I fell asleep beside her, the scent of cinnamon and apples lulling me until my eyes fell shut and I drifted off. The sense of dislocation that had been dogging me since we arrived in Atlanta dissolved in the heat of the body beside me.

Chapter Nineteen

GRIFFEN

I WOKE IN THE THIN LIGHT OF DAWN TO A WARM weight across my chest and legs. Soft skin shifted under my hands, a kitten moan touching my ears as warm breath brushed my chest.

Fuck. I'd fallen asleep beside her, but I'd kept my hands to myself. I had absolutely kept my hands to myself.

Hope was another story. In her sleep, she must have rolled into me, snuggling close until she was draped across me.

I thought about getting up, slipping from beneath her sleeping form and escaping into the bathroom. I could get dressed and head into the office before Hope had any idea she'd been wrapped around me, her cheek to my chest, one leg slung over my hips. She shifted, her thigh brushing my hard cock, and I knew I wasn't going anywhere.

My hands came up to cup her ass, barely covered by a white cotton nightgown. She was more lean than she was curves, but she still filled my hands nicely. Every part of me approved. Wanted more. Still mostly asleep, she stretched up, her mouth brushing my skin. Fingers sinking into her flesh, I shifted her over me, raising her just enough for my mouth to take hers.

She woke and went still as she realized where she was. The slightest hesitation—Would she leave? Was she going to run?—and then her mouth opened to mine, her tongue darting out to stroke mine, and all thoughts of letting her go evaporated.

I rolled, pinning Hope beneath me, settling between her spread legs, rocking my erection into the heat of her as her dazed eyes searched for mine. Her arms wound around my neck, holding on, her lips parting.

Don't tell me to stop, I silently prayed.

I would if she asked. In that moment, I thought I'd do anything if she just asked.

Those pink lips fell apart, but she didn't say a word. She arched her neck, lifting her mouth, her eyes hot and inviting. She was half asleep, turned on, and too innocent to have any idea what I was thinking. What I wanted.

I wasn't going to take advantage, but we had to start somewhere. She was mine. I didn't care about the will. Not here. Not in this bed with Hope's warm, soft body under mine, her mouth moving with a greed I don't think she understood. She wanted me.

Why did that hit me so deep? With everything swirling around us, why did it matter so much? She'd wanted me years before. She'd been a child. In a lot of ways, so had I. There were no children here. I'd lived a lifetime since the last time I'd seen her. So had she.

For all her innocence, Hope was a woman grown, and she was my wife.

148

I kissed her slowly. Deep, drugging kisses. Nothing that would scare her. I wasn't going to rush. I just wanted more. Her heart thundered under my hand as I cupped her breast, the slight curve fitting neatly in my palm. Her nipple beaded at my touch. Hooking my fingers in the strap of her nightgown, I pulled it down, baring her skin, and closed my mouth over her.

A moan slid from her, a little desperate and edged with need. She went stiff beneath my sucking mouth. I didn't stop, but every cell in my body was alert to the slightest indication she wanted me to.

A push on my shoulder, a sound of hesitation, and I'd end this.

Like the day before, she trembled under my touch. Unlike the day before, I didn't let her go. I didn't soothe her down. I sucked harder at that sweet nipple, savoring every gasp, every moan, the pounding of her heart and the strain of her muscles.

Needing more, needing all of her, I pushed aside her nightgown and moved to her other breast, cupping it in my hand, plumping it for my mouth as my lips closed around her.

Her gasp set me on fire. Slowly, giving her time to stop me, my fingers trailed over her ribs, her soft belly, the curve of her hip until they found the heat between her legs.

She was wet. So fucking wet. I could feel it even before I nudged her panties aside. At the touch of my fingertip, she jerked, her eyes flying wide with shock. Fear? Or pleasure?

With a final, lingering swipe of my tongue, I released her breast, propping myself up on one elbow and working my finger against her. Her pupils were dilated, cheeks flushed, breath coming in short pants. My lips brushed over hers, tasting her rising pleasure.

I needed to see her come. I needed to make her come. For me. I had to have that from her. To know I'd given it to her.

I needed her to know I could give her something good.

Something that was just for her. Fuck the rest of it. My family, the will, her uncle, the house. Fuck them all. I needed to give her this.

I couldn't find any words. I kissed her, absorbing every little sound she made as I sank one finger deep into her slick, tight heat. Little begging growls in her throat, her mouth attacking mine, our kiss an anchor as waves of pleasure dragged her under. I wanted to spread her legs wide, to drop between them and put my mouth on her. To suck her clit like I'd sucked her breast.

I also didn't want to give her a stroke. Later, I'd get my mouth on her later. For now, I drove a second finger beside the first and ground the heel of my palm into her clit. Her hips rocked, her body knowing what it needed even if her mind was drowning. She rode my hand, sucking my tongue, wild beneath me as her orgasm broke.

I pulled my mouth from hers. I wanted to watch. Her eyes, those warm cognac eyes, flew wide with disbelief as her pleasure crested and crashed through her, dragging a keening sound from her throat.

Hope in orgasm was the most beautiful thing I'd ever seen. Making her come once wasn't enough. It would never be enough.

I fought the urge to drive her up again. To give her more. To see that beauty spread over her face again. And again. I couldn't let her go. Not yet. I kissed her. Soft. Gentle. Slid my hand from between her legs and rolled us, settling her on top of me.

With a sweet, languid sigh she relaxed into me, her heat branding my belly, nudging the tip of my cock. It would be so easy to push down my boxers, slide her panties out of the way and—

Not yet. Hope wasn't ready for that.

Slowly, she came down from the high of orgasm, her body going stiff, her brain clicking into gear as she realized she was half-naked on top of me, realized my fingers had been inside her, that she'd come apart for me.

With a squeak of embarrassment, she moved to roll off of me. My arm clamped over her back, holding her in place.

"I've never done that before," she confessed in a rush, her lips hot against my neck.

Shock spiked through me. Never? "Hope—I know you said you were a virgin but—you've never had an orgasm?"

She jerked in my arms, trying again to free herself. I wasn't letting her go anywhere. I rolled us again, landing between her legs, the length of my erection solid against her soft heat, wanting more than anything to get inside.

I framed her face with my hands, chasing her eyes with mine. "Really?"

Her eyes glued to my shoulder, she mumbled, "Not with someone else."

I couldn't stop a groan at the picture that invaded my head. Hope naked, one hand between her legs, the other cupping her breast, working her clit as she pinched her nipple and moaned my name.

My hips jerked against her. It took every ounce of control I had to stay where I was. Fucking hell. Fucking, fucking hell. I had to see that. Not today. Not for a while, probably. But eventually. Fuck yes. For now—

"Do you want to do it again?"

Her eyes went so wide I thought they'd pop out of her head. I hadn't expected to laugh, but her shocked look was so adorable I couldn't do anything else.

"Again?" She shifted beneath me and froze, suddenly aware of my erection. "But you, don't you want me to—?"

So fucking adorable.

I almost said it, but I didn't think she'd find the situation as cute as I did. Pissing her off was the last thing I wanted. Not now that I'd had her. Hot, wild, giving me everything.

Hope was wound up so tight most of the time, but when I got my hands on her, she was all mine.

"Next time, Buttercup. This time was all for you."

"But, don't you—" Her teeth sank into her lip. "I don't know what to do. I mean, I do, but I—" She squeezed her eyes shut.

Fucking adorable, but I had to put her out of her misery. When I was a teenager, skill and experience had been a turn on. Skill and experience could always be a turn on, but I'd learned they weren't necessary. Not in the face of Hope's brand of honest passion. I didn't need technique. I didn't need her to know what she was doing. I just needed Hope.

"Not this time. Next time I'll show you what to do. For now, I'd better get in the shower and down to the office before Cooper and the guys come looking for me. I'll make coffee. You can sleep a little longer. Alice won't be here for an hour or two."

I rolled off the bed, not missing the flash of skin as Hope scrambled to pull up the sheet. I wanted to count every freckle. Her eyes scanned me, jumping away after they landed on my cock comically distending the front of my boxers. Her teeth sank into her lip again, her cheeks so pink.

Eventually, she'd get used to this. As far as I was concerned, she could take her time.

Eyes squeezed shut, she said, "I don't need you to buy me clothes."

"Hope, look at me." Her gaze fixed studiously on my face. Fighting a grin, I said, "I need to buy you clothes."

Her eyes got squinty. "Because you don't want to see my ugly suits?"

"Do you want to wear those suits? Honestly? If you could wear anything you wanted, that's what you'd pick? Because if you really like them, wear them. Go out with Alice, take my credit card and buy ten more."

"I don't get it. I don't know what you want."

"I want you to be happy," I said. "I want you to be Hope. I want you to pick clothes you like. Because they make you feel good. Not because you think I like them or they're appropriate. Fuck appropriate. Fuck what anyone else likes. I can't set you free, Hope. I can't change the past. There are so many things I can't do for you. But I have money, and I can do this. Alice loves to shop and she loves clothes. She's also fun, and loyal, and a great friend. Let her take you shopping. Let me do this."

Hope stared back at me, clearly still confused, but she nodded her head. I disappeared into the bathroom and started the shower. The second I stood under the hot spray, I closed my soapy hand around my cock and squeezed, starting a slow rhythm, water beating down on the top of my head, my brain filled with the memory of Hope's orgasm.

The heat of her squeezing my fingers. The taste of her skin. I haven't come that fast since I was a teenager. If I hadn't needed to get to a meeting I could have done it again before the hot water ran out, just thinking about Hope moving beneath me, lost in pleasure.

Chapter Twenty

HOPE

I PRETENDED TO SLEEP UNTIL GRIFFEN QUIETLY LET himself out of the apartment. Cowardly, I know, but I needed a timeout. I'd had no idea. No clue. I couldn't believe I told Griffen I'd never done that with anyone else. I was thirty-one years old, for God's sake.

So embarrassing, and still not as embarrassing as admitting I'd made myself come. He wasn't even here and I had to squeeze my eyes shut at the thought. I blamed post-orgasm insanity.

Nothing I'd ever done at night under my covers bore any resemblance to what had happened in that bed with Griffen. Not even close.

When Harvey said it had to be real, when I knew I'd have to have sex with Griffen, I'd been half-terrified. The other half of me had been an unruly combination of aroused and excited and intrigued and giddy. But the overwhelming emotion was terror.

Griffen had been a player when I was a teenager. Calling him experienced didn't really cover it.

Everything *I* knew about sex came from romance novels and rom-coms. Comparing that to what Griffen knew—we weren't even close.

I took a quick shower, ignoring the light rash of beard burn on my breasts and the tenderness between my legs. I didn't know what I was doing with Griffen, but I knew I wanted more. I found a robe on the back of the bathroom door and slipped into it, needing coffee before I thought about getting dressed.

I was luxuriating in that first hot, bitter sip when a quick rap sounded on the front door and it swung open. I jumped, barely managing to avoid spilling the coffee all over my robe.

A woman poked her head in, her dark hair cut in a short bob, bangs a straight line across her forehead. Alice. She'd walked me back to Griffen's office when I'd come to tell him about Prentice's death and the will. Had it only been four days ago? It felt like a lifetime.

Alice entered, shutting the door behind her, a smile spreading across her face as her eyes landed on me. "Hi, Hope. I'm Alice. We met a few days ago, but I don't know if you remember. Sorry to barge in on you. The boys are all locked up in the conference room going over security plans for your castle. Did Griffen feed you? I know a great breakfast place if you're hungry."

Her smile was so genuine I couldn't help but smile back. "It was a crazy day, but I remember you, Alice. It's good to see you again. I'd love breakfast if you don't mind waiting a few minutes. I just have to get dressed."

"Perfect. I want to see what you brought. Is the shopping really that bad in Sawyers Bend?"

I looked at Alice for a long moment, weighing my answer. Sawyers Bend wasn't overrun with options for women's clothing unless you're looking for a good pair of hiking pants. Outdoor gear we had. Dresses and suits? Not so much. I could just say the shopping was really that bad and leave it at that. It wouldn't be a lie.

I thought about what Griffen had said. That Alice was loyal and a good friend.

"The shopping isn't great," I admitted, "but the real problem is that I've been working for my uncle for the last—" I rolled my eyes to the ceiling. "For forever. He has horrible taste in clothes, but he thinks mine is worse. He badgered me into letting him buy my wardrobe. It was easier to give in. But I'm not working for him now, and Griffen said he doesn't care what I wear as long as I like it."

Alice's grin spread wider. "And if he's paying..." She shot me a wink.

I shrugged and grinned back. "It seems to mean a lot to him, so I figure we might as well let him have his way."

Alice placed her hands on her hips and scanned me from head to toe. I tried not to squirm under her sharp gaze. Instead, I scanned her back. She was small, the top of her head even with my shoulder, her bones tiny, reminding me of a pixie. Delicate but packed with energy.

I got what Griffen meant when he said she knew how to shop. She must because her sense of style was unique, and it was clear she'd spent time putting it together. She wore a long-sleeve boatneck dress in kelly green with a fitted bodice and full knee-length skirt. I thought I caught sight of a crinoline under the skirt.

The look was modern and 50's at the same time. Fun and pretty. Her style wasn't mine. I didn't want to draw attention the way I was sure Alice did, but I'd love to find something that suited me the way her dress suited her.

Done with her study, Alice gave me a nod and said, "Lay out everything you brought on the bed."

Tightening the belt of my robe, I did as she asked. Aside from the red dress Griffen had talked me into wearing, I was looking at a sea of boring. Khaki. Black. Beige. Boxy cuts. Bland fabrics. Alice walked around the bed looking at everything, shaking her head in silence. On her second pass, she picked up three items. The red dress, the jeans Griffen had liked, and a gray cashmere sweater with fitted sleeves and a cowl neck. The only things I'd brought that I truly liked.

"Do you like these three?"

"Yes. Absolutely."

Alice glanced at what remained on the bed. "Anything I missed that you like? Even if you're not crazy about the color or the fabric, anything that's really comfortable or you think makes you look good?"

That was an easy answer. I shook my head. "No. To be honest, I haven't really put much thought into my clothes. I don't have that much to work with," I said, making a vague gesture at my curveless body and neutral coloring.

"There wasn't really anyone to show off for, and my uncle was so—" I searched for a nice way to describe his constant criticisms. Nothing was ever good enough for Uncle Edgar. Definitely not me.

Alice's eyes warmed with sympathy. "Get that out of your head. You have plenty to work with. I'd kill for your height, for one. A good bra can give you curves, but there aren't any heels made that can make me as tall as you are."

"Then maybe I need a new bra," I mused, thinking about what she'd said. I hadn't done a lot of lingerie shopping. I hadn't done a lot of shopping at all.

Alice gave me another slow, assessing scan, this one focused above my shoulders. "You have great skin. Clear, creamy, but not washed out. I love the freckles. Some women try to hide their freckles, but yours are perfect. Just enough for character but not so much that they overwhelm you. And your hair is great. Thick, shiny, I bet it holds a curl."

"I've never tried to curl it. I mostly just throw it in a bun or a ponytail."

Alice walked closer and did a turn around me, reaching out to sift her fingers through my freshly dried strands.

"Would you be open to a cut? Some help with makeup? My stylist sometimes takes last-minute appointments if I beg and bribe her. She's saving up for her wedding right now. Totally susceptible to bribes."

I reached a hand up to finger my hair, eyeing Alice's short bob, the line of bangs across her forehead. Her hair was perfect for her face and her 50's style, but it was not subtle.

I was open to a wardrobe change, even a haircut, and I could use some help with makeup, but I was never going to be bold. Subtle was my thing. I just wanted to find a way to be subtle without being bland.

Alice caught the look on my face and laughed. "Nothing extreme, I promise. Your hair is gorgeous."

"It's brown."

Alice made a dismissive *pff-fff* and spread my hair across my shoulders, smoothing it out. "Calling it brown misses the point. You've got a lot in here. Caramel, some threads of blonde, some red undertones. The shine is great, but it's so heavy. You need layers. Maybe even some highlights. Can I call Danielle? I promise I won't rope you into anything you won't like later. I swear. Understated elegance all the way. You just need a little polish, that's all."

Understated elegance. I liked the way that sounded. Like Hope, just more dressed up. What it didn't sound was bland.

"I'm in your hands," I said, only a little nervous.

"Perfect. Grab either the jeans and sweater or the red dress and get dressed while I make some calls. Do you mind if I invite Lily? She's Knox's wife. Evers' wife, Summer, is out of town. She travels a lot for work. Too bad because she loves to shop almost as much as I do. Lily isn't a competitive shopper but she's the best for moral support."

"Sounds great," I said, a little breathless.

"Good deal. You scoot, get dressed, and I'll take care of everything."

Alice was as good as her word. She was a miracle worker. I heard her bright voice through the door, and by the time I'd thrown on the red dress, swiped mascara over my lashes, and brushed my teeth, she had everything arranged.

"You're in luck. Danielle was happy to work you in for a donation to her wedding fund." Alice gave me a saucy wink. "We have just enough time to pick Lily up and get some breakfast. Ready?"

I thought I was ready. I was wrong.

Alice was a whirlwind. In a lot of ways, the opposite of Lily, who was sweet and quiet with a gentle smile that eased my nerves. When we pulled up in front of a fairytale cottage not far from the Sinclair Security building, Lily ran out clutching her purse, her cloud of dark curls flying behind her. She jumped into the car with a laugh.

"I can't believe we stuck the guys with both kids for the day. Don't they have a ton of work to do on Griffen's house?"

"It's more a castle than a house, and there are four of them, plus they pulled in Lucas and Riley. They can handle it," Alice said. "Lily, this is Griffen's Hope."

Lily gave me the first of her gentle smiles and held out her hand. "It's nice to meet you, Hope."

"Nice to meet you, too," I said lamely, shaking Lily's hand. Her brown eyes were friendly as they flicked between Alice and me. "Not that I mind, but why are we shopping?"

"Because Griffen gave us his credit card and told us to buy Hope clothes. And no sane person turns down a fully-paid shopping trip. Especially someone with a huge closet to fill," Alice answered.

"Mmmm. Tell me more about this huge closet," Lily said. "Is the house really a castle?"

Chapter Twenty-One

HOPE

AT BREAKFAST, I STUFFED MYSELF WITH FRENCH toast and drank way too much coffee. I filled Lily and Alice in on the details of Heartstone Manor, keeping the personal stuff to myself. I didn't know how much Griffen had told them about Sawyers Bend, but I had a feeling it wasn't much.

Stomachs full, we piled back in Alice's car and she drove us to a sleek salon tucked into a shopping center between two boutiques. We'd barely entered when a statuesque blonde pulled Alice into a hug and led us to the back, away from the other customers and into a private treatment room.

The din of a busy salon faded away behind the closed door. Propping her hands on her hips much like Alice had, the blonde gave me the same head to toe scan before saying, "Layers,

IVY LAYNE

definitely. And I'm thinking a deep, side-swept bang. Something you could tuck back if you needed to."

I could work with that. "But you'll keep it long?"

"I love the length. How would you feel about highlights? I don't want to change the color—you've got a nice, rich brown with good natural variation, but you could use some pop around your face."

Giddy from too much caffeine and maple syrup, I just said, "Whatever you want sounds great."

Smart move on my part. I chatted with Alice and Lily and Danielle about everything and nothing as Danielle worked. I learned that Cooper and Alice had recently taken custody of Cooper's toddler sister and that Lily watched her during the day along with her own son—the kids they'd left with the guys while we embarked on Project Save Hope's Wardrobe.

Danielle and her fiancé were planning on starting their family as soon as possible, and the three of them talked all things kids while I listened, torn between longing and worry. I'd never really thought about having kids. Only in a vague *one day, maybe* kind of way.

Now, there was Griffen, and the will, and the understanding that a lot of things would be simpler if I just got pregnant.

I didn't want to get pregnant.

Not a concern yet. I still remembered sex-ed. I had to have sex first. Or something a lot closer to sex than what we'd done so far.

We hadn't discussed birth control. I wasn't using any because I hadn't needed it. Maybe Griffen wouldn't want me to.

"Hope, what do you think?"

I snapped out of my musings on sex and birth control to look in the mirror. What I saw drove all thoughts of sex from my mind.

Was that me? It couldn't be. The woman in the mirror looked beautiful. Confident. Her hair wasn't brown. It was

164

cinnamon and honey and caramel with blond streaks around her face.

I hadn't quite been paying attention to what Danielle had done with the makeup, but my eyes looked deeper. More dramatic. She'd left my lips natural, but all of a sudden, I had cheekbones. Where had those come from? Was it the haircut or the makeup?

I blinked, taking in the changes. I was me but not me. I looked... I looked pretty. Really, truly pretty. I looked like a woman who deserved to wear more than boxy, ill-fitting suits and dull colors.

I looked like the woman who had bought that red dress. Maybe I looked like the me I'd always wanted to be.

"I love it. I love the hair and the makeup. Everything. But you have to show me how to do this at home. I should have been paying more attention but—"

Danielle patted me on the shoulder. "I've got you, honey. Alice is going to take notes, and I'm going to walk you through it. It's a lot of impact, but not a lot of work. I promise."

She was as good as her word. We left a half-hour later with a bag of makeup and hair products as well as video, pictures, and notes on how I could do it all by myself.

As Alice and Lily led me through the mall, I couldn't stop staring at my reflection in every mirror we passed. It was a good thing I was dazed by the makeover. Otherwise, I might have argued more about the clothes, the expense.

Griffen had been right. Alice was an excellent shopper. She knew where to look for the right styles and the best deals, and she quickly grasped exactly what suited me and what I liked.

Lily was the perfect moral support. Kind and funny, she distracted me or made me laugh every time I started getting overwhelmed. In a few hours, I'd amassed a collection of shopping bags I wasn't sure we could carry back to the car, much less fit in Alice's small trunk. Somehow, we managed.

Our last stop was a small boutique tucked into an upscale shopping center in Buckhead on the way back to the Sinclair Security building. I walked through the door on autopilot and stopped as soon as I saw the filmy bits of lace and satin filling the racks of the store. Lingerie. I'd forgotten I'd meant to buy lingerie. Sometime in the last few hours, my recklessness had begun to wear off.

I followed Lily and Alice through the store, listening as they joked about how long the men would let them wear the filmy bits of nothing before tearing them off. My cheeks burned at the thought. I couldn't even pretend sophistication here.

I bought my underwear from the big-box store off the highway, usually in bulk packages. One bra for seventy-five dollars? Did it come with an extra set of boobs? I couldn't even comment on the matching scrap of lace for almost fifty. Fifty dollars and it wouldn't come close to covering my butt.

Okay, I knew I was missing the point of lingerie versus underwear, but still. I didn't belong here. Not even with my new haircut and pretty makeup. I didn't know what to do with any of this.

I stood in front of a floor-length midnight-blue nightgown fingering the soft silk and delicate lace. I wanted it. It was soft and beautiful and I wanted it. Not because it was sexy—maybe there was too much fabric for it to be sexy.

I didn't know what Griffen found sexy. I didn't know what any man found sexy. I had no business wearing sexy clothes. Not me. Not Hope.

All of the confidence I'd gained from the makeover drained away. I stood there listening to my new friends laugh and wondered what the heck I thought I was doing.

Was I going to seduce Griffen? Why?

So he could break my heart and leave me later when my use-fulness had run out?

I was temporary. A stop-gap measure with a five-year expiration date.

The day so far had been about me, and I was glad we'd done it. I loved my new hair and the piles of new clothes. But this? Sexy underwear would only lead to heartbreak.

"You okay?" I looked down to see Lily standing beside me.

"Yeah. Just, uh, tired, I guess."

Lily didn't buy it, but she let me off the hook for the moment. Flipping through the nightgowns I'd been looking at, she found one in my size and took it off the rack. "You should try this on. While you're in the back you can get fitted for new bras. This place is pricey, but everything is great quality."

I let her lead me to the back of the store, passively standing there as the saleswoman stretched a measuring tape around me and pronounced my bra size—not the size I'd been wearing all these years, by the way—and told me to pick out some fun things while she put together a selection of bras to choose from.

I followed Alice and Lily to a wall in the back covered in camisoles, bustiers, bras, and panties so brief I wondered why they bothered to exist. They didn't cover anything. And I mean *anything*.

Alice pinned me with that incisive stare I'd grown familiar with. "Spill it. What are you stressing about? Is it the lingerie? Is it Griffen and the lingerie? Because you don't need to buy anything for him, you know. That's the big secret. Men think this stuff is for them, but really, it's for us."

"Well, sometimes it's for them," Lily said with a secret smile.

"Sometimes," Alice agreed. "But not today. Today it's about Hope. We can worry about Griffen later."

"I don't know what I'm doing with him," I heard myself say in a whisper. "I can't control myself when he... I haven't ever...

I don't…" I forced myself to choke out the words now that I'd begun. "We're married. And we haven't had sex yet." The last words came out in a rush of breath. "Every time he touches me it's like my brain shuts off and I just—I can't breathe and I can't think and I… I want. I don't even know *what* I want. I don't know what to do about it and it's scaring me to death."

I squeezed my eyes shut, too embarrassed to look at either of them. I bet neither of them were virgins. I mean, I knew neither of them were virgins. They were both happily—and actively—married. But I bet neither of them had been virgins when they'd met their men either. Or for long after adolescence.

I was a freak, and a dork, and I was way out of my league with Griffen Sawyer.

The silence stretched until I thought I might die of humiliation. My eyes flicked open in surprise as Alice's strong arms squeezed me tight.

Alice said quietly, "It's okay to be scared. Falling in love is scary. It's dangerous. You risk your heart and you don't know. You don't know what's going to happen. Cooper scared the hell out of me. I was so terrified of him I ran to another state."

While I was digesting the idea of Alice being afraid of anything, Lily cut in, "Cooper deserved that. He was a moron."

"True. But still, I should have known how he felt. I was too scared to see straight."

"I'm not in love with Griffen," I said, knowing it was mostly a lie. I didn't know how I felt about Griffen, but I couldn't pretend I felt nothing. No one was going to believe that, least of all me.

Ignoring my protest, Lily mused, "I thought Knox was going to kill me. At first. But *he* thought *I'd* killed my husband, so it evened out. Then the Russian mob showed up and we realized we were on the same team."

I couldn't get my head around that. How could anyone think Lily was a murderer? Now I wanted to meet her Knox.

"You aren't scared of Griffen like that, are you?" Lily asked.

I shook my head. "He'd never hurt me. But he's going to break my heart. I can't stop it. And I want him anyway."

Chapter Twenty-Two

HOPE

I COULDN'T EXPLAIN WHY I WAS SO SURE HE'D BREAK my heart. The terms of the will meant I had to lie about the reason for our marriage. It didn't matter. Alice knew Griffen hadn't wanted to see me a few days ago. They both knew he wasn't in love with me, knew there had to be another reason he'd married me.

"We're not falling in love," I whispered, staring at the scraps of silk in front of me without seeing them. "That's not what this is. He'll never love me. He can't."

Lily stroked a hand down my hair. Alice wasn't as soothing. "Forget about that. Love will take care of itself, one way or another. The real question is do you want to have sex with him?"

"I do," I admitted. "But everything's upside down when he kisses me. I feel too much and I can't think. I don't know what I'm supposed to do."

Lily stroked my hair again, her touch gentle. "You can trust Griffen. You don't need to know what you're supposed to do. Not like that. He'll show you."

"Does he know?" Alice asked. "That you haven't—"

"I kind of told him accidentally after my uncle told him to get me pregnant."

Lily's hand flew over her mouth as she choked back a laugh. I couldn't help it, a smile cracked across my face as I heard what I'd said. I shook my head. "My life's such a mess right now."

"Don't worry about that," Alice said. "Lily's right. You can trust Griffen. All you need to do is pick out what you like here, put it on, and he'll take care of the rest. That's a guarantee."

Could it be that simple? Just trust Griffen? It made more sense than anything else. I sure as heck didn't know what *I* was doing. And if the way he touched me was any example, Griffen absolutely knew what he was doing.

I wanted him. I'd always wanted him. This was my chance to have him, if just for a little while. I didn't want to waste it because I was scared.

For all these years, I'd thought nothing could happen to me if I was with Uncle Edgar. He'd rescued me. He could keep me safe. And he did.

What I didn't realize was *nothing could happen to me* if I was with Uncle Edgar. If I spent my life hiding, nothing would *ever* happen to me.

I thought about that morning, Griffen's hands, his mouth, the way he'd touched me. The way I'd come. I wanted more of that.

I wanted something from this wall of silk and satin and lace. Something that would make Griffen crazy.

Crazy for me.

I took a deep breath, pushed away my fear, and reached out for a confection of blush pink silk and creamy lace.

"What about this?" I asked my partners in crime.

"That would be perfect."

I couldn't look at the total on the register when Alice paid. Three huge shopping bags filled with everything from everyday bras and panties to a merry widow and stockings, the nightgown I'd been drooling over, matching robe, and so much more. Too much more.

Originally, I'd planned to pay him back, but considering the meager contents of my savings account, that would take years. Uncle Edgar hadn't paid me much, coolly implying that years of room and board and a college education were expensive.

If I'd been content to remain under his roof I would have had more disposable income. Apartments on Main Street didn't come cheap, and I'd paid dearly for that small taste of freedom. Too dearly to have a nest egg I could toss at Griffen to make up for all we'd spent. I tried to shrug it off. He was the one who'd handed Alice his card and told her I needed everything.

I tried not to dwell on it as we drove back to Sinclair Security. Alice had hidden the receipts, so unless Griffen told me, I had no idea what we'd spent. Alice pulled into the garage, parking next to Griffen's Maserati.

Opening the back passenger door of his car, she said, "Let's put everything in here, that way you don't have to haul it upstairs and then back down again. Are you staying another night, or do you have to get home?" Shaking her head, she added, "It feels so weird to think of Griffen's home not being here. You're going to visit, right?"

"I'd like to," I said honestly. "But you might have to come to Sawyer's Bend for a while. Did he tell you about the will? We can't be away from the house often."

"Then we'll visit," Alice said. "I want to come stay in your castle. Summer stayed at the Inn with Evers once and said it was amazing."

We talked on the ride up to Cooper and Alice's floor—about Savannah and the massive task she had ahead of her, about the Manor and the state Prentice had left it in. About what it would be like sharing the place with Griffen's estranged siblings.

I let myself get distracted by the conversation, almost forgetting what we'd been doing all day. I was tired and starving despite the coffee and cookie we'd grabbed at the mall a few hours before. And somehow, between my mini-freakout in the lingerie shop and the comfortable conversation with Lily and Alice, I forgot about my makeover.

We walked in to a rush of sound, two small bodies hightailing it across the foyer to barrel into Lily and Alice. Lily's little boy looked nothing like her with his platinum hair and blue eyes, but he threw his arms around her waist and babbled up at her about a movie or a video game, such love in his eyes I had no doubt they belonged together.

Alice hefted her little girl into her arms, the toddler almost too big for her to carry. The little girl had dark hair and ice-blue eyes in a delicate face. She nestled her head into Alice's shoulder, murmuring something in a lightly accented voice.

The guys weren't far behind. I caught sight of three tall men, almost identical with their dark hair and broad shoulders. The one with ice-blue eyes just like the little girl's made his way to Alice, scooping the girl from her arms and murmuring something in her ear that made her laugh.

I started to say hello when a hand closed around mine, dragging me through the foyer to a hallway off to the side.

Griffen.

"You aren't even going to introduce us?" a laughing male voice called after us. Griffen didn't bother to respond.

In the quiet of the hall, he took my hands in his, his eyes warm with something I couldn't read. At least he didn't look shocked or repulsed. That was something.

"Do you...? Do you like it?" I couldn't help asking. "Alice thought I could use a haircut and she—the stylist—showed me some things with makeup and—"

"I want to say you look beautiful, but that would imply you weren't already beautiful. And you were. You are. You've always been beautiful, you were just good at hiding it. Or maybe not seeing it. So, the real question is, do you like it?"

I didn't know what to say. Tears welled in my eyes at the steadfast assertion in his voice, as if he had no doubt that beauty had always been a part of me. As if he'd always known.

I hadn't known. I don't think anybody knew. And even with the hair and the makeup, I wouldn't call myself beautiful. Pretty. I could settle for pretty.

I wasn't going to say any of that. Wasn't going to tell Griffen he was wrong if he thought I was beautiful.

A tear welled over my lid and slid down my cheek. Griffen brushed it away with the ball of his thumb. "You see it, don't you?"

I didn't know what he was talking about, but I did know the answer. "I like it. I don't know why I never did this before."

I did know. We both knew. But I didn't want to talk about Uncle Edgar and his horrible taste in clothes and his belief that a woman could be smart or pretty but not both. He was wrong, and I knew enough intelligent, beautiful women that I didn't need Griffen to tell me so.

I said the only thing that felt true even though it didn't make sense. "I feel like me. Like this is Hope."

"Hope is beautiful. And she always was." He grazed the side of my cheek with his thumb before lowering his mouth to mine. I ignored the wolf whistle from behind us and pressed my lips to his. Alice and Lily had been right.

I didn't need to know what to do with Griffen. Griffen knew plenty. I just had to follow his lead. My body wasn't the least bit confused. My lips moved under his, my tongue tasting, loving the growl in his throat when I kissed him back.

"You two want pizza or Chinese?" I didn't recognize the voice, but I resented the interruption. All of a sudden, it occurred to me that I was kissing Griffen in full view of a bunch of people I didn't know and all I could think about was kissing him more.

One orgasm, an hour in a lingerie shop, and my mind was firmly in the gutter.

Griffen stepped back, breaking our kiss. I turned around, Griffen's arm sliding around my shoulders, and looked up to see avid curiosity on all the faces at the end of the hall except Alice and Lily, who were both giving me satisfied smiles.

"Do you want pizza or Chinese?" Griffen asked in a low voice. "If I get my vote, I'd rather take you to bed, but these clowns aren't going to leave us alone."

He'd rather take me to bed. I wasn't sure I was ready for that, but I wasn't going to turn him down. Not after that kiss. Going for the easy answer I said, "Pizza."

Six pizzas later, everyone was full. We were parked on one of Cooper's huge couches watching a basketball game, my head on Griffen's shoulder, my eyes drooping. Before they slid shut, I felt him loop an arm behind my back and lift, pulling me into his lap.

"I'm too heavy," I mumbled, trying to force my eyes to open.

"You're not." Griffen settled me in, his fingers trailing through my hair, the gentle tug and release too relaxing to fight.

"K," I whispered, my eyes closing all the way. I don't know how long I slept there. I surfaced once at the sensation of being carried, only to hear Griffen telling me to close my eyes and go back to sleep.

I woke to an empty bed, a note on Griffen's pillow.

Working out downstairs, be back to take you to breakfast.

My new clothes were all in his car, but I did my best with my old jeans and gray sweater. Griffen didn't seem to mind when he came back, deliciously sweaty, his eyes glued to my butt in the worn denim.

We met Cooper, Alice, and Petra for breakfast, then all headed over to Evers' house. His wife, Summer, was home from her trip, and we spent the day hanging out, the guys still refining the security plan for Heartstone Manor, the rest of us watching the kids and getting to know each other. I'd never had a day like it. The easy camaraderie, the open welcome.

Like Alice and Lily, Summer seemed to accept me without reservation. It was more than I'd expected, and I wasn't quite sure what to do with it except just enjoy myself.

All too soon, we had to leave. We pushed it later than we should have, but neither of us wanted to go. This was family. The Sinclairs had given Griffen a home when his own people had thrown him out. Back in Sawyers Bend, we faced uncertain welcome, a barely functional place to live, and—oh, yeah— someone who'd murdered Griffen's father and might be after Griffen.

With all that waiting for us, was it a surprise we didn't leave Atlanta until late Sunday night? We might have stayed into Monday, but Griffen and I were in agreement. We wanted a day to settle into Heartstone Manor before the rest of his siblings arrived.

Our time in Atlanta had run out.

After a long dinner of steaks grilled on Evers' deck, we said our goodbyes, mine only a little tearful, Griffen's filled with plenty of back slaps. The guys would be at Heartstone to over- see the security install, so it wasn't good-bye forever. Not really. And yet, it was. Griffen was quiet as we got in the car. I reached out to tangle my fingers with his.

The Sinclairs would always be his friends. Family. But his life in Atlanta was over. This wasn't good-bye forever, but it was still a good-bye. Griffen squeezed my hand and let out a long breath. That was the extent of his emotional release. Men.

I couldn't change the terms of the will or force Griffen's family into accepting him. I couldn't replace what he was losing in leaving Atlanta and Sinclair Security. As I stared out the window and watched the road flash by, I swore I'd do everything I could to make it worth it, to make up for everything he'd lost when Prentice had died and turned his life upside down.

Chapter Twenty-Three

GRIFFEN

I CALLED SAVANNAH ON THE WAY BACK, TALKING QUI-
etly so I didn't wake Hope. Not long after we left
Atlanta, she'd balled up her jacket under her head,
tucked herself into the corner of her seat, and fallen asleep. Her
face at rest was compelling. More than pretty. More than beautiful.

I'd told Hope the truth when I said she'd been beautiful
without the haircut and the makeup. Despite what Edgar had
made her think, she'd always been beautiful. Now everyone else
could see it, too. She hadn't looked like she was wearing a lot of
makeup, but whatever she'd done had made her eyes deeper,
mysterious. Her hair had a sleek shine it had been missing.

It wasn't any one thing. Not her hair or her eyes or her full,
pink lips. It was all of it together. Maybe it was just confidence
from making friends and having fun spoiling herself for once.

I didn't know and it didn't matter. Not really. What I did know was that, unexpectedly, I hadn't wanted to linger in Atlanta with the people who'd become my family. Not that I was looking forward to dealing with my actual family. They weren't scheduled to show up until Tuesday, and I wanted time alone with Hope.

Savannah assured me that things were well in hand at Heartstone Manor. I found that hard to believe. Not because of Savannah, but we'd only been gone a little more than forty-eight hours.

How much could she do in forty-eight hours?

I soon learned that Savannah Miles could work miracles in forty-eight hours.

Hope's eyes fluttered open as we pulled up in front of the house. Half asleep, shopping bags looped over her arm, she followed me up the steps, blinking in the light as Savannah swung open the heavy door.

Here, things weren't much different. The chandelier was still dusty. *Everything* was still dusty. Following my eyes as they took in the room, Savannah said, "I started with the living spaces. That seemed most efficient. Are you hungry? Hope?"

"I'm fine," I assured her. "You need anything, Buttercup?"

Hope slanted me a look that was partly disgruntled and mostly pleased. She liked it when I called her Buttercup. So did I.

"I'm fine, Savannah, thanks. Just tired. It was a long day. Good, but long."

Savannah stepped forward to take the bags on Hope's arm and finally got a good look at Hope. She stopped in surprise before breaking into a wide grin. "Hope, you look fantastic. Did you get your hair cut?"

"Haircut, highlights, makeup, and Griffen's friends took me shopping. I got way too much. And I might need your help with the makeup tomorrow."

"I'm no expert, but just give a shout. I love your hair. Is this all your bags?"

"There's more in the car," I said, "but I can get it tomorrow."

"Don't worry about it. That's my job," Savannah said with a smile. I listened to her and Hope talk about the stores Hope had visited in Atlanta and something about Savannah settling on a uniform for the house. The day was catching up with me. More than anything, I just wanted to be alone, in bed, with Hope.

I wasn't planning on starting anything. She was obviously exhausted. I wasn't much better. I hadn't slept much the night before. I could use a solid eight hours before we faced the rest of what was to come.

I was lost in thoughts of the pile of work on my father's desk—of having to face my father's desk at all—when I walked into the master suite and got my first pleasant shock since coming back to Heartstone Manor.

Savannah had transformed the room. Hope's living room was reproduced in the spacious sitting room, augmented by pieces Savannah must have grabbed from here and there in Heartstone Manor. She'd taken everything else from Hope's apartment. The huge velvet couch, the side tables and bookshelves, right down to the stacks of books just as Hope left them.

Hope let out a gasp of pleased surprise and turned in a circle, her eyes wide and bright. "How did you do this? You even got my drapes."

Savannah treated us to a smug smile. "They're not actually your drapes. If you look a little closer, you'll see these are a few feet longer and a darker shade of green. I found these in one of the guest rooms and moved them over here."

I followed Hope to the master bedroom where, again, Savannah had reproduced Hope's apartment. My eyes fixed on that lush brass bed overflowing with soft pillows and blankets. As in the sitting room, Savannah had found pieces around the house to fill the space, Hope's small bedroom no match for the expansive master suite of Heartstone Manor.

What she'd chosen went perfectly with Hope's belongings. A chaise lounge in red damask with a delicately arched reading lamp. A mahogany dressing table with tufted stool and three-part mirror. And on the other side of the room, a huge leather chair and ottoman with a side table perfect for a mug of coffee and a book.

"I left the fairy lights," Savannah said, "because I didn't want to stick that many pins in the plaster here, but otherwise, I tried to move your place to Heartstone. Anything you want to change—"

"It's perfect! It's amazing. Thank you so much. How did you manage this? We weren't gone that long."

"I put Billy Bob to work," Savannah said as if that explained everything.

It must have because Hope replied with a knowing, "Of course. Good thinking."

"Who is Billy Bob and how did he get all this done in barely a day?"

"Billy Bob is my cousins, Billy and Bob. Bobby if you're referring to him in the singular. They've been joined at the hip practically since birth. My aunt took to calling them Billy Bob as a joke and it stuck. I put them on the payroll for the time being. They work hard, and between the two of them, they can do almost anything. Plus, they can always come up with extra hands to get a job done. When we moved your apartment," she said to Hope, "they made one phone call and ten guys showed up. Way cheaper than movers, and I had the place emptied out and put back together over here in only a few hours."

"You're a miracle worker," I said, grateful she'd taken the job.

"I'll show you the rest tomorrow. You two look like you're about to fall down where you're standing. If you decide you need anything, text me. I haven't had a chance to test the bell system. Oh, and I set you up for the little things."

She nodded to an ornate cabinet in the corner of the sitting room. We followed her over and she opened it to reveal a mini-fridge, set of drinking glasses, water decanter, mugs, tea caddy, single-serve coffee maker, and an electric kettle, all arrayed on cleverly designed shelves.

"I found this in the attics. I like the way this room is set up. Your own little apartment inside the Manor. Once the hordes descend on Heartstone, you might not want to leave if you want a drink or a snack."

She pulled out a basket filled with small bags of pretzels, chips, oranges and apples, and a few plastic-wrapped brownies.

"Text me a half-hour before you want breakfast. I'm on duty in the kitchen, but I have an interview with a potential cook tomorrow so hopefully, that won't last much longer. Beyond breakfast, my skills are fairly basic."

"Thank you," Hope said. "You don't know how much it means to come home and find home."

"That's how I hoped you'd feel." Savannah gave her a quick hug and headed for the door. "I'll bring the rest of your luggage up. If you think of anything you need in the next hour, just text."

Hope was wavering on her feet, so tired I was half-afraid she'd pass out where she was standing. I was still holding the suitcase she'd packed the day before and handed it to her. "I'm going to help Savannah get the rest of our stuff. You go ahead and get ready for bed."

Her face pale with exhaustion, Hope nodded and disappeared into the bedroom. I knew by the time I got back she'd probably be out cold. That would be for the best since she was too tired for more than a kiss good night. I wasn't sure I could stop at that.

As it was, when I climbed in beside her warm body, I didn't resist pulling her into my arms, settling her against me and smiling as her arm wrapped around my waist, her leg hitching over my thigh. She gave a sleepy murmur into my shoulder and settled in to sleep. With a long deep breath scented of cinnamon and apples, I relaxed and did the same.

Chapter Twenty-Four

GRIFFEN

WHAT FIRST?" HOPE ASKED, HER PEN POISED ABOVE A blank page in her ever-present notebook. Her full breakfast plate sat in front of her, a steaming cup of coffee to her left, but she ignored them in favor of getting a jump on the day.

We sat at the end of the table in the massive formal dining room, the dark-beamed and white-plastered ceiling a full two stories above us, the great iron chandeliers cobwebbed and dark. It felt odd to eat here, just the two of us, the wide expanse of the long table stretching across the room, empty and unused.

There was a breakfast room at the far end of the dining room, a separate space with a wide, curving bay window that looked out into the front courtyard. The breakfast room was almost as formal as the dining room, and its small size was only relative to the expanse of the dining room. All the Sawyers would have fit neatly in the breakfast room with seats to spare, but the space was friendlier, less imposing, and far more comfortable for a quiet breakfast for two.

Unfortunately, the breakfast room was even dustier than the chandeliers above my head. Years ago, it had been papered in silk of light green and gold, a sparkling crystal chandelier above the table. Vaguely, I hoped Savannah could save the silk wallpaper. Breakfast in that room was one of my few good memories of this house.

Through the open doors of the dining room, the house bustled. Savannah calling out orders, Billy Bob's slow easy drawls in response. I'd met Savannah's cousins briefly on my way to the dining room, both of them giving me a firm handshake and an easy, "Good to have you back in town," before they headed off to carry out their marching orders.

"Put the list away and eat your breakfast, Hope. We can figure out the day when you've had some food."

Hope didn't put the pen down. "I can't relax and enjoy my breakfast when we have so much to do and I have no idea how we're going to get it all done."

Taking a sip of coffee, I went over the list I had in my head. "Fine. There's that stack of mail on Prentice's desk. Then I guess you should walk me through the most pressing issues you know about."

"What about Ford?" she asked carefully. "And Cole? Don't you need to talk to Cole, see what's going on with Ford's defense?"

My gut gave an immediate, *No*.

I needed to deal with Ford. I couldn't ignore him. But not today. Not now.

"Later," I said.

Hope shook her head but dropped it. "I don't know everything about Prentice's business. The best person for that is Ford, but—"

"We'll work around him," I said and bit into a biscuit. "Eat your breakfast."

With a *harrumph* of a sigh, Hope shut her notebook and pushed it away, picking up her fork and taking a bite of eggs.

Watching her eat I had a new sensation in my stomach as it twisted and turned over, uneasy. Uncertain. Was this nerves? Was I... Nervous?

The box in my pocket dug into my leg. It shouldn't be a big deal. We were already married.

Only an hour before while Hope had been doing something with her hair with a thing that looked like a giant clamp then fussing with bottles and tubes at the vanity, I'd gone to the safe hidden behind the shoe rack in the master closet.

Harvey had told me about it. New closet, new safe, same combination. Almost as tall as me, a small room unto itself, the safe held everything from decades-old stock certificates to passports to jewelry handed down from generation to generation. I knew exactly what I was looking for.

My great-great-grandmother's ring. Lady Estelle Ophelia Sawyer. She'd traveled to North Carolina after a whirlwind romance with my great-great-grandfather, William Reginald Sawyer. He'd built Heartstone Manor for Lady Estelle, determined to give her a home worthy of her sacrifice in leaving England and her family for the wilds of America.

I remember my father showing me her ring decades ago, telling me that was the ring I'd give my wife one day. A ruby flanked by diamonds in aged yellow gold. I'd half expected to see it on Vanessa's hand the day Prentice announced her marriage to Ford.

Vanessa had given me back the diamond I'd bought her, replacing it with Ford's. Both rings had been ostentatious and obvious. But then, Ford and I had been young and stupid. Back then, it hadn't occurred to me to ask Prentice for Lady Estelle's ring.

Not just because I knew he'd never allow me to give it to Vanessa.

This ring was part of the Sawyer legacy. It was our history.

At twenty-two, I'd wanted to rebel against that legacy. I'd wanted to give Vanessa something that was just mine. As it was, I was glad the grasping viper never got her hands on any part of the Sawyers' history.

It should have bothered me that Prentice intended for me to give this ring to Hope. My knee-jerk reaction was to deny my father anything he wanted. He'd taken enough, meddled enough.

It didn't matter anymore. Prentice was dead. He'd trapped us with his will, but aside from compelling us to marry and spend a certain amount of time in Heartstone Manor, his influence was gone.

I wasn't giving Lady Estelle Ophelia Sawyer's ring to Hope because Prentice wanted me to. I was giving her the ring because she was my wife. She was Hope Sawyer. I needed to see it on her finger, needed to make this real.

Taking another sip of coffee, I set the box with the ring on the table in front of her.

"I know we did this in the wrong order, but I want you to have this."

The greasy, cold twist in my stomach cranked up a notch. It only got worse when Hope didn't move.

She eyed the ring box as if it held explosives and not jewelry.

I reached for her hand, catching the tips of her fingers with mine as she jerked her arm back, her elbow slamming into the side of her plate, sending silverware clattering to the floor.

Her cheeks pink, she protested, "I don't need a ring. I don't need jewelry or anything. This isn't—" A furtive glance to the open doorway and I knew what she'd been about to say.

This isn't real.

She was wrong. This was real. Hope and I were real. Those kisses were real. I watched her carefully, trying to figure out the best way to get through to her. She sat across from me, polished and beautiful, comfortable yet stylish in a dark green cashmere sweater and skinny jeans that tempted me to fill my hands with her ass.

Beneath the veneer I could see young Hope staring at me apprehensively, her cognac brown eyes tinged with fear when she looked at that antique velvet ring box. Why?

Seeing echoes of the child she'd been in the woman she was shook me. When I opened my mouth to speak, I didn't have the right words. I didn't have any words.

Like a clod and a fool, I shoved the box across the table at her and said, "Open it."

Nice proposal, jackass, I told myself. Hope reached out one hand for the box, closing her fingers around it tentatively before she pried open the lid and let out a shocked gasp.

"You can't give me this. This is a Sawyer ring. It's over a hundred years old. This is the ring you're supposed to give to your—"

"My wife," I finished for her. "My wife is sitting right in front of me."

Hope stared at me as if I were mentally challenged. I set my jaw and waited. The ring was for my wife. Hope was my wife. I didn't see why it had to be more complicated than that.

Her fingers trembling, she reached out and tugged the ring from the box. It slid on her finger, a perfect fit. She stared down at it, her eyes wide, twisting the band back and forth on her finger, the ruby and diamonds catching the light. It looked right.

I'd never given that ring to Vanessa because that ring belonged to Hope.

"I'll give it back," Hope said quickly, her eyes flashing up to mine. "After the five years," she whispered, "I'll give it back."

I swear, I kept forgetting about the five years. Did she really think after five years we'd sign some papers and that would be that?

I shifted in my seat at the uncomfortable realization that Hope might think exactly that.

What if she was just biding time with me, doing what she had to in order to save the town, to pay me back for what she saw as her betrayal. What if she was just counting down the days until she had her freedom?

I looked at the ring on her finger. I'd do everything it took to keep it exactly where it was.

"We'll worry about that later. For now, it fits?"

"It fits," Hope said, stretching out her fingers and then making a fist.

"Good. That's one thing we can scratch off our list. Now, if you're done with breakfast—" I raised my eyebrows at her mostly empty plate, "We should hit the office and start digging into the mess Prentice left behind."

Standing in the door to my father's office, I thought the word *mess* had been a gross understatement. "Harvey said the room was cleared as a crime scene," I commented. There were scraps of yellow tape at the sides of the doorway and smears of finger-print powder here and there. Savannah had said she'd done a cursory cleanup, but, as my siblings were descending on the house the next day, most of her attention had been focused on getting the bedrooms, bathrooms, and kitchens up and running.

Prentice's office had been spared the worst of the dust and cobwebs plaguing the rest of the house. Probably because he'd used this room right up until the moment of his death. My skin crawled just standing in the doorway.

I hated this room. I'd always hated this room.

It wasn't the room itself. Much like the rest of the house, it had dark woodwork and tall windows. They should have let in the light, but Prentice had always kept the heavy damask drapes pulled closed. Two of the walls had built-in bookcases, each with its own brass and oak ladder to assist in reaching the higher shelves almost 15 feet from the floor.

On the other two walls where I would've hung oil paintings, my father had chosen dead animals, each shot by Prentice himself. I don't have anything against hunting. I knew plenty of people who loved to spend a weekend laying perfectly still in the woods waiting for just the right moment to pull the trigger.

Venison was no stranger to the dinner table around here. As civilization encroached on the mountains, we had too few predators and way too many deer. I'd gone hunting myself occasionally, though I didn't have the patience to do it often.

I didn't mind hunting, but I hated every one of my father's trophies. I had too many memories of standing in front of that massive desk, being stripped down by Prentice, his sad, dead animals a silent audience for my failures.

I was never good enough for my father. Now he was dead and I'd never have the chance to prove him wrong.

I hated this room, but for now, I was stuck with it. Once we got the rest of the house in order, I'd ask Savannah to look into redecorating. Or see if Hope had any ideas. I thought briefly about finding another room to use. Maybe the gold drawing room Darcy had loved or a corner of the library.

No, both drawing rooms were in total disarray, dusty and barely furnished. The library was better, but the desks in there were too small. It would have to be my father's office.

My office now. Mine and Hope's.

Resigned, I crossed the threshold and made my way to the desk. Here the heavy mahogany desk glowed from an application of polish that left this part of the room smelling like beeswax and lemon. Savannah had been here, anticipating we'd need the space. A pile of mail at least a foot high was stacked in the black leather inbox, Prentice's laptop front and center on the matching leather blotter.

I flipped open the lid and the home screen popped up.

"No password?" I asked.

"He used to have one. Then he kept forgetting it." Hope pulled up the chair Savannah must have put beside my father's and nudged my father's big leather desk chair back from the desk. I sat.

The sooner we got started, the sooner I'd have a handle on my father's business. Once that happened, it wouldn't be Prentice's business anymore. It would finally, truly be mine.

A spark of anticipation lit inside me as I thought about that, really thought about what it would mean to take charge of everything that had been stolen from me. I'd loved my time in the Army and with the Sinclairs. If I hadn't been shot, if Prentice hadn't died with this ridiculous will, I would have happily stayed in Atlanta.

But this, taking the helm of Sawyer Enterprises, this was what I'd wanted to do since I was old enough to understand what it meant to be a Sawyer. I had a flash of grief that Ford wasn't sitting beside me. Or Royal. Or Tenn. Any of them. We were supposed to do this together.

As if she knew what was going through my head, Hope reached over to give my hand a gentle squeeze, the flash of diamonds on her finger chasing away my melancholy.

Clearing her throat, she said, "Okay. I've been thinking about it and we need to start here—"

Reaching over me, she opened a file on the desktop, and we were off. Hope had been right. She didn't know everything about Sawyer Enterprises. Unlike her job with Edgar, she hadn't been Prentice's personal assistant. That didn't matter. She'd still done just enough that if she didn't know an answer, she knew where to find it.

We'd made our way through most of the mail, determining what was important and what could wait, when the deep tones of the front doorbell rang through the house. Moments later, the click of heels on hardwood came toward us. As one, Hope and I braced.

Chapter Twenty-Five

HOPE

AYBE IT WAS MY SIXTH SENSE FOR BITCHES, BUT I knew exactly who those high heels belonged to before she strode into the office. The Viper. Otherwise known as Vanessa Sawyer. Ford had divorced her years before, but Vanessa hung on to his name. She'd sold her soul for the Sawyer name and she'd let it go over her dead body.

She propped her hands on her hips, one leg cocked out to the side, her shoulders angled to give the best view of her cleavage. Tossing her shiny, ebony hair over her shoulder, she pursed full red lips and glared at Griffen before she let her face melt into a sweet smile. "You're in town three days and you don't come see me? Griffen. I thought we had more than that."

Griffen leaned back in the big leather chair, propped his ankle on his knee, and gave her a cool look. "Since the last I saw of you you were married to my brother, I'd say we didn't have anything at all."

I didn't know Vanessa well, but I wasn't an idiot. I knew why she was here. Griffen and his bank account. And this house. I also knew she wasn't going to get any of them. Griffen was loyal and expected loyalty in return.

Vanessa had blown her chance years ago and she wouldn't get another. At that thought, I remembered my own crimes, my own lack of loyalty. I couldn't change the past, but I wasn't going to let Vanessa bother Griffen. All of this was hard enough for him as it was.

"What do you want, Vanessa?" I asked, trying to copy Griffen's cool, detached tone. I don't think I succeeded, but at least my voice wasn't shaking. Vanessa's take-no-prisoners bitchiness had always made me nervous.

Striding deeper into the room, Vanessa took a position in front of the desk, her hands still on her hips. Tilting her head to the side, she said, "Hope Daniels. How cute. Did Edgar send you over to help Griffen sort out all of this?" She waved her hand at the neatly-stacked pile of mail.

"Something like that," I said bitingly.

Griffen laughed, and the sound was anything but cold. Rolling his chair to close the distance between us, he slid an arm around my back, reaching over me with the other arm to catch my left hand in his. He pressed a light kiss to my fingertips before raising my hand, angling my fingers so the light from the tall windows hit the ring on my finger.

Lady Estelle's ring. No, my ring. That still hadn't sunk in.

Griffen missed the flash of Vanessa's dark eyes, choosing to press a slow kiss to my jaw instead. Despite my nerves and Vanessa's sharp gaze, I shivered. Griffen's lips on my skin always did that.

Vanessa lost her hold on sweetly bitchy and slid right into openly catty. "Trying to make me jealous, lover?"

196

Griffen kept my hand in his as he leaned back to look at Vanessa. "Hope and I are married. Considering the circumstances, I convinced her to quit working for Edgar and help me out over here."

Vanessa's composure slipped. Her jaw dropped, dark eyes wide and fixed on my ring. Vanessa was speechless for a whole five seconds.

Good, because I had no clue what to say. Vanessa was deluded if she thought she had a chance with Griffen, but still, it was a little absurd.

Had Griffen really married plain, mousy, inexperienced Hope Daniels when he could have had someone like the glamorous, adventurous Vanessa? I couldn't blame her for being shocked.

Vanessa finally found her voice if not her composure. "Don't be ridiculous, Griffen. Obviously, this is some kind of joke. This is Hope. Don't tell me you couldn't do better than Hope Daniels. I came here to offer you another chance. If you aren't interested you could just say so. You don't have to lie to me about hooking up with—" She waved her hand at me. "That."

Griffen's eyes flared with temper. He looked like he was ready to pick Vanessa up and toss her out the door. While I kind of liked that idea in theory, Vanessa wouldn't hesitate to press charges for assault.

The last thing we needed was another Sawyer in jail.

Under my breath, I murmured, "Don't. She's not worth it."

Vanessa tossed her hair. "Oh, like you are. Please. You were panting after him when you were a teenager. You ruined our engagement because you wanted him for yourself. You probably killed Prentice, orchestrated this whole thing so you could end up with that ring on your finger."

I rolled my eyes. Vanessa scared me a little, but this was just too much. Either I was poor, pathetic little Hope Daniels, or I was a criminal mastermind. I couldn't be both.

I wasn't either one. I was just Hope, and I wasn't putting up with this bullshit.

I pushed back my chair and stood, putting a little space between me and Griffen. I needed space to say what I had to say. It would hurt, but it had to be done. Both of these people were way overdue for my apology.

"I'm glad you're here, Vanessa. I've never had the chance to say I'm sorry. To either of you. I did ruin your engagement. I was sixteen and I had a horrible crush on Griffen. I knew—"

I met Griffen's eyes, glad to finally—*finally*—be saying this straight out. "I knew she would make you miserable. It doesn't excuse telling Uncle Edgar you were going to elope. I betrayed a confidence, and I know you'll never forgive me for that. All I can say is that I was young and I wanted the best for you. I knew I wasn't doing the right thing, and I did it anyway, and I'm sorry."

Vanessa sucked in a breath for her comeback. I cut her off. "I'm sorry for what I did, but I'm not sorry about the way it worked out." I thought for a second and then concluded, "Well, I'm sorry for Ford, and I'm sorry about the way Prentice treated Griffen. But I'm not sorry I stopped the two of you from getting married because you didn't love him. You would have made him unhappy."

Beside me, Griffen quietly chuckled. Vanessa's eyes flashed fire. It occurred to me that I'd just made an enemy. I'd deal with it. My soul felt clean. Maybe my apology should have been more abject. Maybe I should have said I was sorry for all of it. But I wouldn't lie to him. Not again. The truth might not make me look good, but at least it was the truth.

"I don't accept your apology," Vanessa said with a thrust of her hip and another toss of her hair. I wondered what kind of serum she used to make it so shiny. Not that I would ask. I'd forgotten how annoying her constant hair tossing was. "Are you going to let her talk to me like that?" she demanded of Griffen.

Griffen raised his eyebrows as he stood, moving to my side and winding his arm around my waist, holding me close.

"Hope can talk to you however the hell she wants."

Vanessa sucked in a breath, gearing up for another assault. She'd always reminded me of Snow White, with her black hair and red lips, but, despite her looks, she wasn't the princess from the story. Vanessa was the apple. Shiny and lovely on the outside, her beauty masking the poison within. Who knew what venom she was getting ready to spew next? I decided to save her the time.

"Vanessa, you and I both know why you're here. With Ford in prison and not working, he's not drawing a salary, which means you're not getting any alimony. I'm sorry if you didn't put anything away for a rainy day, but that's not Griffen's problem. If you're running low on funds, I'd suggest finding yourself another sucker. Griffen isn't available and he's too smart to fall for your act a second time."

Griffen's grin was a little wicked, his green eyes twinkling as they rested on my face. Eventually, he turned to look at Vanessa. "What she said. Whatever you were getting from Ford, it has nothing to do with the Sawyer estate. Maybe you should go down to the prison and have a chat with him. In the meantime, I'll be alerting security that you aren't welcome at Heartstone Manor."

Vanessa drew in a deep breath and let it out in a shuddering sigh, sinking into one of the chairs facing Griffen's desk. I let out a short sigh of my own.

Act Two, here we come.

Playing with the hem of her skirt, Vanessa let her hair fall forward to shield her face, and when she looked up her eyes swam with tears. If I hadn't known better, I would have thought she was miserable and defenseless. Poor, sad creature.

Unfortunately for Vanessa, I did know better, and so did Griffen. She went for it anyway.

"You don't know what it's like. Ford's been so unkind, and now he's gone and I don't have any money. Everyone sided with him when we divorced. I'm going to lose my home, my car, and I don't have anywhere to go. I'm a Sawyer—"

Griffen cut her off. "Let me save you some time, Vanessa. Number one, you aren't a Sawyer. You manipulated my brother into marrying you and it sounds like you soaked him for a fortune. Not my fault if you didn't bother to save any. If you're having money troubles, I'll give you the same advice I got when you married my brother and I was thrown out of town. Get a job."

"You want me to work? Like—" she waved her hand in my direction again. "Like her? Like an office drone or waitress or something? I can't work."

"Then I'd take Hope's advice and go find yourself another sucker. There's got to be someone left in the Southeast who doesn't know what a grasping bitch you are."

Unable to stop myself I murmured, "Maybe she should try the West Coast. The Southeast isn't as big as it seems."

Fuming, Vanessa shot to her feet. "I see how it is. You say I should find another sucker, but I loved you and I loved Ford. Meanwhile, the woman you married ruined your life, Griffen. She's the reason Prentice ended our engagement. She lied to you and got you kicked out of your home and now she's won you over with her 'poor little me' act. You call me a grasping bitch, but I'm an amateur next to your wife."

Vanessa strode out of the office, hips swaying, tossing her shining hair back over her shoulder. Her parting shot shouldn't have struck home. I knew better. I did. I still felt sick to my stomach.

Apologizing to Griffen's face and to Vanessa's had felt good. Cleansing. Now, I just felt dirty again. It was half a lifetime ago, but she wasn't wrong. I'd—

"Don't let her get to you, Hope," Griffen said.

I shook his arm off my shoulders. "I'm not. I'm not. It's just Vanessa. She's always been mean. I shouldn't have been so rude. I rubbed her nose in it. I just—" I needed to get my head together. "I'm just going to make sure she actually leaves and then take a break. Unpack some things. You can keep working on the mail and save anything you need me for. I'll, uh, be back later."

Chapter Twenty-Six

HOPE

I NEEDED A BREAK. NEEDED TO GET OUT OF THAT room, away from the miasma of Vanessa's cloying perfume and poisonous words. Needed to remind myself that for better or worse, Griffen and I were married. At least for the next five years. And even if we weren't, he'd never go back to Vanessa.

I strode down the hall, ignoring Griffen as he called my name, reaching the front door in time to see Vanessa's car pull away. Savannah came up beside me. "That was fast," she commented dryly.

"Griffen says she's banned from the property. Once we get real security in, that is."

"Good news. I never liked her. But I don't have a penis and a fat bank account, so she's never bothered to be nice to me."

I burst out laughing. Savannah caught my eye and giggled along with me. Staring at the now-empty driveway, I tried to shake off a sense of foreboding. "I'm going to go upstairs for a little while, unpack and see if I can do any damage to that gigantic closet. Is there anything you need help with before everyone shows up tomorrow?"

"Nope. Cross your fingers that the interview with the cook goes well. After that, I have a few more interviews with maids, and if those work out we'll have a skeleton staff."

"That sounds great. Give a shout if you need me. I'll be upstairs."

"Lunch is in an hour," Savannah's voice followed me as I jogged up the curving staircase to the second floor.

Walking into the master suite was a balm to my aching soul. Savannah had done a brilliant job reproducing the feel of my apartment, and I longed to throw myself on my soft velvet couch with a book and a cup of tea and forget everything outside the door.

There was too much to do for that. Sawyer Enterprises had been neglected for too long. I'd take a quick breather up here, but then it was back to work until Griffen had a handle on things.

I couldn't throw myself on the couch with a book, but I could have a cup of tea. Silently thanking Savannah for her brilliance in setting up the snacks and drinks, I opened the cabinet in the corner, popped a pod for tea in the machine, and peeled open the cellophane on one of the brownies.

The sticker showed a candy-pink hand-drawn heart with the words Sweetheart Bakery in the center. My mouth watered in anticipation. Sweetheart Bakery was a town staple, the go-to place when anyone wanted a treat. Everything was great, but Daisy's brownies were divine. We'd bonded over my love for her baked goods, but with everything going on I hadn't seen her in over a week. I'd have to find time to stop in. Later. First, the closet.

I took my tea, half a brownie, and as many shopping bags as I could carry to the closet. Putting everything else out of my mind, I folded and stacked and hung and sorted. I left most of my old clothes in the boxes I'd packed before Griffen and I went to Atlanta. I didn't hang up a single ugly suit.

The master closet was huge. My side was at least as big as my bedroom in my old apartment, and though my shopping bags had practically filled the back seat of Griffen's Maserati, the contents barely made a dent in the closet. That was okay. I could always go shopping again, and I was covered for a while.

All I had left were the bags from the lingerie shop. Deep in the corner of a closet, I'd found a section of shallow drawers designed for storing lingerie. The top drawer was actually for jewelry, with velvet trays and a lock on the drawer. I'd have to see if I could find the keys. Not that I had much jewelry to put away aside from the ring on my finger. I wasn't planning on taking that off. Not until I had to.

I gently removed the tags from bras and panties, the midnight-blue silk nightgown and matching robe. It wasn't until I got to the blush-pink camisole with cream lace and matching thong that I stopped, smoothing the delicate fabric between my fingers and wondering if I would find the courage to put it on. Under my clothes, sure. Maybe.

But the camisole wasn't meant to be worn under clothes. It was meant to be worn alone over bare skin and very quickly taken off. Could I do that? My cheeks felt hot. How could I be embarrassed thinking about sex when there was no one here to see me? I needed to get over it and stop being such a baby.

I needed to do what Alice and Lily had suggested. Just put it on, let Griffen see and then—

"What do you have there?"

I shrieked, starting so hard I jumped and tossed the silk camisole in the air. It landed on my head, blinding me, but I didn't need my eyes to know who'd walked into the closet.

Griffen. Well, I'd wanted to show him the camisole. Though not while I was screaming like a dork. With a nervous laugh, I untangled the straps from my hair and twisted the fabric in my hands.

Griffen strode forward and tugged the camisole free. Threading his fingers through the straps, he held it up against me, his eyes heating as they took me in. "Did you buy this in Atlanta?"

I nodded.

"Did you buy it for me?"

I shook my head.

"No?" His eyes scanned me, taking in the way the silk draped over the curve of my breasts, the thick cream lace at the hem stopping just above where my hipbones were hidden under my jeans.

Finding my courage, I said, "I bought it for me to wear for you."

"Isn't that the same thing?"

Another shake of my head. "I bought it because I liked it. I liked the way I thought I would feel wearing it. And I thought you would agree."

I don't know where I got the courage to say that. It was the truth, but with Griffen so close, holding that pink silk against me, my heart trying to pound its way out of my chest—I was half-terrified.

Half-terrified and breathless with anticipation. I knew what that look in his eyes meant. Or I thought I did.

Griffen leaned in and my heart skipped a beat. "Try it on."

I swallowed hard past the knot in my throat. Try it on? Like, for him? *Of course, for him, you idiot. That's why you bought it, isn't it?*

Obviously. But I'd been feeling a lot more brave with Alice and Lily, Griffen nowhere in sight. Now we were alone and Griffen wanted me to—

"Okay," I squeaked out. "But you have to—" I made a shoo-ing motion with my hands.

Try the lingerie on for Griffen? That I could do. I hoped.

Do it with him watching? No flipping way.

With a quirk of his lips, Griffen handed me the pink silk cam-isole. "Yes, ma'am. I'll be waiting."

He disappeared through the door of the closet. I attempted not to have a heart attack. Then I decided not to think about it at all. I stripped off my jeans and sweater, then my underwear and bra, wondering if I should find perfume, or take a shower, or—I didn't know. I'd never done this before.

I settled for going to the bathroom, washing my hands and splashing some cold water on my face. I could do this. Millions of women did this every day.

This was Griffen. Everything would be okay.

This was Griffen, so everything would be better than okay.

Just put it on and he'll do the rest. One thing at a time. Just put it on.

I did, my rear end feeling very exposed and cold, considering there was no fabric covering it, just a narrow silk string giving me a wedgie. I stared at the closed door of the closet. I could not walk out there like this. I should. It should be no big deal, but it was.

My chest tight, fingertips tingling until I thought I really was going to have a heart attack, I snatched the midnight-blue robe from its hanger and pulled it on, my knuckles white from my tight grip on the silk.

Before I could talk myself out of it, I opened the closet door and walked through to the bedroom. Griffen's mouth spread into a smile. He shook his head in amusement and crossed the room to me, blocking my view of my big brass bed. Good. Every time I looked at the bed, I got a flutter in my chest.

"I thought you were going to model the pink thing for me." He pressed a fingertip into the hollow at the base of my throat and slid it down, down, down until he parted the lapels of the rope and traced the inner curve of my breast.

My breath caught in my throat. I forced out the words, "It's under here. I just couldn't walk around mostly naked."

Griffen's eyes flared on the word naked. "That's okay. I always loved unwrapping my presents slowly."

Closing his fingers over mine, he massaged my tight hand, gently easing the tension out of my fingers, loosening my grip on the robe.

With a deep sigh, I dropped my arm. Griffen hooked his thumb in the silk collar and nudged it back, baring my shoulder, then my upper arm, until the silk slid free and exposed most of the left side of my body.

He didn't say anything. He just looked at me, taking in the way the pink silk clung to my breast, the length of my leg, naked all the way to my hipbone. Moving into me, his hand skimmed my waist and my hip, curving around to squeeze my ass.

"I've been wanting to do that all day. And I've been meaning to tell you I really like your new jeans." Another squeeze. "A lot. Later, I really want to peel them off of you. If you had any idea what I was thinking while we were going through the mail you would've run screaming."

I gave a nervous, breathless laugh. I probably would have.

I didn't want to run screaming now.

Griffen's lips brushed the side of my neck, his breath so warm. The light bite of his teeth sent heat shooting through me. His mouth moved to the other side, nibbling and tasting, nipping my earlobe and sliding down to that sensitive spot where my shoulder met my neck. Somewhere in there, he tossed the robe off my other shoulder, and it hung at my elbows, ready to slide to the floor.

I didn't know what I was doing. I didn't have a strategy or a plan. I didn't need one. Griffen knew, and everything he did felt so good. I straightened my arms and let the robe fall.

Griffen made a choking sound in the back of his throat and pulled away, his eyes burning as they took me in, moving from the top of my head, over my breasts, my hips, my legs, all the way to my feet.

"You're so goddamn beautiful, Hope."

I didn't know what to say to that. Under his burning gaze and gentle hands, I felt beautiful for the first time in my life. Beautiful to him and beautiful to myself.

I didn't know what to say, but I thought I might know what to do. Heart pounding, I raised my hands and reached for the top button of his shirt. My fingers fumbled at first, but as his golden skin was revealed inch by inch, I sped up. He'd seen me, now I wanted to see him.

Griffen Sawyer did not disappoint. He had more muscle than I'd expected, his strong arms corded with it. I traced my fingers over a pink scar on one shoulder and down over his chest, circling his tight, small nipple, delighting in the sharp intake of breath at my touch. I rubbed the back of my fingers down the front of his stomach, smoothing over the ridges and furrows.

When my hands reached the button of his jeans, Griffen was done. He let me undo the button, let me lower the zipper, but before I could push the denim over his hips, he drew back.

I had a moment to wonder if I'd done something wrong, then his hands came up on either side of my face and his mouth took mine in a hungry kiss that blotted everything from my mind but Griffen.

I held onto his jeans for balance, my lips hard against his, just as hungry and just as desperate. This wasn't like the other kisses. This was dangerous. Too much. I was falling, losing myself, and I didn't care because it felt so good.

Griffen's hands held my face, the calluses on his palms rough, his touch gentle as he fed from my mouth. I moaned into him, drinking in the feel of his skin under my hands, his touch making me crazy, driving off all my inhibitions. I didn't care about anything but getting more of Griffen.

His hands fell from my face and he was backing me up, lifting me, dropping me on the bed. The brass frame rattled from the impact of my body, then his as he came down on top of me.

I didn't remember taking off the camisole or the thong, they were just gone and I was naked, and I needed him so much I wasn't even embarrassed that he could see everything.

His jeans were gone, too, and I could see every inch of his beautiful body, including his more than impressive erection. He was hard and thick and I wanted to touch. I reached down and closed my fingers around him. Squeezed.

Griffen's face landed in my neck, his mouth sucking at my skin, his fingers between my legs finding me wet and open. Ready. I was so ready. I needed.

I squeezed again, loving the way his chest hitched, his breath ragged in my ear, the way he throbbed and jerked in my hand.

His finger slid inside me. One finger, then another. I spread my legs wider, lifting my knees, opening myself to him, needing him so badly. I was empty inside and I wanted this—I squeezed again, tugging, demanding—I wanted him inside.

With a groan, Griffen gave me what I wanted. Rolling on top of me, settling between my legs, he moved my hand aside and pressed into the soft heat at my core.

I gasped at the burning stretch of him. There wasn't a sharp pain like I'd expected, just a slow burn as he pushed in and in and in. Slow. So slow. When he was seated to the hilt he stopped, propping himself up on his elbows and brushing the hair out of my face.

A tear trickled from the side of my eye. I didn't know why I was crying. It didn't hurt that badly. It wasn't that, it wasn't pain. I was so full. My body. My heart. So full of Griffen, and it was more than I'd imagined. Better. So much better.

He kissed the tear from my cheek. "Hope. You feel so fucking good."

Then he started to move. Slow, steady thrusts, his hips rocking between my legs, his hand where we were joined, and suddenly, I didn't feel the burn. Suddenly, I was on fire. Rocking up into him, my fingers sank into his shoulders, holding on with everything I had as we moved together.

This orgasm was nothing like the one from the day before. That one had left me dazed and drunk on sensation. This one blew off the top of my head. All I knew was pleasure, rising, drowning me until I was no more than the points that connected us. Griffen inside me. My hands on his shoulders, his chest pressed to mine. My mouth on his skin, teeth sinking in as stars exploded behind my eyes and bliss washed over me, sharp and sweet and perfect.

Griffen went still, his breath harsh, his lips pressing, kissing, soothing as the pleasure ebbed slowly, leaving me limp and sated.

I didn't think I could move. Not just because Griffen was pinning me to the bed. Every muscle in my body was wrung out, too happy to do anything more than just lay there. Alice and Lily were right. I didn't have to do anything but put on the lingerie.

Griffen took care of the rest, and wow, did he. I blinked up at the ceiling, idly appreciating the delicate vines carved into the woodwork, my mind drifting, when Griffen slid to the side and rolled us. I splayed over him, my backside suddenly cold.

Griffen's head popped up, and instead of the lazy satisfied expression I expected, his eyes were stark.

Chapter Twenty-Seven

GRIFFEN

"FUCK. DON'T MOVE. FUCK."

Goddamnit. I hadn't just fucked up. I'd fucked up big. She was a virgin, for fuck's sake. Bad enough I'd taken her hard and rough with little warning and almost no foreplay, I hadn't used a goddamn fucking condom. I had no excuse. I had them, right there in the bedside drawer.

Hadn't I thought about this already? I'd decided. Despite that stupid fucking will and Edgar's warning, I would not get Hope pregnant. Not until she was ready. Not until she wanted it as much as I did. Then I took one look at her holding up that scrap of pink silk and all my good intentions went out the window.

I slid her off of me, my cock sliding free of her body, the friction a painful pleasure. Fuck. I'd only just come and I already wanted back in there.

In the bathroom, I grabbed a washcloth off the neat stack and ran the hot water. The least I could do was take care of her. Fuck. She was still laying there, one knee cocked up, hugging the pillow, a little smile on her face despite the shadow of concern when she looked at me.

She didn't look pissed so I couldn't have fucked up that badly.

Don't fool yourself, asshole. You know you fucked up.

She'd be sore. She needed a bath. The sun streamed through the un-curtained windows, a spotlight on her beauty: those long limbs spotted with cinnamon freckles, the indent of her waist, the curve of her hip. She tried to squeeze her legs shut, throwing an arm over her breasts.

Gently, I eased her legs apart, pressing the warm cloth between her legs, soothing and cleaning her at the same time. I nudged her knees apart, pressing the washcloth more firmly to her sweet, well-fucked pussy.

"Don't. Let me. Fuck, Hope. I wasn't planning on this. Not yet. We didn't use anything. Tell me you're on the pill."

The happy, sated smile fell from her face. Her eyes drained of heat and affection and contentment. "Oh, no. I'm not on the pill, Griffen. I never—I didn't think I'd—" Her eyes slid shut, her face twisted in a grimace.

Fucking fuck.

"I'm sorry, baby. I thought we'd wait. I was going to wait and I saw you with that pink thing and all those freckles and I fucking lost my head. I'm sorry."

"It should be okay," she said, staring past me at the ceiling. I imagined she was doing calculations with the calendar in her head. More confidently, she repeated, "It should be okay. It's a little late in my cycle for me to get pregnant. I think. I'm not exactly up on the details of conception considering, you know, I hadn't done this before."

Fuck me. I might have just screwed up both our lives and she was being cute. I should have been relieved that Hope had cute in her at this moment. Perversely, I wasn't.

It's not that I didn't want a baby with Hope. I was starting to think that might be one of the things I wanted most in life. A family with Hope. But not like this. Not ever like this. Not so she would think it was a ploy. A way to trap her and save myself.

I didn't want her with me for a baby or the will. Not for guilt or duty. I wanted Hope to want me for me.

Not sure what to say, I helped her to her feet, ushering her into the bathroom. I pulled her under the warm spray of the shower, careful to keep her hair clear of the water. "A bath would be better," I said, smoothing my hands down her arms and around to cup her breasts. "But Savannah's going to ring the lunch gong any minute, and I'm assuming you don't want to explain why we're missing the meal."

Hope's teeth sank into her lower lip, her cheeks flushed pink. She shook her head, unable to meet my eyes. So shy, even after what happened in that bed.

"You're okay?" I had to ask. "I didn't hurt you?"

Another shy shake of her head. "It was good," she whispered. "Really good."

"I wasn't too rough?"

I'd lost control. Not completely, but enough. More than I ever had before. I didn't know why. It was just... Hope. She was so responsive, so in the moment, and her passion was so real. She'd wanted me enough to give me something she'd saved her entire fucking life.

She seemed fine. A little sore, a little shy, a little shaken about the condom thing but otherwise, fine.

I watched her step out of the shower and grab a towel, self-conscious in her nudity. Probably not wanting to tip off Savannah, she grabbed her discarded jeans and sweater from the closet floor and got dressed after smoothing on her apples and cinnamon lotion.

I didn't watch, I swear.

I mostly didn't watch.

I was pulling my shirt over my head when the lunch gong sounded. I'd forgotten that thing until I came home. Some long-ago Sawyer ancestor had brought it over from the Far East, a big brass disk hanging from two leather straps in a wooden frame. It had been used for generations to call the Sawyers to the dining room.

Hope looked up at me with a grin. "I forgot about that thing. It's loud."

I grinned in agreement and followed her out of the bedroom. I was stuck in my head, in my heart, all of me turned inside out by Hope and the gift she'd given me. She practically skipped down the stairs, sending Savannah a brilliant smile as we walked into the dining room and took our seats at the end of the table.

You should be glad she's not freaking out, I reminded myself. And I was. I didn't want to hurt her. I didn't want her scared. If forgetting the condom meant she ended up pregnant, we'd deal.

I didn't want her scared or hurt, but I wanted her to feel... something. Hadn't she been in love with me for most of her life? She'd just given me her virginity. Now she was sitting down to a turkey sandwich like nothing had changed.

Everything had changed.

For me.

Maybe not for her. Maybe this was just scratching something off her bucket list.

Finally fuck Griffen. *Check.*

I never thought I'd end up married to Hope. Never thought she'd be in my bed. She'd been a kid when I left. At best, my friend, and at worst—at worst she'd been the architect of my exile. Except she hadn't been. In truth, at worst she'd been an occasional nuisance.

I hadn't been planning to sleep with her. Not yet. I'd planned a lot more foreplay, a lot more teasing and kissing and touching. But she'd been so hot, right there with me, her moans when I kissed her and the heat of her body impossible to deny.

She'd given me a gift. Not just her virginity, though that meant so much more than I'd expected it would. It wasn't that I cared if she'd slept with other men. I didn't have any hangups about purity. That would have been pretty hypocritical considering my own past.

It was her trust that meant so much. She'd spent her entire life protecting herself, never sharing her body with anyone. Until me. She'd trusted me with that, known I'd take care of her, that I wouldn't hurt her.

I hadn't been looking for this. Hadn't expected it. But Hope was the most precious gift life had ever thrown my way and it killed me that what we shared didn't seem to have touched her beyond the pleasure of it.

My world had been rocked, turned upside down and inside out. I didn't want a fucking turkey sandwich. I wasn't hungry. I wanted to drag Hope back up to the room, to pull her into a warm bath, to kiss her and make her come again and again.

I wanted the world to be just the two of us until she was right there with me feeling everything I was feeling.

That wasn't going to happen. Not anytime soon.

We ate in silence until Hope said, "Are you okay about seeing Vanessa?"

I looked up sharply, "Vanessa? Sure. Are you? Okay?"

"I guess. It was a little weird. She's mean, but she's never paid much attention to me."

"You're a threat."

"What?" Hope looked confused.

I clarified, "She thinks you're a threat. The hair, the new clothes. You want to be seen and she sees you. What she sees is a threat."

Hope tilted her head to the side as if examining this new idea. "Am I a threat?"

"No," I said, without thinking.

Her face fell. "Oh."

I realized my mistake. "To say you're a threat to Vanessa implies that she has a piece on the board. She doesn't. She has no position to threaten. She's nothing."

"What?" Hope still looked confused. She'd lived her whole life in the shadow of her uncle Edgar, and even Prentice and Ford. Doing their bidding and letting them push her aside. She didn't realize she'd always been important. Now, with them out of the way, everyone else would realize it too.

"Hope, you are so far above Vanessa she doesn't even factor. She's been sitting around wasting her life, probably alienating half the town while living off alimony from Ford. She doesn't have any skills and she probably doesn't have any real friends. Now she's running out of money, and the best she can do is come here in some halfhearted attempt to seduce some cash out of me. She's nothing like you. You're so far out of her league she shouldn't be able to see you."

"She didn't like that I was wearing this ring," Hope commented, staring down at her hand where the Sawyer ruby burned among fiery diamonds.

"Of course, she didn't. Even back then she was never going to get that ring. It didn't even occur to me to give it to her, to be honest. Obviously, it didn't occur to Ford either."

"Prentice used her. To punish you and keep Ford on a leash," Hope said, taking a sip of her iced tea, her eyes sad.

"I guess he did. She didn't seem to mind."

Hope looked down at her finger again, turning her hand so

the ring caught the light. "Not much has changed. At least I got a nice ring out of it."

A direct stab to my heart. "That's not what this is," I protested. "That's not what you are. Prentice isn't using you to control me."

"No, he isn't, is he? He used the town to control you. I don't know why I'm even here."

The bitch of it was I didn't know why she was here either. It still didn't make sense. Prentice didn't need Hope to get me to stay. Starving the town of funds was enough to do that. In fact, he'd used the town against Hope as much as me.

Edgar must have had something on Prentice, some way to strong-arm him into putting Hope in place as my wife. But if so, why did the prenup leave her with nothing at the end of our marriage? Why put a time limit on it at all?

I didn't know the answers, and I was starting not to care.

It didn't matter why Hope was here, I was just glad that she was.

Chapter Twenty-Eight

GRIFFEN

*I*T LOOKED LIKE MY SIBLINGS WERE KEEPING THEIR distance until the last possible moment. Hope and I ate dinner alone—again—in the formal dining room. It should have been romantic. The great iron chandeliers were working, but Savannah had found candelabras somewhere and we dined by candlelight, sitting diagonally, me at the head of the table and Hope just to my right.

Hope was reserved. Distant. I couldn't tell if she was shy, or worried, or pissed off at me and not sure how to tell me. She could have just been exhausted. We'd spent the rest of the afternoon and early evening plowing our way through my father's inbox. Reaching out to business connections on the phone and by email, setting up meetings, and just trying to get a picture of the modern version of Sawyer Enterprises.

When I'd been involved in the company it had been made up of a collection of traditional industries. Sawyer Enterprises had owned a logging company, several quarries, furniture manufacturing, and commercial real estate all over the Southeast. Back then, the Inn at Sawyers Bend had been our only investment in the hospitality industry, and more about legacy than profit.

Prentice had sold off the quarries, the manufacturing, and the logging company. These days, Sawyer Enterprises was made up of the Inn at Sawyers Bend, Quinn's guide company, Avery's brewery, and all the commercial real estate we owned in Sawyer's Bend and across the Southeast.

Beyond those interests, Prentice had invested the profits from logging, manufacturing, and the quarries into investments in various companies. Overall, it was a smart move. We were far more diversified than we'd been in the past, better able to weather changes in the markets. If one of our interests was down, another would be up, and at the core, the Sawyers maintained an iron grip on the town Alexander Sawyer had founded over two centuries before.

While Prentice's strategy for Sawyer Enterprises was a good one, it meant we had a lot more moving parts to track down. While my siblings oversaw the real estate, Inn, brewery and guide business, Hope and I were still digging into the investments, seats on various boards, and all the other ways Prentice had his fingers in businesses across the country.

If I had to read another email or look at another quarterly report I thought I'd go blind. Once I had a handle on everything, I knew I'd love the challenge of tweaking and changing, searching for new investments to make our portfolio thrive. That was later. Right now, I had a mountain of paperwork and communications to put in order and the headache to go with it.

Hope squinted down at her plate. I was reading too much into her mood. She probably wasn't mad at me. She probably had the same pounding headache I did.

"Tired?" I asked.

With a look of relief, she nodded. "My head is killing me."

"Me too. I have a plan for that."

Hope raised an eyebrow. I only smiled in answer.

Dinner finished, I caught Hope's hand in mine and led her upstairs. Savannah, with brilliant foresight, had placed bath salts and scented candles beside the clawfoot tub. The tub was massive, and for once, I didn't fault Prentice for his need to have everything bigger and better. The tub would fit both of us easily and it was exactly what I needed.

I started the hot water, lit the candles, and added the scented bath salts before I went looking for Hope. I found her at the window in the sitting room looking down into the courtyard below. When Hawk arrived, I was sure he'd whip the scraggly bushes and overgrown weeds into shape. For now, all I saw was neglect. I hoped it was only the sight of the abandoned property that had put that sad, strained look on Hope's face.

Catching her hand with mine, I tugged, drawing her attention from the view outside. "Come on," I said. "I promised you a bath."

Pulling her hand from mine, she leaned closer to the window, squinting into the darkness outside. "Hold on," she murmured, swatting at my questing hand.

"What?" I gave up trying to drag her away and joined her at the window.

"Did you see that?" Hope shifted, then backed up and crossed into the bedroom, looking out the window there. I glanced out of the sitting room window, saw nothing unusual, and followed her to the bedroom.

One hand pressed to the glass, Hope stared down into the courtyard. "I wish we had lights out there. I swear I saw someone."

"Someone or something?" It was night, and we were deep in the woods. Who knew what was roaming around the estate in the dark? It could have been a deer, fox, even a bear. It had been years since anyone had sighted a mountain lion this close to civilization, but they were out there.

"I thought it was a person, but it's dark. I guess it could have been a deer. Or just the shadows."

"Do you see anything now?" I asked, stroking a hand down her hair.

Hope leaned into me, letting out a long sigh. "No. And my head is killing me. It was probably nothing."

"Do you want me to go take a look?" I would if it would help her relax. I was ninety percent sure no one was out there skulking in the courtyard, but if Hope thought she'd seen something, I wouldn't blow her off.

"No." She turned, pressing her forehead into my neck, fatigue coming off her in waves. It had been a hell of a long day. She was exhausted, that was all.

I tried not to think about my father's death. Whoever killed him hadn't bothered skulking around in the night. His murderer had walked right in and shot him in broad daylight.

Was Hope jumpy because she was tired and stressed out, or was she worried about Prentice's killer out there somewhere? This time he'd be aiming for one of us.

Now I was being jumpy. The house was locked up tight. Prentice was dead. If there was someone out there who meant us harm, I could keep Hope safer here, my weapon only feet away, than if I left her alone while I wandered around in the dark outside.

"Time for a bath." Stopping to get my weapon from the bedside table and place it on the small bench by the tub, I led Hope into the bathroom.

Hope followed me in silence, standing behind the rapidly filling tub, her eyes wide and impenetrable. She let me pull the sweater over her head, unbutton her jeans, and slide them over her hips to pool around her ankles. She was still pushing them off her feet, reaching out to grab the side of the tub for balance when the last of my clothes hit the floor. I stepped into the tub and helped her inside with me, settling in with my back against the end of the tub and Hope in my arms.

Exactly where I wanted her.

When she saw the tub she'd grabbed a hairband off the counter, gathering her long strands into a messy knot on the top of her head. It left her neck completely exposed, and I took full advantage, nuzzling her damp skin, smelling the cinnamon and apples scent I'd discovered came from her favorite lotion, now neatly stowed on the bathroom counter.

I liked seeing her things there. I liked having her with me in the tub. I wasn't much of a bath guy, but I could get used to this.

She was tense in my arms. Braced, I assumed, for me to make a move. I'd bungled this whole thing with Hope more than once, but I'd figured out Hope was fine once we got going. It was the getting started part that made her nervous. That was okay. Despite my showing earlier, I could be patient. I could.

I closed my hands over her shoulders and squeezed, her muscles like steel bands under my fingers. Pressing with my thumbs, I rubbed and she let out a moan that had my cock stiffening.

I said I could be patient, didn't I? I could. I would.

"No wonder you have a headache. Is your neck as bad as your shoulders?" Hope didn't answer. I didn't need her to. I lifted a hand and found out for myself. It wasn't as bad as her shoulders, it was worse. "Just relax. I've got you."

We'd worked through the normal dinner hour and it was late. Not quite bedtime, but close enough. Hope's eyes drooped shut, her body easing as she relaxed into me. I worked her muscles with my thumbs and fingers until she was all loose limbs and stillness. She was so still I wondered if she was asleep.

"Hope?"

"Hmmm?"

"Are you tense anywhere else? Here?" Her back plastered to my front, I stroked my fingertips down her shoulders to cup her breasts, strumming her nipples with my thumbs. She squirmed in my lap, my cock flexing against the curve of her ass.

I touched her without urgency. Without demand. This wasn't going anywhere. Not for me. We didn't have an ending in sight, I just wanted to touch and tease. To give her a nice orgasm before she slipped into sleep.

Hope arched her back, letting out a low moan, pressing her breasts into my hands and rubbing against me. I dipped a hand between her thighs and stroked one finger inside, not surprised to find her already wet.

Tomorrow, I reminded myself. *She's sore. You can get back in there tomorrow.* So fucking tight and wet, her hips rocking up into my hand. She might get nervous in the beginning, but once I touched her, Hope's instincts were spot on.

Another stroke of my fingers against her clit, swirling and dipping inside just the smallest bit before going back for another tease of that swollen bud. Hope squirmed, a keening sound vibrating in her throat. Abruptly she rolled, her hands closing over my shoulders for balance as she straddled my lap, trapping my hard cock against the heat of her pussy.

Bliss. Fucking bliss. Being inside her was the only thing better. This was almost as good. Her mouth found mine. With the touch of her lips, Hope unleashed all the hunger, all the demand I'd been holding back.

Hope opened her mouth to mine without hesitation, her tongue stroking, just as hungry. Just as demanding. How could my calm, serious Hope be hiding so much passion? She gave a low, desperate moan as she rocked her hips into mine. My hands closed over her ass and I ground her slick pussy against my cock, thrusting hard, knowing it wouldn't be long before I came.

Not until she did. I had to see her come again, the flush of pleasure across her face, the sounds she made, breathless and greedy and overwhelmed by pleasure. Her knees gripping my hips, she rode me harder, faster, sliding against the slick porcelain until she almost lost her purchase and shoved us both under the water.

Her frantic movements sent the first wave cascading over the side of the tub, the splash background noise to her orgasm. Hope tore her mouth from mine, crying out. Her pussy pulsed against me, scalding my cock, driving me over the edge before I could stop.

Hope owned me.

I was no inexperienced boy. I'd been in charge of my orgasms for a long time. Not anymore. Not since I got my hands on Hope. Coming in the tub was unlikely to get her pregnant, but it wasn't exactly safe sex either. Fuck me. So many years as *Mr. In Control*, and now a few days with Hope Daniels—*Hope Daniels*—and I was worse than a teenager.

Hope collapsed against me, rubbing her cheek against my collarbone, pressing light kisses into my wet skin. "I don't have a headache anymore," she murmured sleepily.

"Neither do I. Are you ready for bed?"

"Mmm-Hmm."

She was half asleep already. I slid her to the side and reached to let the water out of the tub. The floor wasn't an inch deep in water, but it was far from dry. Climbing from the tub, I said, "Stay put for a second," and reached for a towel, looking back to see Hope's eyes slitted open, a satisfied little smile on her mouth.

"Are you checking out my ass?" I asked, amused. She could check out my ass anytime she wanted.

"Maybe."

I tossed my towel on the floor to soak up the water and grabbed another, reaching for Hope's hand. "Careful, it's slippery." I wrapped the towel around her, pressing a kiss to the curve of her cheek.

The bed was so close. I'd tuck her in beside me, naked and warm, and—

The crash of shattering porcelain sliced through the silence beyond the door. Something else falling, breaking, and voices raised in alarm. Tightening the towel around Hope I said, "Stay here. Don't leave this room. Do you understand?"

Chapter Twenty-Nine

GRIFFEN

EAR CHASED AWAY HER POST-ORGASMIC HAZE. HOPE blinked up at me and nodded, eyes grave, closing her fingers around the towel. "Go. I'm okay here."

"Don't leave the room," I repeated, dragging on my clothes, grabbing my weapon from beside the tub, and racing for the bedroom door, my feet still damp from the bath.

The hall outside the master suite was dim, lit only by sconces turned low. The voices were coming from the hall beyond the head of the staircase. The one that led to the wing with my siblings' bedrooms.

I should have gone to check the courtyard. Hope thought she saw something and I was so intent on getting her naked I'd convinced myself it was no big deal. I had to stop letting my cock run my brain. This wasn't just about me. Hope and Savannah were here. I had a family to protect.

I rounded the corner and stopped short.

Sterling sprawled at the top of the steps, arms laid wide, golden hair trailing across her face. Savannah crouched beside her, tugging on her hand. "Sterling, come on, get up."

Sterling rolled to her side, torso heaving before she grumbled, "Don't wanna. Sleeping here."

This was not Savannah's job. We had specifically discussed the fact that dealing with my sister on a bender was not her job. Fucking hell.

"Leave her there," I said to Savannah. "I've got her. Any mess she makes, she's going to clean up."

Savannah let go of Sterling and stepped away. "No argument here. You sure you've got this?"

Grimly, I confirmed, "I've got this."

With a shake of her head, Savannah took off. She was no fool. I had my arms hooked under Sterling's armpits and was hauling her to her feet when I heard a sound behind me.

"She okay?"

Hope.

"I told you to stay in the room." I looked over my shoulder to find her wearing her robe. Not the dark blue silk one I'd taken off her earlier in the day, this one was fluffy and pink. Ugly, but it looked comfortable as hell.

"I know," she answered, watching Sterling with wary concern. "I heard her voice. I knew it was Sterling."

I wanted to argue with her, tell her she should have listened to me anyway, but I didn't have time. Sterling was wobbling on her feet, her body hitching as if she was getting ready to hurl.

"I have to get her to her room," I said, hauling her into my arms and striding to the corridor. Hope followed behind, then raced ahead to throw Sterling's door open. Both of us paused on the threshold, my little sister's room still an unholy pit of disaster.

I set Sterling back on her feet, turning her to face her bathroom. Unsteady, she raised her head, pushed her hair out of her eyes, and spotted Hope. "Hope? What 'ya doin' here?"

Hope reached out to turn Sterling in the direction of her bathroom, murmuring, "We'll talk about it tomorrow. I think you need—"

A spasm shook Sterling's body and she threw up, a fountain of vomit spewing onto Hope and the floor beyond. Swearing under my breath, I moved fast, dragging Sterling into her bathroom. She fell to her knees before the toilet, draped her arm over the seat, and retched pitifully.

I left her there, going back to check on Hope. I expected her to be pissed. She stood in the middle of Sterling's room, her face white as a sheet, shaking, her eyes shocked and wide. This wasn't anger. This was something else.

"Baby. What's wrong?" Hope's eyes settled on mine. Wild. Terrified. I reached out to touch, but she shook me off.

"Take care of Sterling. I'm just going to go—I just need to—I need to get the smell off me. I can't stand the smell. I can't—I can't stand the smell. I'm sorry. I'm sorry, Griffen, I have to go—"

"Go. I'll be there as soon as I can, okay? I just have to make sure she's—"

Hope was gone. She disappeared down the hall, her feet pounding on the hardwood as she took off back to our suite.

Getting thrown up on was gross. No question. And nobody liked the smell of vomit. Hope's reaction had been something else. Something worse. I'd dig into that later. She was right, I had to take care of my little sister.

Sterling had everything under control. Stomach empty, she flushed the toilet and got to her feet without looking at me. After shoving her face under the faucet, she rinsed both it and her mouth.

I stood in the center of her bedroom, staring at the splash of vomit on the carpet and watching as she went through the motions of caring for herself. She was wobbly and off-balance, but she brushed her teeth and pulled back her hair in motions so practiced I knew this happened far more often than it should.

Sterling stumbled out of the bathroom and came up short at the sight of me. "Griffen. Thought you were a dream. I got sick."

"I know. You threw up on Hope."

Sterling shrugged a shoulder. "Sorry."

"I'm not the one you have to apologize to. Get in bed. We need to talk."

"Don't wanna talk." Fully clothed, probably with specks of vomit on her shirt, she climbed into her unmade bed, pulling the covers up around her.

She was sleeping on her stomach. Good news if she threw up again. I drew in a breath, planning to blast her, to lay it out and tell her how it was going to be now that I was in charge.

Tugging the blanket closer to her chin, a whimper escaped. "You left us. Didn't think you'd ever come back."

You left us.

I'd never thought about it like that. She'd been a child. Not even ten years old. She was right. I had left. The others, Royal and Tenn and Finn, even Avery and Quinn, I could have expected to speak up for me. To reach out or answer my letters. But Sterling? She'd been a child, her mother dead, her father disinterested.

From all accounts, Sterling had spent the last decade drinking and doing God knew what else to wipe away her pain. On top of that, she'd just lost her only parent, shitty father though he was. She was grieving.

Maybe I needed to cut her some slack. Breathing in the scent of fresh vomit layered over old, I revised that thought. I could give her compassion. She was my baby sister, after all. I wouldn't be cutting her any slack that ended up with another episode like this.

I sat on the edge of her bed after checking it for puke or grime, and pulled the covers up, tucking them tightly around her. Stroking her hair from her face, I waited until her breath was even and deep, her body relaxed in sleep. Her stomach was empty, and she'd probably feel like hell in the morning, but I didn't think she'd throw up again.

I found Hope getting out of the shower, the color back in her face but something about her still fragile.

"Hey," I said.

Her head rose and she gave me a weak, embarrassed smile. "She okay?"

I shrugged. "As okay as she can be for now. Are you okay?" I waited, expecting her to pretend her flight from Sterling's room had been no big deal.

She didn't answer, disappearing into the closet. I resisted the urge to follow and watch her drop that towel. Instead, I went to the corner of the sitting room and the clever little station Savannah had set up. Brewing a cup of tea, I spooned in a liberal dose of honey.

By the time it was ready, Hope had reappeared in a loose cotton sleep shirt that reached to her knees. She probably thought she didn't look sexy. Little did she know the thin cotton clung to her damp curves in an appealing tease. I sat on the brown velvet couch and held out the tea.

She took it with a grateful smile and sat, sipping, the silence stretching between us.

"I'm sorry I didn't help with Sterling. I—"

"She threw up on you, Hope. I think you get a pass." A ghost of a smile touched her mouth and faded. "You didn't seem grossed out. You looked scared. Why did that scare you, Hope?"

Hope took a slow sip of her tea, studying the brown velvet of

the couch, worrying the nap with her fingertips. It took everything I had not to push. I didn't know why this was important, I
just knew it was. She took another sip. Then another. I waited.

Eventually, "She reminded me of my mother. I haven't
thought about her in so long, but the smell of vomit and the
way she was slurring her words, the way she just didn't care—"
Hope's voice choked off.

I wanted more. I wanted to slide over on the couch, take the
tea from her hands and pull her into my arms. She looked too
alone sitting over there, clutching her teacup and studying the
steam. I didn't move. Hope was lost in memory, and I had the odd
sensation that if I touched her she'd disappear in a puff of smoke.

"I don't really drink," she went on. "I usually avoid being
around people who are drinking. I can't—I know it was a long
time ago, but I can't handle it."

"When was the last time you saw your mother?"

"I was eight. They'd left me. Again. Five days, that time.
Uncle Edgar stopped by. He was in town on business. I wouldn't
have opened the door—I knew better—but I remembered he
was Momma's brother. And I was hungry. The can opener broke,
and I couldn't make any soup."

I was reeling. So much in so few words. She'd been left alone
as a child. She'd been hungry. I cleared my throat. "They left you
alone?"

Hope's haunted eyes lifted to mine. "I knew how to make
soup and peanut butter and jelly. I taught myself how to make
grilled cheese, but once I left the dishtowel too close to the
stove. They were home that time. I got a whoopin' and locked in
my room, but at least I didn't burn the place down."

I didn't want to ask what a *whoopin'* entailed to parents who
didn't mind leaving their eight-year-old alone for almost a week.
I remembered what Hope had said.

"Edgar saved you."

Chapter Thirty

GRIFFEN

E'D VISITED BEFORE. ONCE OR TWICE. THEY always knew he was coming and cleaned the place up. Stayed sober." She considered. "More sober. I don't think I remember ever seeing either of them completely sober. He gave them money. I think it was for me. For food and clothes."

"But they spent it on alcohol?"

"Liquor, drugs. Mostly drugs. Rarely food."

"And they left you? Where did they go?" Stupid questions, but I didn't know what to say. This was so far outside my realm of experience, and the idea of Hope abandoned, neglected, burned deep inside.

I remembered what she looked like the first time Edgar had brought her to Heartstone Manor. So thin and frail a strong wind could have blown her down. I hadn't paid that much attention. I'd been a fourteen-year-old boy. I'd asked my father if she'd been sick and he told me it wasn't my business, that she'd be fine. And she had been.

In answer to my question, Hope shrugged a shoulder and took another sip of her tea. "I have no idea where they went. Somewhere. They came home wasted with a supply of drugs, so I don't know. I never knew what they did to earn the money they used to buy the stuff. I think—there was a man—he came to the apartment sometimes. He—he touched my mother—even that young, I knew a stranger shouldn't touch her like that, but she didn't say no and my father was always—" Another shrug.

"Your father was…?"

"Useless," she finished. "My father was useless. My mother was always some degree of wasted on whatever she could get her hands on, but still, she was the one who made the decisions. When the man came over, she was the one who talked. He liked me. She always told him, 'Not yet.'"

Everything in me recoiled from Hope's words. Her mother. How could a mother—? My own mother had run off with her lover and abandoned Ford and me, but that was nothing like this. She may not have loved us, but she knew we'd be safe and taken care of.

Hope's mother had half-starved her own child, neglected her, and planned to pimp her out to get money for drugs. Fucking hell.

I didn't know how a human being could do that to any child, but when I tried to place Hope in that scene, my brain wouldn't do it. She'd been so sweet. Kind and gentle. Curious and funny. There was a reason we'd been friends despite the difference in our ages.

Looking back, I could see that she'd been so much older than her years. Knowing her past, so much made sense. Her loyalty to

Edgar. Her obedience. The virginity she'd only given up the day before. Oh, God. Had they—

"That man—did he ever—?" I couldn't bring myself to say the words. Couldn't force her to hear them.

A flash of a glance at me, her eyes shamed. Tortured. Hope shook her head. "He, uh, touched me, but not like that. I swear, Griffen, not like that. Just his hand on my face. My knee once. It felt like things crawling on me. He was so creepy and gross. He didn't smell like smoke and vomit like my mother and father, but that just made him scarier. At least with them, I knew they'd pass out eventually. I knew when he came for me, he wouldn't pass out. I didn't fully understand what he wanted, but I knew he'd get it. It was just a matter of time."

I hated the way she protested. *Not like that*. As if it would have made her less if that evil man had touched her. Not sure if it was the right thing to say, not sure if I should say anything at all, I ventured, "You know it's not your fault, right? If he had."

She shook her head hard, and I said, "I'm not saying he did, Hope. I believe you. I'm just saying, of all the people in that fucked up situation, you were innocent."

"I was never innocent," she said bitterly.

"Hope, you're the most innocent person I've ever known."

"If you knew the things I'd seen by the time I could walk—"

"That just makes you more of a miracle, that you were born into that, saw all those things, and here you are. You're kind, and generous, and sweet, and loyal. You're one of the best people I know. Your heart has always been innocent, and it breaks mine to know that the people who were supposed to protect it didn't."

A tear rolled down her cheek falling into her almost-empty teacup. Leaning forward slowly, not wanting to spook her, I pulled the cup from her fingers. "I don't want to crowd you, Buttercup, but I really want to hold you right now."

With a choked cry, Hope threw herself in my direction. I caught her in my arms and pulled her on top of me, turning to stretch out on the wide, soft, velvet sofa. Wrapping my arms around her, I held her as tight as I could, not sure I'd ever let her go.

She was silent in my arms, her face pressed into my neck, her tears hot on my skin. Hope wept for what felt like hours, never making a sound aside from a hitching breath here and there.

Had she learned to cry quietly as a child? I hated the thought. No, hate didn't cover it. Hope, my Hope, was everything good in the world. How she'd come from such desperate beginnings I couldn't imagine.

I rubbed her back, smoothed her hair, so many details falling into place now that I knew.

I already knew I'd been a shit by blaming her for what had ultimately been my father and Ford's machinations. She'd been an easy target and I'd fallen for it. I could forgive twenty-two-year-old me for being a dumb ass. I wasn't sure I could forgive myself for holding a grudge for so long. Against my father, abso-fucking-lutely. Against Hope? No.

I thought of Sterling passed out in her bed. Of Brax, and Quinn, and Parker, and even Avery and Tenn who'd been only fifteen when I left. Ford, Royal, and Finn had been old enough to speak for themselves. To understand what was happening. Maybe they deserved a little bit of a grudge.

But the rest—I was holding onto anger over something that had only been good for me in the end. The woman wrapped in my arms had lived through so much worse than Prentice's bullshit and she'd come out of it with a clean and open heart. I should learn from her and stop being such an asshole.

Hope fell asleep, her tears still wet on her cheeks, her body held tightly in my arms. When I was sure she wouldn't wake, I picked her up and carried her to our bed.

I climbed into bed beside her and pulled her back into my arms, her head over my heart, emotion flooding me as she settled into me with a sleepy sigh. I combed my fingers through her hair and felt her slide deep into slumber, only following when I was sure she'd have sweet dreams.

She didn't. I could have guessed that. Dredging up the past, the scene with Sterling—all of it was custom-made to plant nightmares in Hope's brain. She woke twice, the first time with a start and a gasp, sitting bolt upright and looking around the room, eyes wide in panic.

I slept lightly out of habit, coming alert and catching her before her panic grew too deep. Framing her face in my hands until her eyes locked on mine, I said, "Breathe, Buttercup. Take a deep breath for me." With each slow breath, she calmed, and I pulled her back down, stroking her hair from her face until she fell asleep again.

Later, in the light of early dawn, she tossed and turned, little whimpering sounds coming from the base of her throat. Wounded, frightened sounds. I hated every one. This time, she didn't wake fully but responded to the sound of my voice in her ear telling her she was safe. That I wouldn't let anything happen to her.

I meant the vow all the way to the marrow of my bones. Hope was precious. I wouldn't let anything happen to her. She was mine now. I take care of what's mine.

I watched her wake for the last time just before seven, her eyes fluttering open, dazed and sleepy. Before she could remember too much of the day before, I kissed her. A brush of my lips, my fingers sinking into the silken strands of her hair. Gentle, careful. She was sleepy, but she was definitely awake. I didn't want to overwhelm her.

I wanted her to choose this.

Choose me.

Choose us.

Her lips opened, her tongue stealing out to graze mine. I groaned deep in my throat at her honest, open desire. Would it always feel like such a gift? That she gave this to me with no reservation?

I thought that it would, and cradling her face in my hands, I fed from her mouth, drinking in her sweetness, her passion, the innocence that would always be hers because it was the core of her open heart.

This time, I was prepared. After I slid off her sleep shirt to feast my eyes on her body, after I tasted her breasts, sucking until she cried out, after I slipped my fingers between her legs to find her ready and eager, I drew the condom from beneath my pillow and rolled it on. I wouldn't take any more chances with Hope. She deserved better from me. She deserved everything.

This time, I took it slow, easing into her, relieved to see her face showed only pleasure. She raised her knees and spread them wide, rocking up to take me deeper. I couldn't bear the thought of hurting her. Her mouth seeking mine, her legs wrapped around my hips, I kissed her, drinking in her sighs and moans as I took her slowly, letting it build and grow until the wave of bliss took us both.

I left her for only a minute to take care of the condom, and I was back pulling her into my arms again. She flicked a shy glance my way before resting her cheek on my chest.

"It's moving day. Do you have a plan?" she asked, amusement in the edges of her voice.

"You mean am I going to stand at the door with a clipboard like a cruise director welcoming my errant siblings home?"

Hope giggled. The sound was sunlight in my soul.

"Fuck that," I said—and meant it. "I'd rather go to prison."

Hope propped herself up on her elbow, looking down at me. "About that..."

I knew what she was going to say. I didn't want to hear it.

"Later," I murmured, drawing her face down to mine and kissing her again. The gong would ring for breakfast soon. Just enough time to introduce Hope to one of the many ways I could make her come in the shower.

Chapter Thirty-One

GRIFFEN

*H*OPE HAD A SECRET SMILE ON HER FACE AS WE descended the stairs for breakfast. When Savannah met us at the bottom, clipboard in hand, dressed in a housekeeper's uniform, Hope's secret smile spread into a wide grin.

"Savannah! You look fantastic! Is this what you meant when you said you figured out a uniform?" Hope walked a circle around Savannah, taking in her calf-length, long-sleeve gray dress in a tight herringbone pattern, starched white apron, black tights, and comfortable-looking shoes.

It was similar to the uniform Miss Martha had worn. I felt compelled to say, "You know you don't have to wear a uniform."

Savannah's lips quirked into a grin. "I know, but it just doesn't feel right for the housekeeper of Heartstone Manor to show up to work in jeans. I thought about khakis and a polo—that's the uniform I decided on for the house staff if it works for you—but the housekeeper—"

She spread her arms wide and gestured to the grand entrance hall. It was still dusty, the chandelier wreathed in cobwebs, but I got what she meant. When the house was fully restored to its glory, it would feel wrong to have the housekeeper strolling around in jeans.

"You look great," I said. "I like the gray better than the black your mom used to wear."

"Me too," Hope agreed. "More elegant and easier to keep clean. Black shows dust."

Savannah winked at her. "Exactly what I was thinking. The pattern is even better than the color for that. Keeps it looking neat even when it's not. And the skirt length is actually comfortable. I have a similar style in mind for summer. I also got myself a set of the khakis and polos the house staff will wear for when there's a messy job."

"I don't know how you found the time to get all this done," Hope said as we followed Savannah to the dining room.

"I put my mom on temporary retainer until we fill out the house staff. She knows so much and she can do a lot from home when Nicky's with her. He's in preschool this morning so she'll be training the new cook in the kitchen and serving breakfast. If you don't mind, I'd like to take that time to go over a few things with you."

"Works for me," I said, my hand on Hope's lower back as I ushered her into the dining room. "Have you eaten yet?"

"An hour ago, but I'll have coffee with you." We took our seats at the end of the table, me at the head and Hope to my right as before. I reached out to squeeze Hope's hand after we sat, and she slid it away, her palm leaving smears of moisture on the shiny dining room table, her eyes skipping away from mine.

Was she shy in front of Savannah, or was she withdrawing from me again?

I got it. Or I thought I did. It was second nature to Hope to keep herself safe. Even from me. Maybe especially from me. I kept reminding myself that just because having her in bed had changed everything for me didn't mean it had done the same for Hope.

Didn't that happen to couples all the time? One thinks sex equals love and the other is all about the orgasm.

Internally, I jolted. Love? Is that what this was?

I get Hope in bed and suddenly I'm in love?

I didn't know. I hadn't thought about love in years. Not like that. Not since Vanessa. Love was a trap and a lie. What I had with Hope wasn't some mushy sentiment, it was blood and bone. It was history and loyalty. I owed her more than lies about love. I wanted to give her more than words. I wanted to give her everything.

It was very possible that all she wanted from me was sex. Now that she'd had a taste and discovered she liked it, maybe that was all she was interested in.

The idea of that burned. I reminded myself that we had time for me to change her mind. Time to show her that I was good for more than orgasms.

Miss Martha came in, dressed in her old Heartstone uniform, similar to Savannah's except the dress was solid black. With a wink and a smile, she slid full plates in front of us. "I'll be right back with coffee."

Savannah looked down at her clipboard. "I'd like to give you an update on where we are."

"Go for it. You've worked a miracle in a few days."

"Not quite a miracle, but close enough." Savannah picked up her pen and pointed to the top item on her list. "The bedrooms are ready. All but Sterling's. As ordered, I did not touch that one."

"She can clean up her own mess," I said, irritated all over again by my baby sister's behavior. "When the room is no longer a toxic waste dump, feel free to put it on the rotation."

"Gotcha," Savannah said, underlining something on her list. "We have a cook, and we'll see how she works out. I've hired two day maids. I'm not sure that'll be enough with this many people in-house, but I thought we'd start small and add later."

"Security is a concern," I said, "so, at the moment, the fewer strangers in the house the better. I spent some time with my former employers putting together a security plan for the house. They'll send a team down this week to get started. The groundskeeper I hired used to work with us and he'll head security. I planned to put him up in the gatehouse, but I don't know what kind of state it's in."

Savannah scribbled something at the bottom of her list and murmured, "I'll get out there and take a look. As far as I know, it hasn't been used in years, so it might not be habitable."

"Hawk isn't picky. He'll be fine with whatever we have for him until we get the details worked out. I don't know when he's going to show up. Could be today, could be next week. Hopefully sooner. I'll try to get an update."

"A timeframe would be helpful," Savannah agreed. "As soon as we get everyone settled in today, I'll get our team working on the rest of the house. Unless you want a big crew in here, we'll have to take it room by room."

"Room by room works. Hope and I will be working out of the office here most of the time. Today we'll be out, so we won't need lunch. If anyone shows up to move in before we get back and they give you any trouble, just call."

"It'll be fine," Savannah said evenly. I wasn't so sure, but I liked her confidence.

When we finished eating, we followed Savannah through a hidden door in the rear of the dining room to a butler's pantry with dumbwaiters on either side, two long counters, and storage for linens, flatware, and everyday crystal. At the end of the butler's pantry, we found the elevator, door locked, and the back stairs that led to both the second floor and the lower level. We followed Savannah down, faint voices from below coming clearer with every step.

"I just want to walk you through what we've done down here so if you need anything from the kitchen or the laundry you know where to find it," she explained.

I needed the tour. I hadn't been in the lower level of Heartstone Manor in fifteen years and not often before that. The lower level was the staff's domain, lorded over by Miss Martha when I'd grown up here. Not only were the Sawyers not expected to venture below, we weren't exactly welcome.

While the upper levels of Heartstone Manor were dominated by dark wood paneling, tall windows, and hardwood floors, the lower level felt like it had come from a medieval castle.

The walls and floor were stone, the arching barrel ceiling high, giving the feeling of space while at the same time reminding me of a crypt. Here, the pipes were exposed and electrical wiring ran through conduit drilled into the stone.

The main kitchen was opposite the base of the stairs, doors open wide. A huge room over thirty feet across, it had a massive cast-iron and enamel stove on one end, and a huge island running down the center, shining copper pots and pans hung neatly on hooks along the wall. Woven baskets were organized on tall wood shelves, faded labels reading everything from *Root Vegetables* to *Spices*.

Miss Martha and the woman I assumed was the new cook stood in front of the baskets inspecting what looked like produce. Miss Martha looked up and spotted us. Now that we were away from the formality of the dining room, she was no longer the former housekeeper of Heartstone Manor. She moved to pull Hope into an embrace.

"You look gorgeous. Absolutely beautiful." Stroking a hand down Hope's shiny hair, she cupped her chin and turned Hope's face this way and that, shaking her head and smiling. "I heard you cleaned out Atlanta and brought home a whole new wardrobe. About damn time."

Hope hooked her arm through Miss Martha's elbow and gave her an affectionate squeeze. "When it's time to restock, you can come with me."

With a kiss on the cheek, Miss Martha said, "I'd love to." She caught Hope's left hand in hers and turned it so Hope's ring caught the light. "Exactly where it always belonged."

Hope flushed and Savannah came to her rescue. "Griffen and Hope Sawyer, this is Melissa Stiles. She'll be keeping us fed. For the moment, Mom is walking us through some of the procedures for the kitchen. I'll check with everyone else and see if we have any dietary requirements or food allergies I need to be aware of. I've asked Melissa to plan to serve a full breakfast and dinner every day. I think it's easiest—if it works for you—if lunch is less formal. I know you and Hope will be eating at home most days, but I think everyone else will stay in town. If that changes and we end up having a full crowd every day we can always add lunch to the schedule."

"Works for me," I said. Hope nodded in agreement.

Savannah moved to the door of the kitchen. "As you might remember, most of the lower level is storage. I did want to show you the laundry in case you need something in a rush. And there's a gym, but I'm fairly sure you'll want it updated. I think the others have been using the gym at the Inn, but I'm assuming you won't want to drive into town to work out."

"You assume right. I don't know about everyone else, but Hawk will definitely want workout facilities on-site."

Before we left the kitchen, I caught Miss Martha in a quick hug. "I know you're just helping Savannah get settled, but it's really good to see you here."

"Oh, I'll be around. Don't think you can get rid of me."

"I wouldn't dream of it," I said. With another squeeze, I released her and was following Savannah down the hall when I heard a discordant clang. It continued, sounding almost like a bell but wrong. Off.

"What the hell is that?" I asked, coming to a stop and trying to determine where the noise was coming from.

Chapter Thirty-Two

GRIFFEN

I THINK IT'S ONE OF THE HOUSE BELLS," SAVANNAH said. "I haven't had a chance to test them yet. We've mostly been using text messages."

Turning, she strode down the hall, past the kitchen to the staff dining room where one full wall was taken up by a series of neatly-labeled brass bells connected to wires that spread through the house, each one going to a different room.

The bell clanging so loudly was labeled *Rose Room*. Sterling's room. I rolled my eyes and gritted my teeth. "Ignore it. I'll deal with her in a few minutes. We'll have to come up with a better system than the bells. Unless you plan on having someone hanging out in here all day."

"Not likely," Savannah agreed. "I'll think of something. Maybe a messaging app? The Inn has an app the concierge uses, tagged to the guest so they can keep track of who needs what. I'll ask Royal how it works."

"I'm open to suggestions," I said, pretending not to hear my sister's demanding ring. The others followed my lead, and as one, we ignored Sterling. "Let's take a look at the gym and you can show Hope the laundry while I go upstairs and deal with Sterling."

"Better you than me," Hope murmured.

Savannah had been right; the gym needed a complete rehab. It was big, even had a hot tub and a sauna, though the hot tub was bound for the dump. I promised Savannah I'd get her a list of what we needed and jogged up the stairs to the main level. The sooner I got to the second floor, the sooner I could drag my sister's finger off that goddamn button.

I could move quietly when I wanted to. I crept down the hall to Sterling's room, swinging her door open with no warning to find her leaning against the wall, her face pasty and gray, her finger jabbing the button by the light switch over and over.

"What the fuck are you doing?" I demanded. All my sympathy for the grieving girl was gone, drained away by the incessant press of her finger on that button. "What do you want? Everyone in this house is busy. Working. You missed breakfast."

"I'm hungry. And I need my room cleaned," she whined.

"Meals are served in the dining room. You want to eat? Shower and get dressed like a normal adult human and show up downstairs. There will be no trays brought to your room so you can be a lazy slug."

Tears brimmed in Sterling's bloodshot blue eyes. "I don't know why you have to be so mean to me," she complained.

"Maybe because you vomited all over my wife last night after stumbling in drunk, falling down in the hall, and waking up the whole house."

"It was just you and Hope and Savannah. And Savannah is the housekeeper. It's her job to get up."

"The hell it is. Her job is to keep the house running, not to wait on you hand and foot. Don't ring that fucking bell again. If you want something, get your ass up and go get it."

"I bet *you* ring the bell," she muttered.

"It's my fucking house." And goddamn, did it feel weird to say that out loud. Tears spilled over Sterling's cheeks and I felt like an utter shit. "Look, if you want your money, you have to live here to fulfill the terms of the will. But it's my house. I'm sorry if you don't like that. I'm sorry if it's not fair. None of this bullshit is fair, but we all have to live with it."

"I'm over twenty-one. I'm an adult. You can't tell me what to do."

"If you want your money I can. Short of locking you up, I can't stop you from drinking. But if I catch you driving drunk, or if we have another scene like last night, there will be consequences."

Sterling crossed her arms over her chest and glared at me. With a sullen mutter, she said "Whatever, Dad."

I shuddered. I wasn't brother-of-the-year, but I didn't deserve to be compared to my father. "You owe Hope an apology."

"Fine."

Done with the stink of her room and her adolescent attitude, I headed for the door. "Savannah has hired some staff. Two day maids and a cook. You're welcome at meals, as long as you're sober. I've instructed Savannah and the day maids to stay out of your room until you clean it up. Once it's clean they'll help you keep it clean, but I'm not paying any of them enough to deal with this pigsty. Got me?"

"Fuck you, Griffen."

I ignored the slam of the door behind me. I knew this wouldn't be the last time we had this conversation. I felt guilty for the role I'd played in Sterling's lack of an upbringing but not guilty enough to put up with this bullshit.

Sterling wasn't unique among the Sawyers. We'd all gotten a raw deal on the parenting front in one way or another. But she was living in what amounted to a modern castle, all expenses paid, just waiting for a huge inheritance. All she had to do was stay reasonably sober and clean her goddamn room. It was hard to feel sorry for her in light of all that.

Since it seemed to be my morning for facing unpleasant realities, I crossed Sterling off my list and got out my phone. Pulling up the numbers I'd noted down when I'd seen Harvey the other day, I placed the calls I'd been dreading.

I found Hope a little later in the office, scrolling through emails on the laptop. "You ready to go?"

"Go where?" she asked absently, making a note on her pad.

"To see West. And then Cole and Ford." If I sounded grim it's because I felt that way. Finding out my father had been murdered was one thing, but it didn't touch the dread I felt at the prospect of seeing my brother.

Hopes eyes lifted to mine and she set down her pen. "That's quite an agenda. You ready for that?"

"Absolutely not. I have to do it anyway and I'm dragging you along with me. Let's go."

Hope stood and looked down at herself. She wore another sweater, this one a V-neck in soft blue, and another pair of those tight jeans that made her ass look spectacular. "I can't wear this. You have to wait—two minutes. Five minutes. I'll be down in five minutes."

"Hope—" I called after her.

She shouted back, "Five minutes."

She didn't have to dress up. This wasn't a business meeting. I could almost guarantee West would be wearing jeans. I'd known West since grade school. Once upon a time, we'd been good friends. Good enough that he'd given me a couch to crash on the night Prentice tossed me out and had driven me to the army recruitment office in Asheville the next morning.

I'd lost touch with West when I left Sawyers Bend, but unless he'd changed, he'd always been a good guy. Also not one who'd wear a suit to work.

Cole was Ford's lawyer. The Sawyers were paying his bills. He had to wear a suit. We didn't. One of the perks of being the guy writing the check.

Clearly, this logic made no impression on Hope. I don't know how she did it, but not quite ten minutes later, she strode down the stairs completely transformed, and not—thank God—in one of Edgar's ugly suits.

Her hair had been pulled back into a soft bun, a few strands loose around her face, catching the light. She wore a suit, but unlike the others, this one had a fitted jacket and a knee-length skirt that managed to be both completely modest and also make the most of her slender curves.

Discrete pearls circled her neck, one at each earlobe, and a slim gold watch sat on one wrist. She was the picture of professional elegance, and she was undeniably gorgeous. The possessive lover inside of me didn't want to let her out the door looking like that.

Everyone had written her off when she'd been plain, drab Hope. Now that the men in town could see her for the beauty she was, I'd have to beat them off with a stick. Fine, I could handle them. No one was taking Hope away from me.

"Let me grab my notebook from the office and I'll meet you at the door."

I watched her go, taking in the delicate pleats at the back of the suit jacket and the way it flared above her hips. I thought about following her to the office and bending her over the desk.

West wouldn't mind if we were late. Well, yes, he would. But there was always later. There'd be time for Hope and the desk later.

Chapter Thirty-Three

HOPE

THE TRAFFIC WASN'T BAD IN TOWN FOR A MIDMORNING in March. By summer, it would take almost half an hour to get from one end of Main Street to the other. For now, the streets weren't crowded and there was even parking here and there. I spied a spot in front of Sweetheart Bakery and called out, "Wait, stop here," pointing to the empty parking space.

Griffen pulled smoothly into the spot and stopped. He looked ready to ask me what the hell was going on when his eyes caught the sign on the door. "Do they have coffee here?"

"Amazing coffee," I told him. "I'm feeling the need for a cookie. Maybe toffee-chip. And a cappuccino. I thought we'd grab whatever West likes, kind of a peace offering."

"Bribing the police chief?" Griffen asked, one eyebrow raised. The tease in his eyes made me want to lean in and kiss him. I didn't, but I wanted to.

I raised an eyebrow back. "When was the last time you talked to West? Considering how close you two were in high school, I can't imagine you threw him out with the rest of us."

Griffen pressed his hand over his heart and shook his head. He was smiling, but regret was in his eyes. "Direct hit, Buttercup. Yeah, let's go get something sweet and bring the police chief a peace offering. It's been a long time. These better be some damn good cookies."

"Oh, you have no idea."

I hadn't seen Daisy in a few weeks. As expected, she wasn't in the front of the shop. I ignored the line and strolled by the brightly lit bakery cases, my mouth watering at the plates of brownies, cookies, and pastries. Loaves of bread and rows of pies. Cakes. I zeroed in on the toffee-chip cookies. Exactly what I wanted.

Daisy's best friend J.T. stood at the register ringing up a woman buying bread. I caught his eye and tilted my head toward the door to the kitchens. J.T. got my silent message and called in a singsong tone, "Daze. I have a surprise for you."

A minute later, Daisy came through the swinging door to the kitchens, her poof of chin-length curls bright red, eyes shining as she caught sight of me and my new look. Brushing her hands clean on her apron—a futile effort—she came around the end of the counter and pulled me into a hug, rocking me from side to side before she exclaimed, "Oh, shoot!" and jumped back, brushing streaks of flour off my new suit.

Grabbing my hands in hers, she jumped up and down. "Oh, my God! Oh, my God! You look amazing!" She dropped my hands and turned me around, smacking my butt. "Who knew Hope Daniels had an ass like that?"

Behind us, J.T. murmured, "I did." He winked at me and heat hit my cheeks even though I knew he wasn't really flirting. Despite Daisy acting like J.T. was her boyfriend, I was pretty sure if J.T. had a shot at seeing me or Griffen naked, he wouldn't pick me.

Daisy tugged a lock of my hair. "Fantastic cut. Where did you get this done? The highlights are perfect."

"Atlanta." That one word wasn't adequate to cover my adventure in Atlanta, but I didn't have time to tell her the whole story. I hadn't had time to do anything but try to keep up with all the changes in my life. Trying to deflect, I took a good look at Daisy's red hair. "You look great, too. I love the red, but what happened to the yellow? I thought you were going around the color wheel with your hair. Yellow, then orange, then red. Did I miss the orange?"

Daisy lifted a hand to her red hair, ignoring J.T.'s laugh behind us. Before she could answer, he called out, "Daze got tired of looking like a dandelion. Yellow is not a good look on poofy hair."

Behind her back, Daisy gave him the finger. J.T. had been her BFF since middle school and was immune to insult. Ignoring J.T., she said to me, "He's not wrong. You were just too nice to tell me."

I bit my lip and looked at the ceiling in exaggerated innocence. Not even Daisy's pretty features could make up for dandelion hair. A better friend might have told her—J.T. sure had—but Daisy was a smart woman, and she had a mirror. If she wanted bright yellow hair, who was I to tell her to change it?

"So, did I miss the orange?"

"Only kind of. I did it for a few days last week to give the red a good base, but—"

"Orange wasn't much better than the yellow," J.T. added honestly. At Daisy's glare, he said, "Sorry, babe. You know I love you, but I'm not gonna lie to Hope."

Daisy sighed. "The orange wasn't great. I'm not in love with this red, but I think one more layer and I'll have a nice cherry cola color." She brushed her hair back, leaving a streak of flour on her cheek. "So, who's this? And why do you have those rocks on your finger? What have you been up to?"

Uhh... I'd been planning to tell Daisy about Griffen and I getting married, I wouldn't have stopped in if I didn't want to, but now that the moment was here, my tongue was tied in knots.

Griffen saved me the trouble. Stepping closer, he wrapped his arm around my waist and held out his other hand. "We haven't met. I'm Griffen Sawyer. Hope's husband."

Daisy shook his hand, her brown eyes dazed. "I'm sorry, what? Hope's husband?" Those familiar eyes sharpened and turned to me. "How do you have a husband? I literally saw you two and a half weeks ago, and not only did you not have a husband, you didn't even have a boyfriend."

Griffen squeezed his arm around me and gave Daisy his best charming smile. "It's a long story, and we're on our way to see West. We thought we'd stop in and bring him a coffee."

Daisy got what he was saying and finally recovered, returning his handshake. "Well, it's nice to meet you, Griffen Sawyer. It's good to have you back in town." She said the last with a question in her voice, sending a raised eyebrow in my direction as if asking, *Is it? Really?*

"It's very good to have him back," I confirmed.

"And you're okay? This is good?"

"It's complicated," I admitted with a sideways glance at Griffen, "but good. I'm sorry I haven't told you before this. Things are kind of rushed and it's been absolutely crazy."

From behind Daisy, J.T. rolled his eyes. "You have to ask if she's good? Just look at the hottie standing next to her and the smile on her face. I've never seen Hope look so good. I have to go get Grams."

"We really can't stay long—" I said, but J.T. was already gone.

Daisy shrugged. "Grams would kill us if we didn't tell her you were here. Considering your news and all. But I'll get your order started."

"You know what West likes?" Griffen asked.

With the quirk of a grin, Daisy said, "Large Americano with a splash of half-and-half and a chocolate chip cookie or the cof-feecake. The police chief has a sweet tooth. And for you?"

"Get me whatever you're getting West," Griffen said, "that sounds great. Hope?"

"Butterscotch latte and two toffee-chip cookies." West wasn't the only one with a sweet tooth.

"How many of the toffee-chip cookies do you have?" Griffen asked. "We'll take at least half a dozen."

"That's about what I've got left."

"We should bring one of these cakes home," I said, my eye on a black forest cake in the case in front of me. The cherries gleamed against the rich chocolate frosting. "We're going to have a full house for dinner tonight. Maybe a little cake will smooth the way."

"I don't know if it'll survive driving around all afternoon, but I wouldn't say no to cake," Griffen said.

Handing Griffen his coffee and cookie, Daisy added, "I'll box it up for you and put it in the fridge in the kitchen. You can pick it up on your way back through town."

"Do it," Griffen said and broke off a piece of his cookie. As soon as it hit his tongue, his eyes slid shut with pleasure. That look. God. I wanted to get a dozen cookies and feed them to him naked.

Such an un-Hope thought. Griffen was turning me into a sex fiend.

Griffen's eyes opened and he swallowed the cookie slowly. "I'm going to need another cookie. This is amazing."

Daisy grinned. "My chocolate chip cookies are the best."

"Do you supply any of the businesses in town?" Griffen asked. "Savannah stocked our room at the Manor with your brownies. I bet the guests at the Inn would appreciate the same thing."

"I have a few arrangements with local businesses. The sandwich shop under Hope's apartment and a few others. I've never talked to anyone at the Inn, though."

It was a great idea. I was surprised I hadn't thought of it before. "We'll mention it to Royal when we meet with him this week."

Daisy had just given me my latte, though to be honest, I was more interested in the cookie, when Grams pushed through the swinging door from the kitchen, her gray eyes bright with anticipation. She swept around the counter, a tall, broad-shouldered woman with long gray hair in an intricate braid. She might have been the image of an elderly matron if not for the pink streaks in her hair and the Grateful Dead T-shirt she wore over a long denim skirt.

"You look beautiful, baby girl." She pulled me into a hug and rocked me side to side before closing my left hand in hers and examining the ring on my finger. Without comment on the ring, she looked up at Griffen.

"Griffen Sawyer. I wondered if you'd ever roll back into town. Don't blame you for staying away. I'd say I'm sorry to hear about your father, but I try not to lie."

Grams managed to startle a laugh out of Griffen. He held out his hand to her. "I'm sorry, I don't remember you."

"Eleanor Hutchins. I was a friend of your mama's. And Darcy. I'm not surprised you don't remember me, but I can promise you I won't be the only one in town glad to have you back. You can imagine, gossip has been swirling. Not that these two would know, Daisy always in the kitchen and J.T.

spending most of his time in school. You going to get your brother out of jail?"

"We're on our way to talk to West now," Griffen confirmed. I was surprised he said anything to a woman he claimed not to remember. Maybe it had been the mention of Darcy. Everyone had a soft spot for Darcy.

"Well, good luck. West wouldn't of locked him up if he didn't have a reason, but I just can't see that boy shooting your father. There was a long line of people who wouldn't mind putting a bullet in Prentice's head, but Ford was always too smart for those kind of shenanigans. I would've gone with poison, myself. Always a little surprised one of those wives didn't take care of the problem on their own. But then, Prentice could be a charmer when he wanted to be."

Again, I expected Griffen to be annoyed, but he just shook his head with a wry smile on his face. "When you think about it, it's almost a miracle he lived as long as he did."

Grams threw back her head and laughed, patting Griffen on the arm. "You always were a clever boy. We'll let you get settled in, but then we'll have you over for dinner one of these nights."

"We'd like that," Griffen said.

Grams' gray eyes shifted from friendly to hard. "You take good care of Hope. It's about damn time she got out from under Edgar's thumb. I don't want to see her under yours."

"No, ma'am," Griffen agreed. "Hope doesn't belong under anyone's thumb. I'm lucky to have her at my side, and don't think I don't know it."

Grams squeezed his arm before stepping back and turning to head to the kitchen. "Like I said, you always were a clever boy. And a good one, despite what your father did." To J.T. and Daisy, she said, "Finish up their order and let them go. They've got business to see to."

Another eye roll from J.T. "Yes ma'am," he called out. "I'm just going to box up this cake and tag it in the fridge. We close at five, but I'll be upstairs if you're running late."

Daisy finished up with our order and sent us off after tugging me aside and saying, "Late lunch? Later in the week or the weekend?"

"Definitely. Saturday? I can come into town or you can come out to the house."

Daisy's eyes widened. "You're staying in the Manor, aren't you? Of course, you are. Oh, I'm coming to the house. I'll bring lunch."

I gave her a hug, not minding the flour on her apron. "I'll see you then. Thanks for the cookies."

Griffen was halfway finished with his first cookie by the time we got back in the car. He hadn't bothered with the treats Savannah had left in our room, but he answered that question before I could ask. "If I'd known her baking was this good I would've eaten the brownies before you got to them."

"Over my dead body," I said without thinking.

My mind skipped back to the look on Griffen's face at his first bite of cookie. He wasn't stealing my brownies, but I could share. Especially if it was naked sharing. I squirmed in my seat.

Business, Hope. Sex later, business now. I sighed. I'd rather have sex now and forget our *business*.

Chapter Thirty-Four

HOPE

"WHAT WAS THAT FOR?"

I blinked at Griffen. What was what for? Oh, the sigh. Heat flooded my face. I was not going to tell him what I'd been thinking about. No way. I settled for, "Just thinking about how long a day it's going to be." Not entirely a lie.

He gave my hand a squeeze. "Things will settle down soon. Then we can find a new normal."

A new normal? I was married to Griffen Sawyer, living in Heartstone Manor. I hadn't seen my uncle Edgar in days. None of that would ever be *normal*, new or not. A twinge of guilt hit at the thought of Uncle Edgar, one I tried to push away.

He replaced you, I reminded myself. *He told you to go off with Griffen and have babies. And it's not like he's called. Not once.*

From Uncle Edgar, my mind skipped to the idea of babies. Griffen's babies.

I let out another sigh. There was too much stuff on my mind, and most of it I couldn't do anything about. Griffen and I were being safe, except for that one time. There wouldn't be any babies any time soon.

And Uncle Edgar was a grown man. He loved me in his own way. I had to believe that. He'd sacrificed years of his life to raising a child he'd never wanted. Who was I to expect him to want me around forever?

He'd given me a home, an education, a job. Apparently, he'd even given me a husband. For a while. That was a heck of a lot more than most people got.

The car came to a stop and I looked up in surprise. We were here already? I had to love early spring traffic in town.

The Sawyers Bend Police Department was adjacent to the Town Hall, connected by a covered breezeway. With their tall, arching, white-framed windows and white columns, both the police department and the town hall were stately, the epitome of turn-of-the-century charm.

We climbed the brick steps to the big white doors and pushed through to find the receptionist waiting for us. I couldn't remember her name, but she knew mine. Her eyes skittered past Griffen to me. "Hope. And, uh, Mr. Sawyer. The Chief is waiting for you. I'll show you back to his office."

She glanced over her shoulder at Griffen again before turning away. We followed her down the hall where she left us at a door bearing the nameplate *Weston Garfield*. Griffen rapped his knuckles twice on the door before pushing it open.

West was already standing and coming around the desk, hand held out in front of him, a smile on his face. "Griffen, good to see you. Sorry for the reason you're back in town, but it's good to see you."

Griffen took his hand in a firm shake and leaned in to clap him on the back in that thing men did that was kind of a hand-shake and kind of a hug. West clapped him on the back in return, and I thought I saw a flash of relief in his eyes.

They separated and West held out his hand to me, not missing the ring on my finger or my new clothes. Weston Garfield never missed much. "Hope, thank you for coming. Please, sit."

He gestured to the seats in front of his desk, smiling when I handed him his coffee and cookie. "For me? From Sweetheart?"

"Hope needed a latte and a toffee-chip cookie. We asked Daisy what you liked," Griffen said, taking the last bite of his own cookie.

"Thanks. You have no idea how much I needed this." West took a sip of his Americano and ran his fingers through his thick, dark hair. "The morning has been a week long already."

"Everything okay?"

"Just life," West said, rolling back his shoulders. "Car acci-dent. Two break-ins. A tourist claims his room at the Inn was robbed."

Griffen straightened in his chair. "Was it? Is there a problem with break-ins at the Inn?"

"Not until recently, but you might want to talk to Royal and Tenn about that." West broke off a piece of his cookie and looked deliberately from Griffen to me and back again, stopping for another glance at the ring on my finger. "Are the rumors true? You two are married?"

"They're true." Griffen reached over to take my hand in his. West stared at both of us for a long moment, and I knew that he knew our marriage had to do with Prentice and not anything between the two of us.

I pulled my hand from Griffen's and broke off a piece of my own cookie. I didn't mind the fiction of our whirlwind courtship and marriage with the rest of the town, but West was smart and he wasn't interested in gossip. He was interested in the truth. I didn't want to talk about the truth.

"Hope? Are you good?"

Why did people keep asking me that? Did I seem that helpless? "I'm great, West."

His eyes rested on my hair, then my face for a moment too long before his lips curved into a smile. "I can see that."

Making a disgruntled noise in the back of his throat, Griffen reached out and took my hand again, holding it tightly in his. Leaning forward, angling his shoulder closer to me he said, "You don't need to look out for Hope, Weston. That's my job."

West nodded like he'd acknowledged some message from Griffen in man code that I'd completely missed. "I can see that, too. You're going to want to keep an eye on her. We have your brother in jail, but that doesn't change the fact that your father was shot in the head in his own home in broad daylight."

"You don't think Ford did it?" Griffen asked.

"It doesn't matter what I think, Griffen. What matters is the evidence. It all points at Ford. We have numerous public arguments in the weeks leading up to Prentice's murder. Open threats to disinherit Ford and cut him out of the family businesses. Ford's car seen leaving the Manor at high speed right around the coroner's estimated time of death.

"The murder weapon was found in Ford's closet with his fingerprints on it. Footprints from his shoes were in the flowerbeds outside the sunroom by the office. We think he parked in front and then came in through the French doors to take Prentice by surprise."

"And there's nothing else? Nothing to show that someone else could have been in the house?"

"Nothing we've been able to find. I swear to you, Griffen, I went over that house and the grounds with a fine-tooth comb. Ford doesn't have an alibi. Do I think he walked in the house and shot your father in the head? No, I don't. I just can't see it. The list of people happy to see your father dead is so fucking long I don't know where to start. But the truth is I don't have to because we have the murder weapon and it was in your brother's possession."

"What does Ford say?"

"You haven't seen him yet?"

"We're meeting up with Cole in half an hour to head out to the county jail."

"Have you seen him since—"

"Nope."

West the Police Chief disappeared and Griffen's old friend took his place. He shook his head in sympathy. "Sorry, man. It's good to have you back in town, but this is a bitch of a situation to walk into. I wish I could help, but my hands are tied. I won't compromise the evidence. Not even for an old friend."

Griffen let out a sigh. "I wouldn't ask."

I was relieved to see West give a nod of understanding before changing the subject.

"I know you left this town in the dust, but I kept an eye out. I know who you used to work for. Did a little digging. Your army record has some interesting blank spots. Considering all that and what happened to your father, I'm assuming you have plans for a security upgrade at the Manor."

"We were in Atlanta a few days ago. The Sinclairs are coming down with a team." Griffen propped his foot on his knee and took a long sip of his coffee. "Man, it's a mess. I don't think the locks have been upgraded in forty years. Forget the alarm system. What they have is barely worth it. We'll have a team at the house for a while. My old office manager is salivating at the invoices she's going to throw my way."

West let out a low whistle. "I don't want to think about what it's going to cost for Sinclair Security to secure a property the size of Heartstone Manor. Even if you're getting the former employee discount."

"Tell me about it."

"What about on-site security? I heard you got Savannah to take over Miss Martha's job. Good move there. She was wasted waiting tables. Heard she's got Billy Bob on the job and is doing some hiring. Please tell me on-site security is on the list."

"I've got a guy. Hawk Bristol. He was in the Army with the Sinclairs and me. You could look into him, but if you think my record has blank spots—" Griffen shook his head. "Hawk's not what I'd call social, but he's a genius at finding a weak spot, and he's relentless. The Sinclairs managed to get him to Atlanta, but the city is too crowded for him. He's an outdoor guy and he's into gardening. I don't know if you've seen the state of the grounds at Heartstone, but he was all over the chance to run security and get his hands in the dirt at the same time. Added bonus for being surrounded by thousands of acres of mountain and an hour from the closest city."

"Are your guys going to be pissed if I show up and check things out during the install and when Hawk gets here?"

Griffen shook his head again. He broke off a piece of his second cookie, chewed and swallowed, thinking before he said, "I've been gone a long time, West. Aren't many people I missed, but you're one of them. Hope trusts you and I trust her judgment. You're always welcome at Heartstone. When the dust settles I wouldn't mind going out to get a beer."

West cracked a grin. "I was hoping you'd say that. Look, there's nothing I can do about Ford. Not as things stand right now. But if you need anything else, you know where to find me."

Griffen leaned forward to set his empty coffee cup on West's desk. Something about West's words had caught his instincts. *You know where to find me.* "What do you know?"

West gave him a level stare. "Nothing concrete. But Prentice had his fingers in a lot of pies and he never minded pissing people off. Now you're back, and the whole family is moving into the Manor, bringing it back to life. You married Hope. That's a lot of change. Some people might see it as a new beginning, but there are a lot of people who'd love to see the sun set on the Sawyer empire."

"I'm not my father," Griffen said.

"And thank God for that. I don't know how you two hooked up, and I'm not asking, at least in an official capacity. Maybe I'll get it out of you over a beer." At that, Griffen let a wry smile curve his lips, and I ducked my head. West went on, "But for a lot of the town, seeing Hope happy will make a difference in how they see you."

I wasn't sure I liked the way that sounded. I *was* happy. Mostly. Freaked out about the situation we were in and everything being upside down so fast, but being with Griffen made me happy. Not the thought that it would end in five years, but everything else.

The way West had put it reminded me I was a tool, put into place by Prentice and my uncle Edgar for reasons we still didn't know.

I was useful to Griffen. I wanted to be useful to Griffen. Of course, I did. I cared about him. I more than cared about him.

I wanted to be useful, but I didn't want to be a tool. Anyway, I wasn't sure West was right. Why would the town care if I was happy?

"I'm not sure my moods make that much of a difference," I said, sipping my butterscotch latte and suddenly wishing Griffen and I were back in his office going through paperwork, the door shut against the rest of the world.

The smile on West's face was gentle. "Was Griffen behind this change?" He gestured at my hair and suit. I nodded, my throat tight, not sure where he was going with his question.

"Nice to see he doesn't underestimate you. Edgar did. And so did you. You've always underestimated yourself. I don't think there's a single person I know who doesn't like you, Hope. You're kind and generous. Thoughtful. The people in this town appreciate that. They appreciate you. Gossip about you two getting married has been spreading like wildfire, and while nobody's quite sure what to think of Griffen, everyone is hoping for a fairytale for you."

I had no idea what to say to that. I loved this town. I always had. When Harvey read the will, when I realized what I'd have to do, I hadn't had a question. Not just because it was Griffen. Because it was Sawyers Bend.

It never occurred to me that the town might love me back.

Knuckles rapped on the door, saving me from coming up with a response. West called out, "What is it?"

Chapter Thirty-Five

HOPE

HE DOOR SWUNG OPEN TO REVEAL A TALL, LEAN MAN with short dark hair and horn-rimmed glasses. With his expensive suit and shiny shoes, blue eyes and square jaw, he looked like a model in an upscale menswear ad. Except for the shadows in his eyes.

Cole Haywood had always been a top-notch defense attorney, but since his wife died in childbirth, he'd become a different man, burying himself in his work. I didn't know him well, but I did know he used to smile. It had been a while since anyone had seen Cole Haywood smile.

"Sorry to interrupt," he said. "I can wait if you aren't done. I saw Griffen's car and thought I'd catch you here. We can ride together to county."

Griffen stood to shake Cole's hand. "How did you know it was my car?"

"Not many Maseratis in Sawyers Bend."

"Probably true," Griffen agreed.

The walk out to Cole's Mercedes sedan was awkward, to say the least. His cool blue eyes rested on Griffen and myself for only moments, but they left me with the sense that he saw all the way to the bone.

West was sharp and didn't miss a detail, but underneath it, I always felt like he was on my side. On Griffen's side. Not so with Cole Haywood. Cole was on Ford's side. As he should be, considering he was Ford's defense attorney. I guess I'd expected him to be comforting. He was anything but.

We were pulling out of town when he spoke. "Harvey wouldn't let me see all of Prentice's will. He claimed aspects of it are confidential." In the rearview, his glance landed on me before moving to Griffen. Again, I had the feeling he knew more than he should. More than anyone should.

"Harvey was Prentice's lawyer, not mine," Griffen said, evenly. "But I can confirm that Prentice had written Ford out of the will."

"That's what Harvey said. Only a few weeks before he was killed."

"You think he did it? Ford?" Griffen asked. I hated the tone in his voice. Distant. Cold. I couldn't help remembering that he and Ford had once been like twins. The best of friends.

"It's not my job to decide if he did it. My job is to convince a jury that he didn't."

"Do you think you can do that?" Griffen asked, and now his voice wasn't cold. It was dangerous. For all his anger at his brother, Griffen believed wholeheartedly that Ford was innocent of killing Prentice.

Cole shot a frustrated glance at Griffen before shaking his head. "I'm not a magician. West reviewed the evidence with you?"

"He did."

"Then you know what we're dealing with. Telling a jury that Ford is too smart to have hidden the murder weapon in his closet along with the shoes the murderer was wearing—that doesn't sound like much, considering the prosecutor is going to bring up the fights, Ford being disinherited, and your father's general assholery."

"And isn't that your job?" Griffen asked tightly. "To make them believe it?"

"Do you want to risk your brother's life on that?"

"Ford didn't kill our father," Griffen said.

"You don't know that," Cole countered, annoyance breaking through his cool veneer. "Neither do I. And if we can't know it, I can't promise you that I can make a jury believe it. Not with the evidence stacked against him."

Griffen's jaw tightened. He stared out the window in silence before saying, "Then what's your plan? Are you just going to give up?"

"Of course not. Not that it should matter, but I consider Ford a friend. I don't want him rotting in prison for a crime I'm pretty sure he didn't commit. But sometimes it's not about innocent or guilty. Not when innocence looks like guilt. Not when insisting on that innocence could land him in prison for the rest of his life. Or worse, with a needle in his arm. My job is to look out for my client's best interests."

"And those are?" The dangerous tone was back in Griffen's voice. He didn't like what Cole was saying any more than I did. Right and wrong, black and white, guilt or innocence. On paper, it seemed so clear-cut.

Quietly, Cole said, "The prosecution is open to a plea."

"No fucking way. If he pleads guilty to murder it'll follow him for the rest of his life."

"If he pleads innocent and he loses, the rest of his life will be spent behind bars. If he's lucky and he has a rest of his life. The prosecutor is suggesting she'll ask for the death penalty."

Griffen's jaw went tight again. He focused on the trees flashing by outside the car and said nothing else. Not when we pulled into the parking lot at the county jail. Not when we went through security. Not when Cole turned to me and said, with an accusing look at Griffen, "Hope, you shouldn't come in. Why don't you wait here? We won't be long."

I slipped my hand into Griffen's and squeezed tight. "I'll stay with Griffen, but thanks. Don't worry about me."

Cole shook his head and turned to the visiting room. I kept my eyes straight ahead, very aware of Griffen's fingers wrapped around mine. He hadn't let go. He was holding onto me with everything he had. I wished I could blink my eyes and spirit us anywhere else.

I don't know what I expected to see when Ford walked into the room. That Ford had changed, I guess. That he was pale and thinner. Whatever I expected, it wasn't what I got. The door to the sparse, concrete block room opened and Ford walked through, looking just like he always did, except wearing an orange jumpsuit instead of a suit.

I definitely didn't expect how odd it was to see him in the same room with Griffen. I'd forgotten how much they looked alike. Ford's hair was dark brown to Griffen's sandy blond, but otherwise, they could have been twins.

I must have blocked out how much Ford reminded me of Griffen for all those years we worked together after Griffen left.

Seeing them face each other across the metal table, my heart ached for all they'd lost. Ford had screwed Griffen over, no question. Griffen had a right to his anger. But I knew that Ford regretted it. Knew he'd missed his older brother. And, knowing Ford, I wasn't surprised he had too much pride to show it now that they were face to face.

Ford sat, resting his chained hands on the metal table in front of him. "Did you come to gloat?"

Griffen said nothing, just stared at his brother in silence and waited. For what, I didn't know.

Ford turned his hard gaze to me. "Hope. What the hell are you doing here? What was Edgar thinking letting you visit the county jail?"

"Don't talk to her like that," Griffen said.

Ford leaned back, a sneer distorting his mouth. "Oh, so it's like that. You have plenty of forgiveness for Hope, but nothing for the rest of us?"

"Hope doesn't need forgiveness. She didn't do anything wrong," Griffen said, his eyes as hard as Ford's.

I blinked, sure I'd misheard him. Did he have temporary amnesia? Everyone in this room knew what I'd done. Griffen most of all.

"Right," Ford said, giving me a look of confusion before he aimed one of disgust at Griffen. "Because I remember her torpedoing your engagement and getting you thrown out of town—"

Griffen's eyes were ice, but his voice was calm. "Funny you remember it that way. Because I remember you selling me out to Dad, marrying my fiancée, and cheering Dad on as he threw me out of my home. And then I remember the bunch of you blaming the whole thing on a teenager who told a secret. A big secret, sure, but Hope made *one* bad decision. That doesn't stack up next to what you and Dad did. So, let's just drop this story of Hope being the bad guy in that scenario."

Both Ford and I stared at Griffen in shock. When had he decided I wasn't the bad guy?

The idea wouldn't fit in my brain. I'd been the villain in this story for so long. Was Griffen just trying to needle Ford, or did he really believe what he'd said? I was afraid to trust that he might have forgiven me.

Griffen rolled a shoulder back as if shrugging off the past like an old coat. "I didn't come here to talk about ancient history. I'm not the same boy who walked out of Sawyers Bend fifteen years ago. None of us are the same. I don't care about all that. I care about now. What are we going to do to get you out of here?"

I don't think I'd seen Ford show so much emotion in years. He was usually so in control, so calm and even-tempered. Now, his eyes flared wide with shock yet again.

Before he could speak, Cole cut in. "The judge refused to grant bail."

Ford shot an annoyed look at his lawyer. Eyes back on Griffen, he said, "You don't think I did it."

"I know you didn't do it."

"How? Because you did?"

At that, Griffen laughed. "I wouldn't waste my time killing Prentice. He got all of me he was going to get years ago. And I have a rock-solid alibi."

"Do you have an extra? Because I could use one."

They shared a grin, and for a millisecond I shot back into the past when these two men had been boys who grinned at each other exactly like that ten times a day. All too soon the moment ended.

"Don't enter a plea," Griffen said. "Not yet. Prentice has only been dead a week. West hasn't been able to find anything new, but let me look around. Investigations aren't my specialty, but I used to work with the best. I'll get someone down here to dig up something Cole can use—"

"The clock is ticking," Cole said from where he leaned against the wall. "The prosecutor isn't going to leave the plea deal open forever. And once it's gone— The rest of your life is a lot to gamble with."

Ford looked away.

"It's been a fucking week," Griffen growled at Cole. "A week. We need more time."

Cole shook his head. "You don't get it. This is an open and shut case. It doesn't matter if he did it. What matters is they have a mountain of evidence against Ford and this is a high-profile case. Have you thought about the optics? Ford Sawyer, heir to billions, murders his father in an attempt to take control of the Sawyer empire and gets caught in the act. It's a miracle the town isn't overrun with news vans right now. If your father hadn't been so insistent on privacy, kept the Sawyer name out of the papers, they'd be here already. A case like this will make the prosecutor's career. She can't wait to put him on the stand and make him look like an entitled, rich asshole who thought he could get even more by killing his father."

"I didn't kill my father!" Ford shouted, slamming his hands on the table, the chains clattering against the metal.

"It doesn't fucking matter," Cole roared back. "She's going to destroy you, Ford. She'll drag up the past—you conspiring to get Griffen disinherited and stealing his fiancée. Gradually taking over more and more of the family business. It shows long-range planning. You got rid of the original heir, edged out your other siblings, and when the time was right, you took out your father so you could have it all."

Ford opened his mouth, but Cole cut him off. "Shut the fuck up. Unless you can hand me a single piece of evidence that disproves the prosecution's case, then just shut the fuck up. I'm not here to defend your honor, you asshole. I'm here to save your life."

"They're not going to give him the death penalty," Griffen said.

"And you know that for sure? You can guarantee it? Because that's what the prosecutor wants. I'll give it everything I have to get her to back down to life in prison, but goddamn it, Ford, is that what you want? Life in prison? Is your honor worth giving up your future?"

Griffen took a deep breath. I wanted to take his hand again, to offer comfort, but I didn't like the way Ford was looking at us.

"Give me three weeks," Griffen said, reaching across the table to his brother. "Three weeks. If my guy can't find anything, then we can reconsider. We've got a lot of shit between us, but you're my brother. I'm not going to give up on you. Don't give up on yourself."

Ford stared across the table, examining Griffen for an endless minute before shrugging a shoulder. "Why the hell not? It's not like I'm going anywhere."

"Ford," Cole cautioned.

"Three weeks," Griffen said, ignoring Cole's scowl.

"Three weeks," Ford agreed.

Cole barely spoke to us on the ride back to town. I didn't know anything about criminal law, but I'd always thought these things took forever to get to trial. Why was he in such a rush to get Ford to plead guilty? He was known as one of the best— Prentice had always joked that if he ever got caught he'd want Cole Haywood on his side.

Caught at what, I didn't want to know.

Maybe Cole didn't want a high-profile loss on his record. He'd said there would be media coverage. Was he trying to avoid coming out the loser?

Cole dropped us off at the police station with only, "I'll be in touch," as a goodbye. That was fine; I think Griffen and I were both tired of hearing what Cole had to say.

We retrieved the black forest cake from J.T. and headed back to Heartstone Manor. It was late afternoon, and we'd both missed lunch. I was about to suggest texting Savannah to ask for a snack when we pulled up to the end of the drive, right at the point where we could continue straight to the courtyard in front of the house or turn left to drive around through the porte-cochère to the garages.

We'd been parking in the garage for the last few days, an easy choice, considering they were one of the only places in the house in good condition. And an easier choice just then considering the cars that crowded the front courtyard.

It looked like Griffen's siblings had finally come home. I glanced over at Griffen, saw the fatigue drawn on his face. "Why don't we forget work for the rest of the day? You were saying earlier you needed to go for a run. I'll cover for you. Go change and get out of here for a little bit. Clear your head before you have to face dinner with the family."

Relief washed through his eyes, but he shook his head. "I'm not abandoning you to my family."

"I have to live with them, Griffen, and I know your family. At this point, probably better than you do. Anyway, I wasn't exactly going to mingle. I thought I'd see if Savannah needed any help getting everyone settled, and if she didn't, I'd hide in our room until dinner."

Griffen's green eyes warmed. He reached up and rubbed the back of his fingers across my cheek. "I'm a lucky bastard, you know that? I don't deserve you."

"Maybe not, but you're stuck with me anyway. Now go, get some fresh air. Shut your brain off for a while."

He leaned in and pressed a hard kiss to my mouth before parking in his spot and heading into the house. We went our separate ways, me looking for Savannah while Griffen peeled off up the back staircase to change and escape Heartstone Manor. Just for a little while.

Chapter Thirty-Six

GRIFFEN

MY FEET THUDDED ON THE GRAVEL IN A FAMILIAR rhythm that set my mind at ease. It was March in the mountains. Cold and damp, the sun already dropping in the sky though it wasn't yet five o'clock.

I didn't care about the cold or the damp. How did Hope still know me so well? I'd needed this. The fresh air in my lungs, the solitude. I felt guilty leaving her at the house, though not guilty enough to stay. I hoped she didn't regret her suggestion.

I was still reeling from seeing Ford. It had been like looking in a mirror. All these years apart, and somehow, I'd imagined he'd changed, imagined he'd look as much like a stranger as he felt. I'd been wrong.

I needed to call Cooper, see if he could send someone down to look into things a little more. I understood West when he said his hands were tied. I didn't blame him, but Ford was my brother. He hadn't killed our father.

I couldn't stand the idea he'd serve time for a murder he didn't commit. Part of me hated him, but only a part. He was still my brother, and while he hadn't looked changed by his week in jail, decades in prison would turn him into another person. I didn't want that for him. How could I?

At the end of the long drive to Heartstone Manor, I turned right, heading up the mountain, further away from town. My legs and lungs burned. I ran hills in Atlanta on a regular basis, but Atlanta hills had nothing on the mountains. Maybe I wouldn't get out of shape living here after all.

The rumble of an engine sounded behind me, growling up the mountain, drawing close faster than I would've expected. The turns were tight up here. Most people took it slow. I glanced over my shoulder, realizing twilight had set in while I'd been focused on my burning quads. In the shadows, I'd be difficult to see. I should have grabbed my reflective jacket, but I hadn't bothered. I'd just wanted to get the hell out of the house and clear my head.

I slowed down and moved to the uneven gravel on the side of the road. The road opened up ahead, giving the truck a wide sightline and plenty of room to hit the gas and pass me by.

It didn't. The rumble of the engine slowed and the truck drifted to the edge of the road, the tires crunching gravel as it drew closer. Closer.

Another glance over my shoulder. In the shadows of twilight, it was too dark to see who was at the wheel. Not short. Not wide. Other than that, it could have been anyone.

When that anyone slammed their foot on the gas and bar-reled straight for me, the revving engine a roar in my ears, I didn't have to think. I dove off the side of the mountain, catching myself with my hands and rolling, letting the rocks and fallen trees beat me to a pulp. Better the rocks and trees than getting flattened by a pickup truck.

The screech of brakes penetrated through the crack of tree limbs and the thud of my head on the dirt. Deliberately, I kept my limbs loose, not fighting gravity, using my arms to protect my head and neck. The incline was steep enough to keep me moving but not so steep that I was plummeting dangerously fast.

I weighed the risks. What was worse, slamming into a rock or tree trunk the wrong way or stopping myself while I was still in view of the truck?

Whoever had been driving had planned to hit me. That much was clear. If they'd come with the intent to kill me, they'd be armed. The light was bad, and I was shielded by trees, but I wasn't going to bet my life on my would-be murderer having bad aim.

A spray of gravel, the squeal of tires, and the truck took off— as far as I could tell. I slowed my descent, rolling to a stop at the base of a narrow pine tree.

Fuck. Once upon a time, I'd known these mountains like the back of my hand.

Once upon a time was a long fucking time ago. I'd left my phone back at the house, just wanting quiet for my run. Stupid. Stupid and careless. My father was dead, and his killer was still out there somewhere. I couldn't afford to be stupid and careless.

My life wasn't just about me anymore. If I died, everything Sawyer would pass to Bryce. My siblings would lose their liveli-hoods, their home. Hope would be alone with no one to look out for her.

Looking back up the side of the mountain, I thought about the direction I'd run, and how far I'd come after I'd turned off the Heartstone drive. Below me, the fading light showed an endless sea of trees and not much else.

I could drag my bruised and bleeding body back up the side of the mountain and follow the road back to the house, but I'd be exposed and vulnerable if the pickup truck came back for another shot. Or I could risk a hike through the woods and hope I knew where I was.

I thought I did. Standing, I used the tail of my shirt to wipe my face, aggravated to see the gray fabric rusty with blood. Fuck. Another glance at the sky and I started to move. I'd come a long way by the road, straight out from the house and then right on the main road perpendicular to the drive. Theoretically, if I headed away from the road, angled back the way I'd come, I should end up near Heartstone.

My brisk pace turned into a trudge sooner than I would have liked. With each step, I felt every rock and branch and log I'd bounced over as I'd rolled down the side of the mountain. Somewhere, I'd slammed my still healing shoulder into a log or a rock and it ached like a bitch. I had a cut on my forehead that wouldn't stop bleeding, the salty, warm fluid stinging my eyes. Despite the cold, I wanted to take off my shirt and use it to bandage my head, but the temperature was dropping as the sun set. Until I found a solid landmark, I wouldn't run the risk of hypothermia.

No water, no food, no phone. Fucking idiot. As I followed the bearing I'd set, I castigated myself. No more running without a phone and a weapon. Maybe no running by myself for a while. I'd have to get the gym at the Manor set up.

I kept my mind busy running through lists of things to do. Otherwise, I'd start to worry. What if I didn't find the house? What would happen when Hope realized I was missing?

Ignoring my aches and pains, I stepped up my pace as the ground leveled out. A glimmer of light peeked through the trees. Finally. I never thought I'd be grateful Heartstone Manor was so fucking big. Gradually, step by step, the house took shape through the trees, looming over the flat land surrounding it. Lights flickered in windows here and there.

Relief flowed through me and I found the energy to break into a slow jog. I just had to get to the house. Call West. Get cleaned up before anybody saw me. I headed for the side door by the mudroom. Nobody used it since everyone came in through the garage or the front door, but I was betting it would be unlocked with everyone moving in. If I could get through the mudroom, I'd use the elevator to go upstairs, and from there it was a short walk to our room.

The door handle resisted before it turned, the hinges squeaking as I pushed my way into the mudroom, relieved to find it empty. I strode across the hall to the elevator, also empty. So far, so good.

A short ride up, the elevator doors opened, and I ran out of luck. Royal was walking by and stopped, startled by the sound of the metal grate as I pushed it out of my way. His eyes landed on me and his face went pale. I must look like shit.

"What the fuck happened to you? You look like you got hit by a car."

"Close enough. Lower your voice," I said, checking the hall. Empty. I turned and jogged toward my room, Royal on my heels. "Do you have your phone?"

"Yeah, why?"

"Do you have West's number in there?" I asked. I didn't want to call in front of Hope if she was in the room, but we needed West.

"Yeah. What you want me to tell him?"

"Tell him there was an accident and I need him at the Manor but to keep it quiet. Come in the side door by the mudroom."

Royal focused on his phone but followed me, lingering just outside the door of the master suite, knowing without my saying that I didn't want Hope to hear the call. If I could jump in the shower before she saw me, she wouldn't worry.

I opened the door, Royal talking quietly behind me. The coast was clear. He followed me in, shutting and locking the door behind us. I heard him say, "Yeah, good, I'll meet you downstairs and bring you up. No, he's in one piece but he looks like hell. Didn't tell me what happened."

"You'll let him in?" I asked, scanning the room for Hope.

"Yeah, I've got it, but what the fuck, Griffen? What happened?"

"Griffen?" Hope's voice came from the bedroom or the closet. Crap. Then louder, "Griffen! Oh, my God, Griffen!"

I turned, holding my hands up. "It looks worse than it is, I swear." I had no idea if I was lying. I was pretty sure I wasn't. I didn't feel great after taking a nosedive off the side of the mountain, but head wounds bleed like a bitch and all the blood on my T-shirt made things look worse than they were.

She crossed the room and stood in front of me, arms tight around her chest, hugging herself, breath coming in rough gasps.

"I'm fine, Buttercup. Don't freak out. Everything is okay."

"What happened? Tell me what happened right now, or I swear to God—"

"I'd like to know what happened, too," Royal added, his arms crossed over his chest, his expression far more concerned than I would have expected.

"Hold on a second, and I'll tell you." I went to the bathroom and grabbed a washcloth, running water on it. The sight of my face in the mirror told me exactly why Hope was freaking out so badly. My attempts to wipe up the blood had only spread it all over the place, my hair crimson and sticking up in spikes. The cut on my forehead was close to the hairline and not that bad, but it still bled sluggishly.

I shoved my head under the sink faucet, letting the water wash away sweat and dirt and dried blood. Knowing Hope and

Royal only had so much patience, I grabbed a towel and dried my hair and face, keeping the washcloth to hold against the cut.

I came back out to the sitting room to find Royal positioned by the window, probably watching for West's car. Hope hovered in the middle of the room, her eyes stark, still hugging herself.

"Tell me what happened. I'm not waiting for West to get here," she demanded.

Chapter Thirty-Seven

GRIFFEN

I WAS ON THE ROAD, ON MY RUN, AND A TRUCK CAME UP behind me. I thought it was going to pass, but instead, it tried to run me down. I jumped off the shoulder, rolled down the mountain a little, and walked back to the house. I look worse than I am, I promise. I got banged up a little, but I'm not hurt."

Hope reared back at those words and swung her fist into my sore shoulder. "Don't tell me you're not hurt, you asshole. There's blood everywhere. Your legs are scratched up and your clothes are torn. We should take you to the hospital. As soon as we talk to West, we'll go to the hospital." Her words spilled out in a rush, gaining speed with each one.

"I don't need the hospital, Hope. Calm down."

"Don't tell me to calm down. Now is not the time for calm. You got hit by a truck!" The last came out in a screech.

"I didn't get hit by a truck," I hedged. "I'm fine." She wasn't buying it.

Fists flailing, Hope screeched again, "Don't tell me you're fine. You're covered in blood."

"Hope—" I sent Royal a beseeching look. I couldn't remember ever seeing Hope this wound up. Ever. With everything we'd been through, she'd been cool as a cucumber. She'd walked right into the prison earlier and hadn't blinked.

It occurred to me that the stress of the last week had been piling up on her, all while she acted like our lives were business as usual.

Eventually, it would have been too much for anyone, but this? Her new husband coming home beaten and bloody after admitting he'd almost been run over? That was enough to push even the calmest person over the edge.

Royal gave a helpless shrug but said, "Hope, he's okay. West is on his way and we'll figure out—"

"Don't you patronize me, Royal Sawyer. Just because he says he's fine and you say he's fine doesn't mean he's actually fine. We need to go to the hospital. He could have internal bleeding or something."

Not sure what else to do, I crossed the room and roughly pulled Hope into my arms, wrapping her tight. Her pulse fluttered in her throat, her breath shallow. Her fingers closed on my shirt, gripping tight. "Griffen," she breathed.

I dropped my mouth to her ear. "I promise you I'm okay. I wouldn't lie to you, especially not about this. Do you trust me?"

She leaned back and looked up into my eyes, the warm brown of hers brittle with fear. "You know I do. I wouldn't be here if I didn't."

"Then trust me when I tell you I'm okay." From the corner of my eye, I saw Royal straighten and head for the door. West was fast. Taking advantage of being alone, I cupped Hope's face in my hands and kissed her, trying to tell her everything I didn't have the words for with the press of my mouth to hers.

When I pulled back, she said, "You promise you're okay?"

"I promise. I'm banged up and I'll probably be bruised all to hell tomorrow, but I didn't break anything, and the cut on my head feels like the worst of it."

Hope drew in a deep breath, straightening, pushing away her fear and panic. My wife was so strong. Raising a hand, she probed around the edges of the cut on my head. "I think it's done bleeding. You need a hot shower. Maybe a bath."

"I'll get a shower after we talk to West."

Royal pushed open the door and West followed him in. West's reaction to the sight of me was better than Royal and Hope's, probably because I'd cleaned up a little, but it wasn't great.

He shook his head. "I just saw you a few hours ago. What the fuck happened?"

I gave him a quick rundown of the events since the truck had pulled up behind me.

"Did you get the plate? See the driver?" West asked.

"The light was already going. I can tell you they weren't short or fat, but other than that, I couldn't see much. The truck was dark. I'd say navy or black, but I can't be sure."

"Not much to go on," West said. "Did it hit you, or did you get out of the way fast enough?"

"It didn't miss me by much, but it missed me. You'll probably get DNA samples from half the trees and rocks on the side of the mountain, but I didn't leave any evidence on the truck."

West turned to Royal. "Where were you when this happened?"

All three of us looked at West in surprise. He thought Royal could have done this? West stared back at us as if his reasoning were obvious. "If something happens to Griffen, Royal's next in line since your father disinherited Ford. That's a helluva motive."

The confusion washed from Royal's face, replaced with disgust. "You know me better than that, West."

"He would've had to be fast," I said, rolling the idea through my mind. I didn't like the idea that Royal might have tried to kill me, but someone had. "I rolled halfway down the mountain, and I think I took a direct path from where I landed straight back to the house. He wouldn't have had much time to ditch the truck and make his own way back, but he could have done it."

Royal stared at me, fists clenched at his side. I wanted to apologize, but the truth was I didn't know Royal anymore. I wanted to believe my brother wouldn't try to kill me, but it wouldn't be the first time one of my siblings betrayed me. I'd be an idiot to assume everyone around me was on my side. Especially considering I knew at least some of them would like nothing more than to see me gone.

"That's a helluva motive," West repeated.

Hope looked to me and then said, "Except Royal isn't next in line." When I didn't signal her to stop, she gave Royal a sympathetic look before explaining, "Prentice's will wasn't straightforward. He removed Ford from the line of succession. But unless Griffen and I have a—unless there's a—if anything happens to Griffen before Griffen has an heir, Bryce inherits everything. Royal only comes in to play after there's a child. Not before."

"Bryce?" West asked, incredulous. "Your cousin Bryce? That fuckwit? Last time he was here, I had to give him a DUI. Does he know about the will?"

"He hasn't had any communication from Harvey," I said, "but that's not a guarantee he's in the dark."

Royal shoved his hands in his pockets, shaking his head in disbelief. "God knows I don't want it. Seriously, I don't. But Bryce? I guess I'm headed out to buy you two a crib. I was going to give you shit about getting married so fast, but if that's the way the will rolled out, you better get working on my niece or nephew."

At the sight of Hope's stiff face, I said, "Shut it. We're not having a baby just to protect the Sawyer line of succession. That's fucked and you know it. Hope is not an incubator and I'm not some stud to carry on the Sawyer genes. We don't have to worry about it. Nothing is going to happen to me."

"It will if you don't stop being an idiot," Royal said, echoing my own thoughts. "Dad is dead. You don't believe Ford killed him any more than I do. But someone walked into this house and shot him dead in the middle of the afternoon. That person is still out there. As long as we don't know who it is or why they did it, we don't know that any of us are safe. Especially you. And if Bryce is what we get if something happens to you, then you'd better fucking start being smart."

West agreed with him. "No more going running by yourself. Get a treadmill or come to town and I'll go for a run with you when I'm off shift. Don't go anywhere without your weapon and your phone. Don't go anywhere without telling someone where you'll be and when you're getting back—"

"You do know what I used to do for a living, right? I don't need a lecture on personal safety."

"You do as long as you're being a dumbass. Just because you used to be a Ranger and security to the stars doesn't mean you're invulnerable," West reminded me.

"Obviously," I said, gesturing to the scratches and streaks of dirt covering me. I let out a huff of breath, hearing myself and knowing I was being an ass. "I'll be careful. I know what happened to Dad," I said to Royal. "I assumed whoever killed him did it because of something isolated to Prentice. A grudge or a business deal gone wrong or something. We all know most of the people who knew him hated him."

West shook his head. "I think we can throw that theory out the window. If this was about a grudge or business deal, it wasn't isolated to Prentice. Either the motive was connected to you, or this isn't about you at all. It's about your family."

Royal threw his hands in the air. "Well, that's not vague. If we're looking for people who might have a grudge against the Sawyers, that list isn't any shorter than the list of people who hated Prentice. What are we supposed to do? Just hang around and wait for him to try again?"

"Or her," Hope added. We all turned to stare at her. She raised an eyebrow. "You guys have tunnel vision. Whoever killed Prentice did it with a gun. They had to have been a good shot because you only recovered one bullet, right?"

West nodded in confirmation.

"Nothing says a woman can't be just as good a shot as a man. And when you're looking at the list of people who had a reason to hate Prentice, there are probably more women on it than men, considering. This could have started with Prentice, but now it's about all of you."

She turned to West. "You said it this afternoon. Griffen coming home, everyone moving back into the house—if the killer wanted to end the Sawyers, that's only going to piss them off. And there are just as many people who hated Prentice over his personal life as there are who hated him because of business."

Royal dropped his head to stare at the carpet. "Fuck. Good point. As far as I know he wasn't involved with anyone. Not for a while. There was someone a few years ago—I don't know who—just that he hinted it was getting serious and then he never said anything else about her."

"You never know," West added. "People can hold a grudge a long time and then one day—" He made his fingers in the shape of a gun and mimed firing a shot. "I need you to come in tomorrow and make an official report. If anything else happens I want to make sure we have it all on file."

I nodded and glanced at the clock. "If we're done, I need to get in the shower. Savannah's going to call us to dinner any minute, and I don't want to show up like this."

"I'll walk you out," Royal said to West.

I looked to Hope after they left. "You okay?"

She clenched her teeth, shaking her head. "I'm fine. I'm sorry I lost it, I just—you had blood everywhere and—"

"Don't apologize. I'm sorry I scared you. I'm sorry I was careless and left my phone and my weapon back here. I won't do that again."

"See that you don't," she said tartly.

I caught her hand in mine. "Want to join me in the shower? Wash my back?"

Hope bit her lip and glanced at the clock. She stared at the ceiling for a heartbeat before tilting her head to the side. "You can't get my hair wet."

"It's a deal," I promised. I didn't get her hair wet in the shower, but I did manage to take her mind off my attempted murder, if only for a few minutes. The shower was quick, but I made the most of every second.

Chapter Thirty-Eight

HOPE

THEY ARRIVED IN TWO HUGE BLACK SUVS, STUFFED TO the gills with gear. The Sinclair brothers, Cooper, Knox, and Evers, and another man I hadn't met when I was in Atlanta. Hawk Bristol. Griffen greeted them with a warmth that reminded me how distant he was from his own family. He might be surrounded by Sawyers, but these were his people.

The size of the Heartstone Manor project had nothing to do with the reason all three brothers had come to Sawyers Bend. They'd come because Griffen was part of their family and they wanted to see for themselves that he was okay. I already liked them after my trip to Atlanta. I loved them for that.

The group of them filled the front hall of Heartstone, making the room seem almost normal-sized.

Savannah met us there. "I've arranged to serve dinner in two shifts. The rest of the family is about to eat. There'll be drinks and appetizers in the office for all of you, then dinner as soon as the first group has cleared out. I thought you'd prefer that."

"That's great, thanks, Savannah," Griffen said.

With a satisfied smile, Savannah continued, "I have rooms for the four of you," she nodded at the Sinclair brothers and Hawk, "but I understood you'd be bringing a team?"

"They'll be here tomorrow," Cooper said. "Six total."

"We can put them up at the Inn, maybe, if we don't have room," I suggested.

Evers laughed. "In this place? Not have room?"

Savannah and her cleaning team had spared a few hours for the front hall, and while it wasn't up to its former glory it no longer looked derelict and abandoned. She smiled. "You'd be surprised. Heartstone has plenty of rooms but not all of them are in decent condition. And speaking of—" She looked to Hawk. "Long-term, you'll be in the gatehouse. I'm sure you saw it as you drove in. At the moment it's not entirely habitable. It seems a family of mice made themselves at home and we're working on getting rid of them."

Griffen added, "Welcome to Heartstone. We have the space, acres of it. We don't necessarily have working plumbing or anywhere to sleep in a lot of the bedrooms, but the roof doesn't leak and we mostly have electricity. Savannah has been working on the more central rooms. Guest rooms haven't been at the top of the list."

"I think I can handle accommodations for six," Savannah added, "but if I can't, I'll let you know by morning."

"Don't worry about it," Cooper cut in. "We're already going to soak Griffen for the security set-up. I don't want to add lodgings to the bill. My team will take whatever you have for them."

Savannah nodded. "Then, if you'll follow me? You can leave your things in the hall. They'll be delivered to your rooms by the time you finish with dinner."

Knox settled his bag on his shoulder. "Will you carry them upstairs or is there a footman lurking around?"

Savannah only smiled. Evers picked his bag back up and gave her a charming grin. "Why don't you show us where our rooms are? We'll drop our own stuff off, then I'll be ready for a drink and some food."

"Hope and I will show you," Griffen said. "Thanks, Savannah."

Griffen led us up the main stairs. Cooper fell into step beside me. "It's good to see you, Hope. You look great."

I gave him a shy smile, feeling the heat of a flush on my cheeks. Cooper and Alice were tight, and I could guess he probably knew more of the details of our shopping trip than I'd like. It didn't matter; he was a nice guy, and he was Griffen's friend. "Thanks."

"Alice wanted to come, but given what happened yesterday with Griff, I didn't want Petra here, and Alice didn't want to leave her behind, even with Lily. Alice made me promise to tell you that as soon as I feel like the house is safe, we're coming back for a visit. All of us."

"That's good news. And I completely understand. It's one thing for us to choose to take the risk of being here, another to bring Alice and Petra when we're not sure it's safe. But when you think we're ready, I'd love to have all of you back."

We followed Griffen down the hall to the left of the stairs. I hadn't spent much time here since we moved in. Just a quick check with Savannah to see that most of the rooms were in various states of abandonment or disrepair. She'd managed to get the four best guest rooms cleaned and ready, but another six would be tough. If anyone could do it, it was Savannah.

Bags stowed, we all tromped back down the stairs and settled in the office. Savannah had trays of hors d'oeuvres on the coffee table by the couch, armchairs, and a fire burning merrily, chasing off the early spring chill. The small bar by the built-in bookcase was stocked and everyone but me fixed a drink. I hadn't slept well the night before. If I had a drink it was possible I'd fall asleep in my soup.

"I looked at pictures," Evers said, "but I still wasn't prepared. This place is like a castle. I stayed in Rycroft Castle for a job when Summer and I got together, and I thought that was over-the-top, but it still has nothing on Heartstone Manor."

"Yeah, well, Rycroft was a good try, but it's still not a genuine Gilded Age mansion," Cooper reminded him. "Most of the houses like Heartstone Manor have been abandoned or opened to the public."

"That was one the conditions of my father's will," Griffen said. "He left us money to maintain the place, and God knows we're going to need it, but one of the restrictions is that we can't, as he said, '*turn it into a tourist attraction*'. He was an asshole, but he loved this house."

"It's amazing. It'll be even better when you have it back in shape, but it's going to be a nightmare to secure," Knox said, getting straight to the point.

"I'm aware," Griffen said, wryly. "We'll walk the house and the property tomorrow, but I'm already thinking Hawk is going to need help."

Hawk hadn't said much since he'd walked in. His dark eyes were alert, taking in everything. Thick dark hair fell across his face as he studied the French doors to the sunroom. I had a feeling everywhere he looked he saw a potential security breach.

Lifting his face to look at Griffen, he said, "Calling this place a nightmare to secure is an understatement. I'm going to need at least two more on-site. Four would be better. We can make up some of that with electronic surveillance."

Griffen pulled a pad off his desk and sat with his whiskey, leaning forward to take notes. "I've already thought of that. I agree a team of four would be best. I need to check with Harvey—our lawyer and the one who holds the purse strings on the house budget—but I already said I'll cover what we need out of my own pocket if I have to."

"We're not draining your savings account to keep you from getting shot in your own house," Cooper said with annoyance.

The nonchalant way he mentioned Griffen getting shot sent a chill down my spine. I suddenly wished I was having dinner with the rest of the family. I wasn't sure I was up for hanging with these guys who threw around the threat of a bullet like it was no big deal.

Griffen shrugged. "My whole family is here, and we have no fucking clue what's going on. Someone has it out for us. We don't know why or what they want. I don't know how long it's going to take to get to the bottom of it, but until we do, I don't care how much it costs. I want my family safe."

"Harvey will free up the money," I said quietly. "I'll call him tomorrow morning and get specifics."

Griffen smiled at me. "Thanks, Buttercup."

Knox snorted at the endearment, but Cooper and Evers just smiled. Hawk looked vaguely annoyed. Griffen wrote something on his pad and then said, "So, here's what I'm thinking —"

I zoned out as they ran over ideas for security. It sounded like it would take years to install. Sensors on every window and door, motion detectors, cameras everywhere. A room on the lower level would be repurposed for surveillance, and there would be someone walking the grounds and someone on cameras twenty-four hours a day. Just the idea of that made me feel safer. If Harvey balked at the budget, whatever it turned out to be, he'd have to answer to me. I'd make it my mission if I had to.

By the time dinner was ready, all I wanted was bed. I hadn't slept well the night before, visions of Griffen dripping blood waking me over and over. He hadn't been hurt aside from some bumps and bruises and the cut on his head, but when I'd walked in, there had been so much blood.

I knew I'd fallen for Griffen all over again, but I hadn't realized how hard I'd fallen until I saw him dripping blood and thought I might lose him. In the night, as he slept beside me, I stared at the ceiling and came to a realization.

Our marriage had a time limit.

Fine. Everything in life has an ending.

At least I knew when ours was.

But Griffen was mine for now, and miracle of miracles, he seemed happy about it. I wasn't his true love, I was the wife he'd been forced to marry, but he cared about me. He was sweet, and kind, and fun, and a better husband than I'd imagined he would be—and trust me, I'd imagined a lot back in the day.

I had five years with him before it was over. I was going to make the most of every one. If leaving felt like ripping out my heart, I'd deal with it then. For now, I was going to enjoy every day like we didn't have an expiration date.

It turned out that was easier than I thought.

For one thing, we were so busy there wasn't time to worry about the future. I'd been right about the security install. It took them two days to work up the plans. By Friday, the Sinclair brothers were on their way back to Atlanta with promises to come back for a long weekend sometime soon. Hawk had set up a cot in the guest house, claiming he liked mice more than people anyway. Savannah didn't argue much. She had her hands full, and if he wasn't complaining, neither was she.

I managed to talk Harvey into the proposed security budget, including the team of four under Hawk's command. He grumbled and reviewed some numbers, but when I reminded him that if Griffen got killed he'd see everything but the house fund drained by Bryce, he'd agreed that Griffen's safety was the priority.

Considering that so far, even Sinclair Security's crack investigator hadn't been able to find a shred of evidence on Prentice's real killer, caution seemed wise.

Griffen spent his mornings with me in the office handling anything I couldn't do on my own. We had lunch together, usually at the desk, and then he was off with the security team and Hawk working on the install: running wires, setting up cameras, sometimes disappearing with the team for hours to hike the property.

He'd come back for dinner most of the time, and we'd fall into bed at night exhausted. Exhausted, but never *too* exhausted. If I'd known what sex with Griffen would be like, I might have jumped him right after we said our vows. He was endlessly inventive, never too tired to peel off my clothes and make me dizzy with orgasms.

I'd waited a long time to have sex, but I was making up for it. In bed, in the shower, on the velvet couch in our sitting room, over our desk. On top of our desk. Once in the woods against a tree, out of range of the cameras. We were busy, but never too busy for sex.

I didn't see much of Griffen's siblings over those next few weeks. They were hit or miss at dinner. Usually, Parker and her husband were there. Sometimes Finn, and almost always Sterling. The rest of them worked late more often than not. The will said they had to live in Heartstone, not that they had to be there every spare moment.

Savannah made progress on the house, getting the breakfast room cleaned and set up, the extra staff housed, and eventually chasing off the mice in the gatehouse thanks to an exterminator.

I can't say Sterling never had a drink, but there hadn't been a repeat of her sprawl on the steps or the rest of it. She'd finally cleaned out her room, and it had taken six trash bags to empty out the junk. According to Savannah, she was even managing to keep it reasonably clean.

March eased gently into April, bringing warmer weather most days, though a cold front had blown in. The lawn around Heartstone Manor was frosted with a thin layer of snow, making everything look like a wonderland. The main house was deserted for once, empty of staff and quiet. Fat, lazy snowflakes had begun to drift from the sky, making me wish for hot chocolate and a roaring fire. For a snuggle under a blanket. Or in bed.

Looking down at the contract I was reviewing, I forced myself through the last page before I closed it, making a note on the section I wanted Griffen to take another look at. Griffen. He hadn't joined me in the office that morning or for lunch. If he wasn't too busy he might be interested in my snuggling in bed plan.

He wasn't answering my texts, wasn't in our room or anywhere else I'd looked. I made my way down to the lower level to see if Savannah had seen him. I found her in the kitchen refereeing a fight between Finn and the cook. She stood between Miss Stiles and Finn, arms held out as if trying to physically keep them apart.

Yikes. Miss Stiles' cheeks were flushed with temper, Finn's blue eyes sparking with anger. I hadn't talked to Finn much one-on-one, but we'd all heard the comments under his breath at meals. The eggs were too dry. The chicken was salty. The cook didn't know the meaning of al dente.

I didn't hear Finn's last words, but Miss Stiles' face went beet red and she screeched, "Get out of my kitchen! Get out!"

He ignored her, his hand darting forward to grab a carrot and take a bite, wincing as it hit his taste buds. "What did you do? Soak it in syrup? I know we're in the South, but that doesn't mean you have to deep fry or sugar coat everything you serve us."

"What would you know about it?" Miss Stiles yelled in outrage. "I've been cooking since before you were born and—"

"I trained at the Culinary Institute of America and spent a year at Cordon Bleu in Paris, not to mention cooking my way through some of the best kitchens in Europe and the States. Where did you learn to cook? A roadside diner?"

Savannah, Miss Stiles, and I stared at Finn, all three of us stunned silent.

Finn was a trained chef? And not just trained, but based on the shock on Miss Stiles face, a very well-trained chef. How did we not know that? And if he was, then why did we need a cook? It's not like he was working.

Savannah narrowed her eyes on Finn. "If that's all true, then what are you doing here? Shouldn't you be in Asheville? Or working at the Inn with your brothers?"

"I'm here because I have to be. The second I get my money, I'm using it to open my own restaurant. In the meantime, I have to live in this house, but I don't have to suffer through her mediocre meals."

Miss Stiles shrieked and threw her syrup coated spoon at Finn's head. She stormed out, shouting over her shoulder, "I quit, Savannah. I don't have to work under these conditions."

Savannah turned furious eyes to Finn, covering a smirk at the sight of the wooden spoon stuck to his thick, dark hair. Maybe Finn had a point. There was an awful lot of syrup on that spoon. Still, we needed a cook, and unless Finn wanted to do it—

"Do you want to take over her job?" Savannah asked with deadly sweetness, already knowing Finn's answer.

"Hell, no. Do I look like a private chef? It's bad enough I have to be here in the first place."

"You don't have to be here at all," Savannah pointed out, stabbing her finger through the air at him. "You're only here because you want the money your father left you. Don't pretend you're better than everybody else. You're just hanging around waiting for your payday, thinking you're too good to work like the rest of us. You haven't changed since high school, Finn Sawyer. You were an arrogant snot then, and you're even worse now."

"Savannah—" Finn protested, taken aback. He tugged the spoon from his hair and held out his hand, but Savannah pushed past him.

"I don't want to hear it," she said, "I'm going to go find Miss Stiles and beg her to reconsider. If she quits, you're in the kitchen until I replace her. And if she doesn't quit you're banned from the kitchens and storerooms permanently."

She stormed out, leaving Finn staring at her retreating back with a bemused smile on his face. Looking at me, he shrugged a shoulder. "She's right," he said conversationally, "I was an arrogant snot in high school. But she's wrong. Now I'm only an arrogant snot in the kitchen. If I cooked for you, you'd know why."

I watched him stroll out and crossed my fingers in the hopes that we'd still have a cook when Savannah was done working her magic. That had been an interesting little byplay. I had to tell Griffen, but first I had to find him.

It didn't take that long. I heard the clang of weights in the gym and opened the door to see Griffen on his back on an exercise bench, a loaded metal bar above him. Sweat gleamed on his smooth skin, his muscles corded and bunched with the effort of lifting the heavily-weighted bar.

He was ridiculously, seriously hot. Looking over and seeing me, he shot me a grin that sent my temperature skyrocketing. My head felt light as I crossed the padded floor to his side. Maybe it was the heat in the room, but I was pretty sure it was all Griffen. His sweaty skin, those muscles, that mischievous grin...

He racked the weights and peeled himself off the bench, holding me off with one hand. "I'm sweaty, Buttercup."

"I like you sweaty," I said, my head buzzing as he leaned in to press my lips against his. Everything went gray for a second, and I stumbled against him.

Griffen's arm caught me and he pulled me close, kissing me again, murmuring against my lips, my cheek, "You okay baby? Did you get dizzy?"

I straightened, taking a deep breath and liking the salty scent of Griffen more than the musty smell of the basement gym. "I don't know, I think it was just hot in here. Maybe I didn't eat enough lunch. My stomach was off. I'm okay now. It's snowing and I was ready for a break, then I couldn't find you. And on the way here I found out something funny. Well, maybe *not* funny, I guess we'll see."

Griffen grabbed a towel and wiped off his face and chest. "You sure you're okay?"

"I'm sure, really, it was just a thing for a second. I'm fine. But I was in the kitchen and—"

I filled him in on what I'd witnessed and he shook his head in annoyance. "If Savannah can't get Miss Stiles back, Finn's taking over until she finds someone else whether he wants to or not. But really? Culinary Institute of America and Cordon Bleu? That's impressive. I knew he left home after high school, but I didn't know he was a trained chef. And he wants to open a restaurant? Interesting."

"I know. Now I really want him to cook for us. I want to know if he's any good after all that bragging. And speaking of cooking, do you want to raid the kitchen? I didn't eat much lunch and you skipped it altogether. Then I was thinking maybe some hot cocoa and a fire in our bedroom. So we could watch the snow and, um, other stuff."

"Hmm, some of that sounds good." Griffen scooped me up in his arms, sweat and all. I didn't mind. In Griffen's arms was one of my favorite places to be.

He strode from the room, explaining, "I'm taking you upstairs, and you can help me wash off all this sweat. And then I'm going to make you come at least twice, maybe three times, and then I'm going to feed you a brownie, in bed, while we watch the snow. How does that sound?"

"That sounds just about perfect."

Chapter Thirty-Nine

GRIFFEN

I LEANED OVER THE LAPTOP, SCROLLING THROUGH THE contract we were reviewing. "Tricky bastards. They keep trying to slip something in." A click and I deleted the extra lines before moving on. "I'll be glad when we're done with these clowns. By the time this contract expires we need to have an alternate supplier in place."

"Got it," Hope said, adding it to the list in her ever-present notebook.

A quick double rap sounded on the door and both of our heads popped up. Royal stuck his head inside the office. I thought he'd headed out to the Inn after breakfast. Maybe he'd come back.

"Come in," I said, closing the laptop. "I'm ready to take a break from this anyway."

A little hesitant, Royal crossed the room and took one of the big leather chairs in front of the desk. He sat, propping an ankle on his knee before he leaned forward.

"I know you haven't had a lot of time to get up to speed with the business, and it's even harder with Ford... gone."

"We're getting there. I'd be lost without Hope."

Royal gave Hope a surprisingly affectionate smile. "I can see that," he said. "It was a surprise, you two getting married, but it's good to see you both happy."

I leaned back in my chair, taking Hope's hand with a smile that probably showed more than I meant it to. I didn't care. Hope smiled back before dropping her eyes, still too shy for public displays of affection.

"Is that what brought you in today?" I asked. "Here to wish us happy?"

"Not exactly. I had some thoughts about the Inn that I wanted to run by you. I'll be honest and tell you that I ran most of this by Dad and Ford. Ford was in favor of it. Dad was not."

"If you're trying to get me on your side, that's a good start," I said.

"That's what I was hoping," Royal said with a hint of his charming grin. "The first thing is the guest cottages. We have more land along the river and the cottages have been selling out on a regular basis, year-round. I put together some numbers—"

Royal handed me a manila folder. A quick look showed spreadsheets and graphs. "Tenn and I believe the investment would pay off within a few years, if not sooner. On top of that, we'd like to do more coordination with the rest of the family businesses. Dad was determined to keep us all separate. Islands unto ourselves and all that. We have a great restaurant at the Inn, but we should coordinate more with Avery's brewery, and I know she'd like to add a restaurant at some point, which would be great as an alternate place to send a guest for a meal and still keep them in the family. Ditto for offering activity packages through Quinn's guide business."

"Hope and I haven't reviewed the family concerns since I knew the rest of you had them under control, but I assumed all of this was already going on. I didn't know about Avery wanting a restaurant, but the rest of it. Why would Dad hamstring you like this?"

"Paranoid, I think, that we were plotting against him. Or he was just being an asshole. With Dad, it's hard to tell."

"True enough. I can't see any reason we shouldn't do everything you suggested. Hope and I will take a look at these numbers you put together, but if they look as good as you think they do, we can start talking construction plans."

Relief washed over Royal's face. He let out a breath as if steeling himself and went on, "There's something else. I never mentioned this before because, well, I wasn't interested in working any closer with Dad than I had to. I don't know how Ford did it. He acted as a buffer for the rest of us, and I appreciate it, but I didn't want that job."

"Dad's gone," I said, flatly. "And I don't know when Ford is coming back."

"I know. I'd like you to consider letting me take Ford's place," he said carefully.

I have to admit, I was surprised. From my siblings, I'd gotten mostly contempt and dismissal. They'd been ignoring and avoiding me for the most part. That was fine, honestly.

I had enough on my plate between taking over the business and getting the house in shape, a new wife and a new life—if they wanted to give me space I'd take all I could get.

Not sure what Royal really wanted—or if I could trust him—I raised an eyebrow and said nothing.

"I don't want to leave the Inn completely, but we're growing there and need more than just Tenn and I at the helm. I thought

313

we could bring on a CFO. Tenn could officially have the CEO position, and I could split my time between the Inn and working for Sawyer Enterprises."

"Why?" I had to ask.

"Look, I love the Inn. I'm proud of everything we've accomplished there, but sometimes I want to do more. Sawyer Enterprises is so diverse, you're always doing something different. I guess I'm restless."

"And Tenn? How would he feel about this?"

"Tenn loves the Inn, loves everything about it. I talked to him about the idea and he was open to it. He doesn't want to go anywhere. He likes having control over all the moving parts of the property. Truthfully, he doesn't understand how I could be restless. Every day at the Inn is different. New guests, new challenges. I guess I just want a different kind of different."

I stared at my brother, lost in thought. I couldn't deny it would be helpful to have another hand on deck, assuming I could trust him. I didn't have a reason to *distrust* him any more than he had one to distrust me. Wasn't it time I took a chance on one of them? Didn't I have to eventually?

"Let me think about it," I hedged. Royal's face shuttered. "I'm not saying no. I just need to think about it and go over everything you've given me. It's a big decision and I'm still getting my feet wet here. I can't just say yes."

Royal looked between Hope and me and nodded. "Fair enough."

"Now, to save some time, why don't you walk me through some of this—" I gestured to the manila folder he'd given me.

Royal opened the folder and spread sheets of paper across my desk. Cost projections, a map of that section of the Inn property, complete with sketches of proposed cottages. Noticing that one of them could be moved to catch a better view of the river, I reached for my pen and found it missing.

Shuffling through the papers, I was about to pull a new one from the drawer when I looked down and saw the pen by my foot. "One sec," I said, leaning down.

A sharp crack of glass, a deep thud sounded, and my chair rocked back hard, knocking me to the floor. I hit the carpet hard on my hands and knees, momentarily stunned.

What the fuck was that?

Turning, I spotted a neat hole in the back of my leather chair exactly where my head had been. A bullet hole. The broken window closest to my desk had a matching hole, spiderwebs of cracks reaching out from the center across the clear glass.

What the fucking fuck?

Hope jolted upright in a rush, reaching for me as her face drained of blood and she crumpled to the floor.

"Hope!" I lunged across the carpet for Hope, shouting to Royal, "Call Hawk. Tell him we have a shooter on the grounds."

I vaguely heard Royal talking into his phone as I checked Hope for injuries. No blood, nothing broken. She hadn't been shot. I forced myself to take a deep breath. Hope hadn't been shot, she'd just stood up too fast and fainted.

She was already coming to, her fluttering hands batting me away as I rolled her over to double-check that she didn't have any injuries.

"Are you OK?" she asked, voice weak but gaining strength fast. "Griffen! Did someone shoot you?"

"I'm fine, they missed. Why did you pass out?"

"I don't know, I just got up too fast. Maybe it was the shock. You leaned over and then the window cracked and there's a hole in your chair. Griffen, someone shot at you? Is Royal talking to West?"

"No, Hawk." I looked to Royal, who hung up his phone.

"Hawk started a search, told me to stay with Hope, said you should get out there."

IVY LAYNE

"What? No!" Hope's hands closed over my arm and held on tight. "There's someone out there with a gun and they're trying to kill you. You can't go out there. Are you crazy?"

I pulled my loaded weapon from the holster at my lower back. "I'm armed," I reminded her gently, "and this is what I'm trained for. I need you to trust me, Hope. I have to go out there."

Royal took my place, helping Hope to her feet. "Hawk told me to get her to the lower level, away from any windows, and call West. Go, before he gets away."

I pressed a quick kiss to Hope's mouth and promised, "I'll be back as soon as I can. I promise."

I hated leaving Hope behind, but she was safer in the house with Royal and I needed to do my job. I ran through the house, past the unused family gathering room and out through the side door, not far from the edge of the woods. I called Hawk as I ran and learned that he'd picked up the shooter's trail a few hundred yards west of my location.

It had been years since I'd been in the woods on that side of the house, but as I curved around the back of the property to meet up with Hawk I realized the shooter was retracing his steps back in the direction of the area where I'd been run off the road. Fuck.

Keeping low, my weapon in hand, I moved as fast as I could and still stay alert to my surroundings. As far as I could tell, I was alone in this part of the woods. Hawk was fast and he had a head start. He'd also spent the last few weeks learning every inch of the house and surrounding property. He might have been a newcomer, but he knew his way around better than I did.

I came over the rise to see Hawk staring up the hill in disgust. He shook his head when he saw me. "Fucking bastard was fast. Took off like a bat out of hell. I'd say he didn't even stick around to see if he hit you. Just took the shot and ran. Smart. This about where you got run off the road?"

I didn't have to look around to answer. "Yep. I rolled down that hill and hiked this way back to the house."

"I heard a truck engine start up and take off a few seconds after I got here. That's not much proof, but my gut says whoever tried to run you off the road took the shot."

I holstered my weapon at the small of my back. The holster wasn't my first choice, but I hadn't wanted my weapon at my side where Hope would see it.

"Well, fuck. Suggestions? Do we need to put in a fence?" I scanned the woods surrounding us. The idea of a fence didn't sit right. Forgetting the fact that it would be expensive as hell, a fence would be an annoying disruption to everything and everyone, cutting through our hiking trails and trapping local wildlife.

Hawk shook his head. "No. It would take too long and it wouldn't be worth the cost. I can put up an electronic perimeter. I have some of the equipment and can order the rest. We'll get a lot of false positives, but we'd get those if we had a wired fence anyway. And I'd rather send the guys out or go check myself and have eyes on the property. It'll only take a few days. Let's get back to the house and talk to West."

"Yeah, I want to get back to Hope. She hasn't been feeling well, and she passed out after that asshole shot through the window. Said she stood up too fast but—"

Hawk raised an eyebrow. "She pregnant? Already? Didn't you two just get married?"

"It's not that," I said automatically before turning the word over in my mind. Pregnant? No. It was too soon to know, wasn't it? We'd been careful, except for that one time... I couldn't process the thought.

It seemed to take forever to get back to the house. West was walking through the door when we got there. I shot him a wave. "I'll be right back. Meet me in the office."

I sprinted up the stairs and down the hall to find Hope lying on the sofa in our sitting room, cradling a cup of tea in her hands, a worried line etched between her eyebrows. She sat up when I came through the door, almost spilling her tea.

"You're all right," she said.

"Of course, I'm all right. We chased him through the woods, but he got away. Hawk thinks it could be the same guy with the truck from a few weeks ago. He's going to put up a perimeter around the house. No one will get close enough to take a shot at us again."

"Are you sure?"

I sat on the edge of the sofa, urging her back until she was lying down. I brushed her hair off her face, wanting to chase the worry from her eyes. "This isn't the first time someone has tried to kill me. Hopefully, it'll be the last. I don't want you to worry."

"Not worry? Are you insane? How could I not worry? Someone shot you!"

"Someone shot *at* me. Trust me, I know the difference," I said, thinking of my shoulder. Big fucking difference.

Hope scowled. "Smartass. I don't want anything to happen to you."

"I'm being careful. I promise. I have to go talk to West and Hawk, see what we can do to make sure we're safe. I wanted to check on you first. Are you better? How are you feeling? You went down hard. That's the second time you fainted."

"No, it's not. I just got a little dizzy the other day, that's all. I've been lightheaded. Maybe I'm drinking too much coffee or something."

I narrowed my eyes on her, thinking back. "You haven't been drinking coffee at all lately. You said your stomach felt funny."

I thought about what Hawk had said. Thought about asking Hope straight out and immediately pushed the idea way. She'd tell me if she was. Wouldn't she? The last thing I wanted to do was give her more to worry about.

"It's nothing, I think I have a cold. I've been a little stuffy and I had a headache the last few days, that's all. I always feel lightheaded and tired when I have a cold. Don't worry about me. I'll text Savannah if I need anything. You go figure out security stuff with Hawk and West. I'm just going to close my eyes after I finish this tea."

A cold. She had been drinking a lot of tea and sniffling the day before. That made sense. I wasn't expecting a flash of regret at her simple explanation. Just a cold. Nothing to worry about.

I wanted to stay, to curl up on the couch with her and just *be*. More, I needed to know she'd be safe. I pulled a soft blanket over her, dropping a slow kiss on her mouth before I finally dragged myself away and headed down to plug the holes in our security with Hawk and West.

I had no intention of being shot, but I wasn't going to be a prisoner either. One way or another, we'd figure this out.

I'd never been an overly optimistic man before. Maybe Hope had softened me up. Maybe I was just happy.

Or stupid.

I should have been more suspicious.

I should have been more careful.

I should have remembered how quickly things can go bad, just when you least expect it.

Chapter Forty

HOPE

I CLOSED MY EYES AND SLEPT FOR SIX HOURS. GRIFFEN woke me for dinner, concern in his eyes. I lied and told him it was just a cold and truthfully admitted I was starving. That was my pattern lately. I woke late with my stomach turning over, wasn't hungry until afternoon, and then I ate like a pig at dinner.

I wanted it to be a cold. The flu. A random virus I'd picked up somewhere. As each day passed and it got worse, I was afraid it was something else.

I was late.

My period wasn't regular. It wasn't irregular either, it was just kind of vague. I'm not one of those women who knows the exact day it's going to show up, but I did have a general idea and that general idea had passed about a week before. My breasts were tender, and I was dizzy. Queasy when I wasn't starving.

I hadn't figured out what to do about it. I wanted to know one way or the other. But how?

Of course, I could just tell my husband. Everything in me rejected that idea. I wasn't ready to accept the thought that I might be pregnant. I'd sure as heck wasn't ready to talk about it with Griffen.

It wasn't like I could run out and buy a test. There was only one drug store in town and I knew everyone who worked there. Ditto for the grocery store. The last thing I needed was for everyone to find out Hope Sawyer had been seen buying a pregnancy test. Griffen would get a dozen calls before I made it back home.

I could get one somewhere out of town, except that I never left town without Griffen. Usually, when I ran into a store he came with me. I couldn't think of a way to ask for privacy that wouldn't seem awkward and weird. Maybe I could order one online. Or ask Daisy or J.T. to get me one. J.T. drove into Asheville every morning for school. He wouldn't mind stopping at a drugstore.

So far, I hadn't been able to bring myself to ask. I was holding on to my current plan of ignore, ignore, ignore. Stupid and immature, I know. Ignoring it wouldn't make the problem go away, but I didn't want it to go away. I just wanted the whole thing to be a lot less complicated.

I'd always wanted children. A family. If I were being brutally honest, I'd always wanted both with Griffen. But not like this. I'd wanted it as his real wife. The wife he chose for himself. The wife he loved. Not someone he'd divorce in four years and eleven months.

I wanted to be a mother to my child all the time, not just when I had custody. By now, I knew Griffen wasn't the kind of man who'd keep me from my child, but that was just a fact of divorce. It wasn't like I'd keep living here—

Horror spread through me at that thought. I could. I could stay and raise my child and watch him move on without me. I couldn't imagine how awful that would be. Sitting at breakfast with Griffen and his new wife, watching him dote on her while I was alone, pining for him.

I was in love with my husband and he didn't love me back. Not like that. As an old friend, sure. Griffen had love for me, I knew that, but there were so many different kinds of love. The love he felt for me wasn't the one I wanted.

I'd been trying to go with the flow, to enjoy him while I had him and all that. A child would change everything. I rested my hand over my lower belly, wondering if there was really someone in there.

Maybe I was worrying for nothing. Maybe I had a bug just like I'd told Griffen. I wouldn't know until I took the test, and so far, I hadn't figured out a way to do that without alerting the entire county.

Just call Daisy and J.T., I told myself.

I loved Daisy and adored J.T., but I didn't want a crowd involved in this. Not yet. I didn't want to process the results with an audience.

"Not hungry this morning?" Griffen asked, looking across the breakfast table at me.

I gave him a weak smile. "Just this cold," I deflected. "I'll be fine, I just need to get going." I forced myself to take a bite of eggs, swallowing the bile that rose in my throat.

I was going to eat my breakfast and we were going to have a normal day. I was not going to get dizzy or throw up.

Griffen was watching me, concern in his eyes. Concern and something else I couldn't read. He was studying me like I was a puzzle he wanted to solve. I didn't like it. I didn't want to be figured out. I had enough to figure out myself.

"If you're not feeling well, we can postpone the trip to Asheville. We'll do it another day and you can go lay down."

"No," I said. "Brax rearranged his schedule so he could show us the Asheville properties today. Better to get it done. I'm fine. I'm going to ask Savannah for a tea to go and I'll be good for the ride."

That turned out to be a lie. I'd never been prone to car sickness, but the eggs went sour in my stomach and I sipped at my herbal tea, praying everything would stay put. Mountain roads are no good with an unhappy stomach.

With every curve and dip, my stomach tried to turn inside out. I should have taken Griffen up on his offer to reschedule or just told him to go without me. I gritted my teeth and wished desperately for a ginger ale.

Brax's office in Asheville was less than an hour from Heartstone Manor. The drive took forever. By the time we got there, I thought if I had to ride for one more mile I was going to hurl all over Griffen's gorgeous car.

Brax met us at his office, taking a quick minute to show us the small yet elegant space before guiding us on a whirlwind tour of commercial office space, retail locations, and small apartment buildings, most of them in the downtown area.

I barely paid attention to anything Brax said, making random notes and knowing all the while that Griffen could read me like a book. He knew something was wrong. He knew it was more than my having a cold.

Or maybe he didn't know anything and I was just paranoid. Paranoid and freaked out and scared.

What if I was pregnant? A lot of people would be happy. I just didn't know if I was one of them. I wanted to be. Oh, how I wanted to be. Having a baby with Griffen... How could I not be happy?

I would be happy, ecstatic, except that every time I looked ahead I saw that deadline. Four years, eleven months. A lifetime of loving him, loving our child, and only having one of them. Of putting on a brave face, never letting anyone know my heart was broken when Griffen moved on without me.

It made me realize that the issue wasn't really whether I was pregnant. Baby or no baby, I was in love with Griffen Sawyer, and I always had been.

I'd loved him when I was a girl for being handsome and kind. For always having time for me. I loved him now so much more than that girl had ever dreamed. I loved the life we had together. Working side-by-side, seeing him first thing when I woke and as I fell asleep.

It's always the little things with me. I'd never wanted grand gestures. I loved that he brought me Daisy's toffee-chip cookies when he went through town without me. The way he smiled at me. The way he held my hand. The way he asked what I wanted, and what I liked, and what I thought.

And—I had to be honest with myself—the sex didn't hurt. He'd said I was innocent. I disagreed. I may have been a virgin, but I'd seen plenty of live shows by the time Edgar took me from my parents. I was very clear on the mechanics, and I'd read more than my share of romance novels.

I thought I knew all about sex, but wow, had I been wrong. No one would ever be as good as Griffen Sawyer. I already knew that.

I'd thought I could handle a temporary marriage to Griffen. Now that there was the possibility of a baby I realized I'd just been fooling myself. What had my plan been, anyway? After five years was I just going to leave town and move away?

I was always going to have to see him move on without me, was always going to have to watch him fall in love with someone else, to build a life with another woman. And now? Knowing that if we had a child together I could never move away, would never do that to our family—whatever form it took—could I live with that?

This whole thing was a mess. How many times had he said he didn't want to bring a baby into this situation? Someone was trying to kill him. What if getting pregnant turned that gun on our child?

And I couldn't forget that every time someone told him my getting pregnant would make things simpler, Griffen insisted he didn't want a child with me. He'd been very clear about that.

Then he should have stayed out of my bed.

A wan smile curved my lips. What did they say in health class? All it takes is once. I tried to force myself to take a deep breath. I didn't even know if I was pregnant. It was probably just a virus, and I was late because I was stressed.

I kept my eyes open all day for the chance to run into a drug-store on the excuse of grabbing cough drops, but when we finally stopped, Griffen said easily, "I'll come in, too. I need a water and I ran out of toothpaste."

"I'll grab you some," I offered, but he turned me down with a smile. Foiled again.

The drive home from Asheville was longer than the drive there thanks to five o'clock traffic, but it felt faster. We sped towards Sawyers Bend, all my worries looming over us, Griffen sneaking questioning glances at me through the silence.

I rolled my window down to get some air and break up the quiet in the car. It was cold outside but not freezing. Spring was finally on its way.

I never heard the gunshot.

We were zipping down a straightaway and out of nowhere the front end of the hood dipped on Griffen's side, the car lurching down and to the left, speeding into the opposing lane of traffic. A car swerved out of our way as Griffen swore, wrestling the steering wheel until he could pull the vehicle back into our lane.

He hit the brakes. The car heaved and jerked, the wheel yanking itself out of Griffen's hands. We careened off the road, tilting to the side, every cell in my body straining to be upright as the car leaned and leaned, and I knew in my gut we were going over the edge of the embankment.

The fall started so slowly. I was on my side, then my feet were over my head and we flipped again, gaining momentum as gravity took over.

The mountain flew up to the window—or we were flying down—I didn't know anymore. Fire erupted in my arm, we rolled again, and everything went black.

Chapter Forty-One

HOPE

*L*IGHT SLICED INTO MY EYES. I BLINKED, SQUINTING AS a shadow eclipsed the sun and everything went dark again. Voices. Griffen and someone else. A stranger.

The strange voice was a man, distant and tinny in my ringing ears. "I couldn't believe it! I swerved to get out of your way and when I looked in the rearview, you flipped! Man, you went over like five times," he said, breathless with shock.

Griffen's face came into focus above mine, his eyes stark with fear.

"Hope. Oh, my God, Hope. Look at me."

"So much blood," the stranger said.

"The ambulance is on the way, baby. Please say something."

"I'm okay," I gasped out, lying because I couldn't stand seeing Griffen so scared. "Are you bleeding?"

Griffen's face went blank. Softly he said, "No, baby. You are. You had your window open and a branch got you in the arm. I don't know how deep it is, but I'm going to leave it until the paramedics get here."

"Just my arm?" I asked, suddenly feeling the deep burn in my upper arm, the sticky heat of blood growing chill and clammy the further it flowed from the source.

Griffen had an expert poker face. He didn't answer my question. "We'll know more when the paramedics get here. Just stay still, okay?"

"Don't I have to get out of the car? In case it explodes or something?"

The tiniest smile quirked the side of his mouth. "The fuel tank isn't leaking, Buttercup, and I don't want to move you unless I have to."

The stranger kept babbling. "I can't believe it, I thought for sure you'd both be dead."

Griffen looked over his shoulder at that. "Shut up. I'm fine. She's fine. Don't freak her out."

"Sorry, sorry, I've just never seen anything like this. Sorry." The briefest pause. "Oh, my God, is that a Maserati? Did you just total your Maserati? Oh, man, what a waste."

Griffen ignored him to brush my hair back off my face. "Just hang in there for me, okay? Try to stay awake and hang in there."

Hang in there? How much was I bleeding? Griffen looked over his shoulder again, his features relaxing from their expressionless mask.

A second later, everything was noise and motion. Griffen was pulled away, and a man and a woman in dark uniforms were poking and prodding me, asking questions, making me move my fingers and my toes, probing the branch stuck in my arm until I gasped in pain.

Finally, they unbuckled my seatbelt and eased me out onto a stretcher. They moved fast, the blue sky flashing above me, the air cold on my cheeks, and I was being lifted and shoved into the back of the ambulance. They moved around me, attaching monitors, shoving oxygen in my nose, and talking over me in words I didn't understand.

Griffen joined me in the back of the ambulance, taking my hand but staying silent to let the medics work. They decided to leave the branch where it was until we got to the hospital. That decision made, one of the paramedics went to the front and we started to move.

"ETA less than 11 minutes," the paramedic beside me told us. "If you had to flip your car, you picked a good place to do it."

"I didn't flip the car," he corrected the paramedic and pulled his phone from his pocket. After a few taps on the screen, he said, "West, Griffen." A pause. "Not great. I'm in an ambulance with Hope headed to the E.R. We were coming back from Asheville on Boylston Highway and somebody shot out my left front tire." Another pause. "I'm okay. The car flipped a few times and Hope has a branch stuck in her arm. We'll know more once we get to the hospital." He waited, listening, and then said, "You can't miss it. When you're done, you know where to find me. Yeah, I know."

I tried to catch his eyes from my prone position, but he was avoiding me, staring across my body at the paramedic holding a bandage on my arm, her eyes on my vitals.

Giving up on catching Griffen's eye, I looked at the paramedic. "Did someone check him over? Make sure he didn't hit his head or something?"

She gave me a well-practiced smile of reassurance. "We gave him a quick look. We can check in again at the hospital, but I think you got the worst of it."

Griffen turned to look at us, his smile of reassurance forced and stiff. "I'm fine, Hope. She's right. You got the worst of it."

Their reassurance wasn't the least bit reassuring.

I stared at the ceiling of the ambulance and tried to think. Someone had shot out Griffen's tire? We'd considered canceling the trip after the shot taken into the office the day before, but everyone had agreed it was unlikely the shooter knew our plans, and so far, the attacks had centered on Heartstone.

Guess everyone had been wrong. Somehow, the guy with the gun had known exactly where we'd be, and when. Someone must have talked, but who?

It occurred to me that it could have been anyone, and not necessarily out of malice. We had no idea who the shooter was, which meant the person who mentioned our plans for the day probably hadn't attached any significance to the conversation. We'd been shot at twice and still had no idea who was behind it.

I snuck a glance at Griffen. He stared at the other side of the ambulance, his jaw tight, fists clenched on his knees. The ambulance rocked up and rolled to a stop. Everyone sprang to life, the back door swinging open, people talking over my head and around me. I was lifted and rolled through the doors, down a glaringly-white hall, and straight into a room.

Someone in a white coat carrying a tablet corralled Griffen, asking him all sorts of questions about my medical history and insurance and then, to my surprise, taking his credit card and swiping it through a reader plugged into the tablet. Efficient. I was mostly being ignored as the paramedics filled in the doctor and the doctor took a closer look at the branch still sticking out of my arm. It wasn't much of a branch, really, no more than seven or 8 inches long and skinnier than my pinky finger. Still hurt like hell.

"Okay, Hope?"

I nodded up at the doctor, wondering if it was time for somebody to tell me something.

"We're going to take this stick out of your arm. It's probably going to bleed more and I don't want you to panic. I'm going to clean it out and then stitch it up for you. I'll give you a local anesthetic so you shouldn't feel anything. If it hurts, I'd like you to let me know, okay?"

It took a few seconds to process what she was saying. Once I did, dread filled my heart. This was it. I was officially out of time. I glanced over at Griffen and then up into the doctor's friendly but impatient eyes.

"I... uh... will the local anesthetic be bad if... um... if I'm pregnant?" When I said the p-word, I shot a panicked look at Griffen. He froze. A heartbeat later he was at my side, taking my hand and looking down at me. I couldn't read his eyes. Maybe I was afraid to look too closely, afraid of what I'd see.

"You think you might be pregnant?" he asked in a carefully neutral voice.

"I... uh... I'm late. And I—"

"You fainted twice," Griffen reminded me as if I didn't know.

"Only once," I corrected, looking at the doctor. "The other time I just got dizzy. I've been dizzy and my stomach's off, but—"

"The local anesthetic should be fine if you're pregnant, but just in case, we'll do a test. How about that?"

I nodded in agreement.

"How late are you?" she asked, making a note on her own tablet.

"I'm not perfectly regular so it could be a week or it could just be a couple days."

"All right. I don't want to try to get you in the bathroom with this tree sticking out of your arm," she winked at me, "but we can do a blood test instead of a urine test."

I barely noticed as she drew blood for the test. Griffen was staring down at me, his eyes fixed on the injury to my arm, his face pale.

The next thing I knew there was another needle, and then another, the doctor injecting a local anesthetic. "We'll find out soon if you're pregnant, and if you are, I can give you a quick exam, but this won't do any harm to the baby. The risk of infection outweighs any potential risk from the treatment. It's easier if you don't look."

Griffen caught her meaning and pulled up a chair on the other side of the bed, taking my hand in his. He reached out to run a finger down my cheek, turning my face away from my right arm.

His eyes locked on mine. "Just look at me, Buttercup. She's going to get that splinter out of your arm, clean you up, and you'll be good as new. Okay? Just keep your eyes on mine and don't worry about what she's doing over there."

"Got it," I said, my gaze melting into his clear, green eyes, no longer remote and closed off. I still couldn't read them.

Was he freaking out? Angry? Happy? Shouldn't he be something?

I was all of the above.

Well, not angry. But freaking out and happy and confused and scared and also freaking out. Did I mention freaking out? I was a jumble of emotions, but I read none of them in Griffen's calm gaze.

"Just keep your eyes on me," he repeated. My arm moved. Something was pulling on it and I realized the doctor was taking out the piece of wood. I had to look, was already turning my head when Griffen's palm cupped the side of my face and turned it back to his.

"Don't look."

He ignored his own advice and watched with the doctor was doing. I wanted to watch. I also didn't want to lose my lunch, so I kept my eyes on Griffen.

"I won't look, but how big is it?"

He sounded a little sick as he said, "I'll tell you later."

I swallowed hard. Maybe I didn't want to know.

I didn't feel much of anything as the doctor cleaned the wound. A cold liquid on my skin, like she was rinsing it, and then more tugging. Griffen kept his eyes on me, holding my hand and stroking my hair back from my forehead. I tried to breathe, to relax, to think about anything except for the hole in my arm. And that I'd told Griffen I might be pregnant and he hadn't said anything.

A nurse came into the room just as the doctor was lifting her head to place tools in a tray beside her. Ignoring me, the actual patient, the nurse passed the doctor a sheet of paper and took over with the instruments.

"Well, Mr. and Mrs. Sawyer, congratulations. That was a good guess. You're pregnant."

"Is the baby okay? How would we know? Can you do an exam or an ultrasound or something?" My heart raced. It was one thing when the baby was theoretical. I'd been able to separate the possibility of a baby from the accident and all that blood. The piece of tree in my arm.

But now, knowing our barely-there baby had been through that car accident with us, tossed around as I bled so much—"How do we know if he's okay?"

"It could be a she," the doctor said in a gentle tease. "I'm going to help you slide to the end of the bed and I'll give you an exam. That's the best I can do at this point. It's a little early to see anything on an ultrasound. You need to make an appointment with your OB/GYN, and in a few weeks you can go and get your first baby pictures."

With her and Griffen to help, I scooched to the end of the bed where the doctor unfolded cleverly-hidden stirrups. "I don't care if it's a girl or a boy as long as the baby's okay," I said. Griffen silently squeezed my hand in what I hoped was agreement.

The doctor flicked her gaze up to him. "Are you comfortable having this exam with your husband present?"

335

"If he wants to stay," I said, my cheeks burning at the idea of Griffen watching me get a pelvic exam. Never mind that if I really was pregnant that was probably the least of what he'd see. Still, I wasn't there yet.

"I'm staying," Griffen said, his voice low.

I tried to pretend I didn't have my knees hiked to my chin with the doctor leaning between them. She put on a fresh pair of gloves, took the equipment the nurse handed her, and said, "You'll feel a touch now and some pressure." That was an understatement. I never really thought about how big a speculum was but... ouch.

"Try to relax," she murmured, shoving the speculum in deeper. I don't remember a pelvic ever hurting before.

Griffen squeezed my hand again, drawing my attention. He stroked his fingers down my cheek, rubbing gently. "Relax, Hope. Every muscle in your body is locked tight. Take a deep breath and relax."

He was right. I was holding my breath, utterly terrified, tensed against the bad news I was afraid was coming. I let out the breath I'd been holding and drew in another, this one long and slow. Gradually, breath by breath, I relaxed my body, the exercise mostly taking my mind off the doctor poking at my cervix.

Okay, not mostly. It took my attention a tiny bit off the doctor. I was still more terrified than relaxed.

Finally, she straightened. "Everything looks good. I don't see any signs of bleeding, and your cervix looks great. I can't make any promises, considering you just came through a car accident, but I don't see any cause for concern. I'd call your OB tomorrow and have them schedule you for your first appointment in the next few weeks. We'll get your discharge papers together and then you can head home."

I said a weak thank you and slid into cruise control as we waited to go over discharge instructions and final paperwork.

Griffen held my hand through it all, but he said almost nothing.

Was he angry? He must be. He'd said he didn't want to have a baby with me.

Now he was stuck.

Forever.

With me, the wife he hadn't wanted.

Chapter Forty-Two

GRIFFEN

I CALLED ROYAL WHILE HOPE WAS WORKING ON HER discharge paperwork. "I need a favor," I said, trying to focus on our immediate needs. My head was too crowded by the sight of Hope covered in blood, her scared eyes.

She was pregnant. I couldn't begin to get my head around that.

When I found whoever had pulled that trigger, I was going to kill him.

"Sure," Royal said easily, "What's up?"

"Hope and I are at the hospital. Someone shot out our tire and my car flipped. We're okay, but we need a ride home."

"You're okay? You and Hope? What the fuck, Griffen?"

"We're fine. Hope had to get stitches, but that's it."

"I'm on my way. I'm at the Inn, so I won't be long."

"Thanks. Meet us at the Emergency entrance. We should be out soon."

I called Hawk as soon as we hung up. He swore a blue streak, then said he'd meet me at the house as soon as I got Hope settled. I listened to Hope and the nurse with half an ear, frantically thinking through our options.

It was one thing for someone to try to kill me. I wasn't a fan, but I could handle it. Putting Hope in danger was a different story. She hadn't signed on for this. I could keep her safe if we never left the house, but what kind of life was that?

"Are you ready?" Hope's question interrupted my racing thoughts, her face tight with pain but her eyes calm.

I looked into those warm cognac eyes and everything inside me settled.

I knew what I had to do.

Hope wasn't going to like it, but that didn't matter. Not anymore.

"I'm ready," I answered, resolved to follow through, no matter what.

Royal was pulling up to the Emergency entrance of the hospital as we were wheeled out. Hope let me help her out of the wheelchair and into the backseat. I slid in beside her.

None of us talked much on the ride back. Hope was exhausted, the pain and shock finally catching up to her. Once we were on our way Royal asked, "Did you talk to Hawk? Does he have a plan?"

"We're working on it," I evaded. It wasn't just Hope who wouldn't like my plan. I couldn't have cared less.

No, that wasn't true. I cared. I didn't like it either. But, sometimes, life throws you into trouble and shows you what really matters. I'd faced that moment once before when my father had kicked me out. I thought I'd needed to be a Sawyer. Instead, I'd learned I had everything I needed as Griffen.

I knew, with crystalline clarity, that this was another of those moments. I wouldn't make the wrong choice, no matter how hard the right choice might be.

Royal dropped us at the front door. Hawk was waiting. "Give us a few minutes," I said, my arm around Hope. "Can you check with West to see if they found anything on the shooter?"

He nodded and pulled out his phone. I ushered Hope up the stairs before she could ask any questions. Once we had the door shut firmly behind us, I laid it out.

"I know your arm must hurt like hell, but tell me what you need to bring and I'll do all the work." I strode for the closet, muttering to myself, "I can have Savannah send anything we leave behind."

"What are you talking about? Bring where?"

"Bring with us," I said, impatiently dragging my suitcase from the back of the closet.

"Bring with us where? Where are we going?"

Had she hit her head in the accident? "To Atlanta. The Sinclair safe house to start. If West can't catch this guy, then maybe we'll stay there."

"What?" Hope stood in the closet door, staring at me blankly, swaying a little. Fuck. She needed to sit down.

"Never mind, I can figure out what to pack." I took her hand and pulled her to the couch, nudging her to sit. She did but stared up at me in bewildered confusion.

"We can't go to Atlanta, Griffen. We have to stay at Heartstone. The will—"

"I don't give a fuck about the will," I said. "I can't keep you safe here. We're leaving."

"We can't leave. We only get fourteen days away a quarter and we might need them for something else."

"We're not leaving for fourteen days, we're leaving and we're not coming back until I know it's safe," I said, feeling time ticking away. I had to get us packed. We needed to get moving.

"Griffen, we can't. If we're gone too long, you'll lose every-thing. The whole point of this is to keep your inheritance. To protect the town. If we leave it was all a waste."

I froze in place, not sure I'd understood her words. "A waste? What the hell are you talking about? What do you think we've been doing here?"

Hope took a slow breath before she said flatly, "I think that less than a month ago we walked into Harvey's office as strang-ers and we walked out married. I think that we have four years and eleven months until we're not married anymore. I think I'm not going to be the reason you lose your legacy. I think if we leave, there won't be anything to come back to. That's what I think."

I sank down on one of the chairs opposite the couch, prop-ping my elbows on my knees and resting my forehead in my palms.

"I really suck at this," I muttered.

Here I was, happily falling for Hope, and she thought I was looking for the end of the line.

How could she not know I was completely in love with her?

Hope was the only thing that mattered. Not the money or Sawyer Enterprises. Not this fucking house or my family. Not even the town.

I wouldn't let the town sink for my own sake, but to keep Hope safe, I'd do anything.

I'd burn the whole fucking place to the ground if it would keep her out of danger.

I'd fucked around long enough, assuming I could protect her, assuming whoever was after us would give up. She could have been killed today. I wasn't going to let that happen.

I stared at her, trying to think of what to say. If she didn't already know, then words weren't enough. I thought I'd been showing her how I felt, but obviously, I'd been fucking that up.

I could stand here and tell her I loved her all day, but the words wouldn't make her believe it if my actions hadn't gotten through.

I stared up at Hope's warm eyes and I knew.

I knew what I could say. What I could do.

Every step of Hope's life had been arranged by someone else, for their motives. Their interests. She was thirty-one years old, and I wondered if anyone in her life had ever asked her one simple question.

"What do you want?" I asked, holding her eyes with mine. "If you could have anything in the world for yourself, what would you want? What's your dream?"

She stared at me, mute, and I read the fear in her eyes. If she couldn't trust me even this much, I really had fucked everything up.

I stood and crossed to her, kneeling in front of where she sat on the couch, taking her hands in mine. "Trust me, Hope. Trust me enough to tell me your dream. The thing you want more than anything. Forget the will and this town and what people expect. Tell me what you want."

Hope sucked in a breath, opened her mouth to speak, but nothing came out. I squeezed her hands tighter. "I promise, Hope. You can trust me. With your dreams, with your heart. Please."

A tear spilled over her cheek. "Don't you get it? It's the same thing. My dreams and my heart are the same thing. And I—" Her voice cracked and she broke off. It was enough. The little she'd said was enough.

"I love you, Hope. In one way or another, I've always loved you."

More tears. Then her eyes fell and she whispered, "It's the baby. You said you didn't want the baby, but now—"

"It's not the baby, Hope." I released her hands and stood, facing away before turning back to her. All I could give her was the truth.

"I've been thinking about a family with you pretty much since we left Harvey's office the first day. The only reason I said I didn't want a baby was because of this exact situation. This was my nightmare, that you'd think I only want you because you're pregnant. I didn't want you to feel like a pawn. I wanted to wait so you'd know I wanted you. Just you. Not as a package deal or a way to save my inheritance. How can I prove that it has nothing to do with the will and everything to do with you?"

Hope stared up at me in mute wonder. Of all the things she'd been thinking, that I was in love with her clearly had not been on the list. Hope. Usually so observant, but she had a huge blind spot when it came to her own self-worth. I was going to spend a lifetime teaching her exactly how amazing she was.

"I can't prove that I love you," I said. "You have to believe. Tell me what you want. If there's any chance I can give it to you, I'll spend the rest of my life trying to make your dreams come true."

"Anything?" she asked, tilting her head to the side as if considering. Didn't she know? Surely, over all these years, she'd stored up a dream or two.

"Anything, Hope. Whatever it is, I'll find a way to give it to you. It's about time you got what you want for a change."

"And if I want to leave you? To be on my own for the first time? What then?"

Chapter Forty-Three

GRIFFEN

ER WORDS STABBED STRAIGHT THROUGH MY heart. I knew that was a risk when I'd asked. She'd spent her whole life being organized by other people. Maybe her wildest dream was just to be on her own.

I tipped my face to the ceiling, searching the plaster for an answer. None came. I went for blunt honesty.

"I know this is the part where I'm supposed to say '*Yes, even that*'. I can't. I can't say those words. Don't ask me to." I swallowed past the knot in my throat. "But I'd do anything to make you happy. Anything. So…" I shrugged. "I think it might kill me to watch you leave. But if that's your dream…." I swallowed again, my throat so dry it clicked.

Hope tilted her head to the side, the corner of her mouth tipping up as she watched me squirm. "You're my dream, you idiot. I can't believe you even had to ask."

Pure relief washed through me. I'd hoped, but I didn't know. "I thought, for once, someone should ask. I don't want you with me out of obligation. Because you think you need to save the town or protect my inheritance. I want you with me because you love me. Because you believe I love you. Edgar said I have a target on my back until you got pregnant, but you being pregnant moves the target to you. I thought if we waited until the five years were over we'd be safe. But life isn't safe and I want you. I want our baby. Tell me what you want me to pack so I can get you to Atlanta and we'll figure out the rest after that."

Hope looked at me, her eyes spilling fresh tears and glowing with love. I wasn't ready for what came out of her mouth.

"No. We're not going anywhere."

"Hope, I don't want to argue about this."

"Neither do I. My arm hurts. I'm tired. I'm hungry. I love you and I just want to curl up on the couch together. Or in bed. I don't care where, but this is a stupid plan."

"Hope, we can't stay here. What if you'd been shot yesterday? You could have died today."

"If we leave, your cousin Bryce gets everything. Am I the only one who remembers that?"

"I don't care," I ground out. "I don't care about the will and I don't care about Bryce. Let him have it. I care about you and our child."

Hope gave me a flat stare. She stood slowly, wiping tears from her face with the back of her hand before she crossed the room and started to make a cup of tea.

Wasn't she listening? We didn't have time for tea. We needed to get on the road. We needed to leave. We needed—

"*I care* about your legacy," Hope said. "And I'm not going to be the reason that you lose everything."

"As long as I have you, I'm not losing anything," I said.

She turned and gave me a patient, mild look. The look I imagined she'd give a toddler who wasn't listening. "You'd lose your family, Griffen. They're your real legacy. Not Sawyer Enterprises. Your family. You can't leave them now. We finally have everyone back under one roof. Together. Sterling is drinking less. Royal wants to work with you. You talked to Ford. We're not leaving."

"Hope, this isn't the time to get stubborn. Don't you understand? Your life is on the line."

"Griffen, you are one of the smartest men I know, but you're not thinking clearly. Understandable, considering we almost got killed, your car is totaled, and you just found out you're going to be a father. But you need to think. Your father was murdered. Unless you believe Bryce did it because he knew the details of the will, then the will doesn't have anything to do with this.

"We can leave, but you're still Griffen Sawyer. In Sawyers Bend, Atlanta, Fiji. You're still Griffen Sawyer, and I'm still your wife, and this is still your baby. I don't think this is about the will at all. I think this is someone who has a grudge against the Sawyer family. We're safest together."

I sank back into the chair and stared at Hope as she calmly stirred honey into her tea and sipped. Goddamnit. We'd talked about this the day before, but I'd still been thinking about it from the wrong angle. The will, the company, Bryce—all of it pointed me into seeing money as a motive.

Hope was right. If money had been the motive in my father's murder, then who stood to gain? Me. Possibly Bryce, assuming he knew about the will when no one else had.

If this wasn't about money, if it was about a grudge against the Sawyers, then Hope was right. We could run, but if someone had it out for us they'd follow. My father was dead. Ford was in prison. Was someone trying to knock us off one by one? Was Royal next?

Making a decision, I stood up, turned on the gas fireplace so the flames flickered warm and cheerful. Grabbing a blanket off the back of the couch, I said, "Come here."

Hope crossed the room to me, cupping her tea in both hands. I drew her down on the couch, putting her tea on the coffee table and pulling her close.

"How bad is your arm?" She couldn't take any decent pain-killers this early in pregnancy. I knew it had to hurt like a bitch.

Typical of Hope, she said, "It's fine."

I pressed my lips to the top of her head, settling inside now that she was lying against me, her body warm in my arms. "Liar. I know it hurts. I'm going to call down to the kitchen, get you something to eat, but we need to talk to Hawk first. Are you up for that?"

"As long as I don't have to move," she said, resting her cheek against my shoulder. I pulled the blanket up over her, careful not to put any pressure on the bandage on her arm.

"You're not going anywhere. You're right, leaving isn't the answer. I lost my head there for a minute."

"You're entitled," Hope murmured.

"Keep that in mind because we're not leaving, but I'm about to go a little crazy on security."

"Should I be worried about what that means?"

"Do you trust me?"

"You know I do."

"And you acknowledge that we're in danger until we find out who's behind all of this?"

Hope paused, knowing I was leading her down a path with my questions. "Considering you almost got run down, then shot at, then shot at again until your car was totaled and I had a tree stuck in my arm, then yeah, I'll acknowledge we're in danger."

I flicked her lightly on the nose. "Don't be a smartass." Hope didn't comment. I pulled up my phone and called Hawk, asking him to meet us up in our suite. Then I called Savannah and asked if we could get soup and a sandwich for two.

Hope struggled to sit up as Hawk came in, wincing as she moved. I handed her the mug of tea and we got down to business. Hawk was already working on the electronic perimeter around the property. We agreed to a second perimeter closer to the house and additional cameras.

I'd talk to Cooper and Alice in the morning and see about ordering a new car from wherever they got the vehicles Sinclair Security used. No Maserati this time. I wanted one of the armored SUVs we'd used for high profile clients. Short of a rocket launcher, it was impossible to take one of those things down. Along with the armored car, Hope learned she was getting a full-time bodyguard and driver.

As I'd known she would, she objected. "I don't need a bodyguard. I have you. We're together almost all the time and this is what you were trained for. This was your job. Are you saying there's somebody better than you?"

Maybe it was relief that she was okay, that she loved me, but I grinned at her peevish objections. "Of course not, Buttercup. No one is better than me. But two is better than one. I'm not going to let anything happen to you. I don't trust the hospital staff to keep their mouths shut. Everyone in this town is going to know you're pregnant by tomorrow. Even if this isn't about the will, if this is someone with a grudge, you being pregnant is only going to piss them off more."

Hope looked at Hawk. He shrugged a shoulder. "Griffen knows his business. You think he's overreacting, and I'm telling you he's not. We have extra people coming in, we're setting up a perimeter, and I'll get on ordering a new car and finding the driver/bodyguard. But until all of that is in place, as your head of security, I'm telling you that I want you to stay in the house and away from windows. Curtains are closed and no strolling the property. Understood?"

Hope just stared at him.

"My job isn't to make you happy, Hope, it's to keep you safe. Listen to your husband and listen to me. Make it easy for us, yeah?"

"Okay," Hope whispered. She didn't like it, but she got it.

Hawk stood. "I'll call Cooper now and get the ball rolling. I'd expect your phone to ring as soon as I get off. They're not going to take this well. You're one of theirs, and no one comes after one of theirs."

He left and Hope sagged against the back of the couch, her face pale. "I wish you could take something for your arm," I said.

"Me too. I just need to eat, I think. I get so queasy in the morning and then I'm starving at night."

"Are you happy? About the baby?" I almost didn't ask. I didn't want to hear a *No*.

Hope sipped her tea again and gave me a wan smile. "About the baby? Yeah. I'm happy about the baby. I'm happy about us. I'm not happy about the hole in my arm and someone trying to kill us, but I can't do anything about that, so I guess I just want some dinner, sleep, and you."

"I can give you that. Savannah's on the way with some food and then we'll curl up in bed. Maybe watch a movie, go to bed early."

"That sounds perfect." And it was.

It was perfect right up until dawn—when everything went to hell all over again.

Chapter Forty-Four

HOPE

T WAS MY ARM THAT WOKE ME. IT HAD ACHED AND stabbed at me through the night, prodding me from sleep far too often. I blinked gritty eyes against the weak dawn light peeking through the curtains.

Just as I thought about drifting back to sleep, I shifted to take the pressure off my arm. At the movement, my stomach hitched.

Not again.

Griffen rolled toward me, propping himself up on his elbow. The smile on his face was nothing I'd ever thought to see in real life. Open, happy, and overflowing with love. For me.

The pain in my arm faded into the background. A goofy smile spread across my face. I couldn't help it. I was so in love with Griffen Sawyer, and he loved me back. A miracle like that deserved a goofy smile.

Blinded by the look on his face, the light in his green eyes, I leaned up to kiss him only to collapse back on the mattress with the yelp of pain.

Dumbass. How could I have forgotten the hole in my arm?

The stab of pain stole my breath and tried to turn my stomach inside out. Saliva flooded my mouth. Crap. I wasn't getting off easy this time.

The goofy smile long gone, I scrambled from the bed, ignoring the pain and nausea, ignoring everything on my race for the bathroom. I almost didn't make it. I fell to my knees on the marble floor and wrenched up the lid, just in time.

I hate vomiting. I don't know anyone who likes it, but I really, really hate it. I especially hated knowing that Griffen was standing right behind me, watching me heave my guts up. I wanted to wave him off, but I was braced on my good arm and I wasn't willing to risk moving the bad one. Someone needed to invent a decent pain med for pregnant women.

After the first heave, I caught my breath and lifted my head up. "Don't watch."

"Tell me how to help," Griffen said, sounding a little desperate.

I took a slow breath and managed to get out, "Ginger ale," before the next heave hit my gut. I wasn't ready for anything to drink yet, but the ginger ale—actually ginger beer so spicy it burned going down—was the only thing that settled my stomach. Griffen disappeared and was back seconds later.

"The fridge up here is empty. I'll run down to the kitchen and grab one out of the pantry."

I let him go without a word, too busy puking up everything I'd ever eaten. I don't know how long I sat there, the cold floor freezing my bare skin, my good arm wrapped around the toilet seat and clammy forehead pressed to my wrist. Eventually, it stopped.

I waited, just in case, but my stomach had decided it was thoroughly empty, and I was free to go.

I staggered to my feet, flushed the toilet, and headed straight for my toothbrush, catching sight of myself in the bathroom mirror. Yuck. My face was too pale, dark circles bruised under my eyes, my hair a hopeless tangle.

Once I'd brushed my teeth and ran a brush through my hair, I realized that I was hungry.

Hungry? How the heck could I be hungry? Maybe because I'd barely eaten anything the day before and had just spent a million years throwing up.

Whatever, I didn't care. I wanted that ginger beer and then I wanted some food. Wandering back into the bedroom to check the clock, I realized that it was too early for Savannah to be on duty, and Miss Stiles might not be in the kitchen yet. If I wanted food, I'd have to make it myself. Not that I wasn't fully capable. I could manage toast.

I scooped up Griffen's sweater from the floor, the cashmere settling around me, soft and scented of the woods and Griffen. He wasn't getting this sweater back. I pulled on a pair of jeans I'd left on the floor of the closet, shoved my feet into a pair of ugly-but-warm slippers and left the room in search of food.

No one else was up, not that I'd expected them to be. It was barely dawn, the weak light of the spring sunrise peeking through the closed curtains. Remembering that Hawk had told me to stay away from the windows, I went down the back staircase, my stomach growling in demand.

On the lower level, voices echoed down the hall, bouncing off the stone. Voices? Was Miss Stiles here early? With Savannah? I didn't hear a woman, though. Griffen. Griffen and a man I didn't recognize. A strong accent. Someone who'd grown up in the mountains around here.

We didn't have anyone on staff with that accent. I would have remembered. The local accents varied from almost none—like me and my uncle Edgar and all the Sawyers—to a little Southern—like Maisie—to varying degrees of the mountain accents and dialects, some of which I could barely understand, and I'd lived here my whole life.

Whoever was talking to Griffen was somewhere in between town and mountains. Not so strong I couldn't understand, but strong enough. No one I recognized.

I slowed down and listened. The hall was dark. Either Griffen hadn't bothered with the lights, or he'd turned them off. The windows high in the wall of the kitchen filled the room with light, even at this early hour. I stayed in the shadows of the hall, inching toward the open doorway of the kitchen.

I had to smother a squeak of terror when I heard Griffen say, "Put the gun down and we can talk." His voice was solid and calm. Almost conversational. But he'd said *gun*.

Gun? What now?

I knew what Griffen would tell me to do. Run and not stop until I found either West or Hawk.

I wasn't doing that. Not exactly. Not if it meant leaving Griffen. There wasn't time to wander all over the estate trying to find Hawk. I didn't have my phone. I'd left it on my bed-side table. It hadn't occurred to me I'd need it for a trip to the kitchens.

There was a house phone in the gym. I just had to pray it was still hooked up. I tried to remember where else I'd seen the house phones. Some of the bedrooms had them. Savannah's for one.

Savannah. Nicky. They were trapped in their rooms tucked behind the kitchens, unaware of the danger. I had to warn her.

Flattening myself against the far wall of the corridor, I sent a silent thanks to the heavens that Griffen's sweater was dark gray and my jeans a blue so deep it was almost black. I blended into the shadows of the dark hall, almost impossible to see from the far brighter kitchen.

Griffen stood with his back to the door, weapon drawn and pointed at a man, thin and tall, his hair in greasy strings around a gaunt face, a wild look in his eyes. The man held Miss Stiles in front of him like a shield, her ample frame providing his lean one plenty of cover. With a shaking hand, the stranger pressed the barrel of a revolver to her temple.

I crept past the open doorway, seeing a small plate of toast beside three cans of ginger beer. Despite the armed standoff only feet away, my heart warmed. He'd been making me toast. My husband had been making me toast.

"How did you get in?" Griffen demanded as I cleared the open doorway and moved further down the hall.

"You don't put that gun down, I'm gonna shoot you."

"I'll put it down," Griffen promised, "I just want to know how you got in."

"Climbed in the back of this here's car. Bitch never knew I was there 'til I made 'er open the door for me."

I didn't hear Griffen's answer. The second I was all the way past the door I raced down the hall for the gym.

The house phone hung on the far wall, a chart of rooms and numbers beside it. Jackpot. Heart racing, I fumbled for the receiver and dialed the number of the housekeeper's room, praying the sound didn't carry to the armed men in the kitchen.

She answered after three rings with a distracted, "Hello?" I could hear Nicky saying something in the background and Savannah's exasperated, "I don't know, honey, I just handed it to you."

"Savannah?"

"Hope. Is everything all right?"

"No. Stay where you are and be quiet. Tell Nicky to be quiet. I'm in the gym. Someone broke in and he's holding Miss Stiles hostage in the kitchens. Griffen is there, and they both have guns. They don't know I'm down here. You need to call Hawk and then West."

"All right, okay. Hold on." Silence for an endless minute. Then she was back, her voice breathless. "I locked the door to my rooms and hid Nicky in the bathroom. You go back upstairs and stay there, Hope. Get out of the gym."

"I'm okay. I'm safe. Just stay in your room and call Hawk and West."

"Hope! Don't do anything dangerous. Just go up to your room and I'll send Hawk straight to Griffen, I promise."

I hung up. I wasn't going to do anything stupid, but I wasn't running away, either.

I left the receiver hanging from the cord. If Savannah called back I didn't want the ring to echo down the hall to the kitchen, and I wasn't going to waste time arguing.

Savannah was calling Hawk and West. Help was on the way.

I looked around the gym for anything I could use. Not a weapon. I wasn't dumb enough to go running into the middle of the standoff between two men holding guns.

All I needed was a way to give Griffen an edge. Given what he'd spent the last fifteen years doing, he had to be good with that gun. If I could distract the intruder, maybe...

My eyes landed on the medicine balls stacked in the corner. Ignoring the pain in my injured arm, I grabbed two, one the size of a soccer ball, the other small enough to fit in my hand. Moving in silence, I made my way back down the hall to the kitchens, hugging the shadows.

A woman's whimper of fear made its way out of the room. Poor Miss Stiles. The intruder shouted into the quiet, his voice more high-pitched than before. He was starting to panic. "I told you to put that damn gun down. You know you're not gonna shoot her."

"Are you planning to shoot me?" Griffen asked mildly as if they were chatting over a beer and pizza.

"Damn straight, I'm gonna shoot you. Missed you in your office. Fuckin' bad luck you leaning down. I almost had you. And the car flipping. Shoulda killed you. This time, I'm gonna blast off your mother-fucking face."

"Like you shot my father?" Griffen asked, sounding curious as if he hadn't even registered the threat.

"I wish I'd killed that bastard. Give whoever did it a medal. A goddamned medal. No one deserved killing like your daddy."

"Not sure I disagree with you on that," Griffen said in that same maddeningly-relaxed tone. "But why did you want my father dead? What did he do to you?"

Chapter Forty-Five

HOPE

I PEEKED INTO THE ROOM, STAYING OUT OF THE LIGHT. The intruder's hand trembled with rage, his eyes burning, his arm a bar across Miss Stiles' throat.

"That bastard fired me. Said I was unreliable. One time I was drinking on the job. One goddamn time. I lost my job. I lost my wife. She moved away with my boy. Couldn't get another job in town when everybody found out why Sawyer let me go. Whole fucking life ruined because o' your holier-than-thou daddy. And now you're gonna be dead, too. You and all the rest of them."

His eyes flared with a kind of joyous intent, his arm steadied as he took aim on Griffen.

Griffen was stuck. He could fire, but Miss Stiles was not slightly built and her body made a great shield.

I knew Griffen. He wouldn't risk her life.

I would.

I did.

Crouched in the corner of the doorway, mostly out of sight, I rolled the medicine ball into the kitchen, straight at Miss Stiles' feet. I ducked into the shadows, betting the intruder would look up. He did, his arm loosening on Miss Stiles' neck as he turned to see where the ball had come from.

The gun he had pointed at Griffen slid to the side. The second the barrel wasn't pointed straight at Griffen, I palmed the smaller ball in my left hand and pitched it straight at the arm around Miss Stiles' neck. My aim wasn't great. I caught more of Miss Stiles than I'd meant to, but I figured a bruised jaw was better than dead.

The man with the gun yelped in surprise, his arm loosening even more, body turning to the side as he looked for whoever had thrown the ball. I let him see me before diving out of the doorway and flattening my back against the stone wall. He could shoot at me, but a bullet wasn't getting through that stone.

I heard feet scuffle, a shout. A gunshot. My heart froze, but I didn't dare look. I should run, take off for safety. I could be up the stairs and on the main level in less than two minutes. There wasn't anything else I could do to help.

My feet refused to move. I wasn't leaving Griffen.

A woman's sobs leaked into the hall. Griffen's voice, swearing. "Stop moving, you fucking asshole."

I slid closer to the open doorway and risked a look. Miss Stiles was crumpled in the corner weeping into her apron, but I didn't see any blood. Griffen knelt on the intruder's back, both of their guns out of reach on the floor, the intruder's hands wrenched behind his back.

I stepped into the room. "I called Savannah. Hawk and West are on their way."

Griffen glared at me. "Get the fuck out of here, Hope. Are you insane? Did you call Savannah and then come back here?"

Relief flooded through me at the strength in his voice. He was okay. I ignored his questions. "Are you all right? Did anyone get hurt?"

"I'm fine. Everyone's fine. Answer my question. Did you call Savannah and then come back here?"

"Obviously," was my not so brilliant response. Griffen glared at me. I tried to look contrite. Griffen wasn't having it.

"Why would you do such a goddamn stupid thing?"

"I wasn't leaving you. You can yell at me all you want, but I wasn't leaving you."

He shook his head but didn't say anything else. Hawk came in the room from behind me, his eyes like ice. "Hope. Some-one gets in the house, you hide in your fucking room until you get the all-clear from me, West, or Griffen. Got it? You do not—"

Hawk looked around the room, trying to figure out what had happened.

Griffen helpfully supplied, "Roll a medicine ball at him."

Hawk rolled his eyes. "You threw a medicine ball at an intruder with a weapon?"

"It worked, didn't it?"

Neither Griffen nor Hawk deigned to reply. That's because they didn't want to admit it had been a good plan. I'd barely been in any danger *and* I'd distracted the shooter. They should be thanking me.

Instead, Griffen growled, "Go check on Savannah, see if she and Nicky are okay. Then stay with them in their room until one of us lets you out."

I thought about arguing, but at the strained expressions on his and Hawk's faces, I decided to do what I was told. Grabbing the toast and can of ginger beer off the counter, I made my way down the narrow hall in the back corner of the kitchen and knocked on Savannah's door.

"It's Hope. Griffen and Hawk have everything under control, but they want us to stay here while they wait for West."

Savannah opened her door and pulled me in. "You didn't go upstairs, did you?"

I waved her off. It was over and everyone was all right. Now that the adrenaline had worn off, my arm was killing me and I really needed that ginger beer. Popping the top, and deeply grateful it was still cold, I took a long gulp, my eyes watering at the fiery ginger. It hurt to swallow, but nothing settled my stomach like it.

"Are you two okay?" In a lower voice, looking over Savannah's shoulder, I asked, "Nicky good?"

"He's watching cartoons on my tablet and thrilled I'm not rushing him out the door to pre-school. What happened?"

I filled Savannah in and we waited, quickly growing restless as the door to the sitting room remained closed. We could hear male voices, muffled through the solid wood, shouts from a woman—Miss Stiles I guessed—but as hard as we tried, we couldn't make out any words.

Trying to distract myself, I looked around. "I'm going to talk to Griffen about getting a contractor out here. We need to get your cottage put back together so you have more room than this."

"It's fine," Savannah started to say.

"It's not. And I really think you should repaint when you turn it into an office. All this institutional white is depressing."

Savannah shrugged a shoulder. "We'll get to it. For now, I'm worried about finding a new cook. I have a feeling Miss Stiles is out of here."

Savannah wasn't wrong. By the time Griffen opened the door and set us free, the kitchen was empty of everyone, including Miss Stiles.

"West took the guy to the station to book him. We need to follow when we can. Hawk is checking the perimeter and getting security tapes to send to West. Miss Stiles—" He shook his head at Savannah. "Sorry. She quit. Wouldn't even consider staying until we replaced her."

Savannah sighed. "I'll call Mom, see if she can help with breakfast and take Nicky to pre-school. Then I'll set up some more interviews. In the meantime—"

"I'll talk to Finn," Griffen said. "He can dust off all that fancy training for a few days to feed us, or he can take a hike."

"Good luck with that," Savannah murmured.

Griffen didn't speak to me, not really, until we were on our way to give our statements to West.

"Are you going to be mad at me all day?" I asked, trying to tease him out of his mood. It didn't work.

He slanted me a dark look. "Yes. I'm going to be pissed at you forever. You could have been shot."

"I wasn't in danger for more than a second. You had him covered and I was hiding behind a stone wall."

"Hope—"

"Nope, save it. We both know I wasn't really in any danger, and I wasn't leaving you."

"Stubborn," he muttered.

"Get used to it," I said.

"I'm seriously re-thinking our plan to stay at Heartstone."

"Get used to that, too. We're staying."

Griffen sighed. "Unless West gives us a good reason not to, we're staying," he agreed.

West didn't give us a reason to leave Sawyers Bend. "He's not going anywhere," he said of our intruder. "John Fredricks. Former Marine. Went for Marine Scout Sniper and didn't make it, but it wasn't because of his shooting skills. He admitted to trying to run you down in his truck, and to taking the shot at you in your office and at your tire. He also claims he was working for someone else."

"Who?" Griffen demanded.

West shook his head. "Says he doesn't know. He was paid in cash, anonymous drops. Calls came to his cell. I have the number, but I'm betting it's a burner or clone. Voice was disguised. He doesn't know if it was a man or woman. Just that they knew he had a grudge and had sniper level shooting skills."

"So, what now?" I asked.

West gave me a grim smile. "Go home. Keep security high, but live your lives. This isn't over. Whoever hired Fredricks will find someone else eventually, but for now, you have a little breathing room. Enjoy it while it lasts."

Griffen didn't look convinced. Actually, Griffen looked like he was on the verge of packing me up and running for the hills. I wasn't going to let that happen.

I won't say I wasn't scared. It didn't feel great to know someone was out there looking for another hired gun to aim our way. But West was right, we had a little breathing room. I wasn't going to waste it.

"Let's go home," I said when we got back into the car Griffen had borrowed from Royal. "We can ditch work for the day and you can take my mind off my arm."

"How bad is it?" he asked, eyes dark with concern.

"It just hurts. I didn't pull any stitches or anything."

"You're sure? We can go by the hospital if—"

"I'm fine. I swear. But if you wanted to take me home and distract me—"

Griffen finally caught my drift. "Distract you, huh? What did you have in mind? A movie? I could find you a book."

I let my good arm slide over the console between us. My hand landed in his lap. Stroked. "A book? Not exactly."

Griffen hardened under my touch. His green eyes glinted, the worry chased away by my busy fingers. "We have some spreadsheets we could go over—"

"Hmm, not that either. No work today, remember? I was thinking more like naked distraction."

"Naked distraction," Griffen repeated musingly as if his cock wasn't rock hard and straining against his jeans. "What about your arm? You shouldn't move it."

"I thought you could be creative." I squeezed his length through his jeans, loving the sharp intake of his breath.

He shot me a wolfish grin. "Oh, I can do creative, Buttercup."

And he could. Over my protests that I could walk on my own, Griffen carried me up to our rooms, where he carefully stripped me of my clothes and lay me down in my big brass bed.

Our big brass bed. I'd told myself I hadn't thought of Griffen when I'd bought the bed, but I'd been lying. Of course, I'd thought of him.

It was always him.

Always Griffen.

And it always would be.

GRIFFEN

OPE LOOKED DOWN AT THE PICTURE IN HER HAND, a secret smile on her face. To be honest, I thought it looked like a black-and-white blob surrounded by a bunch of static, but the OB swore eventually it would be our baby.

I didn't so much care about the picture, but I kept hearing that fast thud-thud-thud of the baby's heartbeat coming through the speakers. Despite the ER doctor's assurances, we'd both been worried. The car accident. The tree branch sticking out of Hope's arm. All that blood.

The relief of knowing everything was okay was a weight off us both.

We were having a baby.

I didn't really have my head around it yet. I wasn't sure I would until we met face to face. Only seven more months.

Hope turned the picture upside down and squinted at it. "I can't tell which side is up," she admitted. "The timestamp is at the top, I think." She turned it again. "But this just looks weird."

"The doctor said she's about the size of a blueberry. There's not much to see yet."

Hope slid the picture into her purse. "I know. I'm just impatient, I guess."

I reached across the console to take her hand. "I know what you mean. It's going to be a long seven months. And the best early Christmas present ever."

Hope's radiant smile pushed the day right over the top. We'd gotten good news from the doctor and I had my beaming wife sitting beside me.

The day we'd married I'd thought my life had fallen apart. Things had changed—no denying that—but once we'd gotten through the rough parts, this new life was better than anything I'd ever dreamed.

Life wasn't perfect, but we were getting there.

"I don't want to tell everybody yet," Hope said. "Not until we clear the first trimester. I know it's weird with us all sharing the same house, but—"

I didn't like the shadow on Hope's face. I wanted the smile back.

"I agree. Who already knows? Officially." We couldn't account for town gossip. I was pretty sure the doctor who'd seen us in the ER hadn't said a word, but I didn't know about the nurse or any technicians who might have seen the test and Hope's name on it. Added to that, we'd just seen the OB together. Anyone who'd spotted us would know Hope wasn't there for her annual check-up.

But rumor wasn't fact, and it made sense to keep it quiet as long as we could. West had my shooter in jail, and he wasn't getting out anytime soon, but we still didn't know who'd hired him or why.

"Officially?" Hope looked out the window of our new armored SUV as she thought. "Savannah, and I'm pretty sure Royal knows."

"Royal knows," I confirmed. "I didn't tell him, he guessed. Same with Hawk. He figured it out when I mentioned that you'd been fainting."

"I only fainted once." She aimed an affectionate scowl at me. "Hawk's a sharp guy. I shouldn't be surprised."

"Other than them, we'll keep it to ourselves. As long as we can."

We pulled into the long drive to Heartstone, signs of spring everywhere in the daffodils pushing through the soil, the pale green buds on the trees.

Hawk had been too busy with security to do much with the grounds yet. He'd hired a few guys to clean things up, but so far, that was it. Still, the signs of spring, of new life, welcomed us home.

Just before the turn to the garage, I pulled to a stop, my eyes narrowed on the late-model black sedan parked in the courtyard right in front of the stairs to the front door.

"Is that—?"

"Uncle Edgar's car," Hope confirmed. "He knows."

"Looks like it. Do you want me to tell him to leave?" I turned down the lane to the garage and waited for Hope's answer.

She took a deep breath and let it out slowly. "No. I haven't gone this long without seeing Uncle Edgar since he brought me home. Maybe that was for the best, but I think I'd like to see him now."

Savannah met us in the back hall by the mudroom. "Your Uncle Edgar is here," she said to Hope. "I put him in the family gathering room. I didn't think you'd want him in your office unsupervised and that's the only other room on the first floor that's fully furnished aside from the dining room. Do you want me to bring in a tray? Tea and cookies?"

I looked to Hope. My instinct was to tell Edgar Daniels to get the hell out of my house, but it was Hope's call. "No tray. I don't think this will take long."

Edgar rose when we entered, his sharp eyes taking in Hope, absorbing the sight of her as if he'd missed her. I didn't feel too sorry for him. He could have called or stopped by or bothered to acknowledge her existence at all since the day she'd walked into his office to find herself replaced. He hadn't, so my sympathy wasn't running high.

Hope crossed the room to kiss his cheek, gripping his weathered hands in hers. "How are you, Uncle Edgar?"

"Not as good as you, I hear. You two have something to tell me?" His gaze flicked between the two of us, expectant. Just short of demanding.

I looked to Hope. Edgar wasn't on my short list of people to tell about our pregnancy, but I wouldn't stop Hope if she wanted to share the news. Especially since my bet was that Edgar already knew.

Hope hesitated before she made up her mind. She sat on one of the overstuffed couches that flanked the huge fireplace, the flames merrily burning. Smoothing her hands over her knees, she said, "We'd like to keep it quiet for now, but Griffen and I are going to have a baby."

"Good news, good news." Edgar rubbed his hands together, a satisfied smile crossing his face.

"I'd like to know why it's so important to you," Hope asked slowly. "You haven't even talked to me since Griffen and I got married, but you told Griffen to get me pregnant. What does it matter? Why do you care?"

"Don't be ridiculous, girl. Of course, I care. Raised you, didn't I? Got you settled with a good husband. The one you wanted—" The old bastard actually tilted his head and winked at Hope. *Winked.*

I wasn't sure I'd recover from the sight of gruff Edgar Daniels winking. I didn't even mind that he was admitting he'd maneuvered Hope into this position. I'd figured that out a long time ago, and frankly, if his reason was to make Hope happy I wouldn't argue with it.

"Not how I planned to find myself a husband," Hope said mildly, "but I don't understand why it matters that we're having a baby."

"For one, the will," Edgar said as if she were dense. "I know the entire Sawyer estate goes to Bryce if something happens to Griffen before there's a child. I didn't go to the trouble to get you hitched to him to have you lose everything to that fuckwit. And for another, because you'll be a good mother."

Hope straightened in surprise, but Edgar went on.

"Some women shouldn't have children. You know that better than anyone. You're not one of them. You've mothered me plenty the last twenty years. Now you have everything that should be yours. Griffen Sawyer, a baby—Though if you want to keep your husband, girl, you should throw out those jeans and put on something more appropriate."

And right there he crossed the line. Didn't take him long. I sat next to Hope and wrapped my arm around her waist, very blatantly closing my hand on her hip. "I would have thought you'd figured it out already, but I like Hope's jeans. I like everything Hope wears, except those ugly suits you bought her. And I don't think we need marital advice from a lifelong bachelor."

Edgar *harrumphed*, but his eyes were warm as he took in our closeness, the way Hope leaned into me. "Just you know, I have my eyes on you, boy. I get the slightest sign you're not treating her right—stepping out, working too much—I don't care. I get the slightest sign, and I'll take care of it."

I didn't know what to say to that. What was Edgar going to do? Challenge me to a bout of fisticuffs?

No, he'd probably hire a hitman and find Hope another husband.

I tried not to grin at that thought. Edgar wouldn't have anything to worry about. Treating Hope right was my top priority. Always would be.

Instead of taunting him, I said, "I don't think that's going to be a problem. But I want to know—how? How did you know that I'd fall in love with Hope? How did you know I'd be back? That Prentice would die? And how did you get him to agree to force us into marriage?"

Edgar just shook his head. "I didn't know that you'd have feelings for my Hope. Not for sure. I had a hunch. And Prentice? I can't answer that. I don't know who killed him. I just knew he was playing with fire, and it was only a matter of time. I wanted Hope covered in case you didn't come back on your own."

"What does that even mean?" Hope asked, exasperated.

"It means I told Weston Garfield everything I know about Prentice's murder, which wasn't much."

"And what about how you got Prentice to force our marriage in the first place?" I pressed. It was the one thing that made no sense.

"That's not mine to tell, boy. Let's just say your father owed me and I collected. The rest is in the past. Leave it there and focus on your future."

"I don't know that I have a choice, Edgar. Someone seems to have it out for the Sawyers. Feels like the past is coming for me—coming for us—one way or another."

Edgar shook his head. "I can promise you that whatever is going on now, whatever hornet's nest Prentice stirred up before he died, it has nothing to do with what your father owed me. Nothing. Now, what I want to know is when is Hope going to quit working for you so she can concentrate on decorating the nursery and being a mother?"

I glanced at Hope to see her rolling her eyes to the ceiling, shaking her head, a tiny smile curving her lips.

"Hope can do both. Hope can do whatever the hell she wants. What she's not going to do is take orders. From anyone. Is that clear?"

"She's your problem now. If you think you can keep her in line without ordering her around, then by all means...."

"I don't know, I like it when she gets out of line," I said, squeezing her hip and ignoring the affronted look Edgar gave both of us.

He'd been all fired up for Hope to get pregnant. I was assuming he knew how I got her that way. Hope's cheeks were pink as she jabbed her elbow in my ribs.

"I don't know what I want to do, Uncle Edgar," she said, the laugh still in her voice. "I've never had a baby before. I like working with Griffen, and since he works from home, who knows? We'll figure things out as we go."

Not caring that we had an audience, I turned my face to press a kiss to her temple, breathing in her sweet apples and cinnamon scent.

I loved this woman with every fucking inch of my heart. With every cell in my body. I didn't care if she wanted to work with me, or somewhere else, or quit to raise our kids, or do all the above. As long as she was with me and she was happy, I'd have everything I wanted in life.

"You need to be careful," Edgar cautioned, leaning forward, his eyes serious. "Harvey's good, but just because he hasn't spread that will around doesn't mean Prentice didn't share the contents with anyone. I'm glad to see you have security locked down here. Your Hawk stopped me at the gatehouse and escorted me in, wouldn't leave my side until Savannah gave me clearance. He wouldn't give me the details, but he said the grounds are covered, that no one's getting anywhere near the house without him knowing."

"That's right. The house is as safe as we can make it without turning it into a bunker. You don't have to worry about Hope."

"Then you keep your eye on the Inn, Griffen," Edgar warned. "With the house inaccessible, anyone after you is going to target the Inn. That's what I would do. It's too visible, a symbol of the family. Public. And a hell of a lot harder to secure than the Manor. Tell Royal and Tenn to be sharp. They've already had some trouble there, could be the usual, but maybe not."

Edgar levered himself out of the armchair. "I'll be here for Sunday dinner. Tell Savannah to put me at the head of the table near you. I don't want to get stuck down at the end with that sister of yours. She has a smart mouth."

I wondered which sister he meant. They all had smart mouths when they got riled up. Even Parker.

Hope just stared at Edgar. "You're coming to Sunday dinner?"

"Since when do we have Sunday dinner?" I asked. It had been a tradition when I was a kid, but that was a long time ago, and as far as I knew, no one had revived it since Darcy's death.

"You do now," Edgar said. "That's the way it used to be. Sunday dinner at Heartstone Manor. Sometimes the past is best left behind. And sometimes you need to look back and remember what there is worth saving."

With another *harrumph*, he crossed the room and closed his hand around Hope's arm, pulling her into a rough hug. He kissed her cheek and gave her a squeeze before letting go. "I'll see myself out. Be back on Sunday."

Hope and I watched him go. "I guess we're having Sunday dinner," Hope said. "It's a good idea. We should have thought of that already. Make it a house rule. Everyone's here for Sunday dinner."

"I like it. I forgot about those dinners. I hated them back then. Eating with the grown-ups, Darcy combing my hair, making me wear a tie. Then, when she was gone, I didn't want to do it without her. Nobody did."

"Who would have thought Uncle Edgar would be right? Sometimes it is good to look back and remember what's worth saving."

We walked down the hall to the entry, Hope probably thinking about what we had to do for the rest of the day and me planning to talk her into a long afternoon nap. The naked kind of nap. My favorite kind.

"So, what's on next?" I asked innocently.

Hope slanted me a look from beneath her eyelashes. I knew that look. Maybe I wouldn't have to do much convincing after all.

"I'm feeling a little tired after this morning. So much excitement, you know? I was thinking maybe we could lay down. Together."

I loved the way her cheeks still turned pink when she thought about sex.

"I like the way you think, Hope Sawyer. You just saved me trying to convince you to throw out your to-do list and let me get you naked."

She laughed, the sound like bells. "Little did you know. You getting me naked *was* my to-do list."

"Even better." I scooped her into my arms, my heart beating faster at her gasp of surprised pleasure. I strode down the hall, intent on reaching the privacy of our bedroom only to pull up short as Savannah came toward us, her face set, Finn on her heels.

Was I going to have to referee another spat between the two of them? I had much better things to do, namely the woman in my arms.

"You two are going to have to deal with it yourselves," I said, turning sideways to try to pass them. "We're busy."

"No, you're not," Finn said. "Hawk called from the gate-house. We have visitors."

"Is Edgar gone?" Hope asked as I reluctantly set her on her feet.

"He must have passed them on the road," Savannah said.

"You're not going to believe this." Finn turned to lead us to the front door.

Royal came up behind him, an accordion file folder in hand, and looked between the four of us. "What's going on?"

"Visitors," Savannah said grimly and turned on her heel to stride back to the entry hall.

We followed, arriving at the front windows in time to see a classic baby blue Mercedes sedan roll into the courtyard, Hawk's black armored SUV right on its tail.

The Mercedes came to a stop. The driver's side door opened and out stepped a young man. Early twenties, he could have been a twin to Sterling or Brax, all shining golden hair and vibrant blue eyes, with a slim athletic build in a perfectly-tailored suit.

He would have looked like a young Greek God if not for the petulant sneer on his face.

The last time I saw him, he was a child, but I recognized him instantly.

"Bryce," Hope said from beside me.

"Fuck," Royal swore. "What the hell is he doing here?"

"Hawk tried to bar them from the property," Savannah said, "but Bryce had a letter from Prentice saying he could stay in the house."

We watched as Hawk opened the passenger door and reached in to not so gently haul out an older woman with frosted platinum hair and the same bright blue eyes as her son.

"Fuck me," I said under my breath.

Aunt Ophelia.

Hadn't Edgar warned us about trouble?

Well, here it was.

And from the looks of it, trouble was planning to move into Heartstone Manor.

Turn the page for a sneak peek of
SWEET HEART
Book Two of The Hearts of Sawyers Bend

SWEET HEART
DAISY

I SHOULD HAVE BROUGHT A SMALLER BASKET. I FUM-bled, trying to balance the wide, shallow, woven basket against my hip as I searched through the dark for the staff entrance to the Inn.

Another of my bright ideas that didn't quite pan out the way it was supposed to. Lately, I seemed to have a lot of them. I'd been to The Inn at Sawyers Bend hundreds of times, but I'd always come through the front as a guest of the restaurant and bar.

Today I was delivering what I hoped was a tempting selection of treats from my bakery, an example of the kind of thing I might provide for the Inn to leave in guest rooms or sell in the small shop by the front desk. Anything to expand my client base. Right now, I needed every penny I could get.

I usually had a lull in the early morning, after the first wave of baking was done and before our doors opened for the day. Grams could handle our first few customers, and I'd figured I could drop off the basket and get back to Sweetheart Bakery in time for the opening rush. And I might, if I could find the staff entrance.

At the back of the enormous timber and stone building I stared over the gardens, lit with spotlights here and there. Even in the dark the gardens were beautiful, flowing from the back of the Inn, the gravel paths leading to benches, to soft grass perfect for a picnic, and further to the guest cabins scattered along the river.

Fatigue pulled at me, and for a moment I wanted nothing more than to sink on to one of the pretty iron benches, unwrap one of my own cookies, and just take a break.

Not yet. Not for a while, maybe. I'd been running on too little sleep for too long, but I couldn't stop until I'd fixed the mess I'd gotten myself into.

Hitching the basket higher on my hip, I watched as tendrils of light from the rising sun crept through the garden. One more minute. Then I'd get it together, find the staff entrance, drop off my basket and get back to work. As I soaked in the beauty of early morning in the mountains, the burble of the nearby river and the mist rising off the gardens, I realized where I'd gone wrong.

Of course, the staff entrance wouldn't be at the back of the building. During the day this space was mainly used by guests. I'd passed through the guest parking lot as I'd walked from the bakery and had completely forgotten about the smaller parking lot on the other side of the Inn. That must be where I'd find the staff entrance.

My energy renewed, I awkwardly re-balanced the basket and started along the gravel path to the far side of the Inn, hoping I wasn't leaving a trail of prettily wrapped brownies and cookies behind me. Approaching the corner, I took the narrower path to my right, marked with a small sign that read STAFF ONLY, hoping I'd find the door I was looking for.

I wasn't expecting to run into a wall. With a yelp, I back-pedaled, scrambling as the basket tipped, trying to get my feet under me before I landed on my butt.

Not a wall. A man. Tall, in a hooded sweatshirt and jeans, he barreled into me, the cardboard box in his arms bumping my basket and sending it tumbling.

I winced at the thuds of brownies hitting the grass, and shouted, "Hey, wait a sec," but the man flung out an arm, shoving me hard. So much for not landing on my butt. My feet flew out from under me, brownies and cookies raining down on the wet grass.

I stared in stunned amazement at the figure leaning over me, his features hidden by the deep hood of his sweatshirt. For the first time my heart chilled. I'd assumed he was an employee coming into work, or a guest out for an early run. That he'd apologize for bumping into me and we'd laugh and go our separate ways.

He said nothing, only loomed over me, face shadowed, radiating menace.

My heels kicked at the grass, hands scrabbling to pull me backwards, away from this sudden threat. The man in the sweatshirt hesitated, his hands flexing on the box he held before whirling and racing around the corner, exactly where I'd been headed. He disappeared from sight, and I let out a breath of relief.

I should have collected what was left of my treats and gone back to the bakery to try again another time. Or brought what I could salvage to the front desk and dropped it off there.

I should have done anything other than follow the stranger with the box.

I don't know why I did, why I was so sure he was up to no good, or what I thought I could do about it.

I followed anyway. My life had given me good instincts for people who were up to no good. I didn't always listen—and wasn't that biting me in the ass these days—but when I did, I was usually right.

I rounded the corner of the Inn and found the man in the sweatshirt leaning over a metal square protruding from the side of the building. It looked like an HVAC vent or an air intake. He was opening the box, tilting it toward the vent as if getting ready to dump something inside. What the hell?

I fumbled for my phone. My pockets were empty. Crap, I must have dropped it when I'd hit the ground. That would have been the time to run, to head for the front desk and a working phone.

Running would have been smart. Smart, but too slow. If I ran he'd be gone by the time I got the police on the phone, and it would be too late to stop whatever he was doing with that box.

He hadn't seen me. I still had time to get away. Instead I called out, "Hey! Do you work for the Inn? I'm calling security!"

Stupid, I know. Alone in the dark with a stranger I'd already figured out was up to no good and instead of going for help, I shouted at him.

Not my best move.

Not my best move, but it worked.

The cardboard box fell from his hands. In the growing light of the rising sun I watched in horror as it spilled to the ground, a flood of shiny black cockroaches disappearing into the grass. Oh, gross.

Had he been about to dump those into the air intake at the Inn? The ramifications hit me in a split second. I ran an establishment that served food and beverages. I knew exactly how bad a flood of cockroaches would be. On top of that, the sheer size of the Inn would make it nearly impossible to root them all out.

Plus, cockroaches. Yuck.

All of that hit me in a flash, just before I turned to run. Where, I didn't know. He was between me and the fastest route to the front desk and a phone. I took off anyway. Anywhere was better than alone in the dark with a pissed off stranger.

I turned on my heel to bolt. I made it three whole steps before a hand closed over the back of my shirt, yanking me down to the ground. I landed hard, the breath whooshing from my lungs. The man in the sweatshirt was on me a second later, his arm raised, hand balled into a fist.

If he was thinking straight he would have run. I guess that made two of us who weren't thinking. I twisted, trying to throw off his weight, but he held me down easily, muttering, "Dumb nosy bitch. Fuckin' gettin' in my way."

He swung his fist, catching me on the cheekbone. Pain exploded, my head flying to the side, wrenching my neck. I hadn't lived a perfect life, but I'd never been hit in the face before. It hurt. A lot. He swung again, his fist connecting, and a moan slipped out as I struggled to raise my arms to protect my face, unable to knock him off of me.

I'm not tiny, about average size and weight, but he was a lot bigger. He hit me again, this time his fist bouncing off the arm I'd managed to pull free. I screamed with everything I had, knowing sound was my only defense.

Sucking in air for another scream, I braced for the next punch and rolled as his weight was gone, dragged off of me.

I heard a low, "What the fuck?"

I knew that voice. I stopped screaming and sagged into the damp grass, lungs heaving as I tried to catch my breath. A heavy fist struck flesh with a thud, followed by a pathetic moan. Opening my eyes, I watched as Royal Sawyer pinned my assailant to the ground, one knee in the man's back, wrenching both of the man's arms behind him.

"Daisy?" Royal asked, shooting a quick glance my way. "Daisy Hutchins? Are you okay?"

"I think so," I said, slowly. "I was coming by to leave some cookies—Hope said I should drop them off with my card—and I couldn't find the door and I saw him. He—"

"Slow down, Daisy. Catch your breath for a second." His voice was low and soothing. Strong. I lay back in the grass, letting the absolute authority in his tone chase off my fears. No one was going to get through Royal. Everything was okay.

"Hope said you'd be by," he went on. "Why were you back here? Who is this guy?"

I took a deep breath, gathering my thoughts together, and sat up. "I thought I should come in through the staff entrance. I was going to leave the basket so someone could deliver it to your offices before you got in, but it was dark and I realized I didn't know exactly where the door was. I guess I was wandering a little, and then I saw that guy. Oh, God, I think he was trying to dump cockroaches into your air intake system. He was over there—"

I pointed at the spilled box on the ground by the HVAC equipment outside the building.

Royal swore under his breath. "Can you get up? Could you do me a favor?"

I nodded, still trying to get my bearings and, to be honest, a little intimidated by Royal Sawyer. As first meetings go, this wasn't the one I would have chosen.

I was hoping he'd get my beautifully-presented basket of treats, along with the brochure and proposal I'd tucked into the basket, and ask me to the Inn for a meeting. I would have shown up dressed like the businesswoman I was, not in a flour streaked t-shirt with my hair in a messy poof. I definitely would not have been covered in grass stains with a rapidly swelling cheek. Damn.

We'd never officially met, but I knew who Royal was. We'd both grown up in Sawyers Bend. We knew who everybody was. That's a small town for you. I was Daisy Hutchins, part owner of Sweetheart Bakery. My amazing baked goods aside, I wasn't anyone of importance.

He was Royal Sawyer, one of *the* Sawyers of Sawyers Bend. As his name indicated, around here he was practically a prince. Not that he sat around polishing the crown jewels. He and his brother Tenn ran the Inn at Sawyers Bend, and given the way it had taken off in the last decade, they did a hell of a job at it.

Maybe he wasn't actual royalty, but he was still a Sawyer. Wealthy, connected, and did I mention hot? There wasn't a single ugly Sawyer in the whole family.

Their father had been a bastard, but a handsome one, and he'd chosen his wives—according to Grams—mainly based on looks. He hadn't been able to hold on to any of his women for long, but they sure had made some pretty children.

Not that I spent a lot of time ogling male Sawyers. I was too busy for that. But if I did, I would have chosen Royal. Thick, wavy, dark hair he wore a little too long. Deep-blue eyes. Broad shoulders with a lean, powerful build. A smile that was all dangerous charm, one he used easily and often.

I was kind of shocked he knew my name. I'll admit I was a little lightheaded, not just from getting punched in the face, but from the focus in those blue, blue eyes.

"Daisy? You sure you're okay?"

"I'm fine, really." I got to my feet, relieved my head stayed clear.

What a dork. There I was sitting on my butt in the wet grass mooning over Royal Sawyer when there were more important problems at hand. Like the man in the sweatshirt and the cockroaches in that box.

"Can you grab my phone?" Royal asked, those sharp eyes locked on my face, narrowing as they took in the swelling of my cheek.

I nodded and spotted the phone strapped to his arm, the earbuds in his ears. I hadn't realized, but taking in his grass-stained running shoes and the athletic shorts currently stretched across his muscled thighs—*Pay attention, Daisy. Eyes off his legs.*—he must have been out for an early run.

Just like I'd thought the man in the sweatshirt was when I'd first seen him. I guess that explained how Royal kept that lean, strong body when he spent most of his day behind a desk.

Trying not to notice the clean, salty scent of him, I leaned in and unstrapped his phone from his arm. I definitely did not notice the bunch of his bicep under my fingers. Not at all.

"Would you pull West up in the contacts and give him a call, tell him we need him over here?"

I angled the phone at Royal's face to unlock the screen and found West in the list of favorites. Weston Garfield was the police chief of Sawyers Bend and apparently a friend of Royal's. With a few words, he was on his way.

"Do you want me to call Tenn?"

"If you don't mind," he drawled. The comment could have been sarcastic or impatient, but the smile curving his lips told me it was neither. How could he be smiling when he had sweatshirt guy pinned on the ground and that box a few feet away?

The box. Tenn answered, and as I filled him in, I crossed the grass to the box, still laying where he'd dropped it, mostly on its side. As I'd hoped, a few cockroaches still scrabbled at the bottom. Gingerly, I nudged it upright to keep them inside.

I moved to hand Royal back his phone, then shoved it in my pocket when he shook his head.

"Hang on to that for now, would you? Do you have a few minutes before you have to get back to the bakery? West is going to want to take your statement."

"I'm good for now. I just have to find my phone and text Grams. J.T. is working today so he can help her out." The guy who'd hit me was lying motionless under Royal, his chest jerking as he sucked in breath. "Why would he want to dump cockroaches into your air vent? Is he trying to get you shut down?"

"That's a good question," Royal said conversationally. "I'm sure we're going to have all sorts of questions for this guy. I'd like to know if this is the first time he's tried something like this. And if it was his idea, or if he's working for someone else. But West is going to have plenty of time to ask while he's rotting in jail."

"Fuck you," came from the face shoved in the grass.

"Creative. I expected better from someone who was about to dump roaches into the HVAC."

Tennessee Sawyer came around the corner of the building, almost a carbon copy of his brother, except Royal's hair was more of an auburn brown, and Tenn's was pure espresso. Tenn had the same build as Royal, the same perfect Sawyer bone structure, but he'd never done it for me the way Royal did.

Then again, Hutchins women were always a sucker for a charming smile. It was our downfall, generations deep. Royal's was so full of charm it was lethal. Tenn had a nice smile too, but he was straightforward. Serious. Royal had the kind a grin that had a girl out of her panties before she could think twice.

"What the hell is going on?" Tenn demanded, his brow furrowed with concern. "Daisy, are you okay? Hope said you'd bring some samples by, but it's barely dawn."

I gave an embarrassed shrug. "I'm up early to start the baking. I knew the kitchens would be open and I wanted to have the basket delivered before you both got to the office—"

All of a sudden, I remembered the basket of cookies and brownies I'd baked early that morning and and painstakingly wrapped in the ribboned packaging I'd decided on for the Inn, now scattered all over the side lawn along with my phone. Before I called Grams to seriously underplay the reason for my delay, I had to find my phone.

I stood and looked around, catching sight of my basket by the corner of the building, upside down on the grass, the light catching the cellophane wrapped treats that had spilled everywhere. Dammit.

I tried not to think about my tired fingers tying all those ribbons into bows only hours before. I was supposed to make a good impression. To wow them with my delicious treats presented so temptingly in their pretty basket with ribbons that matched the Inn's logo.

Instead everything was scattered all over the grass. The brownies had probably held up, but the cookies would be a crumpled mess.

"One second," I said to Royal and Tenn. "I dropped everything when he ran into me. I have to find my phone."

I went to my knees in the wet grass, turning the basket upright and filling it with as many packages of cookies and brownies as I could find. Royal and Tenn spoke quietly amongst themselves. When I glanced up, I found Royal's eyes fixed on me despite his squirming captive.

I looked away, focusing on my task, surrounded by the disaster of my latest bright idea, the pain in my swelling check a tight throb. I wished I could disappear. I wished I'd never come here. If I were playing that game, I wished I'd done a lot of things differently.

I finally found my phone. I chickened out and sent Grams a quick text instead of calling.

Still at the Inn. Can you open without me?

She answered almost immediately. *On it, baby girl. See you when we see you.*

Grams thought I was working too hard. If only she knew. Grams still lived in the house where I'd grown up. In town, a few blocks from Main Street, it was walking distance to the bakery. I, on the other hand, lived in a small apartment above the bakery which made it easy to hide the long hours I'd been putting in.

Then again, I might be fooling myself. It was never easy to put one over on Eleanor Hutchins. She might be my grandmother, but she was still sharp as a tack. The second she saw my cheek, there'd be hell to pay. But that was a problem for later.

First, I worked on reassembling the cookies and brownies in the basket. With so many broken cookies it would never look as nice as it had when I packed it, but it would do. I'd take the broken cookies back to the bakery and put them to use in something else.

Rising slowly, my muscles aching in protest and my cheek throbbing, I walked back to where Royal and Tenn waited with our captive.

Royal's eyes were still locked on me, his charming grin nowhere in sight. Tenn only had eyes for the basket on my arm. "That looks fantastic. You were going to leave that in our offices so the first thing we saw was that basket of treats?"

I swallowed hard and nodded. At the time, it had seemed like a good idea. Now I was wondering if it was just foolish.

"Pass over one of those broken cookies. I can't wait until I get into the office."

Mutely, I did as ordered, some of my foolishness fading as Tenn's eyes rolled in pleasure at the first taste of one of my chocolate chip cookies.

"Why don't you go up to the offices with Royal and you two can talk about your proposal while you wait for West to take your statement. You need to get some ice on that cheek."

"You ready to take this asshole?" Royal asked, his grip tightening on sweatshirt guy's wrists, wrenching them up and driving man's face into the grass.

"Let's go," Tenn agreed and seamlessly they switched places. Sweatshirt guy tried to roll as Royal stood, but he wasn't fast enough.

Once Tenn had him secure, Royal turned to me and held out a hand. "Let's get some ice on that cheek. Breakfast? Coffee?"

A little dizzy with the quick shift, I slid my hand in his, and with the other gave him his phone. He had it at his ear a moment later. "Two Blue Ridge breakfasts in my office, and a bag of ice." A raised eyebrow at me. "Eggs scrambled? Fried? Regular coffee or do you want a cappuccino or latte?"

Dazed, I did the best I could to hang onto my basket and said, "Scrambled and cappuccino, please."

Royal relayed my order.

"I could have waited with Tenn," I said. "You don't have to—"

"You need ice on that cheek. Considering you got beat up while trying to save the Inn from a cockroach infestation that we both know would have been a monumental pain in the ass, the least I owe you is breakfast."

I couldn't argue with that. I kept an immaculate kitchen, but every time the health inspector stopped by my stomach was still in knots. So many details, so many things that were easy to forget. No one wanted a sign with a bad sanitation score hanging in their window.

I could have stayed with Tenn and sweatshirt guy to wait for West. I probably should have, but Royal's fingers were warm around mine. Strong. I let him lead me through the terrace doors and the lobby to the elevator, noting that he held each door, careful to make room for my somewhat rumpled basket of treats.

The executive offices were on the third floor, quiet and dark. It looked like Royal and Tenn's assistant wasn't in yet. Royal flipped on lights as we passed through the outer office, everything decorated with the same rustic elegance that dominated the rest of the Inn. The wide, tall windows in Royal's office looked out over the gardens. I peeked down to see West hauling sweatshirt guy to his feet, already cuffed.

"West is here," I said needlessly.

Royal gave a quick glance out the window before taking the basket from my arm and setting it on his desk. Using the light streaming in from the window, he tilted my chin and studied my swollen cheek. His thumb grazed my cheek so lightly it didn't hurt but sent a faint pulse of energy shimmering across my skin.

"He got you good, didn't he?" Royal asked, his voice tight. Gently changing the angle of my face, he said, "How many times did he hit you?"

"Twice," I murmured.

Royals thumb skimmed over my lower lip, his blue eyes dark, liquid with some emotion I couldn't define. Nerves skittering through me, I stepped away. "I'm okay."

"It could have been a lot worse. Why did you go after him? You could have just called West. You should have run inside. I don't know how far he was willing to go, but you could have been hurt, Daisy."

"I don't know why I went after him," I admitted. "I couldn't call West. I dropped my phone when he bumped into me. And he just—something about him was wrong. Then I saw him with the box at the air vent. I didn't know what was in it, but I knew it wasn't good. I just—I didn't think."

Royal shoved his hands in his pockets, his lips quirking into a facsimile of his charming grin. It didn't reach his eyes.

"Good thing I came along, huh?"

"Very good thing."

Turning his gaze to the basket on his desk, Royal gestured to the seat on the opposite his own. "This your proposal?" he asked, teasing out the envelope I'd tucked beneath the brownies. My throat suddenly dry, I nodded. "Sit, take a load off while we wait for ice and breakfast. You're here so we might as well do this now."

I tried not to fidget as he opened the envelope and scanned my suggestions and cost projections for bringing a little bit of Sweetheart Bakery to the Inn at Sawyers Bend.

While he was reading, a sharp double knock sounded on the door. Without waiting for an answer, it swung open and a uniformed waiter rolled in a table, filling the room with the scent of coffee, sausage, and buttery biscuits. My stomach rumbled.

Royal looked up. "You can set it up on the desk, and please, give the ice pack to Ms. Hutchins." He winked at me and went back to reading.

I wanted that cappuccino like I wanted my next breath, but my cheek felt like it was the size of a basketball and the whole side of my face throbbed. I went for the ice first, carefully wrapped in a linen napkin, and held it to my face, my eyes closing in relief at the cool burn.

Wanting to have my cake and eat it too, I shifted the ice pack enough to make room for a sip of coffee. Bliss. I hadn't had any coffee since four o'clock that morning. I was way overdue for more caffeine.

Royal set down my proposal and lifted the lids off our breakfasts. "I like how you coordinated your branding with the Inn's. Looks good."

It did look good. The Inn's colors were dark red with accents of Navy and hints of gold. Years ago, when Grams had designed the first logo for Sweetheart Bakery she'd gone with a deep, rich pink, not far from the deep red the Inn used.

For my sample packet I'd gone with navy ribbons paired with those of the same deep pink we used at the bakery and had added navy and gold accents to the Sweetheart Bakery logo on the sticker. It was still very much branded to Sweetheart Bakery but would fit right in on display in the Inn's gift shop.

"Thanks. I laid out some projections, and of course we'll work with whatever you'd prefer, but I thought the third proposal would be the best fit."

"Supplying Sweetheart goods in our welcome baskets for suites and cottages as well as stocking a selection in the gift shop," he confirmed.

I nodded. "That's not a big commitment on your end and gives you a chance to see how it goes. I'd also supply coupons for your regular welcome packets as well as the baskets to give your guests a discount at the bakery."

"We'd include those anyway. We try to promote local businesses as much as we can. I like proposal number three, but I'd prefer to do it on consignment rather than buying outright."

Nerves tickled my stomach. I love running my own business, but these kind of negotiations were not my favorite thing. I'd known they would ask to put the arrangement on consignment.

That didn't work for me. First of all, the accounting would be way too time-consuming, and second, I couldn't afford to be fronting materials in the hopes I'd get paid for them eventually. Not right now. I needed to get paid when I dropped off my stock, not when they eventually sold.

"These are perishable goods, and on the low end of the price range. I don't think consignment makes sense. If you're worried they won't sell I'd rather start with smaller, more frequent orders and be paid when you receive delivery, not later."

"Is this a deal breaker?" Royal sat back in his chair, folding his hands over his flat stomach.

"I think it has to be, yes," I said, wishing I sounded more confident and authoritative. Wishing I'd said *Yes, absolutely* and wasn't terrified he was going to turn me down.

A regular order from the Inn wasn't going to change my life. It certainly wasn't going to solve my cash flow problem. Not on its own. But every little bit counted, and placement in the Inn's gift shop was added exposure to the many tourists who flowed through the Inn at Sawyers Bend.

The Inn was a local landmark, and a lot of people who couldn't afford to stay there still visited the restaurant, gift shop, and bar. They might not buy one of my treats at the Inn, but they'd see the package and recognize my sign when they walked through town.

My free hand curled into a fist in my lap, betraying my nerves. I forced my fingers to uncurl and reach for the cappuccino, pretending this was all no big deal. Like I regularly had breakfast with Royal Sawyer in his office at dawn. Sure, and I'd have tea with the Queen of England later in the day.

Nothing about this was normal.

Without saying anything, Royal unwrapped one of the brownies in the basket I'd set on his desk. Salted caramel. My favorite. He broke off the corner and popped it in his mouth, closing his eyes as chocolate and caramel melted across his tongue, the sharp bite of sea salt making the sugar sweeter. When he opened his eyes, he took a sip of coffee, swallowed and shook his head.

"I can't say no to those brownies. And we owe you one. Let's do it, starting with orders twice a week. I'll expect you to coordinate with the gift shop to make sure you're keeping us stocked and adjust that timing as needed."

"I don't want you to say yes because you think you owe

me," I said, as every instinct for self-preservation urged me to shut the hell up. It didn't matter why he said yes, it only mattered that he did. If my foolish recklessness had helped me get their business, then everything had worked out for the best.

I couldn't help myself. My pride was stronger than that sense of self preservation.

Royal flashed a grin that had me pressing my knees together, and this time it reached all the way to those deep-blue eyes. "I would have said yes anyway, but I would have pushed harder on the consignment thing. What you did this morning was incredibly foolhardy. It was also very brave. Sweetheart Bakery is a lot smaller than the Inn, but I know that you know what would have happened if that guy had managed to dump all those cockroaches into the building. You saved us a great deal of trouble. I understand you don't want us to owe you, but the fact is that we do. And your proposal is a good one. It's a win-win. So, smile and say *Thank you, Mr. Sawyer* and finish your breakfast."

He winked at me. *Thank you Mr. Sawyer*. I couldn't help the quirk of my mouth. I was impervious to flirting by handsome men. The wink, that smile—none of it would work on me. I absolutely did not smile back. This was business. That was all.

Dutifully, I said, "Thank you, Royal," deliberately using his first name to prove he didn't intimidate me. Never mind that he did. A lot. Far more than I wanted to admit. Something about Royal Sawyer left me off-center. Restless.

To cover my discomfort I took another sip of coffee, then set the ice back on the tray and picked up my fork. My last meal had been a long time ago and the Inn's kitchen was one of the best in town. Cinnamon-scented stuffed French toast, fluffy biscuits, scrambled eggs, and crispy links of local sausage.

No way was I letting this go to waste. Royal took my cue and dug into his own breakfast. West didn't knock on the door until we were almost finished.

Sawyers Bend was a little busier than your average small town, given all the tourists that moved in and out on a regular basis, but Weston Garfield didn't typically see a lot of crime. That had changed since Royal's father had died two months before.

Prentice Sawyer had been murdered in the family mansion, and Royal's black sheep of an older brother, Griffen, had inherited everything. Since then, the town of Sawyers Bend had skidded off the rails. Griffen's brother Ford was in jail for their father's murder, though nobody in town seemed to believe he'd done it.

According to Hope, Griffen's new wife and one of my best friends, someone had tried to kill Griffen twice, finally breaking into Heartstone Manor with a gun, intent on taking out as many Sawyers as he could. Added to the rumors that there'd been some trouble at the Inn, I was betting West Garfield had been a busy man.

He greeted Royal like an old friend and took the seat beside mine. Before he got started, he eyed the basket of cookies and brownies. "I know you're not gonna hoard all those for yourselves."

With a shake of his head, Royal passed over a packet with a crumpled cookie and one holding a brownie. West opened the cookie and fished out a piece. "It's a good thing you stay out of trouble, Daisy. I've never been susceptible to bribes, but these cookies might do it."

He sat back in the chair, his eyes fastened to my cheek. I couldn't see what it looked like, but it throbbed, and my skin felt stretched tight. Swollen. It was a good thing I had Grams and J.T. to work the front counter at Sweetheart. I didn't need customers seeing me like this.

"We have your early-morning visitor locked up. Unsurprisingly, he's not talking. He do that to you, Daisy?"

"It was dark, and I was trying to find the staff entrance—"
I ran West through the events of that morning. When it was
happening it seemed like it took forever. In retelling it to West
I realized only a few minutes had passed from the moment I
bumped into sweatshirt guy to Royal pulling him off of me and
pinning him to the ground.

West took careful notes, his face impassive, eyes serious. "Is
that everything?"

"That's it," I confirmed and drained the last sip of my
cappuccino.

West tapped his pen on his notebook before standing.
"What you did was very brave, Daisy. I know Royal and Tenn
appreciate you stopping him before he could cause them more
trouble, but the next time you run in to a stranger in the dark
who's intent on committing a crime, you don't confront them.
You run the hell away. Understand?"

I hung my head. It wasn't that I didn't understand. I did.
I agreed with West. He was absolutely right. And given the
chance, I would have done the same thing all over again.

I was only somewhat stupid, so I didn't tell West that.
Instead I raised my head and said, as contritely as I could
manage, "I understand."

West nodded. "If you think of anything else, let me know. I'll talk
to you later, Royal." He left, closing the door behind him.

Royal looked at me. "You just lied to the police chief, didn't
you?"

I shrugged a shoulder. "Maybe. If I'd had my phone, I would
have called for help." I thought about the man in the sweatshirt
holding that box up to the air intake vent, and I shook my head.
"No, I wouldn't. I mean, I would have called, but I also would
have tried to stop him. I'm not saying it was the smart thing to
do—"

"—but it was the right thing to do," Royal finished for me.

"It was the only thing to do."

I knew better than anyone that sometimes choices weren't about right and wrong.

Sometimes choices were about what you could live with.

I'd be living with this swollen cheek for a while, but if the Inn had to shut down because of a cockroach infestation all of us would suffer. There were other places to stay in Sawyers Bend, but none attracted the kind of high-profile guests with money to spend like the Inn at Sawyers Bend.

Royal contemplated me, his gaze thoughtful as he took another bite of brownie. "What are your plans tonight?"

"What?" I asked, not following his abrupt change in topic.

"Tonight. What are your plans?"

"Um, dinner with my grandmother and J.T., and early to bed since I have to get up before four." It wasn't sexy or exciting, but that was my life.

"Have dinner with me instead," Royal ordered with a flash of that charming grin. The spark of light in his deep-blue eyes would have brought me to my knees if I hadn't already been sitting.

My long-neglected hormones shouted YES! My mouth opened, and instead, I said, "Why?"

Royal's charming grin morphed into genuine amusement. "Because you're brave. And smart. And very, very pretty."

My jaw didn't exactly drop, but it was close. *Very, very pretty?* I didn't have to look down to see the grass stains on my jeans, the flour smeared across my shirt, and my cherry-cola curls falling out of the messy poof I'd stuck them in well before dawn.

At my best I could pull off pretty. I had good genes to work with, after all. But after hours spent in the kitchen, plus a fistfight? No way.

I rolled my eyes. "I don't mix business with pleasure." I said, primly.

"Neither do I, usually," Royal countered.

I rolled my eyes again. "Right. You never date locals, only hook up with hot tourists who come through the hotel. If that isn't mixing with business with pleasure—"

Royal's smile slipped. "Not the same thing. Are you saying you don't want to have dinner with me?"

I ignored his question. "Anyway, I have boyfriend," I said.

Royal shook his head. "No, you don't."

"I do," I insisted.

"Who?" he demanded.

"J.T. Everybody knows that," I said. It was mostly true. Kind of.

Royal leaned back in his chair again, crossing his arms over his chest and raising one eyebrow. "And that's not mixing business with pleasure? He works for you, doesn't he? In fact, if you look at it that way, it's a harassment case waiting to happen."

I laughed at the thought. "J.T.'s been my best friend since middle school. He's not going to sue me for harassment." Realizing that made us seem less like the romance of the century, I looked away. "I appreciate the invitation. I'm flattered. But I have a boyfriend and I'm not interested."

"Lying again, Daisy?"

The heat that hit my cheeks had me standing, putting my napkin back on the tray and pushing in the chair. "Your first order will be delivered tomorrow. I'll include the invoice. It's been a pleasure doing business with you."

Royal stood and followed me out, his fingertips landing lightly on my lower back as he guided me through the door. "You sure about dinner tonight?"

"I told you, I'm not interested."

Royal's laugh followed me into the empty reception area, all the way to the elevator.

"If you say so. I'll be seeing you around, Miss Daisy."
I very much doubted that.
And I was very, very wrong.

ARE YOU READY FOR
ROYAL & DAISY'S STORY?

Visit IvyLayne.com/SweetHeart
to see what happens next!

Never Miss a New
Release:
Join Ivy's Reader's
Group
@ ivylayne.com/
readers
&
Get two books for
free!

Also By Ivy Layne

THE HEARTS OF SAWYERS BEND

Stolen Heart
Sweet Heart
Scheming Heart

THE UNTANGLED SERIES

Unraveled
Undone
Uncovered

THE WINTERS SAGA

The Billionaire's Secret Heart (Novella)
The Billionaire's Secret Love (Novella)
The Billionaire's Pet
The Billionaire's Promise
The Rebel Billionaire
The Billionaire's Secret Kiss (Novella)
The Billionaire's Angel
Engaging the Billionaire
Compromising the Billionaire
The Counterfeit Billionaire
Series Extras: ivylayne.com/extras

THE BILLIONAIRE CLUB

The Wedding Rescue
The Courtship Maneuver
The Temptation Trap

Don't miss
the series that
started it all.
The Billionaire
Club Trilogy.

About Ivy Layne

Ivy Layne has had her nose stuck in a book since she first learned to decipher the English language. Sometime in her early teens, she stumbled across her first Romance, and the die was cast. Though she pretended to pay attention to her creative writing professors, she dreamed of writing steamy romance instead of literary fiction. These days, she's neck deep in alpha heroes and the smart, sexy women who love them.

Married to her very own alpha hero (who rubs her back after a long day of typing, but also leaves his socks on the floor). Ivy lives in the mountains of North Carolina where she and her other half are having a blast raising two energetic little boys. Aside from her family, Ivy's greatest loves are coffee and chocolate, preferably together.

Visit Ivy

Facebook.com/AuthorIvyLayne
Instagram.com/authorivylayne/
www.ivylayne.com
books@ivylayne.com

Made in the USA
Columbia, SC
27 September 2024